PENGUIN BOOKS

Warrior of Rome: II
King of Kings

Dr Harry Sidebottom teaches classical history at the University of Oxford, where he is a Fellow of St Benet's Hall and lecturer at Lincoln College. He has an international reputation as a scholar, having published widely on ancient warfare, classical art and the cultural history of the Roman Empire. Originally from Newmarket in Suffolk, he now lives with his wife and two sons in Woodstock, near Oxford.

King of Kings follows top-five bestseller *Fire in the East* in the epic grand narrative *Warrior of Rome* – a story of empire, of heroes, of treachery, of courage, and, most of all, a story of brutal, bloody warfare.

Visit www.harrysidebottom.co.uk for more info.

Warrior of Rome

PART II

King of Kings

DR HARRY SIDEBOTTOM

PENGUIN BOOKS

PENGUIN BOOKS

Published by the Penguin Group
Penguin Books Ltd, 80 Strand, London WC2R 0RL, England
Penguin Group (USA) Inc., 375 Hudson Street, New York, New York 10014, USA
Penguin Group (Canada), 90 Eglinton Avenue East, Suite 700, Toronto, Ontario, Canada M4P 2Y3
(a division of Pearson Penguin Canada Inc.)
Penguin Ireland, 25 St Stephen's Green, Dublin 2, Ireland (a division of Penguin Books Ltd)
Penguin Group (Australia), 250 Camberwell Road,
Camberwell, Victoria 3124, Australia (a division of Pearson Australia Group Pty Ltd)
Penguin Books India Pvt Ltd, 11 Community Centre,
Panchsheel Park, New Delhi – 110 017, India
Penguin Group (NZ), 67 Apollo Drive, Rosedale, North Shore 0632, New Zealand
(a division of Pearson New Zealand Ltd)
Penguin Books (South Africa) (Pty) Ltd, 24 Sturdee Avenue,
Rosebank, Johannesburg 2196, South Africa

Penguin Books Ltd, Registered Offices: 80 Strand, London WC2R 0RL, England

www.penguin.com

First published by Michael Joseph 2009
Published in Penguin Books 2010
1

Set in 12.5/14.75pt Garamond
Typeset by Palimpsest Book Production Limited, Grangemouth, Stirlingshire
Printed in England by Clays Ltd, St Ives plc

ISBN: 978-0-141-03230-6

www.greenpenguin.co.uk

With love to my mother, Frances,
and in memory of my father, Hugh Sidebottom

Contents

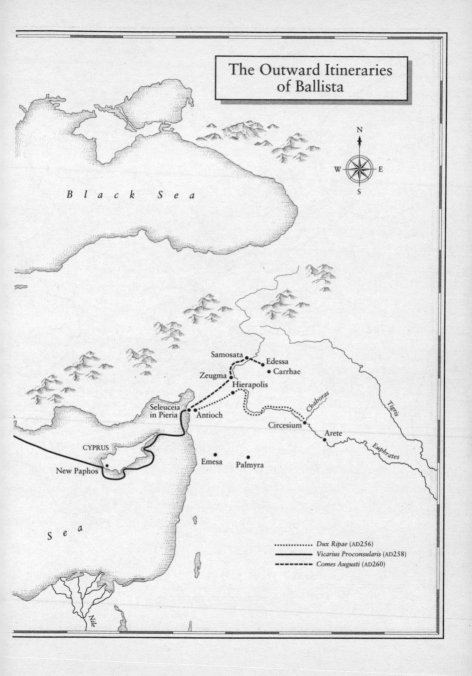

The Outward Itineraries of Ballista

Black Sea

Samosata · Edessa
· Carrhae
Zeugma · Hierapolis
Seleuceia
in Pieria · Antioch
Chaboras
Circesium · Arete
Emesa · Palmyra
CYPRUS

New Paphos

Tigris

Euphrates

Sea

Nile

.... *Dux Ripae* (AD256)
———— *Vicarius Proconsularis* (AD258)
– – – – *Comes Augusti* (AD260)

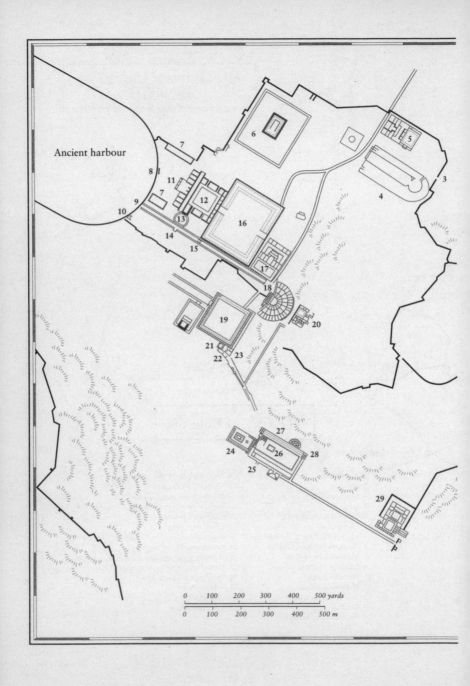

Ancient harbour

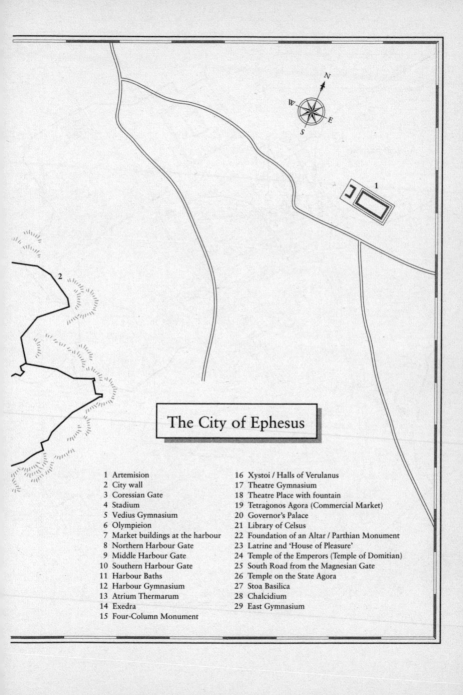

The City of Ephesus

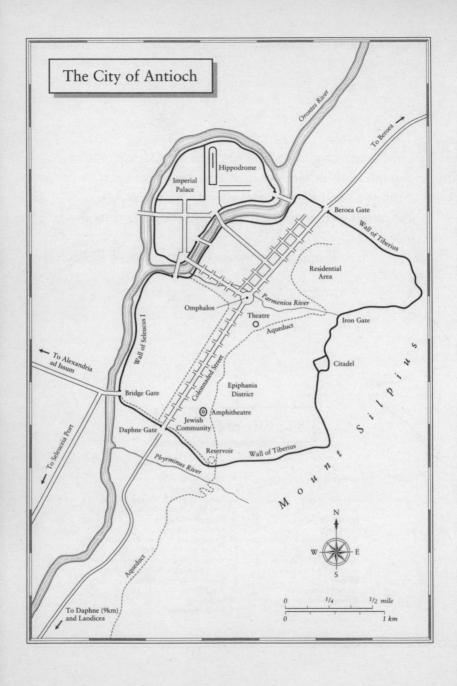

The City of Antioch

'The other crag is lower – you will see Odysseus –
though both lie side-by-side, an arrow-shot apart,
Atop it a great fig-tree rises, shaggy with leaves,
beneath it awesome Charybdis gulps the dark water down.'

Homer, *The Odyssey* (12. 112–115. tr. R. Fagles)

Prologue: The Syrian Desert between the Euphrates River and the city of Palmyra (Autumn AD256)

They were riding for their lives. The first day in the desert they had pushed hard, but always within their horses' limits. Completely alone, there had been no sign of pursuit. That evening in camp among the muted, tired conversations there had been a fragile mood of optimism. It was smashed beyond recall in the morning.

As they crested a slight ridge Marcus Clodius Ballista, the *Dux Ripae*, pulled his horse to one side off the rough track and let the other thirteen riders and one pack horse pass. He looked back the way they had come. The sun was not up yet, but its beams were beginning to chase away the dark of the night. And there at the centre of the spreading semi-circle of numinous yellow light, just at the point where in a few moments the sun would break the horizon, was a column of dust.

Ballista studied it intensely. The column was dense and isolated. It rose straight and tall, until a breeze in the upper air pulled it away to the south and dissipated it. In the flat, featureless desert it was always difficult to judge distances. Four or five miles away; too far to see what was causing it. But Ballista knew. It was a troop of men. Out here in the deep desert it had to be a troop of mounted men; on horses or camels, or both. Again, the distance was too great to make an accurate estimate of the numbers, but to kick up that amount of dust there had to be four or five times as many as rode with Ballista. That the column of dust did not incline to left or right but seemed to rise up completely straight showed that they were following. With a hollow feeling Ballista accepted it for what it was – the enemy was chasing them, a large body of Sassanid Persian cavalry was on their trail.

Looking round, Ballista realized that those with him had stopped. Their attention was divided between him and the dust cloud. Ballista pushed them out of his thoughts. He scanned through 360 degrees. Open, slightly undulating desert. Sand with a thick scattering of small and sharp dun-coloured rocks. Enough to hide a myriad scorpions and snakes; nothing to hide a man, let alone fourteen riders and fifteen horses.

Ballista turned and walked his mount to the two Arabs in the centre of the line.

'Riding hard, how long will it take to reach the mountains?'

'Two days,' the girl replied without hesitation. Bathshiba was the daughter of a caravan protector. She had travelled the route before with her late father. Ballista trusted her judgement, but he glanced at the other Arab.

'Today and tomorrow,' Haddudad the mercenary said.

With a jingle of horse furniture Turpio, the sole Roman officer under Ballista surviving from the original force, reined in next to them.

'Two days to the mountains?' Ballista asked.

Turpio shrugged eloquently. 'The horses, the enemy and the gods willing.'

Ballista nodded. He raised himself up using the front and rear horns of the saddle. He looked both ways along the line. He had his party's undivided attention.

'The reptiles are after us. There are a lot of them. But there is no reason to think they can catch us. They are five miles or more behind. Two days and we are safe in the mountains.' Ballista felt as much as saw the unspoken objections of Turpio and the two Arabs. He stopped them with a cold glance. 'Two days and we are safe,' he repeated. He looked up and down the line. No one else said anything.

With studied calm Ballista walked his horse slowly to the head of the line. He raised his hand and signalled them to ride on. They moved easily into a canter.

Behind them the sun rose over the horizon. Every slight rise in the desert was gilded, every tiny depression a pool of inky black. As they rode, their shadows flickered far out in front as if in a futile attempt to outrun them.

The small column had not gone far when a bad thing happened. There was a shout, abruptly cut off, then a terrible crash. Ballista swung round in the saddle. A trooper and his mount were down; a thrashing tangle of limbs and equipment. The man rolled to one side. The horse came to a halt. The soldier pulled himself on to his hands and knees, still holding his head. The horse tried to rise. It fell back with an almost human cry of pain. Its near foreleg was broken.

Forcing himself not to check the dust cloud of their pursuers, Ballista rattled out some orders. He jumped down from his mount. As endurance was at issue it was vital to take the weight off his horse's back at every opportunity. Maximus, the Hibernian slave who had been Ballista's bodyguard for the last fifteen years, tenderly coaxed the horse to its feet. He talked to it softly in the language of his native island as he unsaddled it and led it off the path. It went with him trustingly, hopping pathetically on its three sound legs.

Ballista turned his eyes away to where his body servant, Calgacus, was removing the load from the one packhorse. The elderly Caledonian had been enslaved by Ballista's father. Since Ballista's childhood in the northern forests, Calgacus had been at his side. Now, with a peevish expression on his ill-favoured face, the Caledonian redistributed as much of the provisions as he could among the riders. Muttering under his breath, he placed what could not be accommodated in a neat pile. He regarded it appraisingly for a moment then pulled up his tunic, pushed down his trousers, and urinated copiously all over the abandoned foodstuffs. 'I hope the Sassanid fuckers enjoy it,' he announced. Despite their extreme fatigue and fear, or maybe because of it, several men laughed.

Maximus walked back looking clean and composed. He picked up the military saddle and slung it over the back of the packhorse, carefully tightening the girths.

Ballista went over to the fallen trooper. He was sitting up. The slave boy Demetrius was mopping a cut on the man's forehead. Ballista began to wonder if his young Greek secretary would have been so solicitous if the soldier had not been so good-looking, before, annoyed with himself, he closed that line of thought. Together, Ballista and Demetrius got the trooper back on his feet – *Really, I am fine* – then up on to the former packhorse.

Ballista and the others remounted. This time he could

not resist looking for the enemy dust. It was appreciably closer. Ballista made the signal and they moved out past where the cavalry horse lay. On top of the spreading pool of dark red arterial blood was a foam of light pink caused by the animal's desperate attempts to breathe through a severed windpipe.

For the most part they cantered, a fast, ground-covering canter. When the horses were blown, Ballista would call out an order and they would dismount, give their mounts a drink – not too much – and let them have a handful of food: bread soaked in watered wine. Then they would walk, leading rein in hand, until the horses had something of their wind back and the riders could climb wearily back into the saddle. With endless repetition the day wore on. They were travelling as fast as they could, pushing the horses to the edge of their stamina, at constant risk of fatigue-induced accident. Yet every time they looked, the dust of their unseen enemy was a little closer.

During one of the spells on foot Bathshiba walked her horse up alongside Ballista. He was unsurprised when Haddudad appeared on his other side. The Arab mercenary's face was inscrutable. Jealous bastard, thought Ballista.

They walked in silence for a time. Ballista looked over at Bathshiba. There was dust in her long black hair, dust smudged across her high cheekbones. Out of the corner of his eye Ballista watched her moving, watched her breasts moving. They were obviously unconstrained under the man's tunic she wore. He found himself thinking about the one time he had seen them; the rounded olive skin, the dark nipples. Allfather, I must be losing my grip, Ballista thought. We are being chased for our lives through this hellish desert and all I am thinking about are this girl's tits. But Allfather, Fulfiller of Desire, what fine tits they were.

'Sorry, what was that?' Ballista realized she had been talking to him.

'I said, "Why did you lie to your men?"' Bathsiba's voice was pitched low. Above the rattle of equipment, the heavy footfalls and laboured breathing of men and horses, she could not be heard beyond the three of them. 'You have travelled this way before. You know we will not be safe when we reach the mountains. There is only one path through the high country. We could not be easier to follow if we were unrolling a thread behind us.'

'Sometimes a lie can cause the truth.' Ballista grinned. He felt oddly light-headed. 'Ariadne gave Theseus the ball of string to find his way out of the labyrinth when he went in to kill the minotaur. He promised he would marry her. But he abandoned her on the island of Naxos. If he had not lied Ariadne would not have married the god Dionysus, Theseus would not have had a son called Hippolytus, and Euripides could not have written the tragedy of that name.'

Neither Bathshiba nor Haddudad spoke. They were both looking at him strangely. Ballista sighed and started to explain. 'If I had told them the truth – that the Persians may well catch and kill us before the mountains, and that even if we get that far they will probably kill us anyway – they might have given up, and that would have been the end of things. I gave them some hope to work towards. And who knows, if we get to the mountains, we might make our own safety there.'

Ballista looked closely at Haddudad. 'I remember the

6

road passes through several ravines.' The mercenary merely nodded. 'Are any of them suitable for an ambush?'

Haddudad took his time replying. Ballista and Bathshiba remained silent. The Arab mercenary had served Bathshiba's father for a long time. They knew he was a man whose judgement was sound.

'The Horns of Ammon, not far into the mountains – a good killing ground.'

Ballista signalled it was time to remount. As he hauled his tired frame into the saddle, he leant over and spoke quietly to Haddudad. 'Tell me just before we reach the Horns of Ammon – if we get that far.'

Night fell fast in the desert. One moment the sun was high in the sky, the next it was dipping out of sight. Suddenly Ballista's companions became black silhouettes and the dark came crowding down. The moon had not yet risen, and, even if the horses had not been fit to drop, it was not thought safe to continue by starlight.

Just off the track, they made camp in near-total darkness. By Ballista's order there were only three shuttered lanterns lit. They were positioned to face west, away from the pursuers, and when the horses were settled they were to be extinguished. Ballista rubbed down his mount, whispering quiet, meaningless endearments in the grey gelding's ears. He had bought Pale Horse in Antioch the year before. The gelding had served him well and he was very fond of the big-hearted animal. The smell of hot horse, as good to Ballista as the scent of grass after rain, and the feel of the powerful muscles under his smooth coat soothed him.

'*Dominus.*' The voice of a trooper leading up his mount broke Ballista's reverie. The soldier said nothing else. There was no need. The man's horse was as lame as a cat. As they so often did when needed, Maximus and Calgacus appeared out of the darkness. Without words, the elderly Caledonian took over seeing to Pale Horse and the bodyguard joined Ballista in checking the other horse. They walked it round, made it trot, inspected its hooves. It was hopeless. It could go no further. With a small jerk of his chin, Ballista indicated to Maximus to lead it away.

The trooper held himself very still, waiting. Only his eyes betrayed his fear.

'We will follow the custom of the desert.' At Ballista's words the man exhaled deeply. 'Tell everyone to gather round.'

Ballista collected his helmet and a pottery wine jar and placed them on the ground next to one of the lanterns, which he opened completely. The small party formed a circle in the light, squatting in the dust. The lantern threw harsh light on to their tense faces, accentuating their features. Somewhere a desert fox barked. It was very quiet afterwards.

Ballista picked up the wine jar, drew the stopper and drank deeply. The wine was rough in his throat. He gave it to the man next to him, who drank and passed it on. Maximus came back and hunkered down.

'The girl will not be included.' Ballista's voice sounded loud to himself.

'Why not?'

Ballista looked at the trooper who had spoken. 'I am in command here. I am the one with *imperium*.'

'We will do what is ordered, and at every command we will be ready.' The soldier looked down as he flatly intoned the ritual words. Bathshiba got up and walked away.

When the empty jar was passed back to Ballista he dropped it at his feet. He raised his right boot and brought it down on the jar. There was a loud snap then a series of sharp clinks as it shattered. Studying what he was doing, he stamped his heel, three, four more times, breaking the vessel into small shards. He crouched down and selected thirteen similar-sized pieces, which he laid out in a row. He picked up two of them. With one he scratched the single Greek letter *theta* on the other. He scooped up all thirteen shards and dropped them, the twelve blank and the one marked, into his upturned helmet and rattled them around.

Ballista stood and held the helmet. Everyone was watching it as if it contained an asp. In a sense it did. Ballista felt his heart beating hard, his palms sweating as he turned and offered it to the man on his left.

It was the scribe from North Africa, the one they called Hannibal. He did not hesitate. His eyes locked with Ballista's as he put his hand in the helmet. His fingers closed. He withdrew his fist, turned it over and unclenched it. On his palm lay an unmarked shard. With no show of emotion he dropped it on the ground.

Next was Demetrius. The Greek boy was trembling, his eyes desperate. Ballista wanted to comfort him, but he knew he could not. Demetrius looked to the heavens. His lips mouthed a prayer. He thrust his hand into the helmet, clumsily, almost knocking it from Ballista's grip. The twelve shards clinked as the boy's fingers played over them, making his choice. Suddenly he withdrew his hand. In his fingers was an unmarked piece of pottery. Demetrius exhaled, almost a sob, and his eyes misted with tears.

The soldier on Demetrius' left was called Titus. He had served in Ballista's horse guards, the Equites Singulares, for almost a year. Ballista knew him for a calm, competent man. Without preamble he took his shard from the helmet. He opened his fist. There was the *theta*. Titus closed his eyes. Then, swallowing hard, he opened them, mastering himself.

A sigh, like a gentle breeze rustling through a field of ripe corn, ran around the circle. Trying hard not to show their relief, the others melted into the night. Titus was left standing with Ballista, Maximus and Calgacus.

Titus smiled a sketchy smile. 'The long day's task is done. Might as well unarm.' He took off his helmet and dropped it, lifted his baldric over his head, unbuckled his sword belt and let them fall too. His fingers fumbled with the laces of his shoulder guards. Without words, Maximus and Calgacus closed in and helped him, lifting the heavy, dragging mailcoat off.

Unarmed, Titus stood for a moment, then bent and retrieved his sword, unsheathing it. He tested its edge and point on his thumb.

'It does not have to be that,' said Ballista.

Titus laughed bitterly. 'A stepmother of a choice. If I run I will die of thirst. If I hide the reptiles will find me, and I have seen what they do to their prisoners – I would like to die with my arse intact. Better the Roman way.'

Ballista nodded.

'Will you help me?'

Ballista nodded again. 'Here?'

Titus shook his head. 'Can we walk?'

The two men left the circle of light. After a time Titus

stopped. He accepted a wine skin that Ballista offered and sat down. He took a long pull and handed the drink back as Ballista sat next to him. Back in the camp the lanterns went out one by one.

'Fortune, *Tyche*, is a whore,' Titus said. He took another drink. 'I thought I would die when the city fell. Then I thought I would escape. Fucking whore.'

Ballista said nothing.

'I had a woman back in the city. She will be dead now, or a slave.' Titus unfastened the purse from his belt. He passed it to Ballista. 'The usual – share it out among the boys.'

They sat in silence, drinking until the wine was gone. Titus looked up at the stars. 'Fuck, let's get it over with.'

Titus stood up and passed over his sword. He pulled his tunic up, baring his stomach and chest. Ballista stood close in front of him. Titus placed his hands on Ballista's shoulders. The hilt of the sword in his right hand, Ballista laid the blade flat on his left palm. He brought the point up ever so gently to touch the skin just below Titus' ribcage, then moved his left hand round behind the soldier's back.

Ballista did not look away from the other man's eyes. The smell of sweat was strong in Ballista's nostrils. Their rasping breathing was as one.

Titus' fingers dug into Ballista's shoulders. An almost imperceptible nod, and Titus tried to step forward. Pulling the soldier towards him with his left hand, Ballista put his weight behind the thrust of the sword in his right. There was an infinitesimally slight resistance and then the sword sliced into Titus' stomach with sickening ease. Titus gasped in agony, his hands automatically clutching for the blade.

Ballista felt the hot rush of blood as he smelt its iron tang. A second later there was the smell of piss and shit as Titus voided himself.

'*Euge*, well done,' Titus groaned in Greek. 'Finish it!'

Ballista twisted the blade, withdrew it, and thrust again. Titus' head jerked back as his body went into spasm. His eyes glazed. His legs gave way, his movements stilled, and he began to slide down the front of Ballista. Letting go of the sword, Ballista used both hands to lower Titus to the ground.

Kneeling, Ballista pulled the sword out from the body. Coils of intestines slithered out with the blade. Shiny, revoltingly white, they looked and smelled like unprepared tripe. Ballista dropped the weapon. With his blood-soaked hands he closed the dead man's eyes.

'May the earth lie lightly on you.'

Ballista stood. He was drenched in the blood of the man he had killed. Maximus led several others out of the darkness. They carried entrenching tools. They began to dig a grave. Calgacus put his arm round Ballista and led him away, quietly soothing him, as he had when he was a child.

Four hours later the moon was up and they were on the move. Ballista was surprised that, after Calgacus had undressed him and cleaned him, he had slept a deep, unhaunted sleep. Wearing new clothes, his armour burnished, he was back on Pale Horse, leading the diminished party towards the west.

One by one the stars faded. When the sun rose again there were the mountains ahead still blue in the distance. And behind was the dust of their hunters. Much nearer now. Not above two miles away.

'One last ride.' As Ballista said the words he realized they were double-edged. He thought a quick prayer to Woden, the high god of his homelands. *Allfather, High One, Death Blinder, do not let my careless words rebound on me and mine, get us out of this.* Out loud, he called again, 'One last ride.'

At the head of the column Ballista set and held the pace at a steady canter. Unlike yesterday, there was no time to dismount, no time to walk and let the horses get their breath back. As the sun arched up into the sky, relentlessly they rode to the west.

Soon the horses were feeling their exertions: nostrils flared, mouths hanging open, strings of spittle flecking the thighs of their riders. All morning they rode, the mountains inching closer. Some god must have held his hands over them. The track was rough, pitted and stony, but there were no cries of alarm; not one animal pulled up lame or went down in a flurry of dust and stones. And then, almost imperceptibly, they were there. The track began to incline up, the stones at its side grew bigger, became boulders. They were in the foothills.

Before the path turned and began to grade its way up the slopes, before the view was blocked, Ballista reined in and looked back. There were the Sassanids, a black line about a mile behind. Now and then sunlight glinted perpendicular on helmets or pieces of armour. Certainly they were within thirteen hundred paces. Ballista could see they were cavalry, not infantry. He had known that already. He estimated there were some fifty or more of them. There was something odd about them, but there was no time to stop and study more. He coaxed Pale Horse on.

They had to slacken the pace as they climbed. The horses

were labouring hard. Yet they had not been in the high country long before Haddudad said, 'The Horns of Ammon.'

They turned left into the defile. The path here was narrow, never more than twenty paces wide. It ran for about two hundred paces between the outcrops that gave the place its name. The cliff on the left was sheer. That on the right rose more gently; a scree-covered slope a man could ascend, lead a horse up, probably ride one down.

'At the far end, where it turns right, out of sight the path doubles back behind the hill,' Haddudad said. 'Place archers up on the right, hold the far end. It is a good killing ground, if we are not too outnumbered.'

As they rode up the defile Ballista retreated into himself, planning, making his dispositions. When they were about fifty paces from the end he stopped and issued his orders. 'I will take Maximus, Calgacus and the girl with me up the hill. She is as good with a bow as a man. The Greek boy can come to hold our horses, and you' – he pointed to one of the two remaining civilian members of his staff, not the North African scribe – 'will come to relay my orders.' He paused. He looked at Haddudad and Turpio. 'That leaves you two and five men down on the path. Wait round the corner, out of sight until you get my command, then charge down into the reptiles. Those of us above will ride down the slope to take them in the flank.'

Haddudad nodded. Turpio smiled sardonically. The others, exhausted, hollow-eyed, just stared.

Ballista unfastened the black cloak he had been wearing to keep the sun off his armour. He dropped it to the ground. It landed with a puff of dust in the middle of the path.

Then he untied poor Titus' purse from his belt. He opened it. There were a lot of coins. A soldier's life savings. He scattered them on the ground just beyond the cloak. As an afterthought he took off his helmet, the distinctive one with the bird-of-prey crest, and tossed that down as well.

Haddudad grinned. 'Cunning as a snake,' he said.

'Among your people that is probably a compliment,' Ballista replied.

'Not always,' said the Arab.

Ballista raised his voice to reach them all. 'Are you ready for war?'

'Ready!'

Three times the call and response, but it was a tired, thin sound, almost lost in the hills.

Turpio brought his horse next to Ballista. Quietly, he recited a poem in Greek.

> Don't cry
> Over the happy dead
> But weep for those who dread
> To die.

Ballista smiled and waved them all off to take up their positions.

'We will do what is ordered, and at every command we will be ready.'

Ballista lay full length on the crest of the hill, an old grey-brown blanket over his shoulders. He had rubbed handfuls of the dun-coloured sand into his hair and over his face. Twenty arrows were planted point down in the ground by his head, looking like a clump of desert grass or camel thorn. Those with him were resting behind the brow of the hill.

Staring at something for a long time in bright sunshine began to have a narcotic effect. The scene seemed to shift and waver, inanimate objects start to move. Twice Ballista had tensed, thinking the moment had come, before realizing his eyes had deceived him. It was not long after noon. They had made good time. The Sassanids must have halted for a rest in the foothills, confident their prey could not escape them.

Ballista blinked the sweat out of his eyes and shifted slightly in the hollow his body had made in the stony ground. He very much doubted this was going to work. Ten fighting men and the girl against at least fifty. Strangely, he did not feel particularly frightened. He thought of his wife and son and felt an overwhelming sadness that he would not see them again. He imagined them wondering what had happened to him, the pain of never knowing.

A movement, at last. The Sassanid cavalry walked round into the defile and Ballista's heart leaped. He saw what had been odd about their column – each Sassanid led two spare horses. That was how they had narrowed the distance so fast. Sixty horses but only twenty riders. The odds were no worse than two to one. And, Allfather willing, he could improve on that.

The leading Sassanid pointed, called something over his shoulder, and trotted ahead. He reached the things lying in the track and dismounted. Struggling to keep a grip on the reins of his three horses, he crouched down and picked them up.

Ballista grinned a savage grin. The others had not halted.

Instead they trotted up and bunched behind the man on foot. Fools, thought Ballista, you deserve to die.

Shrugging off the blanket, Ballista grasped his bow and got to his feet. As he took an arrow and notched it, he heard the others scrambling up to the crest. He drew the composite bow, feeling the string bite into his fingers and the tension mount in the wood, bone and sinew of its belly. Intent on their discoveries, the Sassanids had not noticed him. He selected the man he took to be their leader. Aiming above the bright red trousers and below the yellow hat at the black-and-white striped tunic, he released. A few seconds later the man was pitched from his horse. Ballista heard the shouts of surprise and fear. He heard those with him release their bows. Another arrow automatically notched, he shot into the bunch of riders, aiming low, hoping if he did not get a rider he would hit a horse. Not looking to see where the arrows struck, he released four or five times more into the group in quick succession.

The floor of the defile was a picture of confusion, bodies of men and animals thrashing, loose horses plunging, crashing into those still under control. Ballista swung his aim to the untouched rear of the column. His first shot missed. His second took a rider's horse in the flank. The beast reared, hurling the warrior backwards to the ground. The other two horses he had been leading bolted.

'Haddudad, Turpio, now! Demetrius, bring up the horses!' Ballista yelled over his shoulder. He shot off some more arrows as the crunch and scatter of loose stones grew louder behind him. When the Greek boy appeared with his mount Ballista dropped the bow and vaulted into the saddle. Guiding with his thighs, he set Pale Horse at the slope. From up here it looked far steeper than it had from below, an awkward surface of large slabs of ochre, grey and brown, with patches of treacherous scree.

Ballista leant back against the rear horns of the saddle, dropping the reins, letting Pale Horse find their way. He could hear the others following. Down and off to his right he saw the seven Roman riders, Haddudad and Turpio at their head, thunder into the defile.

As Ballista drew his sword, Pale Horse stumbled. The long cavalry *spatha* nearly slipped from Ballista's grip. Cursing mechanically, he recovered it and slipped the leather thong tied to the hilt over his wrist. The riders with Haddudad had ploughed into the head of the Sassanid column. They had bowled over or cut down three or four of the easterners, but the lack of space and sheer weight of numbers had brought them to a halt. There were loose Persian horses everywhere. Clouds of dust billowed up the scarred cliff face opposite.

Although taken by surprise and now leaderless, the Sassanids were experienced warriors. They were not ready to run. A Roman trooper with Haddudad toppled from the saddle. An arrow whistled past Ballista. Another landed in front of him, snapping and ricocheting away. Everything hung in the balance.

As Ballista neared the bottom, the closest two Sassanids stuffed their bows back into their cases and tugged their swords free. They were at a standstill. Ballista was moving fast. He wanted to use that. At the last moment he swerved Pale Horse at the warrior to his right. The brave little gelding did not flinch and crashed shoulder to shoulder into the Persian horse. The impact threw Ballista forward in the saddle. But the enemy horse was set back virtually on its quarters, its rider clinging to its mane to keep his seat. Recovering his balance in a moment, Ballista brought his sword across Pale Horse's neck in a fierce downward cut. The Sassanids were light cavalry; few of them wore armour. The blade bit deep into the man's shoulder.

Retrieving his sword, Ballista put Pale Horse to cut round the rear of the injured Sassanid's mount to get at the other one. Before he could complete the manoeuvre a third easterner lunged at him from the right. Ballista caught the blade on his own, rolled his wrist to force the Persian's weapon wide and riposted with an underhand cut at the man's face. The Sassanid swayed back. As Ballista's blade sliced harmlessly through the air he felt a searing pain in his left bicep.

Now he was caught between the two Sassanids. With no shield, not even a cloak to guard his left side, Ballista had to try to parry the attacks of both with his sword. He twisted and turned like a baited bear when the dogs close in, steel rang on steel and sparks flew. A hammer-like blow from the right hit Ballista in the ribcage. The Persian's lunge had broken one or two of the mail rings on his coat, forcing the jagged ends into his flesh. But the armour had kept out the point of the blade.

Despite the pain, Ballista forced himself upright and swung a horizontal cut not at the man on his right but at his horse's head. It missed but the animal skittered sideways. Painfully sucking air into his lungs, Ballista swivelled in the saddle, blocked a blow from his left and lashed out with his boot, kicking the Sassanid's mount in the belly. It too gave ground. He had bought himself a few seconds' reprieve.

Ballista looked up. There was nowhere to go. In front of

Pale Horse were four or five loose horses, milling, blocking the way. Again, the fierce dark faces closed in. Again, Ballista twisted and turned like a cornered animal. But he was getting slower. His left arm throbbed. His damaged ribs were agony as he moved. It hurt like hell to draw breath.

Just when it seemed that it could only end one way, Maximus appeared. A deft cut, almost faster than the eye could follow, there was a spray of blood and the warrior on Ballista's left toppled from the saddle. No time for thanks, Maximus spurred on and Ballista turned all his attention to his remaining adversary.

After a time, as if by mutual consent Ballista and his opponent backed their horses a pace or two. Panting heavily, each waited for the other to make the next move. The din of combat echoed back from the rocky slopes and the dust rose up like chaff from a threshing floor. Around Ballista and the Persian the hot battle roared, but their perceptions had narrowed to a space little bigger than the reach of their swords. Ballista's left arm was stiff, almost useless. Every breath he took seared his chest. He noted another rider in eastern dress looming up in the murk behind his assailant. Ballista recognized him.

'Anamu!'

Ballista had last seen him just days before, serving as a temporary Roman officer in the defence of his home town, Arete.

'Anamu, you traitor!'

The long, thin face of the man from Arete turned towards Ballista. The wide-spaced eyes showed no surprise. 'It is not my fault,' the man shouted in Greek. 'They have my family. I had to guide them after you.'

Seeing Ballista's distraction, the Sassanid surged forward. Instinct and the memory in his muscles let Ballista flick the blade aside.

Anamu tipped his head back and shouted, loud, in Persian, 'Every man for himself! Run! Save yourselves!' He kicked his horse. It gathered itself and set off. Over his shoulder he called to Ballista again in Greek, 'Not my fault.'

The Sassanid facing Ballista backed his horse again, four, five steps, then hauled on the reins, jerked the beast round and followed Anamu. Suddenly the air was full of high eastern cries. The rattle of hooves echoed round the Horns of Ammon. As one the Persians desperately sought to disengage and spur their way to safety. The fight was over.

Ballista watched the Sassanid cavalry disappear down the defile. His own men were already busy, throwing themselves off their mounts, slitting the throats of the wounded easterners, stripping them, searching for the wealth they were rumoured always to carry.

'Leave one alive,' Ballista shouted. But it was too late.

Haddudad and Turpio arrived and calmly announced the butcher's bill: two troopers dead, two men wounded, including Turpio himself, who had an ugly gash on his left thigh. Ballista thanked them, and all three climbed stiffly to the ground.

Ballista checked over Pale Horse: a graze on the left shoulder, a small nick on the right flank, but otherwise the gelding seemed unharmed. Calgacus appeared with water and strips of clean cloth. He started to bandage Ballista's arm, swearing volubly as his patient kept moving to stroke his mount.

Bathshiba cantered up. Ballista had forgotten all about

the girl. She jumped off her horse, ran to Haddudad and threw her arms round his neck. Ballista looked away. Something shining on the ground caught his eye. It was the helmet he had discarded earlier. He went over and picked it up. It was buckled. A horse's hoof had trodden on it. The bird-of-prey crest was bent, twisted out of shape, but it could be repaired.

Dux Ripae

(Autumn AD256–Spring AD257)

'Alas, the earth will drink the dark blood of many men.
For this will be the time when the living will call the dead blessed.
They will say it is good to die,
But death will flee from them.
As for you, wretched Syria, I weep for you.'

      – *Oracula Sibyllina* XIII, 115–119

I

Ballista wanted to be a good Roman. Woden the Allfather knew he did. But it was difficult. At times like these it was almost impossible. How could they stand the stupid rules and ridiculous rituals, the stifling impediments of civilization? If a wounded man coated in the dust of nineteen days of almost non-stop travel rode up to the imperial palace in Antioch, staggered slightly as he dismounted, and said that he had news for the emperor's ears only, news of the terrible Persian enemy, you would think that the courtiers might usher him without delay into the presence of the Augustus.

'I am most abjectly sorry, most high *Dominus*, but only those specifically invited to the sacred *consilium* of the emperor Valerian Augustus can be admitted.' The fat eunuch was adamant.

'I am Marcus Clodius Ballista, *Dux Ripae*, Commander of the Riverbanks, *Vir Egregius*, Knight of Rome. I have ridden non-stop from the Euphrates, and I have news of the Sassanid Persian enemy that the emperor needs to hear.' There was a clear dangerous edge to Ballista's voice.

'I could not be more abjectly sorry, most noble *Dux*, but it is impossible.' The eunuch was sweating hard but, metaphorically, he did not lack balls. He was standing his ground.

Ballista could feel his anger rising. He breathed deeply. 'Then pass a message to the emperor that I am outside and need to speak to him and his advisors.'

The eunuch spread his hands wide in a gesture of desolation. 'I fear that it is beyond my powers. Only the *ab Admissionibus* could authorize such a thing.' Rings – gold, amethyst, garnets – glittered on his chubby fingers.

'Then tell the *ab Admissionibus* to give Valerian the message.'

A look of genuine shock appeared on the heavily jowled face – no one in the court would dream of baldly referring to the emperor by just one of his names. 'Oh no, the *ab Admissionibus* is not here.'

Ballista looked around the courtyard. Brick dust hung thick in the air. From somewhere came the sound of hammering. At the foot of the steps stood four *silentarii*, their title eloquent of their function – no man should disturb the sacred calm of the imperial deliberations. They were backed by a dozen praetorian guardsmen by the great doors at the top of the steps. There was no chance that Ballista could force his way into the imperial presence. He listened to the hammering. Although it was almost a year to the day since Ballista had been at the new imperial palace at Antioch, it was still unfinished and much would have changed. There was no real likelihood that he could expect to find an unguarded way to sneak in among the confusion of builders. He knew that his fatigue was making his grip on his temper tenuous. As he rounded again on the functionary barring his way, the eunuch began to talk.

'Not all members of the *consilium* are here yet. The *ab Admissionibus* is expected at any moment, *Dominus*. Perhaps you might speak to him.' The eunuch's smile was placating; his expression was like that of a dog which fears a beating and bares its teeth.

At Ballista's nod the eunuch quickly turned and waddled away.

Ballista looked at the heavens, then closed his eyes as his tiredness provoked a wave of nausea. 'For fuck's sake,' he said in the language of his native Germania.

Opening his eyes, Ballista again looked round the court-yard. The large, dusty square was crowded with men from all over the *imperium* of the Romans. There were men in Roman togas, Greeks in tunics and cloaks, Gauls and Celt-Iberians in trousers. Other groups clearly came from beyond the borders. There were Indians in turbans, Scythians in tall, pointed hats, Africans in colourful robes. Wherever the emperors went, the business of the empire followed them in the form of innumerable embassies. There were embassies from communities within the empire waiting to ask for benefits, both straightforwardly tangible – relief from taxation or from the billeting of troops – and more symbolic: honorific titles or the right to enlarge their town council. And there were embassies from further away, from the so-called 'friendly kings', wanting help against their neighbours or financial subsidies. They always wanted financial subsidies. Now the empire was reeling – attacked on all its frontiers, rebellions breaking out in province after province – those near enough to raid across the borders always got their subsidies.

'Excuse me.' Ballista was exhausted. He had not noticed the man approach.

'I heard you speak in our language.' The man was smiling the smile of someone who thinks that he has come across one of his own race a long way from home. His accent pointed to one of the southern German tribes, one down by the Danube or the Black Sea. It put Ballista on his guard.

'I am Videric, son of Fritigern, the King of the Borani. I am my father's ambassador to the Romans.'

There was a silence. Ballista pulled himself up to his not inconsiderable full height.

'I am Dernhelm, son of Isangrim, the Warleader of the Angles. The Romans know me as Marcus Clodius Ballista.'

The look on Videric's face changed to something very different. Automatically, his hand went to his hip, where the hilt of his sword should rest. It was not there. Like Ballista's, like all other weapons, it had been taken by the praetorians on the front gate.

Two other Borani came up and flanked Videric. The three warriors glowered. They looked much alike: big powerful men, long fair hair to their shoulders, a surfeit of gold rings on their arms.

'You bastard,' Videric spat. Ballista stood his ground. 'You fucking bastard.'

Ballista looked at the three angry men. He had sent his own men, his bodyguard Maximus and the others, to the barracks. He was alone. Yet there was little immediate to worry about. The praetorians did not encourage those waiting in the hope of seeing the emperor to fight among themselves.

'Last year in the Aegean, two longboats of Borani warriors, and you only spared about a dozen to sell as slaves.' Videric's face was very pale.

'Men die in war. It happens.' Ballista kept his voice neutral.

'You shot them down when they could not resist.'

'They would not surrender.'

Videric stepped forward. One of the other Borani put a hand on his arm to restrain him. Videric gave Ballista a look of complete contempt. 'And that is why we Borani are here to collect our tribute from the Romans. While you . . .' Words failed him for a moment. Then he laughed, a harsh snort. 'While you wait like a slave for your orders. Maybe your Roman master will see you after he has handed his gold to us.'

'I live in hope,' Ballista replied.

'One day we will meet again where there are no Roman guardsmen to protect you. There is a bloodfeud between us.'

'As I said, I always live in hope.' Ballista turned his back on them and walked away to the centre of the great courtyard. Wherever you go, old enemies will find you.

A deep metallic boom rang out from the inner gate. Ballista turned. Around him all conversation died as almost everyone turned and gazed up at the gate. High up on the second storey was a gilded statue of a naked man. In his right hand the statue held a tall stake. Nine large golden spheres were suspended at the top of the stake; three more rested at the bottom. Despite his fatigue,

Ballista found the mechanical water clock caught his attention. Obviously, one of the spheres slid down at the start of each of the twelve hours of daylight. It was the third hour. Conventionally, this was when the *salutatio*, the time for receiving visitors, ended and the courts began to sit. The autocratic powers of the emperors had long ago blurred such distinctions.

As the reverberations died away a low hum of talk returned. The water clock was new. It had not been there a year earlier. The engineer in Ballista made a mental note to find out how it worked. He looked away, scanning the courtyard. The great fortress-like walls with their embedded Corinthian columns dwarfed the crowd. The Borani were near the inner gate, still gawping up openmouthed. Ballista moved away towards the outer gate.

A small group of peasants, thin men in much-patched tunics, shifted to one side as Ballista sat on the ground. The big northerner settled himself to wait. His elbows on his knees, his head in his hands, he shut his eyes. The sun was warm on his back. The peasants started talking softly in a language Ballista did not know. He thought it was Syriac.

His mind drifted. Once again he saw the flames engulf the city, the strong south wind pull long streamers of fire into the night sky, the eruption of sparks as a roof gave way. Once again he saw the city of Arete die. The city that he had been charged to defend.

Inexorably, Ballista's thoughts turned to the nightmare flight from Arete. The hellish, relentless pursuit through the desert. His sword slicing into Titus' guts. The trooper gasping out his life breath. The vicious fight at the Horns of Ammon. Then two days crossing the mountains.

Hunched in the saddle, sharp, gnawing hunger driving out all other thoughts. Their staggering journey from one brackish watering hole to another.

Ballista's thoughts moved on. Down from the mountains at last. The first Roman-held village. Clean water, food, a bath, the news that the emperor Valerian had set up his court in Antioch. Then on down a broad Roman highway to the caravan city of Palmyra. And there he had left Bathshiba. Left her and Haddudad. It had been a hurried, tense parting for the three of them, with much left unsaid. There had been little time to say anything, and Ballista had lacked the words. He had not known what he wanted to say.

The rest of the journey had been physically easy. Good Roman roads all the way. West from Palmyra to the next great caravan city of Emesa. Then north up the lush valley of the Orontes River. Ballista again felt the motion of the horse under him as they plodded through the water-meadows towards Antioch, towards the imperial court and the report that he must give today. *The city fell. The Sassanid Persians took it. I failed.*

Click, drag, step. Click, drag, step.

The sounds jerked Ballista awake.

From under the arch of the outer gate came Macrianus. Click went his walking stick, his lame foot dragged, and his sound one took a step. Click, drag, step. The crowds parted as he moved into the courtyard. He was followed at a couple of paces by two other men in togas. In all bar one respect they were younger images of himself; the same long, straight nose, the receding chin, the pouches under the eyes. But the sons of Macrianus walked easily. There was a lithe, confident swagger in their step. Ballista had never seen the sons before, but he had met Macrianus once or twice.

Marcus Fulvius Macrianus may have been old and lame, and his low birth was widely known, but he was not to be taken lightly. As *Comes Sacrarum Largitionum*, Count of the Sacred Largess, as well as being in charge of clothing the court, the army and the civil service – the imperial dye works answered to him – he controlled all the money taxes in the *imperium*, the gold and silver mines, the mints that produced the coinage and, most potent of all, he paid both the regular cash salaries of soldiers and officials and the not infrequent donatives to the military. As *Praefectus Annonae*, Prefect of the Grain Supply, he fed the city of Rome and the imperial court. He had agents and depots in every province of the *imperium*. More to the point, he had the ear of the emperors.

Macrianus had risen high. Now he shone in the sunlight, his toga gleaming white, the golden head of Alexander the Great which topped his walking stick flashing. Click, drag, step. Neither he nor his sons looked right or left as they made their way towards the inner gate and the imperial *consilium*.

Ballista hauled himself stiffly to his feet.

'*Ave, Comes. Ave*, Marcus Fulvius Macrianus.'

Click, drag, step. The lame man paid no attention.

'Macrianus.' Ballista stepped forward.

'Out of the way, you filthy barbarian. How dare you address the *Comes Sacrarum Largitionum et Praefectus Annonae*.' The contempt in the son's tone was not feigned.

Ballista ignored him. 'Macrianus, I need to talk to you.'

'Speak when you are spoken to, you piece of barbarian shit.' The youth was closing on Ballista.

'Macrianus, it is me.'

The lame man did not break his slow progress, but he looked at the long-haired, dirty barbarian who was speaking to him. There was no immediate recognition on his face.

'Macrianus, it is me, Ballista, the *Dux Ripae*. I have news of the Sassanids . . .' The blow to the left side of his head cut off Ballista's words. He staggered a few steps to his right.

'Let this be a lesson to you.' The youth waded forward, ready to punch again. Ballista crouched, one hand to his temple. He turned slowly, as if dazed, to face his attacker.

When the youth came close enough Ballista lashed out a straight right, hard and fast to the crotch. The youth doubled up, both hands clasping his balls. He tottered three steps backwards. The toga was a ceremonial costume, its very impracticality its point. Romans wore it on special formal days when they were neither doing physical work nor fighting. Now the youth's toga caught round his legs. He sat down hard.

Ballista straightened up and turned to Macrianus.

'Macrianus, it is me, Marcus Clodius Ballista, the *Dux Ripae*. You must take me with you into the *consilium*.'

Macrianus had stopped. He stared into Ballista's eyes. Something more than recognition, some guarded calculation, as if he had never expected to see Ballista again, played across his face.

'It is vital that I talk to the emperor.' Ballista heard men running, hobnailed boots pounding, others scrabbling out of the way. He kept his eyes on those of Macrianus. A small smile began to spread across the face of the *Comes Sacrarum Largitionum*.

Ballista was knocked sideways and crashed violently to the ground as the praetorian tackled him. The guardsman rolled off Ballista and got to his feet. Another praetorian arrived. He punched the butt of his spear into Ballista's back. Despite the sickening surge of pain, the northerner tried to get to his feet.

A blow to the head stopped Ballista. Another to the stomach dropped him to his knees. He covered his head as a flurry of spear butts rained down on his arms and shoulders.

'That's it. Beat the barbarian pig. He threatened the *Comes Sacrarum Largitionum* and attacked my brother Quietus. Beat him senseless, then throw the dog out into the street,' the other young man was shouting.

Ballista was curled up into a ball, the paving slabs gritty under his cheek as he tried to cover himself. After a short time the beating stopped. Ballista heard Macrianus' voice.

'My son, Macrianus the Younger, is right. Now throw him out into the street.'

Strong hands grabbed the northerner and began to drag him to the outer gate. Ballista twisted his head, and got a blow round the ear for his pains. But he saw Macrianus and his two sons resuming their rudely interrupted progress to the imperial *consilium*.

'Macrianus, you cunt, you know that I am the *Dux Ripae*.' Although he must have heard, the Count of the Largess did not pause. Click, drag, step. He vanished up the steps and into the inner gate.

Almost gently, one of the guardsmen punched Ballista in the side of the head.

'Keep a civil tongue in your head when talking to the nobility, you barbarian fucker.'

Ballista ceased to struggle. He let his head loll. The toecaps of his boots were dragging on the ground. Expensive boots – that will do them no good, he thought inconsequentially.

'Halt.' The voice was one accustomed to being obeyed. The praetorians halted. 'Let me see him.'

The guardsmen let go of Ballista, who collapsed onto the flagstones.

'Put him on his feet, so that I can see him.'

The rough hands that grasped Ballista were almost solicitous as they manoeuvred him to his feet. Seeing the northerner sway, two of the praetorians supported his arms.

A long, thin face swam into Ballista's view. It came very close, the big eyes squinting. Ballista thought it was strange: he was so light-headed with fatigue that he felt no real pain. His forehead tickled as blood ran down from a cut on his hairline. He tried to wipe it away with his left hand, but only succeeded in smearing it over more of his face.

'Gods below, is it really you, Ballista, under all that filth?'

Ballista stared back at the man. The long, thin face was oddly asymmetrical. It looked familiar.

'Cledonius, it has been a long time.' Ballista smiled. It hardly hurt at all. Although not a close friend, Cledonius, the *ab Admissionibus*, had long been something of an ally of Ballista's at the imperial court.

'What in Hades has happened to you?' Cledonius sounded genuinely concerned.

'You mean before the praetorians beat me?'

Cledonius rounded on the praetorians. 'On whose authority did you do this?'

The praetorians came to attention. 'The order came from the Count of the Largess, *Dominus*.'

Cledonius' face gave nothing away. Life in the palace did not encourage wearing your heart on your sleeve. He turned back to Ballista.

'The last I heard, you were *Dux Ripae*.' Cledonius opened his mouth to say something else but stopped. Ballista could almost see the thoughts running through the other man's mind. *You were appointed* Dux Ripae. *You were ordered to defend the city of Arete from the Sassanids. You are here hundreds of miles away in Antioch, wounded, covered in dirt. The city has fallen. You have failed.*

'We had better clean you up a bit. Then you can tell the emperor what happened.' The look on Cledonius' face now was not all that different from that which had been on Macrianus' earlier: closed, careful calculation. At an autocrat's court, advance knowledge could be turned to advantage, but close association with some newsbringers could also be dangerous.

Cledonius made a courtly gesture with his arm. The two praetorians let go of Ballista and, together, he and Cledonius set off across the courtyard. The crowds parted. Although his head ached and his shoulders and back were stiff, Ballista found that he could walk quite normally. As they neared the inner gate he saw the three Borani warriors scowling. At the steps the *silentarii* moved aside. The praetorians saluted and swung back the great doors.

Cledonius and Ballista walked through into another courtyard. This one was long and narrow compared with what had gone before. A colonnade of free-standing Corinthian columns linked by arches ran down either side. The doors shut behind them. It was quiet and almost deserted. Their footsteps echoed as they walked. Statues of deified emperors of the past looked down at them. At the far end was the third gate, a relatively modest affair only three or four times the height of a man set in the middle of four more Corinthian columns.

Another squad of praetorians saluted and opened the doors. Cledonius and Ballista passed from the sunlight through into the near-darkness of the imperial vestibule. They stopped, letting their eyes grow accustomed to the gloom. Dark, rich, purple hangings seemed to absorb what little light was shed by two rows of golden lamps. The air was heavy with incense.

A fat eunuch approached, his hands decorously hidden in his robes. Ballista was not sure if it was the one he had seen before. Cledonius spoke quietly and the eunuch waddled away.

'Wait here,' Cledonius said. 'The eunuch will bring you some water and towels. Wash the blood off your face. I will come and get you.' With no further ado the *ab Admissionibus* went on through the hangings at the far end, leaving Ballista alone.

The eunuch returned. Ballista cleaned his face. Wetting his hands, he pushed back his long blond hair. It lay lank on his shoulders. He slapped some of the dust from his tunic and trousers. Most of his body ached. He needed to sleep. It was very quiet in the vestibule. Four praetorians stood to attention. Now and then court functionaries crossed the room with silent, purposeful tread.

Ballista wondered if, at the very limit of his hearing, was the sound of distant hammering. At last, after the endless ride, here he was. Time to make his report. *The city fell. The Sassanid Persians took it. I failed.* Then the worm of suspicion was back in his mind. *I failed, as you always knew I would.* Men sent on suicide missions cannot expect to be welcomed as heroes if they return.

Ballista knew that he had done what he had been sent to do. The *imperium* was being attacked on all sides; its forces were stretched beyond breaking point. North Africa was ablaze with a native revolt led by a charismatic warrior called Faraxen. In the west Valerian's son and co-emperor Gallienus had based himself at Viminacium in a desperate attempt to hold back beyond the Rhine and Danube the hordes of the north – the Franks, Alamanni, Carpi, Iuthungi, Danubian Goths and many other peoples. Valerian himself had come east to Antioch to try to repel both the barbarians from the Black Sea, the Heruli, Borani, Black Sea Goths and what most saw as the greatest threat of all, the Sassanids from beyond the Euphrates. Yes, Ballista had done what he had been sent to do. He had held up Shapur, the Persian King of Kings, for a whole campaigning season. Through the spring and summer, and into the autumn, the great Sassanid horde had sat before the walls of the city of Arete. They had sweated, laboured and died in their thousands, their every assault thrown back in bloody ruin. Ballista had bought the Romans a year's grace.

But it would have been less embarrassing for the empire if Ballista had died sword in hand in the ruins of Arete. Dead, he could have been a hero. Alive, he was the walking proof of heartless imperial duplicity, a continual reminder that the emperors had cynically sacrificed two units of Roman soldiers and an entire city for the greater good. *You bastards, you lied. There never was a relief force. You sent me there to die.*

The hangings parted and Cledonius reappeared. He gestured Ballista to come. The asymmetrical face was mask-like, revealing not a flicker of emotion. Ballista began to smile at the contrast between the short, neatly trimmed beard and carefully forward-combed hair of the *ab Admissionibus* and his own long, filthy locks and several days' stubble.

The hanging fell behind them and they were plunged into almost complete darkness. They stood still, just listening to their own breathing.

With no warning, the inner hangings were pulled back and Ballista was momentarily blinded by the rush of light. Squinting, he peered into the audience chamber of Imperator Caesar Publius Licinius Valerianus Augustus, Pontifex Maximus, Pater Patriae, Germanicus Maximus, Invictus, Restitutor Orbis.

As befitted his role as mediator between mankind and the gods, the emperor Valerian appeared suspended in mid-air. He was bathed in bright sunlight from the windows of the great apse where he sat. His toga gleamed painfully white and rays flashed from the golden wreath on his head. The emperor's face was immobile. His gaze was fixed on the distance, over the heads of mere mortals, far beyond the confines of the palace. As the Romans deemed right, the emperor looked as remote as a statue.

As Ballista's eyes adjusted, he saw the low altar where the sacred fire burned at the foot of the steps up to the throne.

He took in the Praetorian Prefect, Successianus, standing at the right shoulder of the emperor, the row of secretaries behind his left.

Cledonius touched Ballista's elbow and they set off to walk slowly the length of the long audience chamber. In front of the pillars on either side sat the members of the *consilium*, a dozen or so of the great men of the empire, as still and quiet as cowed schoolboys. Out of the corner of his eye Ballista saw the sons of Macrianus glowering. The face of their father, longer schooled in the ways of the court, was expressionless. Near them, Ballista saw another man he thought that he recognized. The artfully curled hair and beard, the supercilious expression reminded him of someone. In his fatigue the recognition remained tantalizingly out of reach.

They stopped just short of the sacred fire.

'Marcus Clodius Ballista, *Dux Ripae*, Commander of the Riverbanks, *Vir Egregius*, Knight of Rome.' The voice of the *ab Admissionibus* was reverent but carried well.

Valerian remained motionless, his gaze still far away.

At a sign from Cledonius, Ballista advanced to the foot of the steps and performed *proskynesis*, adoration. Hoping that his reluctance was not evident, the northerner lowered himself to his knees then prostrated himself full length on the floor.

Still Valerian did not look at him. But after a while the emperor held out one of his hands. Ballista got to his feet and, bowing, kissed the proffered heavy gold ring, set with a gem cut with an image of an eagle.

At last the emperor looked down at the man in front of him. The thin, delicate leaves of the golden wreath rustled.

'*Ave*, Marcus Clodius Ballista, *carissime Dux Ripae*, my dear Commander of the Riverbanks.'

Ballista looked up at the emperor. There was the prominent chin, the fleshy cheeks and neck. Now the sparse, carefully groomed moustache and whiskers framed a mouth that was set, eyes that contained no warmth. The word *carissime* was never more of a formality.

The emperor looked at Ballista. The northerner looked back at the emperor. A Roman would have looked away, would have respectfully dropped his eyes. Ballista was buggered if he was going to look away. Motes of dust moved lazily in the sunlight.

At length the elderly emperor nodded, as if to confirm something to himself, and spoke.

'Marcus Clodius Ballista, tell the sacred *consilium* the things that have happened to you and the things that you have done. Take the floor.'

Ballista carefully walked a few steps backwards, stopping just beyond the low altar of the imperial fire. Cledonius had melted into the background. Ballista was alone in the middle of the chamber. He was very aware of the members of the *consilium* seated on either side, but he kept his gaze and all his attention on the old man on the elevated throne.

What has happened to me! No one knows better than you what has happened to me. You and your son betrayed me. Gave me false promises and sent me to my death. You bastard! Ballista swayed slightly. He was light-headed. He knew that he had to control himself. He started to talk.

'Last autumn, following the *mandata*, instructions, given to me by the emperors Valerian and Gallienus, I travelled to the city of Arete on the Euphrates River. I arrived thirteen days before the *kalends* of December. The seasonal rains began the next day. Over the winter I readied the defences of the city. The Sassanid Persians came in April when there was grass for their horses and no more rain to dampen their bows. They were led by Shapur, the King of Kings, in person.'

A faint rustle like a shiver ran through the *consilium* at the mention of the great enemy of Rome, the eastern barbarian who had the audacity to claim equality with the Roman master of the world.

'The Sassanids assaulted the walls first with siege towers, then with a huge ram. We threw them back both times. Many of Shapur's men died. The plain before the city was a charnel house.'

Ballista paused, fighting his weariness to put his memories in order.

'The Sassanids built a siege ramp to overtop our walls. We collapsed it. They undermined a stretch of the city wall and one of the towers, but our earth banks held the defences upright.'

Ballista took a deep breath.

'Shapur ordered one final assault. It failed like the others. Then . . . then, that night, the city was betrayed.'

There was an audible intake of breath from the *consilium*. Even the emperor involuntarily leaned forward. Ballista did not wait for the inevitable question.

'Christians. The Christians were the traitors.'

There was a low babble of voices. Valerian shot a significant look at one of his advisors – which one? Macrianus possibly? – then again nodded as if something had been confirmed to him.

The rising murmur of voices ceased like a lamp snuffed out as a *silentarius* stepped into view.

The emperor sat back on his throne, recomposing himself into a suitably dignified immobility. After a time he spoke.

'The city fell, and you are here.' The imperial voice was neutral.

Ballista felt a hot jet of anger rising in himself. 'With a few companions, I cut my way out of the city. Nothing in my *mandata* said that I had to die there.'

Valerian betrayed no response, but on either side the members of the *consilium* grew even stiller. Ballista was tired and he was angry, but he knew that he had to be very careful or his words would yet see him executed. Everyone waited for the emperor's next words. The emperor's will was law. There was no appeal from his verdict. As a Roman citizen, Ballista would have the advantage of being beheaded and not nailed to a cross.

'Our nature is merciful. We are filled with *clementia*, clemency. Let no one think that we would ever order one of our subjects to his death. We are not an oriental despot like Shapur the Persian, intent on enslaving the world, but the bulwark and embodiment of *libertas*, freedom.' A mutter of assent ran round the *consilium*. 'Who has a question for the *Dux Ripae*?' Valerian gestured.

Ballista half-turned. The man rising to speak was the one who had looked familiar as Ballista entered the audience chamber. That long, artfully curled hair, a short, neatly barbered beard, with at its bottom a ruff of hair teased out – *Allfather, if I were not so tired, I would be able to place this man*.

'What happened to my brother?'

Ballista stared stupidly. His mind was blank.

'My brother, the commander of the legionary detachment in Arete, my brother, Marcus Acilius Glabrio.'

Memories flooded into Ballista. He wondered how to say what he had to say.

'My brother?' The voice was tense, impatient.

'Your brother . . . your brother died a hero's death. The Persians were catching us. With one other, your brother said he would delay them. He said that, like Horatius, he would hold the bridge. None of us would have got away without his sacrifice. He died a death worthy of a patrician family of Rome, worthy of the Acilii Glabriones. A hero.'

There was a pause.

'You left him to die.' There was raw fury in the patrician tones. 'A jumped-up barbarian like you left a patrician of Rome to die. You left him to be cut down while you ran away.' The young nobleman's anger choked his words.

'It was his choice. He volunteered. I did not order him.' Ballista was not going to let himself be abused by a spoilt, pampered brat of the Roman nobility.

'You barbarian bastard. You will pay for the death of my brother. I, Gaius Acilius Glabrio, swear it by the gods below.'

The young patrician would have said more, he was even moving towards Ballista, when two *silentarii* appeared and, without words, herded him back to his seat.

'If there are no other questions?' The emperor's words cut across everyone's thoughts. 'Arete has fallen. The road is open for the Persians, to Northern Mesopotamia, to Cappadocia. The time of troubles has returned. Again, as just three years ago, the road lies open for Shapur – to Syria, here to Antioch, to the heart of our empire. Bitter war looms. Each one of us can ponder in private the implications of the news brought by the *Dux Ripae*. We will meet again in four days' time at the tenth hour in the evening after the *circus*. The *consilium* is over.'

The emperor stood up, and everyone else prostrated themselves as he walked out.

Bitter war looms, thought Ballista. When he faced Shapur again he would not fail. He would not let himself be betrayed again.

As they got to their feet, Cledonius quickly took Ballista's arm and led him from the audience chamber.

Outside in the sunshine, the *ab Admissionibus* kept them moving at some speed towards the main gate.

'Impressive, Ballista, most impressive, even by your standards. You have been back at the imperial court for less than a morning and already you have made two lots of extremely dangerous new enemies.' Cledonius adjusted his grip on the northerner's arm.

'First you make an enemy of Macrianus, the *Comes Largitionum*, one of the richest and most powerful men in the empire. A man who has two active and dangerous sons. Then, not content with that, you manage to make Gaius Acilius Glabrio, a strong-willed member of about the noblest family in the *imperium*, to swear an oath of vengeance against you. Very impressive.'

Ballista shrugged. He decided it was not the moment to tell Cledonius about Videric and the Borani – and, anyway, they were hardly new enemies . . .

'Luckily for you,' Cledonius said, as he steered Ballista through the great courtyard, 'very luckily for you, some of my servants are outside the gate with saddled horses.'

'What?' In his surprise Ballista stopped. 'Are you suggesting that I ride out of the city? What – go into hiding or flee across the borders?'

Cledonius' long face split into a huge grin. 'No. I just thought that, in your condition, the horses would make it easier to get across town to see your wife. You did know that she was here in Antioch?'

II

'And that is the Donkey-drowner.' Cledonius' words only registered on the surface of Ballista's thoughts. In truth, nothing had penetrated deeper since the *ab Admissionibus* had said that the northerner's wife was in the city.

'Flooding is a great problem here in Antioch in the rainy season. From November through to March – even April in some years – heavy cloudbursts fall up on Mount Silpius, and the water pours down into the city. Every gully turns into a flash flood – the Parmenios river is the worst, that is why the locals call it the Donkey-drowner.'

Why is he telling me this? Ballista wondered. He had spent a week in Antioch the previous year. *Julia is here. Isangrim, my beautiful son is here.* With a horrible lurch, Ballista realized that he had just assumed that Isangrim would be with Julia. He had not asked. *Allfather, Deep Hood, Long Beard, Fulfiller of Desire, let my son be here.*

'Back in the reign of Tiberius, they had a magician called Ablakkon set up a talisman against the floods. They are very proud of it, not that it seems to do much good.'

Of course, there was no reason that Cledonius should know that Ballista had spent a week in Antioch. *What would Isangrim look like? How tall would he be now?* It was thirteen months and twenty-two days since Ballista had seen him. He would be four and a half now. *Allfather, One-eyed, Terrible One, let the boy recognize me.*

Cledonius was still talking. 'Up there, you can see . . .'

And Julia . . . What would she look like? Ballista pictured the black – very black – eyes, the olive skin, the black hair tumbling to her shoulders. Julia – the daughter of a long line of Roman senators, married to a barbarian diplomatic hostage become Roman officer – how would she welcome him? He thought of her tall but rounded body, the firm breasts, the swell of her hips. Over a year without a woman; Allfather, he wanted her.

'. . . the Iron Gate, a complicated system of sluices.' Sensing Ballista's distraction, Cledonius sounded slightly put out. 'I thought that, as a military engineer, you might be interested.'

'No, I'm sorry, it's very interesting.' I can add it to the water clock at the palace as another piece of hydraulic engineering to study while the emperor decides my fate, Ballista thought sourly.

They turned their horses past the temple of Zeus, out of the *omphalos*, the 'navel' of the city, and into the main street. The great colonnaded street of Tiberius and Herod ran for about two miles right across the city. Unsurprisingly in a city of a quarter of a million people, it was crowded. Numberless kiosks were jammed between the columns on either side. They sheltered a bewildering range of merchants: greengrocers, goldsmiths, stonemasons, barbers, weavers, perfumers, sellers of cheese, vinegar, figs and wood. Ballista studied the cabins with their brushwood roofs. He could detect no order in their arrangement. More respectable trades, silversmiths and bakers, were jammed up against cobblers and tavern keepers.

Cledonius turned. His long, lop-sided face was smiling. 'They say that each clings to his pitch as Odysseus clung to the wild fig tree above the cave of the monster Charybdis.'

Ballista thought about this. The poetry of Homer was common currency among the elites of the *imperium*, its use an empire-wide badge of status. 'Does it mean that the sites are too lucrative to lose, or that if they lose them they will fall into an abyss of abject poverty?'

Cledonius' face did not change; it continued to smile an open, guileless smile, but he looked sharply at Ballista. It was easy to underestimate this barbarian. Never easier than now, when, muddied and bloody, he looked like everyone's idea of a big, witless northerner. It was all too easy to forget that he had been brought into the empire as a teenager and educated at the imperial court. Cledonius thought that only a fool would gratuitously make an enemy of this man.

'Off to our left is the main theatre. It contains a wonderful statue of the muse Calliope as the *Tyche*, the Fortune, of Antioch.' The *ab Admissionibus* resumed his soothing chatter. 'Some of the more ignorant locals think . . .'

After a time they turned left into a side street heading up towards the foothills of Mount Silpius. Soon they were deep in the residential district of Epiphania: on either side, well-built houses of limestone and basalt. The horses stretched out their necks and trod carefully as the street steepened. Over everything loomed the switchback wall of the mountain.

They passed the Temple of Dionysus, and Cledonius

pulled up in front of a large townhouse. The long blank wall of the residence was broken by a gate flanked by two columns of imported marble. A porter appeared.

'Tell the *Domina* Julia that her husband has returned,' Cledonius said.

For a moment the porter seemed confused, looking at the small cavalcade. With a miniscule gesture Cledonius indicated Ballista. Smartly the porter stepped over and held the bridle of Ballista's horse as the northerner dismounted.

'Welcome home, *Dominus*.' The porter bowed. Presumably he was either a hired local or a recent purchase. As Ballista thanked and said goodbye to Cledonius the porter ordered a boy to run and inform the *domina* of the happy event.

'Please follow me, *Dominus*.'

Ballista watched Cledonius and his servants ride on, then turned and followed the porter.

As they entered the house they walked over a mosaic of a naked hunchback sporting an improbably large erection. Obviously the owner of the rented house was a man of some superstition, who feared the envy of his fellow townsmen. Ballista smiled. There were many worse grotesques that could deflect the evil eye from one's front door, and this one to some extent mirrored what was on Ballista's mind.

At the end of a long dark corridor was an open courtyard. Ballista stopped when he emerged into the sunshine. There was a pool in the middle, reflecting dappled light up on to the surrounding columns. He looked into it. At the bottom was another mosaic. This one was an innocent scene of marine life: fishes, a dolphin and an octopus.

Ballista hesitated. He leant on one of the columns and closed his eyes. The reflected sunlight played on his closed eyelids. He felt strangely nervous and unsure. How would Julia receive him? It had been a long time. Would she still want him? With a sick feeling, he faced up to a fear he seldom let himself consider. Had she taken a lover? The morality of the metropolis, let alone that of the imperial court, was not that of his northern upbringing. There was no point hanging around here. *Do not think, just act.* Somehow the mantra that he had used to force himself through so many things seemed singularly inappropriate here.

Ballista opened his eyes and nodded to the porter, who led him across the courtyard and deeper into the house.

They crossed a dining room, more mosaics on the floor and paintings on the wall passing unnoticed. The porter stopped and opened a double door to the private apartments.

'*Domina*, your husband, Marcus Clodius Ballista.' The porter stepped back and Ballista walked into the room. The door closed behind him.

Julia stood very still on the far side of the room. She was flanked by two maids, each a step behind her. Decorously, she stepped forward.

'*Dominus.*' Her voice betrayed no emotion. Modestly, she kept her eyes down. She was every inch the Roman matron of the past receiving her husband back from the wars.

'*Domina.*' Ballista leant down. Julia brought her head up. Their eyes met. Hers gave nothing away. He kissed her gently on the lips. She looked down again.

'Will you sit?' She indicated a couch. Ballista sat.

'Would you care for a drink?'

Ballista nodded. She told one of her maids to bring wine and water, the other to bring a bowl of warm water and towels.

The maids left and the silence stretched. Julia kept her eyes down. Ballista sat very still. He stifled a yawn.

The maids returned. Julia told them that she would see to the comfort of the *dominus* herself. They should go and make sure that the bath was hot. The maids left once more.

She mixed a glass of wine and water and handed it to Ballista. She moved the bowl of water close to him and sank to her knees. He took a drink. With firm hands she pulled off his boots. Taking first one then the other of his feet, she began to wash them. The water splashed up on to his trousers.

'They are getting wet. You should take them off,' she said. Was there a hint of a smile before she looked down and her long black hair hid her face?

Ballista stood and pushed down his undergarments with his trousers and stepped out of them. He sat. She began washing his feet again. The tension was getting to him. His chest felt tight, his palms slick with sweat.

Julia looked up, into his face. She smiled.

With one movement, Ballista got to his feet. Putting his hands under her arms, he pulled her up with him. He kissed her. Her tongue darted into his mouth.

After a few moments she pulled a little away from him. 'My family warned me of this when they married me off to a barbarian – that I would be a slave to his dreadful lusts.'

Ballista grinned. 'Paulla' – he called her by the name her family used, 'Little One', then by his own affectionate diminutive, 'Paullula.' She stepped back and unfastened her tunic, letting it drop to the floor. She was wearing nothing underneath. Her body looked breathtakingly good. He bent and kissed her breasts, licking them, the nipples stiffening under his tongue.

He straightened up and looked in her eyes. 'It has been a very long time.' She did not reply, but taking his hand, turned and led him to a couch.

'Yes, it has been a long time,' she said. Her hands pushed his tunic up out of the way.

There were some other travellers on the road up to Daphne, but even after just three days it was a relief to be free of the crowds of Antioch.

Up to Daphne. It seemed strange to Maximus the bodyguard. He had noticed it when they were here the previous year. No matter where the locals set out from when they travelled to the suburb, they always said that they were going *up to Daphne.* But sure it was a pleasant enough trip. As soon as you cleared the south gate of the city there was the river, the great Orontes, rolling along to the right, and off to the left began the varied gardens, the springs, houses and shrines hidden among the groves. As you went on and the road edged away from the river, on both sides were shady vineyards and rose gardens. And all along, at no great interval, were the things that gave pleasure to a man like Maximus, the baths and the inns, and the lively looking girls around them.

At first they had ridden close together, the three adults on their horses and the boy on the pony. Ballista talked to the son, but Isangrim did not answer. The boy seemed withdrawn, even sullen. You could not expect to vanish from a child's life for over a year and straightaway be welcomed back. Yet it was embarrassing. Maximus and the Greek secretary Demetrius let their horses drop back. They looked around in the autumn sunshine.

Around midday a pleasant breeze began to blow from the south-west up the valley of the Orontes. The sleeves of the riders' tunics rustled in the wind. The boy started to talk. Then he wanted to ride with his father. Things were all right. Isangrim transferred to his father's horse. Ballista threw Maximus the lead reins of the pony. Ballista trotted on. The boy, clinging tightly to his father's back, was laughing.

It had a sly, nasty nature did the pony. Now they were stopped, it tried to sidle up to bite Maximus' horse. The Hibernian put his boot into its shoulder. The pony eyed the man's leg and showed its yellow teeth before deciding better of it and moving away. Maximus leant forward and played with his mount's ears.

'Hey, *Graeculus*, little Greek, come out of there. They will soon be out of sight.' Maximus knew that Demetrius, like all his race, liked to be called a *Hellene* not a *Graecus*, let alone a *Graeculus*, but he was in a mood to tease the boy.

'They will be out of sight, I tell you.' In truth, Ballista and his son were a couple of hundred paces ahead.

Demetrius emerged from the small wayside shrine. He looked absurdly young to Maximus. And he looked happy. That was good. He seldom looked happy. Even using a mounting block, the Greek youth struggled to get into his saddle. He was no horseman.

'The people of Antioch must be some of the most god-fearing in the world,' said Demetrius.

Maximus looked dubious. It was not their common reputation, and he could only think of one reason that the two girls outside the last tavern they had passed might get on their knees.

'Wherever you look are appeals to the gods.' Demetrius smiled. 'You remember the other day, when we rode into the Beroea Gate, I pointed out to you the talisman set up long ago by the holy man Apollonius of Tyana as a protection against the north wind?'

Maximus made an affirmative noise.

'And then, near the palace, the talisman set up by the sage Debborius against earthquakes?'

'You mean the statue of Poseidon that had been hit by lightning?'

'That is the one.' The Greek youth was smiling. 'And then the one in the *omphalos*, the one set up by Ablakkon to guard against flooding?'

'Mmm,' said Maximus.

'Well, now I have found another set up by the holy Apollonius. This one guards against scorpions.' Demetrius was pleased.

'Sure, might not someone with an uncharitable mind see all this as the most terrible superstition?' The Hibernian's question was accompanied by a quizzical look.

The Greek youth laughed. 'Oh yes, it is always important to distinguish true religion from base superstition.'

You should know, boy, thought Maximus.

'And indeed the plebs here, like the unwashed hoi polloi everywhere, are prey to the most ignorant of superstitions.

For example, in the theatre, there is a wonderful statue of the Muse Calliope as the *Tyche* of Antioch. You will never believe what the plebs think the statue represents . . .'

Demetrius chattered on as they trotted to catch up with Ballista and his son. Maximus let his thoughts wander. It was good that the Greek youth was happy. He had suffered badly in their flight from the fall of Arete: the hunger, the fatigue; above all, the fear. The Greek secretary was not naturally suited to an adventurous life. Actually, he seemed fairly unsuited to any life except that of scholarly leisure. Certainly he was unsuited to life as a slave. He frequently seemed unhappy, which struck Maximus as odd. If you were born into slavery, as Demetrius had said he was, surely you would get used to it, as certainly you had nothing to compare it with.

'So you see, the basest superstitions infect the plebs like a disease.' Demetrius was in full flow. 'I will give you another example . . .'

Truth be told, if anyone should find the pains of slavery especially sharp, it should be Maximus himself. He was already a warrior when he was captured in a tribal raid in his native Hibernia. He had been sold off to the Romans to fight in the *Arena*, first as a boxer then a gladiator. It had not been a good time. But then, Ballista had bought him as a bodyguard and things had become better. In some ways, things were better now than they would have been if he had not been captured. Either way, he would have had to fight – which was good: it was his skill and it was his pleasure. And here in the *imperium* the rewards were better: a greater variety to the alcohol and women.

Maximus looked down as they passed a traveller inspecting the hoof of his lame donkey. Demetrius was still talking.

Anyway, Maximus thought, *there is the debt.* Years ago, in Africa, Ballista had saved Maximus' life. There was no question of Maximus seeking his freedom until he had paid back the debt. Ballista kept offering to free Maximus, but the Hibernian could not accept. Maximus knew that he must return the favour, must clearly and unambiguously save Ballista's life, before he could think about freedom.

They caught up with Ballista and Isangrim. There was a grey-green humpback peak straight ahead. They crested a slight rise and there, opening off to their right, was a lush, wooded valley. This looked like good hunting country. They were coming into Daphne.

Demetrius clapped his hands with pleasure and said they were all blessed. The sides of the road were lined with inns and stalls, mainly selling food or souvenirs. It was not quite *meridiatio*, time for the siesta. The weather was warm despite the breeze. The tables outside the inns were full of men finishing their lunch or playing dice.

They walked their horses past the public baths and the Olympic stadium before they came to the tall, tall grove of cypress trees that was the sacred heart of Daphne. Dismounting, they paid a couple of street urchins to look after their horses. Rather more coins secured the services of a local guide.

They were led down shady paths. The air was full of birdsong and the sounds of the cypresses moving in the breeze. There were pleasant smells, smells sweeter than spices.

The guide stopped first at one particularly tall cypress tree, which stood apart from the others. He told them the story of the Assyrian youth Cyparissus who accidentally shot and killed his pet stag. So great was his grief that the gods took pity and changed him into this very cypress tree.

Even Demetrius looked unimpressed by this. Sensing that his audience was not with him, the guide moved swiftly on.

Next he brought them to a gnarled laurel tree. He told them of the god Apollo's lust for the mountain nymph Daphne, his relentless pursuit, her headlong flight, the moment of capture, her despairing plea to Mother Earth, and her miraculous transformation into the laurel tree in front of them.

While this was generally considered a far better story – indeed, Maximus found himself quite stirred up at the thought of the chase – it again seemed to fail to win total credence. Demetrius pointed out in a stage whisper that the story was usually set in mainland Greece, either in Thessaly or Arcadia.

At last the guide led them to the springs of Apollo. These won a far more positive response. Waterfalls cascaded down the rockface. The babbling waters were guided into semi-circular basins and pools. Streams ran on either side of the Temple of Apollo.

All the party except Maximus went into the temple and admired the great statue of the god – hair and laurel crown gilded, eyes made of huge violet stones – that, three years earlier, after the Persians had sacked and burned Antioch, had made Shapur throw away his torch and leave Daphne untouched.

Maximus was standing outside. The Hibernian was not a man given to bothering the gods, but even he recognized that there was something special about this place. Maybe the boundaries between man and the supernatural were especially thin here. Whatever it was, something was making the hairs on the back of his neck stand up. He looked around. There was nothing to be seen or heard except the water and the trees, the cooing of doves high up on the pediment of the temple.

When Ballista had seen all that he wanted to see, he gave the priests some money to make sacrifice and left the grove. The urchins looking after the horses led the party to an inn, which they said would serve them a good lunch even at this late hour. Ballista thought they were probably relatives of the innkeeper or that he paid them a small fee for every customer they produced. But the inn was fine. Vines were trained over trellises to make a pleasant out-of-doors dining room with a view over the distant plain of the Orontes. Having checked with the others, Ballista ordered their meal, a salad of artichoke hearts and black pudding followed by suckling pig.

Ballista thought that his reunion with his son was going as well as one could hope. At first Isangrim had been silent and resentful. *I waited for you. I sat on the stairs all the time. I did not think you were coming back.* But the boy had an affectionate nature, and soon it was as if there was nothing to forgive.

'I love sausages, Pappa.' Isangrim ate hungrily, with both hands. None of the men told him off for eating with the left hand, which was impolite. Maximus asked him what he wanted to do when he grew up.

'When I get as big as you I will be a forester.' Isangrim looked round at the famous cypresses. 'I chop all these trees

down.' He turned to his father, his earnestness unshakeable.
'I have to get up very early in the morning to do all the
work.' The three adults laughed.

The laughter carried clear across the terrace to where,
eating chickpea broth, the cheapest choice, the assassin sat
watching them.

The assassin had been watching for them all day. The client
had led him to the house in the Epiphania district at first
light. The assassin had given the client a threadbare old
cloak and a tattered, broad-brimmed travelling hat. He had
told the client to sit with him under the wide eaves on the
far side of the street, leaning against the wall close by the
closed wine shop, just like the vagrants did. There they had
waited, the assassin occasionally scratching the jagged scar
on the back of his right hand.

It had been a long wait; time enough for the assassin to
begin to really dislike his client. They had not spoken, but
that was not necessary. There was something about these
smooth, rich young men, an assurance and a swagger that
simply putting on some old clothes could not disguise.
They looked life in the eye in a way that a pleb down on
his luck would have had beaten out of him. The assassin
felt nothing about the man he was going to kill. If he was
a bad man, so much the better. If, on the other hand, he
was a good man, let the judges of the underworld send him
to the islands of the blessed. But the client – him he would
very much like to kill. But a man has to eat.

Eventually they had come out. The client had actually
raised his hand to point. The assassin had grabbed his
wrist and dragged it down. He had thought that the young

nobleman was going to hit him. The moment had passed, but neither was likely to forget it.

The assassin had studied them. There were four of them. Two mattered. The target was, as the client had described, a big, blond barbarian. Then there was the bodyguard, a vicious-looking brute with the end of his nose missing. The other two were of no consequence, a delicate-looking youth and a handsome small boy.

'Do you want me to kill the son as well?'

Again the nobleman's eyes blazed with anger. 'What do you think I am? A barbarian like him?'

The assassin had said nothing.

When the horses had been led out, the barbarian and his party had mounted and ridden off to the south. Shortly afterwards, the assassin and his client had got up and walked away. Around the corner, money had changed hands and they had gone their separate ways.

The assassin had walked to the alley, where he had tethered his donkey. He rolled up the disguises and strapped them to the saddle then set off to follow the target. As he knew the town like the back of his hand, there had been no need to hurry. He had killed many men. He was good at killing men. He just needed an opportunity – the barbarian distracted, the bodyguard at a distance. Then he would strike. It might not happen today, but the opportunity would come. Then he would collect the other half of the money, and it would be a good winter.

III

The day of the *circus* dawned, the twenty-fifth day of October, the fourth day since Ballista had told the emperor's *consilium* the fate of Arete. But for most of the inhabitants of Antioch on the Orontes, any city on the Euphrates was a long way away, its fate an irrelevance. Only three years had passed since the Persians had sacked Antioch, but to the average Antiochene that was as distant as the Trojan War.

The day of the *circus* started well. Long before sunrise the vault of the sky was a delicate blue, cloudless and bright. Even at that hour the six bridges to the island in the Orontes were already thronged. Of all the inhabitants of the *imperium* none took their pleasures with quite the deadly seriousness as the people of Antioch. Thousands of Antiochenes could be found who loved the theatre – the thousands who gazed with wonder at the turn of a pantomime dancer's leg. Then there were tens of thousands of devotees of the amphitheatre, their hearts in their mouths when the gladiators clashed and the blood splashed on the sand. But possibly even the gods themselves could not hope to number the inhabitants of Antioch-on-Orontes who lost their heads to the chariot races.

And it was not any run-of-the-mill races that they were thronging towards. This was no regular, local, Greek-style meeting, the teams funded more or less willingly by a member of the town council. This was racing in the grand Roman manner, truly metropolitan, complete with the four factions from the eternal city, the Greens, Blues, Reds and Whites, racing in the imperial style, directly commanded by the emperor, the most pious Augustus Valerian himself. The old emperor's reputation for being tight-fisted was obviously false. The ever-confident Diocles was driving for the Greens. He genuinely believed that he was by far the best; others held him arrogant. Calpurnianus was up for the Whites – if ever a man was on form, it was him. The legendary Spanish horse Candidus, as white as his name suggested, with his driver, Musclosus, and the venerable Mauretanian charioteer Scorpus had been coaxed out of retirement for the Blues and Reds respectively. It was not just politicians who were prepared to follow wherever the emperor travelled.

In the half-light, the queues, as noisy and jocose as only Antiochenes could be at such an hour, stretched back from the great red-brick *hippodrome*. Tickets were free, and no one could doubt that the racing arena would be full to its eighty thousand capacity, or beyond. When finally the chariot of the sun appeared over the jagged crest of Mount Silpius, almost all those waiting turned to the east and either performed complete *proskynesis*, prostrating themselves full length on the road, or at least the minor version of bowing slightly and blowing a kiss. The people of Antioch might or might not be considered god-fearing, but no race crowd was ever anything less than superstitious.

As the sun was coming up over the mountain, Maximus

stepped out of the house in the Epiphania district. There was nothing much to see in the street – a couple of men driving three laden camels, another adjusting some sacks on a donkey and, over the way, just like the day before, a vagrant sitting under the eaves close up to the still-shuttered wine shop. The litter that Maximus had hired was late. He crossed over. The beggar was asleep. Maximus stopped himself from throwing a handful of low-denomination coins. Instead he crouched down and quietly placed the coppers under the man's hand. The man did not move. Maximus noticed a long, dog-legged scar on the man's right hand. He stood up and turned his back. He looked away down the street, waiting.

The litter, a sturdy affair in light blue, rounded the corner. Maximus called to one of the houseboys to tell the *dominus* that it had arrived.

As the litter reached the house, Ballista emerged. His body servant Calgacus was fussing around him. Ballista was clad in a gleaming white toga with the narrow purple band of the equestrian order. The golden ring of that order that flashed on his finger was eclipsed by the blaze of the golden crown on his head. The crown, about three inches high, was in the stylized shape of the walls of a city. Very few men had the right to wear the *corona muralis*, the mural crown that proclaimed that its wearer had been the first to scale enemy battlements. Few men lived to tell the tale and receive the honour. As a youth serving in North Africa, Ballista had been desperate for distinction, and he had been very, very lucky.

Julia emerged, dignified and demure in the *stola* of a Roman matron. She held Isangrim by the hand. The boy's long hair, so carefully brushed, to its owner's fury, shone in the sunlight. He regarded the litter solemnly before announcing that it was blue, and that it was a good omen. Ballista, Calgacus and Maximus exchanged a smile. Although all three men followed the Whites, they knew that the boy supported the Blues. It was no accident that the litter was light blue.

The family were handed in and the litter was lifted on to the broad shoulders of its eight bearers. Maximus sent a couple of burly porters with big sticks in front to clear a passage. He adjusted the sword on his left hip and the dagger on his right. Maximus took his station by Ballista's side of the litter, Calgacus by Julia's. The bodyguard looked round to check that all was well, and gave the signal to move off.

Under the eaves of the wine shop, the vagrant stirred. He picked up the coins and scratched the scar on his right hand as he watched the litter set off. After a few moments he stood up and followed.

The passage of the litter from house to *hippodrome* was not quick. The notoriously independent-minded hoi polloi of Antioch were never keen to show due deference to rank or station. They were remarkably reluctant to move aside, even for big men with big sticks. As the litter passed they called out jibes, some funny, many innovative in their obscenity. The family, Calgacus and the bearers feigned deafness. Maximus shot glowering glances from side to side. Once, Ballista leant out and laid a restraining hand on the Hibernian bodyguard's arm when a pleb was about to pay the price for having the temerity to barge up against the litter. The Antiochene crowd was always volatile. It never took much to spark a street fight, or even a riot.

At length the litter was set down outside the southern end of the *hippodrome*, reasonably close to the gate in the tall, left-hand tower. Maximus and Calgacus helped the family out, then the body servant fussed with the cumbersome swags and drapes of Ballista's heavy ceremonial toga. The bearers kept the worst of the crush away until they reached the gate. Only those with tickets were allowed further. The three members of the family, Maximus and Calgacus went on. In the high, vaulted passageway under the west stand, the press of bodies grew worse. Elbows everywhere, it was impossible not to be jostled. Maximus swung Isangrim up on his shoulder. Julia walked in the comparative shelter between the three men.

Eventually, they came to the stairwells that led up to the seating reserved for senators and equestrians. They passed by the first set of steps, one of those that zigzagged up the back of the building to the very top of the stands. They stopped at the next flight, a straight, broad sweep of stairs that led through the heart of the stand to emerge halfway up, at the bottom of the bank of seating reserved for the social elite. Maximus gently set Isangrim on his feet between his parents. Again, Calgacus straightened Ballista's toga. With a jerk of his thumb, Maximus indicated the next arch, which was the entrance to a passageway which ran at ground level to the very front of the stands – he and Calgacus would not be all that far away, just there in the poor people's seats if they were needed.

Maximus stood still for a few moments. Calgacus waited. Maximus watched the family climb the steps – the small boy flanked by his tall father and mother, each holding one of his hands. Maximus could not understand the fidelity his friend had for this woman. He himself would never want to lead such a life of domesticity. But he knew that he would die before he let harm come to any one of the three.

The assassin watched, as Maximus and Calgacus turned and walked away. Having given them long enough to clear the passageway, he followed them into the section of ground-level seats.

The massed ranks of senatorial and equestrian togas shone in the morning sunshine – a bank of dazzling white with broad and narrow purple stripes. The arena was still crowded, but the threatening crush was gone. Ballista found their seats with reasonable ease. As the holder of the *corona muralis*, his seat and those of his family had been reserved. They settled themselves within the thin grooves on the stone bench that marked the extremities of their three spaces. Ballista called over a boy and rented some cushions and bought a racecard, some drinks, and a sweet confectionary for Isangrim. From somewhere within the folds of her *stola*, Julia produced a toy chariot for Isangrim – in the colours of the Blues.

They were only just in time. A thunderous blast of trumpets, and the gates of the monumental arch in the northern, rounded end of the *hippodrome* opened. As always, Victory led the procession. She seemed to hover over her chariot on wide-spread wings. A great, rolling cheer from the whole audience greeted her. The ivory images of the gods that followed were applauded by their particular devotees: Neptune by sailors, Mars by soldiers, Apollo and Artemis by soothsayers and hunters, Minerva by craftsmen, Bacchus and Ceres by drunks and countryfolk in town for the day.

Venus and Cupid were cheered by all – who could be so dull as to deny ever being touched by any aspect, physical or otherwise, of love? The applause rose to a crescendo as a gilded chariot brought in the *Tyche*, Fortune, of Antioch.

The cheers fell away as the images of the gods made their way down the track to their appointed places on the *spina*, the central barrier. The monumental gate stood empty.

Another loud blast of trumpets, and priests of the imperial cult appeared, carrying the small altar on which burned the sacred fire of the emperor. The crowd rose to its feet. Perfume and rose petals floated down from dispensers high up in the awnings. With stately deliberation, the imperial chariot entered the *circus. Hail Caesar! Hail Imperator Publius Licinius Valerianus!* The chariot was golden and encrusted with jewels. It was drawn by four snowy-white horses, their trappings purple and gold. *Hail Valerian, Germanicus Maximus, Pater Patriae, Restitutor Orbis.* The emperor stood motionless in the chariot, a laurel wreath on his head. He looked neither left nor right. He was as remote yet also as immanent and powerful as the gods that had proceeded him.

The crowd roared. *Hail the theos, the god Valerian.*

Ballista was on his feet with the rest. Like all the other military men, and a good many more besides, he was saluting. He looked down at the isolated man in the ornate chariot. The emperor was wearing the red boots and purple toga of a *triumphator*. Unlike during a Triumph, there was no one in the chariot with him, no slave to whisper in his ear, *Remember you are but mortal.*

Ballista's lips mouthed the rhythmic chants of welcome, but his mind was far away. Caligula, Nero, Domitian – no wonder so many of the emperors had been corrupted by it all. Commodus, Caracalla, Heliogabalus . . . the list went on and on. No one had accused the elderly Italian senator Valerian of any great vices except a certain meanness since his elevation to the throne of the Caesars. But he had not told the truth when he had ordered Ballista to Arete: that there never had been any hope of a relief army. The old emperor was a callous liar, and disturbing rumours of vice floated back from the banks of the Danube and Rhine of the behaviour of his son and co-emperor Gallienus. Ballista carried on mouthing the welcoming chants. As everyone said, *Pray for good emperors, but serve what you get.*

The imperial chariot reached the winning post and stopped. Grooms rushed forward to hold the horses. Valerian dismounted. Servants opened a gate in the wall of the track and, moving slowly, the emperor climbed the broad steps to the *pulvinar*, the royal box.

The strange, low hum of thousands of conversations resumed as the emperor was settled on a throne at the front of the *pulvinar*. The racecard largely forgotten in his hand, Ballista gazed up to his left at Valerian. Flunkeys were plumping up cushions, arranging rugs, setting food and drink near to hand. Already, several secretaries were in attendance. And there also were Successianus, the Praetorian Prefect, Cledonius, the *ab Admissionibus*, and Macrianus, the *Comes Sacrarum Largitionum et Praefectus Annonae*.

Ballista studied the royal box. Open on three sides except for some Corinthian columns, the *pulvinar* gave an impression of accessibility. The emperor could be seen by all eighty thousand of his subjects gathered in the *hippodrome*. The games – the theatre, the amphitheatre and, above all, the *circus*, or *hippodrome* as the Greeks called it – really were the only occasions when the emperor appeared available to large numbers of his subjects. On these occasions, the emperor was expected to attend. His subjects might shout out requests. The emperor was expected to listen. Yet, as Ballista studied the *pulvinar* – raised above and cut off from the stands by cross walls, a double rank of praetorian guardsmen keeping watch at the back – he thought such interaction counted for little. Having spent half of his lifetime in it, the *imperium* had taught the northerner that, in an autocracy, real power lay in physical proximity to the autocrat; it lay up in the *pulvinar* with the officials such as Successianus, Cledonius and the lame Macrianus, or even with the flunkeys placing the finger bowls or holding the imperial chamber pot.

'Pappa, Pappa, the first race is about to start, and I don't even know who is running.' Isangrim was tugging at his father's toga.

The boy was right. The crowd was whistling and, far off to the right in the stewards' box over the starting stalls at the southern, flat end of the *hippodrome*, the lots were being drawn. A groan went up from the crowd – obviously the team of some favoured charioteer had been allotted a bad stall.

With a smile at Julia, Ballista opened the racecard and studied it with his son. The first race was a team event for four-horse chariots. Two teams from the Blues and two from the Greens would run. The first-string charioteer for the Greens was the renowned Diocles. For the Blues it was not the leading driver that drew the eye, competent though

Musclosus was, but the lead horse of the first team, none other than the legend of the *Circus Maximus*, the pale grey Candidus. While stewards, both mounted and on foot, cleared the track, Ballista quickly placed bets on both teams from the Blues. Only the first string had much of a chance, but it had been known for the second string to come in, and it would not do for Isangrim to be disappointed if there was any form of win for the Blues in the prestigious first race.

The loud twang of the torsion-powered starting mechanism was followed a split second later by a hollow clang as the gates of the stalls crashed into the restraining Herms, the stone pillars with the bust of a man at the top and carefully sculpted male genitals at roughly the right height. The noise of the starting stalls always thrilled Ballista. It reminded him of the shooting of artillery.

Trumpets rang out. Thousands of voices yelled, 'They're off,' and the air was full of the smell of racing: hot horse, crowded humanity and cheap perfume.

The teams shot like bolts from the stalls; the coats of the horses and the silks of the drivers gleaming, the dust puffing up behind them. It was touch and go as they reached the central barrier and all the way down the first straight. Three of the teams were going flat out for position. When they emerged from the first turn, Commius, the second driver of the Blues, was hugging the barrier in front. Diocles, the star of the Greens, tucked in behind him, the second driver for the Greens following. Musclosus was holding back the great-hearted grey Candidus and his team.

'Candidus always likes to come from behind.' Ballista smiled reassuringly at Isangrim. 'Musclosus has driven him before. No need to worry – there are seven laps.' What the northerner said was true. But he had not pointed out that it was also true that Diocles and his team always favoured lying second. So it went, for four laps; Commius, the pace-maker for the Blues, led them round, and each stayed in the same position.

On the second straight of the fifth lap the pace got to the horses of Commius. They were weakening. Even from the stands, the Blues' second string could be seen to falter. A feint from Diocles drew them away from the barrier. They did not have the energy remaining to pull back in quickly enough as the Greens' star swept by on the inside. Around the next corner, they pulled wide, allowing both the other teams to overtake them.

Going into the last lap, it seemed that nothing could stop a Green victory; Diocles was several lengths clear in front, and the Green second string was blocking Musclosus. Diocles was already performing his trademark waving to the crowd.

At the penultimate turn, as the Green second string started to turn left, Musclosus made his move. Leaning right out over the yoke, plying the whip on their withers, he forced his horses on into what threatened to be a colli-sion. It was at moments like this that the great-hearted grey, Candidus, proved his courage and his worth. His was the example that his Blue team followed. The Green team lost their nerve; shying away, they carried their chariot way out wide towards the stands.

Diocles was waving to the crowd, performing tricks with his whip. He did not see Candidus coming up the barrier until the last moment. As the Blue team flashed alongside,

Diocles savagely hauled his team over. His reins tied round his waist, he threw his whole body into the desperate attempt to close the gap. The very unexpectedness of the manoeuvre confused his team. The left-hand horse stumbled. It struck into the horse next to it. This horse lost its footing. In a moment the beautiful harmony of the four running horses, man and chariot went down in a tangle of splintered wood and shattered bones. Momentum carried the thrashing tangle along the sand. It left a smear of blood behind.

Miraculously, out of the side of the chaos rolled a figure in ripped, dusty green. Something glittered in his hand. Arrogant bastard though many considered him, Diocles had not won over four hundred races and survived more crashes than he could remember without having his wits about him. Somehow, in the heart of the maelstrom, he had unsheathed his knife and cut the reins that were tied around his waist. He lay still for a moment, then raised himself on one elbow and waved the knife above his head. He sank back to the ground. The crowd roared.

At least ten lengths in front, Musclosus took the last corner wide; no shaving the turning post with the wheel this time. Safely round, he called Candidus and his team for one last effort, all the time looking over first one shoulder then the other to make sure that no god had given wings to the hooves of the trailing Green second string. There was no divine intervention. The Blue team crossed the winning line. The crowd roared again.

That was the high point of the day. From then on, it was all downhill.

It was publicly given out that Valerian supported the

Blues and his son Gallienus the Greens. The latter was true enough, but the former was widely recognized for what it was – a political statement, the attempt of an elderly, rather aloof emperor to appear a man of the people. By the second race, Valerian could be seen doing paperwork with his secretaries and Macrianus. The crowd did not like it. They strongly disapproved. They demanded that their emperors not only attend the spectacles but did so with evident enjoyment. Anything less was to show disrespect to the people, to disrespect their *libertas*. The plebs were very touchy when it came to their *libertas*, thought Ballista. And of what did their *libertas* consist? The liberty to shout such demands as *Lower taxes! Cheaper corn! Free that gladiator! Put on more shows!* Ballista had little but contempt for such 'liberty'.

After four races, not one using all twelve starting stalls, an ugly realization spread through the crowd. The limited numbers in the first race had not been to showcase the return of the legendary horse Candidus but evidence of the tight-fisted nature of the old emperor. Shouts and chants rang out, along the lines of an aged miser coaxing broken-down charioteers and horses out of retirement with a bowl of gruel.

Even though the sixth race, the one before lunch, was a free-for-all featuring three teams from all four factions, it was then that things started to come to a head. Well before the break line, when such things became permissible, Teres of the Whites blatantly left his lane and pulled straight across the favourite, Scorpus, of the Reds. The crowd were on their feet, waving their togas and cloaks, yelling for a recall and restart. The emperor Valerian worked on, ignoring the pandemonium. The race degenerated into a farce, with over half the teams either pulled up or slowed down while a minority raced on. After seven laps, Thallus, the other driver for the Whites, crossed the line first, to derision and uproar.

Valerian sent a herald to the front of the royal box. The herald raised his arm. The crowd fell silent. The herald read out the words of the emperor: 'The race stands. *Prandium*. Time for the midday meal.' The mob bayed.

The lunchtime entertainment made things worse. Some acrobats erected two tall poles on the central barrier. A high wire was strung between them. The acrobats walked the wire and struck some attitudes. The crowd jeered and chanted: 'Gladiators. We want gladiators. Blood on the sand.'

Again the herald came forward. This time the imperial words were not listened to in silence. The herald persevered: 'There will be blood on the sand next summer. The blood will be Persian. Your emperor needs all the money he can get for the coming war. Gladiators are expensive.'

The message could not have hit a worse note. The crowd howled. A chant emerged in unison from thousands of mouths: 'Everything available, everything expensive, cheap corn now!' It was only too true that the presence of the imperial court and a field army in the city of Antioch had dramatically driven up the price of corn, the staple of life. The chant was taken up by more and more of the crowd.

Ballista felt a stab of apprehension. This could quickly turn very ugly. He glanced up at the imperial box. While the emperor worked on, the praetorians at the back were shifting on their feet, hefting their shields tightly, checking their weapons. Ballista looked all around. There was a definite air of unease among the senators and equestrians. The stairs at the top of the stand were a long way away. The ones they had entered through at the bottom were much nearer. The noise from the crowd was increasing.

Yet again the imperial herald appeared. He raised his arm. The chanting faltered and died into silence. 'That is what he wants – silence,' the herald said. There was a stunned silence, then the crowd erupted in fury. The first shower of stones dashed across the front of the imperial box. The crowd had become a mob, surging, baying for blood. The herald scuttled away. The praetorians rushed forward, erecting a *testudo*, tortoise, of shields around the emperor.

Ballista knew it could only get worse. He had to act quickly. Already stones were flying up into the seating reserved for the elite. The heads of the first of the mob were appearing over the low dividing wall at the bottom. They were climbing over, intent on robbery, assault and rape. Senators, equestrians and their families were running up the steps, scrambling over the seats trying to get away, to reach the stairs at the top of the enclosure. Telling Julia to keep a close hold on their son, Ballista started to strip. He struggled out of his toga, wrapped its voluminous folds around his left arm and gripped his *corona muralis* in his left hand.

'Follow me. Carry Isangrim. Keep close.'

Julia started to edge backwards.

'No, we go down.' There was a momentary doubt in her dark eyes, but she made to follow him as he jumped to the step below. The steps were too deep for her to jump while carrying the boy. She had to sit down, swivel, swing her legs over, stand, step forward, then repeat the manoeuvre.

There were ten seats down to the walkway then, some twenty paces to the right, was the entrance to the lower stairs by which they had arrived. They had only descended two steps when two of the mob reached them. They both had knives. The first lunged at Ballista. The northerner caught the knife in the folds of his makeshift shield. He twisted the man's arm outward. With his right hand he lunged forward and gripped the man's throat. He lifted him off his feet and threw him backwards. The man's feet missed the step. He landed on the one below, lost his balance and tumbled backwards, screaming. He disappeared down the hard, unforgiving stone steps. Ballista rounded on the other man.

'Want some?'

Almost politely, the man said no and, giving them a wide berth, clambered away up the seats, looking for easier pickings.

They climbed down another two seats. Their progress was painfully slow. To their right, the steps up across the face of the seating were choked with the mob. From above came a confused roar and high-pitched screams.

'Follow me.' Ballista moved to within a few paces of the mob on the steps. He stopped. He waved the *corona muralis* above his head. The mob stopped.

'Solid gold. A king's ransom,' he called. 'Who wants it?' The mob stared, open-mouthed with avarice. Before they could move, Ballista drew back his arm and threw the golden crown in a high, long arc over their heads. In a second, the steps were empty.

Ballista turned, scooped up his son and yelled for Julia to follow.

They plunged down the steps. In moments they were on the walkway, the entrance to the exit just a few paces away.

Ballista skidded to a halt. There was a man with a knife blocking his way. Julia ran into his back. 'Behind us,' she panted. Ballista turned. At the foot of the steps they had just left was another man with a knife. They were trapped.

Ballista handed Isangrim back to Julia and pushed them both on to the seat behind him. He span round to face the track, watching the men out of the corner of each eye. Ballista adjusted the toga hanging from his left arm. His mind was calm, crystal clear, but it was racing, working out the possibilities and the angles.

For a time they were all frozen like a statue group; the two men with knives facing in towards the unarmed barbarian at bay, his wife and child huddled behind him.

'Wait,' Ballista said loudly in Greek. Quickly, but with no sudden movements, he untied the purse from his belt. He tossed it in the air, letting it fall heavily into the palm of his right hand so the knifemen could hear the weight of the coins. Ballista addressed the man to his right, the one blocking their escape, 'Take the money and let us pass.' The man looked to the other knifeman, obviously the leader. Ballista half-turned.

'Oh, we will, *Kyrios*, we will.' The man on Ballista's left grinned. His teeth were blackened and tangled. 'Just leave the woman with us – it's been a long time since we had an equestrian bitch.'

Ballista's arm was a blur as he threw the purse. The knifeman jerked back but could not avoid the missile, which smashed into his face with a sickening sound of breaking teeth and bones. Ballista swung round and launched himself at the man on his right. Enveloping the man's weapon with the toga hanging from his left arm, Ballista dragged the blade out wide and punched the man hard in the face with his right. The man staggered back a pace or two, but did not go down. The knife came free. It glittered in the sun as the man raised it to strike. Desperately, Ballista caught the man's wrist with his left hand. The man swung a punch with his left. Ballista blocked it with his right forearm and seized his assailant's throat, squeezing hard.

A noise behind him made Ballista glance over his shoulder. The other knifeman, his face a bloody mess, was moving forward, breaking into a run. Ballista started to swing the man he had by the throat around, to block the new threat. The man was struggling. He was too heavy. Ballista could not do it in time. His side and back were open to the knife.

As the bloodied knifeman ran past, Julia tripped him. It was the lightest of taps, but it destroyed the man's balance. Toppling forward, arms flailing, he ran a few more steps, then crashed on his face. The knife skittered out of his grasp as he slid on the hard, marble walkway. In an instant Ballista released the man he was holding, who crumpled, hands clutching his bruised throat. Ballista swivelled rapidly and threw himself on the man on the floor. His weight came down through his knees into the small of the man's back. The breath wheezed out of him as if he were a broken wind instrument.

On his hands and knees Ballista scrabbled after the knife. Its worn leather hilt was warm in his hand. He got to his feet. The tripped man tried to rise. Ballista stamped his left heel down on an outstretched hand. Putting all his weight on his left leg, he swivelled again. There was a terrible scream over the sound of splintering bones.

The half-choked man was up again. Stepping carefully over the prone attacker, now curled into a foetal position and whimpering quietly, Ballista moved forward. He swung the knife from side to side. The other man's eyes were as if mesmerized by the blade. He edged backwards past Julia and Isangrim.

As the knifeman reached the foot of the steps down which Ballista and his family had come, a rioter clambered over the low dividing wall into the elite enclosure. Another two, then another three followed. In some inexplicable dynamic of the mob, a horde of men poured over the wall. The man with the knife was gone, swept away up the stand by its momentum.

Ballista threw away the knife to scoop up his son. One arm clasping Isangrim secure to his chest, he took Julia in his other hand and ran to the head of the exit. There were the stairs, lit here and there by lamps in niches. In strange contrast to the crowded chaos of the seating enclosure, they were completely empty. The way to the safety of the corridor at the bottom was clear. Holding Isangrim gently, the boy's blond curls against his shoulder, Ballista began to descend as fast as he could without risking a fall.

They had gone some way when a change in the light warned him that something was wrong. He looked up. There, at the head of the stairs, blocking much of the daylight, he saw a man – or the hooded silhouette of a man. A weapon shone in his right hand. This was not a mundane knife to peel apples, this was a man-killing blade, an old-fashioned legionary short sword, a *gladius*.

Ballista handed his son back to his wife.

'Go.'

'I cannot.'

'The boy . . .' Ballista gestured. 'Go now.'

Julia turned to leave.

Very deliberately, in a fighting crouch, on the balls of his feet, the man began to descend the stairs. Cursing himself for a fool for throwing away the knife, Ballista again rearranged the toga over his arm. He began to retreat down the stairs slowly, one careful step at a time.

It was very quiet in the stairway. Ballista could hear Julia's retreating steps, heavy with the weight of their son, the son he would not see again. The man was closing the distance quickly, taking two steps to every one backward of Ballista. The reckoning would be soon.

Ballista could hear the oil fizzing in the lamps. Typical, he thought. In my barbarian northlands, the lights would be solid torches, useful weapons for burning a hall or ramming into a man's face, and here civilization has given me delicate little pottery lamps. Still, the hot oil might have a use if he could surprise the man with it. He stopped by one of the niches where a lamp burned.

The man was getting very close now. Ballista caught the glitter of his eyes under his hood. Ballista watched the blade of the *gladius*. The man moved like a fighter. There was a scar on the hand that gripped the blade. Julia's footsteps were growing fainter. The hissing of the lamp seemed unnaturally loud. Ballista could hear his own breathing, harsh, laboured.

The man was just three or four steps away. *Watch the blade, watch the blade.*

Another sound broke into Ballista's concentration. The sound of running feet. Boots pounding up the stairs behind him. *Watch the blade.* Ballista could not turn. His assailant flicked a glance over Ballista's shoulder. The northerner saw recognition on the nondescript face under the hood. Without hesitation, the man turned and ran. In seconds he had reached the top of the stairs and, sheathing his sword, was gone.

Moments later, Maximus reached Ballista.

'Are you all right?'

'Never better. Like a slave at Saturnalia.'

'Sure, but you are a cruel man to be reminding me of my servile status.' Maximus grinned. 'Julia and the boy are safe enough for the moment with Calgacus down below. Want me to go up and look for him?'

'No, he will be long gone, and it's dangerous up there. I do not want you getting hurt by any rough men. Let's all get out of here.'

Maximus turned to go. Ballista paused.

'What is it?'

'Probably nothing,' said Ballista. 'It is just that the others wanted to rob and rape, and that one . . . I think that he was only interested in killing me.'

IV

Solid-looking shafts of light came through the windows of the great apse and shone on to the floor of the audience chamber. Ballista stared at them, his face carefully composed into a look of thoughtful attention. The glass of the windows gave the light a strange, underwater look. Thousands of motes of dust and the odd oily flick of incense smoke moved in it. Ballista thought about the paradox of Heraclitus: no man can step into the same river twice. The imperial council was ever changing, always the same. For some time, the praetorian prefect Successianus had been telling the members of the *consilium* a story they all knew, except for the ending.

The outrages of three days earlier had been confined to the island in the Orontes. As soon as the disgraceful scenes in the *hippodrome* had begun, troops had sealed off the five bridges that led to the city and the one that led to the suburbs. In fact, the unrest had been contained in only a small part of the island – as ever, the imperial palace had been well garrisoned, and a sweep by Batavian auxiliaries supported by Dalmatian cavalry had dispersed any looters, at the cost of only one burnt bath house and four burnt dwellings. In the *hippodrome* itself, the praetorians had promptly escorted the emperor and imperial party to safety. After his sacred majesty had left, there were scenes of the most appalling depravity – four equestrians had been killed, several beaten and robbed, and six women of the equestrian order raped. Much worse than all this, wooden pictures of the imperial family had been stoned, the mob jeering when they splintered, and a bronze statue of the ever-victorious *imperator* Valerian had been toppled from its pedestal, beaten with shoes, broken apart, before street children had dragged the pieces through the dirt. Although the people of Antioch had always been notorious for their unruliness and lack of respect for their betters, it was clear that the outbreak was the work of a handful of brigands – foreigners, for the most part. Selected squads of soldiers had been sent in to arrest the ringleaders. The unpleasantness had lasted just a few hours, having ended soon after dark. It was estimated that some two to three hundred rioters had been killed. All the surviving ringleaders were in custody – forty-five men, seven women and four children. They awaited the emperor's infallible justice.

Words are slippery things, thought Ballista, and these were weasel words. No one who had been there and had a less than blinkered view could believe that the riot had been instigated and carried on by only a few foreign brigands. How, in that seething mass of humanity, had the troops identified these supposed ringleaders? Above all, how in the name of the Allfather, could children have been involved its organization? These were the weasel words that one heard in the *consilium*. Free speech, freedom itself, the much-vaunted *libertas* of the Romans, the *eleutheria* of Greek philosophy – how could they exist when one man was all powerful? How could they exist when one man was, depending on your viewpoint, either the vice-regent of the gods on earth or a living, walking god himself?

In the silence that followed the praetorian prefect resuming his seat, all eyes turned to the emperor. Seated high above his councillors, Publius Licinius Valerianus remained immobile. He stared over the heads of all, into the distance. Eventually the heavy head nodded, the golden wreath rustling in the unnatural quiet. The emperor spoke.

'We are renowned for our clemency. But *clementia* must not be confused with weakness. It is a stern virtue. *Severitas* is its other face. We Romans did not win our empire by weakness. We have not held our empire for over a thousand years by weakness. In the beginning, the gods themselves charged us to spare the humbled but also to crush the proud.'

The emperor paused to let his words sink in. The heads of the councillors nodded approvingly at the echo – the so very apt echo, they might have said – of the Roman imperial epic, the *Aeneid* of Virgil.

'The unbearable *superbia*, arrogance, of Shapur the Sassanid threatens war. This is not a moment to show weakness. The wickedness of these malcontents, if not inspired by Shapur himself, would at the very least bring him joy, confirm him in his arrogance, were it not punished. An example must be made.'

Again Valerian paused. Again his councillors nodded. Belatedly Ballista thought it best to join in.

'We Romans are the children of the wolf. We are a hard race. When our soldiers betray cowardice we decimate them; one man in ten is beaten to death by his comrades.

Justice demands that we must not be harder on our own men than our enemies. The prisoners of high status will be beheaded in the *hippodrome*, the scene of their depravity, and their heads exhibited on pikes across the river in the suburbs. Of the rest, some will be crucified outside the various gates of the city, some burnt alive in the *agora*, and some reserved for the wild beasts in the amphitheatre. The praetorian prefect will see to the arrangements. This is our judgement, against which there can be no appeal.'

Bastard, thought Ballista. You callous old bastard. You want to play the stern old Roman, the man merely following the ways of your ancestors, following the *mos maiorum*, yet surely somewhere in over a thousand years of Roman history there must be an example to follow which would allow you to spare at least the women and children.

The praetorian prefect got back to his feet, saluted and intoned the standard army response: 'We will do what is ordered, and at every command we will be ready.'

Successianus remained on his feet. He had a broad, flat face like a shovel. It was the face of the simple peasant turned soldier he had been a long time ago. No one on the *consilium* would consider that Successianus' face was a clear window on to his soul. The praetorian prefect cleared his throat and spoke again.

'There is something else that we must discuss. Yesterday, a messenger arrived from Aelius Spartianus, the tribune commanding Roman forces in Circesium. On the tenth of October, six days before the *ides* of the month, Sassanid cavalry appeared before the city.'

Ballista felt the air thickening around him. Whether they were looking directly at him or not, for every one of the other fifteen men in the imperial council, he was suddenly the centre of attention. To his discomfort, the northerner realized that this included the emperor himself. Make that sixteen men.

Ballista looked straight ahead across the chamber. The Count of the Sacred Largess, Macrianus, was impassive, but half-smiles seemed to play on the faces of his sons Macrianus the Younger and Quietus and, behind his carefully shaped beard, the young patrician Acilius Glabrio was openly exulting. It was all too easy for Ballista to imagine what thoughts were lighting up those smiles – *Circesium is three days' march up the Euphrates from Arete. The Sassanids are before the walls of Circesium; they can set Mesopotamia ablaze, because a barbarian upstart like you could not even hold the well-fortified city of Arete. With this news your luck has run out. Today the imperial favour that you have inexplicably enjoyed will end.*

There was nothing else for it: Ballista sat upright and set his face into immobility. He sensed a slight movement to his left. A hand touched his arm. The tough, close-cropped head of the young Danubian general Aurelian did not turn, but he patted Ballista's arm again, reassuringly. Ballista felt better to know that he was not without allies, was not totally alone in the *consilium*. And, across the room, did the long face of Cledonius momentarily betray a wink?

'Spartianus' report states that the Sassanids were not led by Shapur in person and did not appear to have siege equipment with them. He believes that it is not the main Persian field army but that, even so, it is a dangerous force of about ten thousand men.'

The praetorian prefect paused, choosing his words. 'All

'. . . ah . . . internal reports indicate that Spartianus is a reliable officer. In this case, his information is partly corroborated by another . . . external report that states that Shapur is journeying back south down the Euphrates to winter in his own territories.'

Internal reports, thought Ballista, a delicate way of referring to the activities of the *frumentarii*, the imperial secret police that swarmed around all men of office. One or two of them might be good men. They might even be necessary. But, in essence, they were an instrument of oppression, causing nothing but fear, inertia or trouble. By contrast, the spy in Shapur's camp who had provided the *external* report, even if a paid traitor to his own people, seemed positively heroic.

'The question before us is simple: what shall we do about this new menace? The emperor wishes his *amici*, his friends, to give him their advice. He commands you to speak freely.'

The opportunity to be the first to obey an imperial command, even one issued indirectly, such as this, was irresistible to an ambitious courtier. With a graceful speed that contained no hint of haste, Gaius Acilius Glabrio was on his feet. Ballista grudgingly admired both the young patrician's quick thinking and his supreme confidence. The northerner himself was still pondering the possible implications of the words of the praetorian prefect when Acilius Glabrio started talking.

'It is an outrage. A terrible outrage to the *maiestas*, majesty, of the Roman people. And it could not be more dangerous. Let no one mistake that. We all know what barbarians are like.' For the first time, Acilius Glabrio's eyes left the emperor and looked round the *consilium*. They lingered just that bit too long on Ballista before returning to Valerian.

'*Superbia*, overweening arrogance, is ever the mark of the barbarian – whether he is a slippery, decadent little easterner or a big, stupid northerner.' Again the eyes flicked to Ballista. 'If the *superbia* of a barbarian is not crushed when it first rears up, it will grow uncontrollably. Already the *superbia* of the Sassanid ruler grows after his triumph at Arete. Let it go unpunished again, and it will know no bounds. Will he be satisfied with Mesopotamia? With Syria, Egypt, Asia – Greece itself? Never. His irrationality allows no limit to his desires. Let Shapur flout the *imperium*, and every other barbarian will think that he can do the same, along the Danube and the Rhine, across the Black Sea and the Atlas Mountains. I see the Tiber flowing with blood. Our very homes, our wives, our children, the temples of our ancestral gods – all are at risk. We must act now, and act decisively.'

Carried aloft by his own rhetoric, the young nobleman glared around the room, every inch the stern patriot of the old Republic.

'What can avert this danger, kill this eastern reptile? Only old-fashioned Roman *virtus*. And where can we find such antique virtue? Here in this very room. After our noble emperor, who could exhibit old-style Roman *virtus* more clearly than . . .' Acilius Glabrio paused, motionless, for dramatic effect, then turned and thrust out his arm towards an elderly, rather portly senator.

'. . . Marcus Pomponius Bassus. A man whose ancestor, 769 years ago, sat in the very first meeting of the free Senate, the very day after the expulsion of Tarquinius Superbus, the last king of Rome. I say that, this very day, Pomponius Bassus should be ordered to gird on his armour, take up his sword and march with an army large enough for the task to eradicate this upstart eastern threat once and for all.'

Silence succeeded Acilius Glabrio's ringing words. If Pomponius Bassus was surprised by this turn of events, he gave no sign of it. He arranged his plump features into an expression of nobility called up for hard duty and in a voice quivering with emotion, real or assumed, he announced that, onerous as the task was, if called, he would not hang back.

End the eastern threat once and for all, my arse, thought Ballista. For over three hundred years, the Romans had fought first the Parthians and now the Sassanids, and they were no nearer ending the eastern threat once and for all than they had been after the first clash, when the Roman triumvir Crassus was killed at the disastrous battle of Carrhae.

The silence stretched. The gods alone might know what subtle calculations, what delicate balancing of favours given and received, rushed silently through the thoughts of the majority of the councillors. Ballista knew that there were depths here that he could not penetrate.

At last, Macrianus slowly rose to his feet, his lame leg impeding him. In a measured voice he supported giving the command to Pomponius Bassus. Following that, there was an almost undignified scramble to agree. In the arrogance of their youth and the reflected power of their father, Macrianus the Younger and Quietus made sure that their voices were heard next. After them came one Maeonius Astyanax, a middle-aged senator with a reputation for both intellectuality and slavishly following the house of Macrianus. Next, ponderously trying to impart an air of dignity, another descendant of the old republican nobility spoke, the polyonymous Gaius Calpurnius Piso Frugi. By now, Pomponius Bassus' attempts to assume an air of dutiful resignation to hard service had failed, and he gave off his more accustomed impression of unreflecting self-satisfaction.

Ballista felt a movement at his side. Aurelian rose to his feet. Not you too, thought Ballista. Surely you cannot think that old fool is up to the task?

Aurelian stood for a few moments. His tough-looking head, with its close-trimmed hair and beard, turned to take in the whole room.

'I hear what Gaius Acilius Glabrio says. I have nothing but the greatest respect for Pomponius Bassus. But he is the wrong man.' Aurelian spoke quietly, his flat vowels, typical of those from the Danube, emphasizing the lack of traditional rhetoric, or subtly pointing to a rhetoric of plain speaking. Involuntarily, the councillors leant forward. 'Pomponius Bassus is not as young as he was. It is many years since he commanded troops in the field. No, what this command needs is a man in the prime of life with a track record of recent military success. Tacitus here is fifty-five and straight from the army of the Danube. He should command.'

The blunt brevity of Aurelian caught all by surprise. Once he was sure that his fellow Danubian was not going to say anything else, Tacitus said that, if commanded, he would serve. Support came in slowly; the professional military men from the north of the *imperium* were far from universally popular with members of the elite from more traditional backgrounds. The first to offer it, however, was an elderly member of the great Italian nobility, one Fabius Labeo. Even Ballista could work out that Labeo was acting out of pique that Acilius Glabrio had proposed Pomponius Bassus rather than himself. Next was a younger senator, one Valens. Ballista had no idea why, but Valens always opposed Macrianus. Quietly, almost apologetically, the officer in command of the imperial horse guards, the Equites Singulares Augusti, a young Italian tribune also named Aurelian, and universally known as 'the other Aurelian', added his voice. When it was obvious that no one else was going to offer their support, Ballista himself briefly announced that he thought Tacitus was the right man.

As he sat down, it occurred to Ballista that, so far, three of the great functionaries had not yet spoken. There had been not a word from Successianus the Praetorian Prefect, Cledonius the *ab Admissionibus* or Censorinus the *Princeps Peregrinorum*. As the northerner sought them out with his eyes, he thought he saw Successianus almost imperceptibly nod to Cledonius. Sure enough, in a moment the latter was rising to his feet.

'*Dominus*, imperial *amici*, we have been offered much good advice, all of it freely spoken in the highest tradition of the *Res Publica* of the Romans. Yet I think that the previous speakers have not explored absolutely all aspects of this case. Possibly there is more that we can draw out.' Cledonius' voice was sonorous, his tone one of helpful reasonableness.

'Both Pomponius Bassus and Tacitus are great men. It would be unfitting to send either into the field without an army large enough to suit their *dignitas*. Yet there may be reasons to suggest that such a course of action would not be a good thing. First, this is only a minor detachment of the Persian army, less than ten thousand men, and it is not led by the Sassanid king himself. Second, to equip a force befitting the *dignitas* of either of the proposed generals, it would be necessary to strip the imperial field army here in Antioch. No one would be so rash as to suggest that the *dignitas* of a subject, no matter how great, should outweigh that of the emperor himself.' Cledonius' face remained blank as he allowed a time for his audience to reflect.

'This incursion must indeed be dealt with, speedily and effectively, but by a small, highly mobile force led by a younger man. There is a man here with very recent experience of fighting the eastern foe. A man burning with a desire for revenge. A small force must be sent to the Euphrates, led by Marcus Clodius Ballista.'

As if on cue, first Successianus then Censorinus spoke in favour of this idea. The two previous candidates, Pomponius Bassus and Tacitus, wasted no time in affirming their loyalty to the emperor by renouncing any interest in the command and most wholeheartedly backing Ballista – now it was mentioned, he was far and away the obvious man for the post. With varying degrees of reluctance – a great deal in some cases – all the remaining members of the *consilium* fell into line.

The emperor Valerian inclined his head – his *amici* had spoken well. Marcus Clodius Ballista, the *Dux Ripae*, would keep his title and, with a force to be determined later, would set off as soon as possible to fight the Sassanids on the Euphrates.

As he rose to his feet and accepted the command, Ballista realized that, for all the years he had spent in the Roman empire, he could still be completely at sea in the ways of the imperial court. Hopefully, Julia would be able to explain the political manouverings to him. But he had what he wanted: he had an army, a chance to redeem his reputation. And yes, he wanted revenge – revenge on the Sassanids who had tortured and killed so many at Arete and, one day, revenge on the man who had ordered it: on Shapur, the King of Kings.

Antioch was a big and confusing city. If you turned off the main street by the Pantheon into the street known as the Jawbone, the one where so many Christians were to be seen, and followed it down through, first, the potters' quarter then that of the tanners, eventually you would reach the Orontes. If you then turned left at the waterfront and, keeping the jetties and godowns on your right, walked south down Mariners' Street, after about a quarter of an hour you would come to the public baths named after a local woman called Livia. Just beyond the baths was the bar with the improbable name of Circe's Island.

The reputation of the bar for food and drink was not that good, but for girls it was excellent. It was a favourite haunt of Maximus. On the evening of 1 November, the *kalends*, he was sitting with another man out on the rickety terrace which overhung the water. The other man was older and strikingly ugly: he had a great dome of a skull and a weak chin with, between them, a thin, sour, shrewish mouth. The man's shoulders were shaking, and he was making an unpleasant grating sound. Calgacus, the body servant, or valet, of Ballista, was laughing. He asked, 'And are you being watched now?'

There was a pause. Maximus clearly mastered an urge to look round at the other few customers on the terrace before muttering, no, he probably wasn't.

'I have seen it before with men such as you,' the old Caledonian continued remorselessly. 'Cock of the walk for years, scared of nothing. Then one day it all goes. Scared of their shadows for the rest of their lives.'

'I wish I had never mentioned it,' said Maximus. 'The gods alone know how Ballista has put up with a miserable old Caledonian bastard like you for all these years.'

'Wiped his arse when he was the age his son is now, paid off the fathers of the girls he fucked back in Germania and fed and clothed the little bastard ever since we came into the *imperium*. Always made myself useful – unlike a bodyguard who thinks he is being stalked. It always follows the same course when it strikes men like you: first, they think about it now and then; after a time, it comes to dominate their thoughts, preys on their mind without cease, gives them no rest – and that is when it begins to affect everything, strips all their pleasures away. It is hard to get it up when you are always thinking that someone is creeping up behind you with a bloody great sword.' The nasty grating sound issued again from Calgacus as he poured himself more wine.

'I hope that Demetrius gets here all right. You know how easily he gets lost, and it is late,' said Maximus.

'Of course he'll get here all right. This is Antioch, the city that never sleeps – its streets are safer and better lit at night than at day. There is a civic police force armed with bloody great clubs, and the key job of its eighteen elected officers, the ones they call the *Epimeletai ton Phylon*, the Superintendants of the Tribes, is to knock up any shopkeeper who dares to let the lights outside his shop go out.'

'I thought the main job of the *epimeletai* was investigating unexplained corpses?'

'Well, that too. But, as I was saying, you are doomed to a life of misery. After a time, the irrational fear never stops preying on your mind. A hot little tart is spread on the bed in front of you, but what can you do? Nothing. Your sword sleeps in your hand. All the time, you are looking over your shoulder.'

Maximus was spared any more by the arrival of Demetrius. As he walked across the terrace, the secretary called to a serving girl to bring them more wine. The Greek youth was growing up, thought Maximus. Possibly the suffering and fear of the siege and flight from Arete had begun to make a man of him.

Demetrius pulled a brazier nearer to the table. A chill wind was getting up; it carried the smell of the first winter rains. 'Good news and bad news,' he said as he sat down. 'The good first: we all have tomorrow off. The *dominus* is going hunting in the mountains towards Daphne with Aurelian. He says that, if he took his secretary, it would look as if he were not devoting himself to the pleasures on offer; if he took his manservant, that he did not trust his host's cook; and his bodyguard, that he did not trust his host himself.'

'Which Aurelian?' Calgacus croaked.

'The Danubian one,' Demetrius continued. 'The Aurelian to whom a strange thing just happened as everyone left the palace. In his haste he mounted the wrong horse. Not his own, but the emperor's. He dismounted quickly enough when it was pointed out to him, but a few people noticed.'

'Something he should keep very quiet about, and something that others should not discuss in public,' Calgacus interrupted. 'So what is the bad news?'

'Aurelian has been appointed a deputy to the *Dux Ripae*.'

'Nothing much wrong with that,' said Maximus. 'Sure young *manu-ad-ferrum*, hand-to-steel, has a quick temper, likes a drink and is a savage one for the discipline. The troops fear him more than love him, but he is a good fighter. They say he killed forty-eight Sarmatians with his own blade in a single day.' Maximus began to sing a marching song:

Thousand, thousand, thousand we've beheaded now.
One man, a thousand we've beheaded now.
A thousand drinks, a thousand killed.
So much wine no one has as the blood that he has spilt.

Maximus had been drinking for some time, but the staff and clientele at Circe's Island were used to boisterous behaviour.

A boat loomed out of the darkness and bumped up against the ramshackle tenement next door. Seemingly from nowhere, dozens of women and children appeared and, with much calling back and forth, set about unloading its cargo of fish.

'The *Dux* has been given two deputies. The other one is the bad news.' Demetrius paused. 'It is Gaius Acilius Glabrio.'

'The brother of that smug little shit at Arete? The one

who has publicly sworn revenge on Ballista for his brother's death? That's insane. What is that old fool of an emperor playing at?' Maximus' flow of words was cut off by Calgacus placing his hand on his arm.

'It is not for us to debate the ways of our masters,' the old Caledonian said sanctimoniously. 'Now, Demetrius, I was just discussing Maximus' little problem. It seems he has been having trouble getting it up.'

'That is it!' Maximus rose to his feet. 'You, over here.' He took the wine jug from the serving girl and put it on the table. 'Do you want to come and watch?'

'Gods below, not in this life,' exclaimed Calgacus. 'I can think of nothing worse than watching *your* hairy arse going up and down like a harpist's elbow.'

The assassin watched Maximus steer the girl to the stairs. It had been a bad moment when the Hibernian said he thought he was being watched. But he was only a barbarian – earlier, he had looked right at the assassin with no glimmer of recognition. Now the assassin knew for certain a time when the bodyguard would be away from the target. Now, he could strike.

The assassin signalled for a girl to come over, paid his bill and walked across the terrace, an unassuming man who drew no attention to himself. At the door, he looked back for a moment at the two still at the table. The ugly old man and the handsome youth sat in a companionable silence, all unsuspecting as they listened to the shrill shouts of the women and children unloading the boat and the heavy slop-slop-slop sounds of the wheels of the watermills on the far bank.

As he stepped outside, it started to rain. The assassin pulled up his hood and set off north up Mariners' Street.

'Magnificent.'

'Thank you very much,' said Ballista.

Julia laughed. 'Actually, I was referring to the political cunning of Cledonius.'

'That is rather deflating.' Naked, Ballista walked down the steps into the sunken bath and sat in the warm water. As the water stilled, he heard the storm outside, rain drummed on the roof and, somewhere in the house, the wind slammed a shutter or door. 'I thought you had told Isangrim's nurse to take him to visit the children of one of your endless cousins and had given the rest of the slaves the evening off so that we would be completely alone, so that you would have complete privacy to take care of your husband's needs.'

Julia was on the other side of the room, pouring drinks, putting some food on a plate. She smiled over her shoulder. 'I might force myself to do that later, but first I want to use this rare moment of privacy to make sure that my barbarian *dominus* understands the intrigues that surround his latest command.' She turned, the drinks and food temporarily forgotten.

'As *ab Admissionibus*, Cledonius cannot be away from the emperor. As he could not take this command on the Euphrates himself, he was determined that no other leading politician should hold it. Acilius Glabrio's candidate, Pomponius Bassus, may be a self-satisfied fool, but he is a great *nobilis*. Things were going badly for Cledonius when Macrianus spoke in favour of Pomponius Bassus, and all the creatures of the lame one fell over themselves to agree.'

Ballista watched as she paused, thinking. She was wearing a thin white cotton robe, held together with a sash. The lamps on the table behind her shone through the material. He could see the outline of her body. She was naked beneath the robe.

'Piso is a bankrupt; Macrianus owns him. There are many rumours, most of them disgusting, but no one knows for sure just what hold Macrianus has on Maeonius Astyanax.' She shook her head to dismiss such distasteful speculations. Ballista admired the way her breasts moved, full and heavy but firm.

Perhaps I really am the thick northern barbarian so many Romans take me for, an irrational slave to my appetites, thought Ballista. Julia was trying to explain something very serious, something which could affect the success of his mission, maybe his life itself, and all he was thinking about was her body. Ballista smiled. No, he may have spent half his life in the *imperium*, but he was not completely irrational. He could give his mind to two things at once, and she did look good.

'Then your Danubian friend Aurelian proposed Tacitus. That was no better in Cledonius' eyes. So he started talking about important men entrusted with big armies, about taking troops from the imperial field army. There was no need to say the word – after the last twenty years, treachery is on everyone's mind. So, when finally he proposes a less grand figure in the court – sorry, my love – with a smaller force, all the *consilium* rush to agree, and you, my *Dominus*, are back off to the wars.'

She picked up a large silver plate and two crystal goblets

of watered wine and brought them over to Ballista. As she crouched next to him, the robe fell open, exposing her legs. She reached forward to pass him a drink. The robe was tight over her breasts. Ballista looked at the dark circles of her nipples. She smiled and walked round to the steps.

'Cledonius has got what he wants. No rival will lead this expedition. But he has alienated two groups of important men. So how does he win back their favour? At the next meeting of the *consilium*, he proposes that the two crucial men, Acilius Glabrio and Aurelian, are appointed legates. Magnificent, but now you are saddled with two ambitious young deputies who will be at logger-heads. And make no mistake: Gaius Acilius Glabrio hates you. He despises you for your origins, but he hates you for the death of his brother Marcus.'

She was standing very still. Outside, the wind was battering fretfully at the house. The loose shutter or whatever it was banged again. Julia looked sharply at her husband. 'Your friend Aurelian . . . he drinks too much, he has a savage temper . . . mark my words, he will not come to a good end.' Ballista said nothing. Somewhere in the far reaches of the house the wind tugged at the unfastened shutter: rap-rap-rap.

Julia laughed. 'You realize this is why I had to come out east. It was not that I was worried the Persians would kill you in Arete but that you would have no idea what was happening in the *consilium* when you got back to Antioch.'

She undid the sash and let her robe fall. 'And now all that is said' – as she raised her hands to untie her hair, her breasts lifted. Ballista gazed hungrily at her large, dark nipples, flat stomach, flared hips, her shaven delta – 'I think it is time that you took care of your wife's needs.' She stepped down into the water, waded over to him and straddled his lap. Rap-rap-rap went the shutter. 'I do not think you appreciate the risks that I run for you. Over a year without a man inside me – there is not a doctor in the *imperium* who would not agree that such abstinence is very bad for a woman's health.' She tipped her head back and laughed. 'Although I am sure that many a doctor would be prepared to help a girl in such a predicament.' She leant forward and kissed him, her tongue sliding into his mouth, her breasts flattening against his chest. Rap-rap-rap.

'Wait a moment. I cannot concentrate with that row going on.' Ballista slid out from under her, running his hand across her slick, wet breasts, the nipples hard against his palm.

'Do not be too long.' She smiled.

He draped a towel round himself and picked up a small lamp. He left wet footprints on the marble floor.

Outside the bath rooms, the house was in darkness. Ballista stood in the main living room listening. There was the sound – rap-rap-rap – it was coming from somewhere in the slave quarters. This was a part of the house that he did not know at all well. He had only set foot in it once, when he had first been given a tour of the whole property. It was a rabbit warren of short, windowless corridors and tiny cells. Once, as the sound receded, he had had to retrace his steps. Eventually, he found the open window, at the end of a corridor up under the eaves.

The rain stung his face when he stretched far out to grab the wildly swinging shutter. Far below, the road ran like a river. The fitful wind blew great gusts of rain one after another down the road.

When he fastened the window, for a moment everything seemed unnaturally quiet. Then other sounds emerged: small creaks and scratching sounds. Suddenly, he thought he heard a footstep. He smiled. It was just an old house cooling as the warmth of the day died out of it, moving gently in the face of the wind. In his small circle of lamplight, he started to head back.

Before he reached the *tepidarium*, he nipped out the lamp. Quietly, he looked round the door. Julia was lying back, her shoulders and arms supporting her floating body. Her breasts broke the surface of the water. She looked superb. He watched for some time before he walked in, dropped his towel and stepped down into the bath.

Leaving Julia asleep, warm in their bed, Ballista dressed and walked to the stables. He saddled Pale Horse and led him out into the night. He rode alone through the empty streets. It was dark, at least three hours before dawn. The rain had eased off but the wind still ripped through the alleys of the potters' quarter.

Once, the northerner thought he heard something. A clink of steel on stone? He reined in, pushed back his hood and sat motionless, listening, hand on hilt, looking all around. Nothing. He could hear nothing but the wind itself buffeting his ears. He could see nothing except the empty, windswept alley. Ballista smiled to himself. Any more of this and he would become as nervous as Demetrius. Of course it was eerie to ride through deserted streets that usually teemed with men and animals. And he was tired. His smile broadened. Julia had seen to that. Allfather but she had tired him out. He could have chosen worse for a wife.

A gentle pressure from his thighs set his mount in motion again. He left his hood down. Jumpy or not, it was worth cold ears to be able to hear properly.

Always blessed with a good sense of direction, Ballista pulled up in a narrow alley. The walls here looked uncared for, damp, the plaster peeling. He got down from his mount and hammered on an inconspicuous door. The lantern hanging over it squealed as it swung in the wind, its light glinting off puddles and the rivulet that ran down the middle of the alley.

The door opened, throwing a yellow rectangle of light. The head of Gillo, Aurelian's manservant, peered out, squinting into the darkness.

'*Ave, Dominus. Ave*, Marcus Clodius Ballista.' He smiled, snapped over his shoulder for a boy to take the *dominus*' horse, and gestured for the northerner to step inside.

Ballista handed his cloak to Gillo, who hung it on a peg in the shabby corridor. From peasant stock, the young general Aurelian had never tried to conceal his lack of money. Those who liked him said his continuing impecunious state pointed to his financial probity – no soldier ever became rich honestly on what the *Res Publica* paid him. For those who did not care for him, it was an ostentatious sham – for sure, no peasant could keep his nose out of the trough. There were dark stories of millions hidden away.

A wave of warmth and noise washed over Ballista as the door to the main room was opened.

'Ah-ha, here he is. Better late than never.' The strong Danubian accent of Aurelian rang out. 'Come in, come in. You know everyone? The esteemed ex-consul Tacitus? My young friends Mucapor and Sandario?' The face visible between the close-cropped hair and beard was flushed. There was a dark-red spot on each of Aurelian's prominent cheekbones. It was hot in the room, and everyone was dressed for hunting, but Ballista noticed the wine cup in his friend's hand.

'Indeed I do, and I am not late.' Ballista stepped forward with his hand out. 'Marcus Claudius Tacitus, it is good to see you again.' The older man turned his heavily lined face to the newcomer, shook his hand, then embraced him. Close up, Tacitus looked all and more of his fifty-five years. The dour, big-nosed face itself was cleanshaven but luxuriant whiskers ran together into a beard underneath the chin.

'It is good to see you, Ballista.' The Danubian accent was less pronounced than Aurelian's. The older man's family had been landowners there, time out of mind. The two men in their twenties, both again from the lands around the Danube, greeted Ballista with wide smiles. Sandario's made him look even more dashing. Unfortunately, Mucapor's did not have the same effect; it made him look even more of a simpleton.

'Drink!' Aurelian bellowed. 'Eros! Where in Hades has that little Greek bugger got to? Eros, bring drinks for our guests.' Aurelian's slave secretary kept his eyes down as he gave Ballista a cup of wine and topped up all the others, except Tacitus, who quietly put his hand over his cup.

'Food!' Aurelian was in tearing form. 'Ballista, I know how you northern barbarians eat. I told Gillo to buy more food than one could imagine. Help yourself.' The young general gestured with his cup to a table at the back of the room, which did indeed appear to be laden with food. Aurelian grinned at Ballista. Everyone in the room got the irony that, for most of the inhabitants of the *imperium*, the men from the Danube were almost as much barbarians as the Angle from the far north beyond the frontiers.

'My dear Tacitus,' Aurelian said in a slightly more respectful voice, 'you are eating nothing. And I specifically told

Gillo to buy all the lettuce he could get his hands on, knowing it was your favourite vegetable.'

Tacitus, who was actually solemnly eating a piece of dry bread, which he dipped now and then in some olive oil, took his time in replying. 'Only in the evenings. Lettuce helps you sleep, cools the desires of the flesh. Last night, I admit, I ate a great deal of it. Usually I read myself to sleep but, obviously, not yesterday, it being the night after the day of the *kalends* – any fool knows that would bring terrible bad luck.'

To hide his smile, Ballista busied himself filling a plate with food: some cold pheasant, ham, cheese, bread, a little of the lettuce. Aurelian was no fool, but he ought to be careful teasing Tacitus, for the older man was no fool either. They made an odd couple. The elder was a circumspect, kindly man, abstemious, almost ascetic, in his habits, much given to superstition, while the younger, 'hand-to-steel', was impetuous, even hot-headed and – possibly Julia was right – altogether too keen on drink and food. It said a lot that they got along well. The very presence of the two puppies Sandario and Mucapor showed how the military men from the Danube stuck together. Ballista knew enough Roman history to know that it was only in the last generation that these Danubians had come to the fore in the army. Really, it was only in the last twenty-one years, since Maximinus Thrax had seized the throne.

Ballista had to suppress a shudder at even thinking the name of the long-dead emperor. He could not help picturing the great white face, the terrible grey eyes. Ballista remembered the final threat – 'I will see you again' – as the emperor died at his hand. All that was long ago. And it was a long time since Ballista's sleep had been disturbed by the unquiet daemon of the late and unlamented Maximinus Thrax.

Ballista sipped his wine. It was red, as was to be expected from Aurelian, made into *conditum*, warmed and spiced, just the thing for a cold morning following hounds.

Aurelian reverted to a topic that he had clearly been pursuing before Ballista's arrival. 'So the legionary, having seduced the wife of the man in whose house he was billeted, gets away with it. No discipline at all, and another bloody provincial who hates the army. If it had been down to me, I would have made an example of the bastard. Followed the lead of Alexander the Great. Find two saplings. Bend them down to the ground. Tie one of the legionary's legs to each. And let the trees go. Rip the bastard in half. A very public warning of what the men can expect if they flout discipline. Let them see what they are going to get before they do it.' Aurelian grinned. Ballista often found it hard to tell when his friend was being serious or was playing up to his nickname. 'Why the fucker could not just use one of the brothels like everyone else, I do not know,' Aurelian continued. 'It is not as if there is a shortage of brothels in this town.'

'They should all be closed,' said Tacitus. The other men looked at him. Was he joking? He had a reputation for strong self-discipline, but the brothels were so much a part of daily life that only the most radical of philosophers would consider getting rid of them. Even stern Cato had thought that a young man should use them in moderation. 'And the baths, the theatre, the *hippodrome*, and the amphitheatre – they should all be closed. After the disgraceful riot in the *hippodrome*, the Antiochenes should be punished. Take away their pleasures for a time; that would teach those shifty little easterners a lesson.' Tacitus' audience were spared further ways of instilling backbone into untrustworthy orientals by the arrival of Antistius, the other manservant of Aurelian, dressed in the embroidered coat of a huntsman, who announced that the horses were ready.

Outside, the night had grown worse. The wind still tore down the alley, and it had started to rain again. Before they had cleared the potters' quarter, let alone crossed the Kerateion, the Jewish quarter near the Daphne Gate, the little party was thoroughly bedraggled and wet. It was as well that torches carried by the servants Gillo and Antistius stayed lit, though they flared and guttered wildly, for the wind had blown out many of the lanterns that hung outside the shops. 'I will tell you what would happen if I were in charge.' Aurelian pushed back his hood to bellow at Ballista. 'I would liven up those bloody Superintendents of the Tribes. On a night like this, you would not find a single one of the *epimeletai* warming his arse by the fire or ramming his wife in bed. Oh no, the buggers would be out here getting soaked to the skin doing their job, making sure these storekeepers obeyed the law and kept their lanterns alight.'

'You could make an example of a couple of them,' Ballista shouted back over the storm. 'Something fitting the crime. Maybe burn one or two alive.'

'Hmm.' Aurelian grinned and pulled his hood back up.

The streets got wider but steeper as they entered the expensive part of the Epiphania district known as the Rhodion, the rose garden. The houses here were bigger, with wide grounds, often encompassing a whole block. There were fewer shops. There were even fewer lanterns. But the rain was letting up. The gatekeeper at the south-east postern was expecting them. Even at this hour he was civil, and in violation of the law he opened the gate. Obviously he had been bribed in advance. They dismounted and, one by one, led their horses through.

Outside, they remained on foot. The path Aurelian pointed out was precipitous. In single file they set off, leading their horses. To begin with, the walls of the town were close on their left, the ravine of the Phyrminus River at a similar distance on their right. Then both curved away, and the path climbed up through stands of trees, mainly firs, with some ash and wild olive. Progress was slow, the path steep. All except the servants used the boar spears Aurelian had given them as walking sticks. The horses laboured.

Over his own breathing, Ballista listened to the wind moving the trees above their heads, the sibilant sound of the leaves, the creak of the branches, a magical sound that reminded him of the sacred groves of his distant homeland. He noticed that the light of the servants' torches was turning a pale yellow. The rain had ceased some time earlier. The sky had gone from black to deep blue to a delicate azure. Scattered black clouds raced low over their heads and away to the south-east, tattered remnants of the night's storm. It was nearly dawn.

Suddenly they came out into the open on the crest of Mount Silpius. They halted, men and horses getting their breath back, stretching out from the hunched postures of climbing. Aurelian said that they should wait there for the huntsman and the hounds.

The great disc of the sun appeared on the horizon, and a pale gold light splashed over them. Aurelian handed his reins to Antistius and prostrated himself on the soaking ground. The others put their fingertips to their lips and, bowing slightly, blew a kiss to the risen god *Sol Invictus*. Ballista stood quietly, remaining upright, his hands not moving. The sun was not an invincible god in the pantheon of his youth. Indeed, at the end of time, Skoll, the wolf that chased the sun, would catch her in the Iron Wood and devour her, bringing darkness to Asgard, home of the gods, and to Middle Earth, home of mortal men.

Aurelian got up, brushing the leaves and mud from his clothes. He smiled almost apologetically at Ballista. 'My mother was the priestess of the Sun in my home village. Burgaraca was a dump. I enlisted when I was sixteen. But I miss *her*. And I think she was right. I am still alive. *Sol Invictus* has held his hands over me.'

They waited in the sunshine, both the men and their horses steaming slightly. Ballista looked back the way they had come. He watched the shadows retreat towards him as the sun rose behind his back over Mount Silpius. The clear sunlight revealed first the wide, flat plain of the Orontes, the little peasant huts small as toys, the smoke from their dung fires plucked away by the wind, then the suburbs of the city and the *campus martius* across the river and, finally, Antioch the Great herself, the half-built fortress-palace on the island, the broad line of the main street, the glint of the river running through her. Ballista looked all around, at the path they had followed from the west, at the citadel further along the crest off to the north-east, at the land to the east to which they had come to hunt, and then the realization struck him. He had not seen it before. In the week he had spent in Antioch the previous year, he had not found time to climb to the crest of Mount Silpius. The climb from the city had been steep, hard going for the horses. It would have been a Herculean labour of winches, pulleys and ratchets to move any siege equipment up from the city to the crest. But to the east, outside the defences, the land fell away gently, in a landscape of broad upland meadows and open woods. At one point near the citadel a saddle of rock almost overtopped the walls. The northerner filed the revelation away for future use. Despite the river, the walls, the fortress-palace, Antioch-on-Orontes, the Roman capital of Syria, the heart of the power of the *imperium* in the east, was almost indefensible.

'About bloody time,' roared Aurelian. A huntsman came into view, thick coat, stout boots, and six hounds on leads surging around his legs. They were gaze hounds, hunters by sight not scent, Celtic by the look of them. Aurelian might not have much money, but he loved his hunting. The huntsman led the party down to where the beaters were in position. It was a good spot; a wide, undulating field of grass with some dense cover uphill. Aurelian explained again the particular northern style of hunting they were to follow. No, they were not going to use nets and stakes. No, the hounds would not hunt as a pack. As each hare broke cover, a pair of hounds would be slipped, so the hunters could bet on the result. The huntsman shrugged – the Danubian was paying, the northerners could do what they liked, but they need not expect him to feign approval – and called the beaters into action. The hunting party tethered their horses. Aurelian and Tacitus each had a hound on a slip lead. They agreed a wager. Sandario and Mucapor placed a side bet. Although far from adverse to gambling, Ballista kept quiet.

They all waited, hounds and men keyed up, expectant. Now and then there was a flash of the red-and-white feathers of a scarer as the beaters moved through the cover. A hare appeared. After a few hops it sat up, looking around impudently. Then it saw the hunting party. As it raced away, Aurelian and Tacitus slipped their hounds. As always, Ballista's heart thrilled with the beauty of the dogs' acceleration, the grace of their running. Aurelian's big, black dog forged ahead, its strides half as long again as those of Tacitus' brindle bitch. The black dog closed on the hare, jaws open for the kill. At the last possible second, the hare jinked. The big dog tried to turn to pursue it but his own speed and size were against him. He lost his footing and went tumbling and rolling, grass and mud flying about him. The neat little bitch was on the heels of the hare. She turned it once, twice, three times, and killed it cleanly. She trotted back, wagging her tail. The big dog cavorted around her, though he kept a discreet distance after receiving a warning growl.

The huntsman took the prey from her jaws, and made much of the bitch. Tacitus took the money from Aurelian but, for a man who, like his host, was renowned for his love of the chase, he seemed strangely subdued. Having settled their wager, Sandario and Mucapor led up their hounds.

Almost straight away, there was much hallooing and crashing from within the cover. The hounds quivered with excitement. A huge stag leapt from the trees. He stood, his magnificent, widespread antlers accentuating the motion as he looked this way and that. Seeing the hunters, he turned and began to run diagonally across the field. Although the stag appeared unhurried, he was speeding away, each bound covering more ground than seemed possible.

Among the hunting party there was pandemonium. All the hounds were slipped. Aurelian and the two young Danubian officers untethered their horses, hurled themselves into the saddle and dashed after the stag. Ballista and Tacitus took a little more time. The two servants would take for ever packing up all the gear. The huntsman and the beaters would have to follow on foot, as they had no mounts.

Ballista cantered beside Tacitus. Across the field, down a steeper slope, and along a track, all in silence. The hounds and the other three hunters had pulled ahead, out of sight. The servants would be an age behind.

The two silent riders came to the top of a rise and reined in. They caught a glimpse of the hounds, already far below in the valley. Not far behind, they saw the flash of a bright hunting cloak. Out of the corner of his eye, Ballista saw another horseman, higher up the mountainside and moving parallel to them. In a moment he was gone, lost in the trees.

As they rode on, Ballista broke the silence. 'Forgive me, my dear Tacitus, but you seem strangely preoccupied, almost out of sorts.'

'I am sorry I am not better company. I have had some strange news from my half-brother, Marcus Annius Florianus.' Tacitus stopped talking. Clearly, he was debating whether to tell Ballista the news or not. They rode further.

In the midst of the completely wild landscape, Ballista's eye was caught by a man-made terrace off to the right, a thin line of smoke rising from it; someone was burning charcoal.

'We were brought up together, Florianus and me. We have always been close. Not long ago we bought an estate together, at Interamna, about sixty miles north of Rome. We are building a family mausoleum there. He arranged for our statues to be erected. Two big, marble statues, about thirty foot high. Rather ostentatious, I thought.'

Tacitus paused, then took a deep breath and continued. 'I received a letter yesterday. Both statues were hit by lightning, blown to pieces. But that is not so much what is on my mind as the words of the soothsayers consulted by Florianus. They declared that it means that an emperor will arise from our family. He will conquer the Persians, the Franks, the Alamanni and the Sarmatians, establish governors on the islands of Ceylon and Hibernia, make all the lands which border the ocean his territory and then abolish the office of emperor, restore the free Republic, retire to live subject to the ancient laws. He will live for a hundred and twenty years, and die without an heir.'

Ballista looked across at the serious face. Tacitus did not look at him.

'Allfather, Bringer of Despair, do not mention this to anyone else,' said Ballista. 'This is treason. Imagine if a *frumentarius* overheard, somehow got wind of it . . . It would not be you alone that would be questioned in the palace cellars. Think of your half-brother, your wife, your friends.'

'Think of you?' There was a hint of a smile on the earnest face.

'Well, I have no great desire to be tortured because of the ravings of some charlatans consulted by your half-brother, a man I have never met.'

Tacitus smiled broadly. 'As you say, they are probably charlatans and, anyway, they prophesied that the emperor would not take the throne for another thousand years.' He threw his head back and laughed. 'Still, it makes you think. Now, let's ride.'

Without warning, Tacitus kicked his heels into the flanks of his horse and was gone. Within but a few paces he had pushed it into something close to a flat-out gallop. Left behind, Ballista more slowly did the same. Yet no sooner had Ballista's mount reached full speed than the northerner felt something was wrong. Gently, he pulled the horse up. He leapt down from the saddle, made the horse walk a step or two, picked up a hoof, studied its leg intently, made the horse take another couple of steps. The horse was lame, near foreleg, but it was only a sprain. Ballista felt a flood of relief. Pale Horse was not badly hurt.

Ballista was now standing in the middle of nowhere, Pale Horse nuzzling his arm. Tacitus had clattered out of sight. The servants were somewhere miles behind. Ballista looked round. The wind had dropped. The late-autumn sun was warm and the birds were singing. It was idyllic, a landscape from a pastoral poem or the beginning of a Greek novel – but Ballista was totally lost, with a lame horse. Over to the right, nearer than before, a thin line of smoke climbed into the sky. Making soft, comforting noises, he led his lame horse in the direction of the charcoal burners.

To burn charcoal, you need a completely flat surface. The charcoal burners had cut a small terrace out of the slope of Mount Silpius. Yet, apart from that, everything was as it had been in the clearings in the northern forests of Ballista's youth when he had helped his father's men tend the stacks: the barren ground where the heat had sterilized the soil; the round hut made of misshapen branches, a stump as a seat outside; the scatter of tools – shovels and spades, a rake and a sieve, a curved ladder. On the far side of the clearing, about half as tall again as Ballista, was the stack itself, looking like an upturned cup. The northerner could tell at a glance that this one had been alight for some time, at least two or three days; the earth crust packed round the wood had darkened to near-black, and from the low vents came a steady trickle of white smoke.

Ballista called. No one replied. A charcoal burner would be along soon. A stack needs looking at three times an hour at least, to dampen the crust, check there are no cracks in it, generally to make sure that the air cannot get to the wood, cause it not to char but to burst into flames. Ballista would never forget the tiredness that came with seeing to a stack overnight when he was little more than a child.

Ballista set to looking after Pale Horse. He unsaddled the gelding, fed him a carrot from the saddlebag and began to rub him down. The northerner's thoughts drifted comfortably. The homely smell of horse in his nostrils and the repetitive, instinctive work of his hands made the ritual of brushing as soothing to rider as to horse. At last it was done. Ballista went to fetch Pale Horse a drink. There was a bucket near the stack, but it was lying on its side, a dark stain next to it where the water had run out. Ballista picked it up. There was a water butt next to the hut, and he filled it from that.

After his mount had had a drink – not too much – Ballista put the bucket back where he had found it. He had been there a long time now, and no one had come. He reached out and touched the earth crust of the stack. It was hot, crumbly and dry under his palm – far too dry. He walked around the stack. There was a circular depression about a foot across in its side. Inside, some of the charcoal must have slumped down, taking its covering of the earth crust with it. So far, the cave-in was still black, but invisible cracks must have opened, for the smoke issuing from the nearest vent was no longer white but blue. The air had got into the stack and, inside, the wood was burning.

A man walked into the clearing. He was carrying an axe slightly awkwardly over his shoulder. 'Welcome to my home, *Kyrios*,' he said. His tunic had a damp stain on the front but, otherwise, was clean. His hands were also clean. On the back of the right one was a jagged scar.

'Good day, woodsman, how are things?' Ballista asked politely. The man looked round the terrace, he studied the stack, and said that, the gods be thanked, things could be worse. Ballista said that he had some wine – would the charcoal burner care to share some? The man said he would.

Ballista turned away. He paused for a moment then turned back. The broad blade of the axe glittered wickedly as it arced through the air. It was coming down vertically, straight at the northerner's head. Ballista hurled himself backwards, losing his balance. The heavy axe hummed just past him and embedded itself in the hard-packed soil. Ballista landed on his arse. His boots skidding wildly on the loose topsoil, he scrabbled backwards to his feet. As he tugged his sword from its scabbard, the other retrieved his axe from the ground.

'The young *eupatrid* sends you this.' The man laughed. He swung the axe horizontally, low, at ankle level. Ballista leapt back. He felt the wind of the heavy blade's passing.

Now, while his opponent was off balance momentarily, was Ballista's chance. He lunged forward, weight coming down through his bent right knee, left leg straight behind him, blade flashing out towards his enemy's guts. Now it was the axeman's turn to scramble backwards.

The initial flurry over, the two circled each other, knees slightly bent, moving on the balls of their feet. Ballista's eyes never left his assailant's blade. The northerner had the hilt of his own weapon in a two-handed grip, the long, shimmering line of the blade pointing up at the man's throat. Ballista's eyes never left the blade of the axe. They moved slowly, intent on their work. The laughter had died out of the man.

Ballista stamped his right foot, as if advancing. The man flinched. Stepping forward on his left foot, Ballista made a one-handed cut from left to right to the head. As the axe came up to block, Ballista pulled the blow, let his arm swing through and out to the right, then chopped diagonally back in, down towards the man's left thigh. Just in time, the man shifted his grip, sliding his right hand along the haft, and got the axe down in the way. Ballista's blade bit a chunk of wood out of the handle between where the man's hands now clasped it, at the base and below the head.

Without warning, the man rammed the blunt top of the axehead into Ballista's shoulder as if it were a spear. The northerner staggered back. The axeman followed, gripping his weapon by the base, raising it over his head to strike. Still off balance, Ballista twisted his body and thrust wildly. The very tip of his blade caught the man's right shoulder. The man howled and took a couple of paces back.

They resumed their cautious circling. Though the wound could not be deep, blood was seeping down the axeman's tunic.

Ballista was taken completely by surprise when the man suddenly threw the axe. Stumbling back, he awkwardly fended the heavy thing away from his face, the handle catching him a painful blow on the forearm.

The man was running now. He had gained a few paces' headstart. Ballista set off after him. The man was unencumbered by a sword and fear lent wings to his feet. Already, as they plunged into a path from the clearing, he was drawing away. They ran on. Branches whipped at their faces. The man disappeared around a bend. The path here was very overgrown. Ballista could not remember if the man had been wearing a blade on his belt. The northerner skidded to a halt. Cautiously, ready for ambush, he edged round the bend. The path stretched away into the distance. The man was nowhere in sight. Blade at the ready, Ballista turned slowly, scanning the trees. Birds sang. Then, from above, came the sound of a horse's hooves. Ballista caught a glimpse of the man's tunic through the foliage. Then he was gone. The drumming of the hooves was receding.

Ballista turned back and found the charcoal burner. He was just off the path. Neatly chopped staves of wood were scattered all around him. He lay on his back, his tunic deeply stained, his sightless eyes to the sky, his blackened hands clutching a ghastly wound to his neck. Ballista cleaned and sheathed his sword. He was out of breath. He leant forward, hands on knees, panting. The sweat was cooling on his back. Someone had just tried to kill him. Who? 'The young *eupatrid* sends you this.' What young nobleman would pay to see him dead? Ballista stood up, went over and closed the charcoal burner's eyes. He put a small coin in the man's mouth to pay the ferryman.

VI

Ballista walked between the marble columns that flanked the door of his house. It was late. He was tired. It had been a long, long day. He glanced down at the grotesque mosaic of the improbably endowed hunchback. Possibly it had done its job, had averted the evil eye. The axeman in the charcoal burner's clearing had failed. Ballista was still alive. It had only been that morning, but it seemed half a lifetime away.

Coming into the courtyard, he paused beside the pool. Its waters were green in the lamplight. With his left hand, Ballista scooped up some water and bathed his eyes. His right shoulder hurt like hell. Blinking the water out of his eyes, he went on into the house.

Julia was waiting for him. Her face, mask-like, gave nothing away as she spoke the formal words of welcome then told her maid to get the *dominus* a drink and prepare him a bath and food. She stood very straight and still as her maid served the drink. She did not speak again until the servant had left the room.

'It is very late.' Her voice was tight, angry.

'I thought I should report the attempt to Censorinus and the *frumentarii* straight away. Otherwise it might look suspicious, as if I had something to hide, as if I were fighting a private war or something. Then Censorinus suggested I go on to the headquarters of the *Epimeletai ton Phylon* in the *agora*. The earlier the local police came to hear of it, the more chance of them catching him.' Ballista stemmed his defensive flow of words. 'I asked Aurelian to tell you I was all right.'

'Oh yes,' Julia snapped. 'Your friend turned up eventually. Some time after lunch. He was so drunk it was a miracle he did not fall off his horse and kill himself. The Danubian peasant said your shoulder was wounded.'

'It's nothing, just bruised.' It always irritated Ballista that she did not like his friend, let alone that she despised his origins.

'Well, I have not been idle while you have been out.' To avoid replying, Ballista took a drink. Julia continued. 'Someone wants to kill you. They may want to harm your family. I will not let anything happen to my son.' She had never liked the barbarian name that Ballista had insisted their son carried. At times like this, Isangrim always became *my son*.

'I have hired three ex-gladiators. They will guard the house. One of them will accompany my son whenever he goes out. I suggest you keep Maximus with you.'

Julia spoke with the icy self-possession that came with two hundred years of senatorial birth. The Julii of Nemausus in Gallia Narbonensis had been given that exalted rank by the emperor Claudius. Roman citizenship had come one hundred years earlier still, from Julius Caesar. By contrast, Ballista was very aware that his own entry into the citizen body of Rome had been just eighteen years ago.

Although the reason was not made public, the emperor Marcus Clodius Pupienus had given it to the young northerner as a reward for killing Maximinus Thrax. Pupienus had been one of the very few who knew Ballista's role in the desperate coup before the walls of Aquileia. Less than a month after enrolling Ballista in the ranks of the *Quirites*, Pupienus had taken the secret to his grave.

'That is good,' Ballista said, 'if they are reliable.'

Julia made a sharp, dismissive gesture. 'They are the best. My family has never been mean.'

To hide his annoyance, Ballista turned away, on the pretence of putting his drink down. Money was a delicate subject between them. When in his twenties, on his return from Hibernia, Ballista had been given equestrian status, the emperor Gordian III had included a gift of 400,000 sesterces, the property qualification for that order. To the vast majority of the inhabitants of the *imperium*, it was wealth beyond the dreams of Croesus. To the daughter of an old senatorial house such as Julia, it was a pittance. Although it was seldom mentioned, much of their lifestyle was funded by his wife.

Ballista unbuckled and took off his sword belt. He reasoned it was just her concern for Isangrim, and even for himself, that was making her so waspish.

'What are you smiling at?' she said testily

'Nothing, nothing at all.' He sat down wearily. 'Who do you think hired him?'

Julia shook her head, as if freshly amazed by her husband's obtuseness. 'Gaius Acilius Glabrio, of course. He hates you for leaving his brother to die in Arete. He has publicly sworn to avenge him. Patricians of Rome keep their oaths.'

'He is not the only enemy I have in Antioch,' Ballista said. 'Valerian has kept Videric at the imperial court as a hostage for the good behaviour of the Borani. There is bloodfeud between us.'

Julia actually snorted with derision. 'Your drunken oaf of a friend said that the attacker told you he had been hired by a *eupatrid*.'

'Yes,' said Ballista. 'He shouted "The young *eupatrid* sends you this." Videric's father, Fritigern, is king of the Borani.'

'No one in the *imperium* would consider the son of some hairy barbarian king *well born*, a nobleman.' As Julia spoke, Ballista wondered if she realized the implication of her words.

'The sons of Macrianus do not care for me.'

Julia sighed. 'Oh, Quietus and Macrianus the Younger are vicious and repulsive. They both loathe you since the fight at the palace, and they are certainly underhand enough to hire an assassin. They are rich, but they are hardly *eupatrids*. Their equally repulsive father started out as a mule driver.'

'Acilius Glabrio it is then,' said Ballista. In truth, he was far from convinced. He very much doubted that a hired knifeman from one of the slums of Antioch would be quite as aware as his wife of the subtle distinctions of class among the very rich. The irritation was draining out of him. Even Julia was looking less angry.

The maid stuck her head around the door, announced the bath was ready and ducked out again. Ballista got up and went over to Julia. He put his hand on her shoulder.

'Gods below, you stink.' She wrinkled her nose. 'Sweat

and horse. Go and get in the bath.' He turned to go. 'Are you really all right?'

He stopped. 'I am all right.'

She smiled. 'I will come through in a while.'

It was *Saturnalia*, the greatest festival of the Romans and one the hedonistic Antiochenes had taken to heart. Seven days of pleasure, of eating and drinking. Seven days of licence, of open gambling and illicit sex. The normal rules of society were loosened, if not completely inverted. Slaves roamed at will. In some households, they were served by their masters. Everyone relaxed their *dignitas* and let their guard down at the festival of Saturn.

Ballista raised his eyes from reading when Demetrius came into the room. The Greek youth looked worried. He had looked that way since the attack on his *kyrios* in the charcoal burner's clearing. Forty-seven days of apprehension were taking their toll. This evening he appeared at the end of his tether.

'It is Lucius Domitius Aurelian.' The words tumbled out of Demetrius. 'He is hurt. Badly hurt. A fall from his horse. On his way back from hunting. In the Kerateion district. Near the Daphne Gate. He wants to see you. There is a boy outside to lead us.'

By an act of will, Ballista forced down his rising panic. He put the papyrus roll down on the table next to his couch, carefully placing paperweights to keep it open at the passage he had reached in Lucian's little treatise *The Dance*.

Ballista followed Demetrius from the room. To avoid thinking about his friend, he forced his thoughts to run over his reading. It was 18 December, the second day of the *Saturnalia*, so he had decided to read Lucian's work on the festival. He had enjoyed it. But then he had started reading *The Dance*. He was not enjoying that as much. It was always the way with Lucian. You read one satire and it was splendid. You went straight on to another and it seemed less good. You read three in a row and you were sick of them.

In the lodge were the porter and Cupido, one of the ex-gladiators that Julia had hired. Most of the servants, including Maximus, Calgacus and the other two ex-gladiators, were on leave. It was the *Saturnalia*, after all. Ballista did not much care for Cupido. He was a large, brutish man, his muscles turned to fat. He was lazy, and he drank. He smelled like the taste of a copper coin carried in the mouth.

When Ballista had put on his boots, buckled up his sword belt and slung a heavy cloak over his shoulders, he saw that Cupido had done the same.

'Demetrius, you stay here. Tell the *kyria* where I have gone.' At Ballista's words Demetrius started to wrestle his boots off again, hopping on one foot. Ballista smiled at him. 'Keep an eye on the house until I return. Oh, and if you can find a slave that is sober, send him to tell Maximus and Calgacus what has happened. They are in Circe's Island.'

Outside, it was starting to snow, the first tiny flakes fluttering down. The boy that was to guide them was standing in the street, shifting from foot to foot in his anxiety to be off. The door slammed behind them and they heard the bolts shut fast. They started walking, the boy leading the way, the two men following.

It was dark. The lamps had been lit in most porches.

Although it was starting to snow harder, there were quite a few gangs of revellers on the streets as they crossed the Epiphania district. The boy called something over his shoulder to Cupido. The ex-gladiator quickened his pace to catch up and snapped harshly at him. They spoke in Syriac. Ballista, behind, could not understand them.

The snow was falling fast now, big, fat flakes that were starting to settle. Wrapped up in his worry for his friend, Ballista hardly noticed the snow drifting into his face, landing in his hair. Julia was right: Aurelian drank too much. Allfather, let the fool be all right.

They reached the Kerateion district, and the boy started to lead them across it by one narrow alley after another. There was next to no one about now. Of course, the Jews did not celebrate the *Saturnalia*. If anything, they would double-bolt their doors and sit tight at home, hoping the drunken revelry of their pagan neighbours did not turn to violence.

The boy dropped back next to Ballista. 'Not far now, *Kyrios*,' he said in Greek. Cupido was marching purposefully a couple of steps ahead. The ex-gladiator was puffing, his breath visible in the cold air.

At the end of the alley stood two figures in dark cloaks, their shoulders powdered white with snow. They were standing so close together that the high hoods that hid their faces were almost touching, although they did not seem to be talking.

Cupido turned off into a side alley. A moment after, Ballista realized his mistake. As he pushed back his cloak and drew his sword, the boy at his side turned and ran. The blade shone in the light of a lamp. Cupido spun round.

His mouth opened, but no words came out. Behind him, Ballista heard the patter of the boy's feet and the crunch of heavy boots in the snow. He swung the blade. Cupido tried to step back. He was too slow. The keen edge of the sword bit deep into his left arm. He screamed. Clutching the wound, he doubled up and crumpled to the ground.

Careful not to slip, Ballista turned – and froze. The two figures were running at him through the snow, swords in hand, dark cloaks billowing out behind. They looked not of this world. Their hoods had slipped back and they had the faces of impossibly beautiful girls. Their long, plaited hair streamed behind them and their faces had an inhuman stillness.

Ballista stood leaden-footed. His heart shrinking inside him, he stared at the apparitions. They had the faces of statues of goddesses, or the masks of heroines from the stage. Masks! He was a fool – they were wearing masks, dancers' masks from the pantomime.

Having recovered from the shock, Ballista hurled himself forward into the path of the man to his right. He swung hard at the man's head. The mask jerked back as the man raised his sword. Dropping on to one knee, Ballista altered the angle of his blow down into the man's thigh. There was a spray of red blood against the white of the snow, a muffled scream from behind the mouthless mask. The man fell.

Ballista quickly got to his feet. His remaining assailant was blocking the way he had come. He looked over his shoulder. Sure enough, there were two more masked men moving up the alley behind him. There were several doors, a couple of them with small porches, but not a single window opening on to the alley. The screams had not encouraged any door to open. A good spot for an ambush.

Ballista backed to the left-hand side of the alley, to the nearest porch. He tried the door. It was bolted. He hammered on it with the hilt of his sword. The sound echoed back dully and the door stayed shut.

The three men were closing in now. Ballista stepped out into the alley and sidled along until the porch would impede an attack from his left and the wall of the house covered his back. The men were fanning out, as far as possible, surrounding him. The one in the centre was directing them. He wore the face of a miserable old woman, heavily lined and pouchy-eyed. There was a jagged scar on his right hand.

'A long way from your charcoal stack, brother.' As he spoke, Ballista lunged forward, his sword seeking the man's chest. At the last moment, a clumsy but effective parry turned the point of the northerner's blade. Without pause, Ballista took two short steps to his right and unleashed a downward cut. The man there leapt backwards. A movement in the corner of his eye, and Ballista swivelled. Automatically, his sword came down across his body. A clash of steel and the assassin's blade was forced wide.

The snow was still falling. It formed a golden corona around the lamps. Weird shadows flickered about the alley as the four men danced their macabre, rhythmic dance: feint, probe, lunge, block, cut. Ballista fought doggedly. His mind was blank. After years of training and experience, the memory in the muscle was keeping the man-killing steel from his body. But he knew that if he made one slip, it would all be over.

The masked men gave a little ground. A man on horseback rode into Ballista's view. He had a drawn sword in his hand. Unlike those of the others, the mounted man's mask was metal, the silver face of a beautiful youth, lips and eyebrows gilded, an expensive, full-face cavalry parade helmet.

The horse stopped. It stamped in the snow. The impassive silver face regarded the frozen tableau of the fighters.

'Finish him. Get in close and finish the barbarian filth, you cowards.' Through the thin mouthpiece, the Latin sounded strange, unrecognizably distorted.

The pantomime masks closed in on Ballista. Faces immobile but eyes wild, long plaits swinging as the swords flashed. They had not the skill of the northerner and they were encumbered by the masks, but there were three of them. A flurry of blows, sparks flying. Ballista was driven back against the wall. No room to move. Off balance, parrying a heavy blow, Ballista was driven to his knees. A sword knocked chunks of plaster from the wall next to his ear.

And then the masks were receding. Ballista scrambled upright, getting the sword out in front, securing some space. Snow deadens sound, but Ballista could half-hear something off to his left, beyond the porch, out of sight. The eyes behind the masks seemed to be flicking glances in that direction. Ballista got his breathing right, waiting for his opportunity. It never came. The face of the beautiful girl and that of the harridan looked in at the swordsman with the scar on his hand. The mask of the miserable old woman jerked. And all three were running off to the right, their boots kicking up flurries of snow.

The horseman looked down at Ballista. The silver face

remained unmoving, but the eyes behind it were full of hate. He pulled the reins and walked his horse after the others, the way Ballista had come.

At the entrance to the alley, the masked man Ballista had cut down had risen to his feet. His leg was pouring blood. The horseman stopped. He held out his hand. A silver ring with the portrait of Alexander the Great glittered. The wounded man stumbled painfully across, his useless left leg dragging. He put up a hand to be helped up on to the horse. The horseman leaned out and gripped the proffered arm with his left hand. A glittering arc of steel, and the blade in the horseman's right hand crashed down on to the man's exposed head. There was a sickening sound like stepping on rotten fruit. Fountaining blood, the man fell away.

The man in the silver mask turned to look at Ballista. The light of the lamps shone on the mask of the beautiful youth. His arm came up. The bloodied sword pointed at the northerner. Then he kicked his boots into the horse's flanks and was gone.

Ballista leant back against the wall. He was drenched in sweat, limbs trembling with fatigue. Blood dripped into the slush at his feet. For the first time, he noticed four or five minor defensive wounds on his forearms.

The noise was getting louder: the sound of men pounding through the snow. Ballista pushed himself away from the wall and raised his sword again. My enemy's enemy is my friend. But you can never be sure.

A flood of torchlight, and Demetrius appeared. He had one of the Superintendents of the Tribes with him. They were backed by half a dozen Club Bearers of the watch.

Ballista lowered his sword and embraced Demetrius, their faces together. 'Thank you, boy. How?'

'I knew something was wrong. Cupido never volunteers for anything.' Demetrius' face was earnest. 'I disobeyed you, *Kyrios*. I went out and found a party of the watch, led them to the Jewish quarter.'

'You showed initiative. It is lucky one of us kept his wits about him.'

Ballista released Demetrius and went over to where Cupido lay. The ex-gladiator was not moving. Covering him with his sword, Ballista searched him for concealed weapons. 'A doctor,' Cupido moaned.

Ballista looked at the wounded arm. He was fast bleeding to death. 'Who hired you?'

'Doctor . . .' The stale copper-coin smell mingled with that of fresh blood.

'Who hired you?'

'A man in a bar. I do not know his name. The one wearing the old-woman mask. Scar on his hand.'

Ballista looked down at him, considering.

'I need a doctor,' Cupido whimpered again.

'Too late, brother.' Ballista lined the sword up and thrust it down into the man's throat. It was finished. The snow was turning to sleet.

VII

It was early, the second hour of an overcast, gloomy day. The black clouds piling up over Mount Silpius threatened rain. It seemed to have rained every day since the attack in the alley. From the second day of the *Saturnalia*, 18 December, to six days before the *ides* of January: twenty-four days, calculated Ballista, counting inclusively, as everyone did. Twenty-four days since the third attempt to kill him and, despite both the municipal *Epimeletai ton Phylon* and the imperial *frumentarii* scouring the city, there was no trace of the would-be assassins.

The dead assassin's mask, the beauty of its young girl's face marred by the blood soaked into the linen, had been no help. There were more than thirty theatrical mask makers in Antioch. Unsurprisingly, none admitted it was their work. And no one had come forward to claim the body.

There was little to go on. Three hired swords: two faceless men and a nondescript man with a scar on his hand – a nondescript man who in the charcoal burner's clearing had shouted, 'The young *eupatrid* sends you this' – in a city of more than a quarter of a million people.

The identity of the young *eupatrid* on the horse was still

a mystery. The type of cavalry parade mask he had worn was very expensive, but they were readily available all over the *imperium*. It need not even have been made by a silver-smith in Antioch. The horseman had spoken Latin. But his voice had been so distorted as to be unrecognizable.

One thing, however, *had* struck Ballista. The silver-masked horseman had called him a barbarian. That would come naturally to Acilius Glabrio, or the sons of Macrianus, yet surely it was unlikely that Videric, the son of Fritigern, King of the Borani, would call him a barbarian – unless he had become thoroughly romanized in his months as a diplomatic hostage. Or unless he had said it deliberately to throw suspicion elsewhere.

There was so little to go on; still, the northerner had hoped that something would have turned up before he had to leave.

Ballista sat on Pale Horse outside the Beroea Gate, wait-ing. He looked up at the nearest window in the great, square, projecting towers of the gate. The bright lamps inside made a halo of golden hair low down in the window. Higher and less distinct, slightly behind the boy, was the dark hair of his mother. Ballista had said he would leave Maximus to protect them, but Julia would not hear of it. She had pointed out that while someone had three times tried to kill Ballista, there had been no attempt on his family. She had stated firmly that the two remaining ex-gladiators would be enough protection while Ballista was away. The northerner felt some guilt at his relief that he would have the familiar presence of his Hibernian body-guard at his side. He waved, and saw the light blur of his wife's and son's hands waving back.

Behind Ballista, his staff were getting restless. It irritated him. *They* irritated him. He did not want them there. It was so typically Roman – the *dignitas* of a man granted *imperium*, command, demanded that he be accompanied by a commensurate number of staff. As *Dux Ripae*, Ballista must have an escort of four scribes, six messengers, two heralds, and two *haruspices*, to read the omens. Whether he wanted them or not was a matter of no moment.

And the members of staff were more than an irritation, they presented a danger. Ballista knew that, concealed among their number, would be at least two, maybe more, *frumentarii*. The reports written by these members of the secret police would fly along the *cursus publicus*, sometimes at more than a hundred miles a day, into the hands of their commander, Censorinus, the *Princeps Peregrinorum*, who would pass them to his superior Successianus, the Praetorian Prefect, who in turn would hand them to the emperor himself. Every move Ballista made would be scrutinized. The only, grim, satisfaction to be drawn from the situation was the marked reluctance of the twelve new members of staff he had chosen from the officially approved lists. There were so many places to be filled because, from the last expedition, only two of the staff had come back alive.

From under the great arch of the Beroea Gate came a clatter of horses' hooves. A trumpet rang out. Gaius Acilius Glabrio, Commander of the Cavalry in the army of the *Dux Ripae*, led out his two units of men. As befitted a scion of one of the oldest noble houses in Rome, Acilius Glabrio and his charger, a glorious, prancing chestnut, were magnificently turned out. Even on this dull day the young patrician seemed to shine with gold, silver and precious gems. The troopers that followed him were less gorgeous, but they were well equipped. There was no complete uniformity, but they were all much alike: heavily armoured men on heavily armoured horses. Wherever one looked, there was mail, scale, hardened leather and, in each right hand, a long spear, a *kontos*. They made an impressive sight, silent apart from the ring of their horses' hooves and the jingle of armour, bridle and bit, red pennants nodding above the Equites Primi Catafractarii Parthi, green above the Equites Tertii Catafractarii Palmirenorum. These were elite heavy cavalry – shock troops; regular units of tough, disciplined professionals. These men knew their own worth and expected to be treated accordingly.

Rank after rank they came out of the gate. As the last rank cleared the fortifications, the ritual shout went up: 'We will do what is ordered, and at every command we will be ready.' There was a perfunctory sullenness to the cry. It could be that they had caught the distaste of their commander Acilius Glabrio for serving under a barbarian *Dux*, but Ballista suspected it was more to do with the reduced numbers of each unit. They had numbered four hundred each; now, they were down to three hundred. Ballista had taken a hundred men from each unit to form a new one, his guard of Equites Singulares, under the command of the Danubian Mucapor.

A fresh round of trumpet calls, and the tramp of marching feet. Lucius Domitius Aurelian, Commander of the Infantry in the army of the *Dux Ripae*, marched out from under the great gate. Ostentatiously, he was equipped in the worn mail and leather of his men and, like them, he was on foot. First at his back were the men of Legio III

Felix. It was a splendid sounding title, but it could not hide that this was a scratch unit of only a thousand men, made up of drafts from the long-established legions III Gallica and IV Flavia Felix. Still, while the unit might be new, the men, in the main, were veterans, and a *vexillatio* of a thousand men from Legio IIII Scythica would join the army when it reached the Euphrates. At the heart of the force would be two thousand of the best heavy infantry in the world, the feared legionaries of Rome.

Four troops of light infantry, all bowmen, emerged next, in no great order. These were not regular units of the Roman army but *ad hoc* bands of warriors, mercenaries, fugitives and exiles from the wilder reaches of the empire: 400 Armenians, 200 tent-dwelling Saracens, 400 Mesopotamians, 300 Itureans. They did not march. The men of the four *numeri* slouched or swaggered, each as the mood took him. At least the Itureans were famed for the deadly accuracy of their black-fletched arrows. They were followed by a new unit of slingers. Ballista had created this by combining a ridiculously small unit of a hundred and fifty sedentary Arabs with two hundred volunteers from the Armenians. He had appointed the young Danubian Sandario to command them.

We will do what is ordered, and at every command we will be ready.

The braying of mules and a stench of camel announced the approach of the baggage train. Ballista had appointed his old subordinate, Titus Flavius Turpio, as *Praefectus Castrorum*, to be in charge of it. The ever-humorous face of Turpio appeared. Ballista was glad to see him. It was important to have as many men as possible in place you could trust. When Ballista had first met the ex-centurion Turpio he had distrusted him intensely. Then, in Arete, he had found him guilty of embezzling funds from his unit. Turpio claimed he had been blackmailed into it, and after that his service, both in the siege and in the desperate flight from the city, had earned him the right to be trusted. Besides, Ballista had grown fond of Turpio. There was something deeply reassuring about the way he reacted to any news, no matter how bad, with just a slight grin and a quizzical look, as if once again surprised by the follies of humanity or the capriciousness of fate.

With shouts, and provoking animal squeals, the civilian porters gradually bullied the baggage train along. Ballista's mind wandered. 'The young *eupatrid* sends you this.' Ballista knew he had many enemies. Who among them would a hired blade from the back-streets of Antioch describe as well born? Gaius Acilius Glabrio certainly. The sons of Macrianus, Quietus and Macrianus the Younger, almost certainly. Videric, the son of Fritigern, the King of the Borani, just possibly, if racial prejudice was set aside. At any event, further attempts were far less likely while Ballista was in the heart of his army.

The squeal of an axle pulled Ballista's mind back to the present. In the midst of the baggage train were five carts. Ballista had given explicit orders that no wheeled transport was to accompany the army. Who had dared ignore his orders? Even as he formulated the question, an answer came to him: the carts were smart, freshly painted, expensive – the carts of a rich man, a high officer. In the interests of discipline, Ballista could not let Gaius Acilius Glabrio flout his orders.

At long, long last, the end of the baggage train passed. The stolid, almost bovine face of Mucapor appeared at the head of the Equites Singulares. It was time to go. Ballista turned in the saddle and took one lingering, last look at the window in the tower, willing himself to remember every detail: Julia's long, dark hair, the boy's golden curls. He raised his hand in valediction. He saw the frantic waving of Isangrim's small hand. He turned Pale Horse away. Breathing shallowly, controlling himself, he rode away down the road to Beroea and beyond to Circesium, the city on the Euphrates he had to save.

They made the discovery in Antioch the day after Ballista rode out.

The superintendent hated this side of things. All the other duties that came with being one of the *Epimeletai ton Phylon* were close to unalloyed joy. Striding through the streets at night, a troop of burly Club Bearers at his back, felt close to being a hero, even a god. The knock on the door at midnight, the placating smiles of the merchants as they hurried to relight the offending, extinguished lamp, the return to the warmth and mulled wine of his official office on the *agora* – it was all good. But this side of things was not. There were eighteen Superintendents of the Tribes, and it always seemed to happen when he was on duty. This was the third in as many days.

'Fish it out.' This turned out to be easier said than done. The corpse was wedged in a grating at the opening of a tunnel where a storm drain ran under a street in the Epiphania district. The heavy winter rains which had been falling up on Mount Silpius meant the water was running deep and fast. One arm of the corpse, about all that could be seen in the dark, swirling water, banged against the metal as if seeking to call attention to itself.

The Club Bearers busied themselves with ropes and hooks. So far, it was impossible to tell if the corpse was that of a man or woman, or even a child. The superintendent, hunched in his furs, looked at the skies. It was not raining now, but a leaden sky looked as if it might presage snow. It would be colder than Hades in the water, the superintendent thought absently.

Eventually, soaked to the skin, the Club Bearers dragged the corpse out of the water. They deposited it at the feet of the superintendent. Part of him wanted to look away, but part of him was drawn to look by a morbid fascination. The gods below knew he had seen enough of the things.

It was a man dressed in just a ripped tunic. If he had ever had them, belt, cloak and sandals were long gone, taken by the water or his killers.

'He did not fall in. No accident or suicide. His throat has been cut.' The superintendent spoke out loud but to himself. He leant over to peer closely at the corpse. It was only a little knocked about; it had not been in the water long. The man had not been dead more than a day or so.

The superintendent straightened up, easing his back. These days, it always played up in damp weather. He hoped that his wife had told the new girl to buy the proper ointment this time. He looked down at the corpse, thinking. The third murdered man in three days. This one was a nondescript man with a jagged scar on his right hand. The big barbarian officer had ridden out the day before, and now here was the corpse of the leader of the street gang of

141

his would-be assassins. The other two corpses from the previous couple of days could well be the underlings who had escaped from the attempt in the alley in the Jewish quarter. The superintendent did not yet see how this got anyone much further forward, but he was still thinking. It was starting to snow.

VIII

'Hercules' hairy arse . . . our heroic general, mooning over a letter like a lovesick girl . . . lost like a man in the Highlands with the fog coming down, oh shite, what chance have we got . . . doomed, we are all fucking doomed.' Then, at the same volume but in a somewhat different tone, Calgacus continued, 'Gaius Acilius Glabrio awaits your pleasure. He is outside in answer to your summons.'

The Caledonian's voice rang round the main room of the post-house of the *cursus publicus* in the town of Batnae, which had been taken over as Ballista's temporary headquarters at the end of the eleventh day's march out of Antioch.

'Well, are you going to fucking say something?'

Although taciturn to the point of monosyllabism when asked about his *dominus* in public, over the years Calgacus appeared to have developed the strange conceit that if, when in private with Ballista and the intimate members of his *familia*, he spoke in a self-reflective tone, as if just thinking aloud, his querulous mutterings would be perfectly inaudible. Volume did not come into it.

'Thank you very much. Once you have shown him in you can go back to bothering the baggage animals.'

Calgacus' thin, shrewish face gazed at Ballista for a few moments then turned away. 'Bother the baggage animals, and when would I find time to get my leg over anything, woman or beast, working my fingers to the bone night and day looking after you?' The tirade was cut off as Calgacus shut the door behind himself. Smiling, the object of his complaints slid the letter, seal untouched, under the daily log of Equites Primi Catafractarii Parthi, one of the several that he had been working through. The further postponing of the reading of it merely served to heighten his anticipation.

'Gaius Acilius Glabrio, *Dominus*,' Calgacus announced. A chamberlain at the court of their sacred majesties could not have sounded more graceful. With a bow, the Caledonian backed out of the room. Ballista stood up and formally welcomed the young nobleman.

'*Ave*, Marcus Clodius Ballista, *Dux Ripae*.' The patrician officer replied with equal formality, and snapped a sharp salute.

Ballista returned it. 'Wine? Well, if you are quite sure?' Although he did not want it, he poured himself a drink rather than be left ineffectually holding the jug.

'The messenger said you wanted to see me, *Dominus*.'

'Yes,' said Ballista. He indicated a seat. Acilius Glabrio declined, saying he had to see to his men. This was not going to be easy. Ballista took his time. He sipped his drink and studied the young patrician. He was an elegant arrangement of scarlet and gold, muscled cuirass gleaming, his *paludamentum*, military cloak, draped just so over his shoulder. The posthouse only ran to clay and logs and no decoration. Acilius Glabrio was dressed as if he were made for an altogether grander stage.

'Before we left Antioch I gave instructions that no wheeled vehicles were to accompany the army.' Ballista paused, then continued with studied civility. 'I must have worded it badly. The order was intended to include everyone. We have only been marching for a few days, the easiest of stages, and already the wagons carrying your possessions have delayed things several times. Admittedly, the road has been surprisingly bad, part hill and part marsh, rocks thrown here and there in the marsh, no order at all, but it is unlikely to get much better.' Acilius Glabrio stood at attention, not responding in any way. Ballista smiled, but as he did so he knew that it would convey no warmth. 'I am sure that you would agree that those of us appointed to high command directly by the emperor must set an example.'

'When I can find suitable alternative means of transport I will send the wagons back.' Acilius Glabrio was tight-lipped. 'Now, if there is nothing else, I must see to the billets of my men.' Ballista nodded. Acilius Glabrio saluted and left.

Ballista watched the space where the young man had been. His elder brother, Marcus Acilius Glabrio, had been insufferable but he had proved himself a good officer and a brave man. So far, this stripling had shown evidence that he was like his sibling only in the first of those things. And who could be better described as 'a young *eupatrid*' than Gaius Acilius Glabrio, the end result of centuries of high birth?

To drive such thoughts out of his mind, Ballista poured himself another drink. He sat down and pulled out the letter. He looked for a time at the seal, the duplicate of his own, a cupid winding back the levers of his namesake, a torsion-powered piece of artillery, a *ballista*.

He opened the letter and scanned it once quickly, fighting down his anxieties, alert for bad news. He reached the end and, reassured, he settled to read it through slowly and thoroughly. Julia opened with the customary greetings, then she told the latest about the assassin with the scar on his hand. One of the *Epimeletai ton Phylon* who had been on duty had shown some cunning. Rather than announce that the corpse of the would-be killer had been discovered murdered, he had given out that an unknown man had been found drowned in one of the storm drains. Sure enough, within two days, a distraught woman had come to view then claim the body. In this way, it became known that the man had been one Antiochus, son of Alexander, a small-time criminal from the tanners' quarter. Despite rigorous questioning, it became apparent that the widow knew nothing of what she called her husband's trade. They were no nearer finding out who had hired the man. The man left three children, all girls.

The remainder of the letter set out clearly some domestic affairs, before closing with a simple sentence saying that she loved and missed him. It was partly her brisk underplaying of sentiment that had made Ballista fall in love with her. He smiled as he tried to imagine her writing flowery, feminine terms of endearment.

There was another sheet of paper in with the letter. Ballista picked it up. It was a drawing by Isangrim: two vertical lines; towards the top, two horizontal lines; and what looked like two wheels near the bottom – a *ballista*.

In crude letters, it was signed. The big northerner put it to his lips and gently kissed it.

Carrying the picture and his drink, Ballista stepped outside. Bats hunted through the bare fruit trees in the middle of the small walled garden. Around the walls stood rows of cypresses. The evening breeze rustled through their leaves. It reminded him of the sacred grove of Daphne. His eyes became hot with unshed tears.

They travelled for another eight days. From Batnae to Hierapolis, and from there to Caeciliana on the Euphrates, the road ran straight and true across the red-brown plain. Orchards and vineyards came down on either side. But it was winter. The leaves had long since fallen from the fruit trees, their trunks were black with rain, and the vines were thin and stark, savagely cut back.

There was mud, but nothing like before. On this stage of the journey, it barely splashed the knees of the infantry, seldom even touched the boots of the cavalry at all. The five carts of Acilius Glabrio's possessions became stuck fast only infrequently. Even someone as impractical and book-ish as Demetrius could see that this was more down to the natural drainage of the high plain than the efforts of the road builders.

On the morning they reached Caeciliana, the weather lifted. They marched into the small town under a cloudless sky. Beyond the mud-brick walls, at the foot of the cliff ran the mighty Euphrates. Here it was divided into several channels, enclosing several greater and lesser islands. Under the cold winter sun, the river was an intense blue.

The small army made a reasonably brave show as it

followed the white *draco*, the personal standard of Ballista, through the gates. A few handfuls of locals had turned out, and cheered with some enthusiasm. In accordance with orders issued long ago, a *vexillatio* of a thousand men of Legio IIII Scythica had marched downriver from their base at Zeugma and was drawn up, waiting, in the *agora*. Much more surprising was the identity of the centurion in command. At first, Demetrius did not recognize him under his helmet. The young Greek was surprised when Ballista threw himself off his horse and hugged the man. There was a dull metallic clash as their helmets met. Laughing, both men stepped back, took off their helmets and tried again.

'Castricius, you old bastard,' Ballista roared. 'I thought you were dead in Arete or a slave in Persia.'

The thin, lined face smiled wryly. 'It takes a lot to kill me.'

'I would bloody say.' Ballista tipped his head back, eyes almost disappearing in laughter. 'A bugger who can survive the imperial mines can survive anything.'

Demetrius winced. Tact was not always the strongest asset of his *kyrios*. It was far from sure that Centurion Castricius would want his legionaries or anyone else to know that, before he had joined the army, he had been found guilty of a crime serious enough to warrant being committed to the living hell of the mines. Demetrius himself had always had the greatest difficulty in reconciling himself to having been enslaved at all. It was somehow easier to pretend to have been born a slave. The young Greek knew he would not have wanted anyone to know if he had been in the mines. Not, of course, that the issue could ever have arisen. He would not have survived.

Castricius just laughed. 'As I tell this rabble, the good daemon that watches over me never sleeps – keeps them on their toes. Let me present the boys.'

'Yes, that would be good. And then, afterwards, you must tell me how you got out of Arete. You shall do so over a proper feast to celebrate. We will kill the fatted pig – or whatever it is the Christians say.'

'The Christians to the lion,' said Castricius as he turned to lead the way.

The inspection passed well. Silent, serried ranks of men. One thousand large, red, oval shields, on each the golden lion and eagle, the latter crowned by two winged personifications of victory. The symbols of Legio IIII Scythica were repeated on the scarlet *vexillio* on its crossbar above their heads. *Hoplites*, thought Demetrius, 'armoured men'. Possibly not quite the same styles of armour as one found on the pots and bas-reliefs of the ancients, but undoubtedly the spiritual descendants of the heroes of Marathon, Thermopylae and Plataea: the embodiment of western freedom once again called on to defy the countless barbarian hordes from the east.

The feast also started quite well. The official house of the *cursus publicus* was, if anything, more spartan at Caeciliana than it had been at Batnae. But at least the main room was warm; a fine fire burned at one end, and braziers placed here and there throughout kept the early evening chill away. The dining room was just big enough. The *Dux Ripae* had invited his three senior officers, the commanders of cavalry, infantry and the baggage train and the commanders of the individual units under them. There were thirteen dining. There should have been fourteen, but Gaius Acilius Glabrio had sent to announce that he was too busy to attend.

First, they stood, sipping a *glykismos*. The sweet aperitif did little to take a certain stiff formality out of the air. The non-appearance of Acilius Glabrio made the three cavalry commanders uncomfortable. It was not really the place for the prefects of the Armenians, Saracens, Itureans or Arab and Armenian slingers to hold forth, good Romans though they all considered themselves, irrespective of the ethnicity of their men.

Things did not improve immediately when they reclined at table. Hard-boiled eggs with salted catfish and spicy black pudding appeared. Then a light, very easy-to-drink white wine from Ascalon went round, Castricius got into his stride with the story of his escape from the fall of Arete, and things began to flow more easily.

By the time the few remnants of the first course had been removed, all had had the chance to exclaim at the Odysseus-like cunning and fortitude of Castricius' escape: the arrows whistling out of the dark, the screams of horses and men, the fall – so he thought – of Ballista, the surge of Sassanid warriors, the flight through the chaos to the tunnels which brought water up from the river, Castricius' employment of the knowledge gained when he had surveyed those self-same tunnels to hide in a dead end in one of the furthest recesses – three, maybe four, days in the dark, licking mois-ture from the rock walls, at last hunger driving him above ground, into an empty world which smelled of wood smoke and something revoltingly like burnt pork: the moonlit shell of a sacked city.

The main course was served. In accordance with prevail-ing medical opinion, as it was winter there were few vegetables, just a couple of cabbages – it was important to prevent the inner man from becoming damp and cold. There was a Homeric quantity of meat: beef, pork, mutton, and one of a pair of ostriches that the officers of Legio IIII Scythica had caught on the march down. There was a great deal of a strong red wine from Sidon – most doctors held that wine warmed the blood. Momentarily, the conversation became general, if not inspired: the ostrich was tough, the wings a bit better, the only good way to eat it was air-dried.

Then, as is the way, the hubbub died down to a respectful silence as the commanding officer began to talk. Ballista told the tale of the fall of Arete. He told it well, turning to Turpio and Castricius to confirm points of detail; it seemed to be relived before their eyes. The numbers of the Sassanids; the dust darkening the sky. The skill of their siege works; the towers, the great ram, the ramp and mines. The horrible ingenuity of the tortures inflicted on prisoners, the blinding and impaling. The fanaticism of their assaults; the thousands who died before they were thrown back. The god-given zealotry of Shapur, the King of Kings; his mission to conquer the world, to make all peoples worship the Bahram fires, the sacred fires of his god Mazda. Finally, when the dangers seemed overcome, the shattering betrayal by Theodotus the Christian.

It was a subject that Demetrius preferred not to think about. As a slave standing at the foot of the couch of his *kyrios*, naturally he was not brought into the conversation. He envied the others their easy familiarity with Ballista. It was not just that they were free and he was a slave. There was a sense of a hard to define but evident relaxed comradeship between them. Possibly, he thought, it came from the largely unreflective nature of military life, and possibly it came from a sense of dangers shared.

As Demetrius poured more drinks, his thoughts wandered to Hierapolis, the holy city through which they had passed a few days earlier. For once, there, the military itinerary had given him two days of rest. Pleasant images drifted into his mind: the beautiful Ionic temple with its golden doors, the exquisite, lingering aroma of incense inside, the eyes of the cult statue of the goddess following him around the sanctuary, the fire jewel on her brow lighting the gloom; sitting by the sacred lake with its bejewelled fish, which came when called, meeting the stranger Callistratus, walking back through the gardens to his house, the long afternoon behind the shuttered windows.

'Demetrius, you are dreaming, boy.' The voice of his *kyrios* cut not unkindly into his consciousness. 'We all need more to drink.' The others cheered.

'Absolutely arseholed, every one of them,' Calgacus whispered in his ear. 'Our revered leader the worst of the lot.'

More drink in their hands, more drink inside them, half a dozen conversations flourished. Sandario was telling a long story about a young noble Tribune who found a camel on parade when he arrived at a lonely desert outpost. Again Demetrius' thoughts wandered back to Hierapolis, this time less pleasantly, to the hordes of *Galli*, the eunuch devotees that thronged the precincts. He was glad his visit had not coincided with the hideous ceremony when worshippers maddened by the goddess Atargatis seized their own manhood and, the obsidian knives glittering in the pitiless sun, publicly castrated themselves. Self-mutilated and shameless, they would run through the streets of the town until they chose into which house they would hurl their bloody, severed genitals. It was unspeakably barbaric. Demetrius wondered if these eastern provincials had less in common with Hellenes and Romans than with the Sassanid Persian enemy. In a war, how loyal would they prove to the *imperium*?

'No, my dear Tribune, the men use the camel to ride to the nearest brothel.' Sandario's joke was hardly novel but, helped by the wine, it won a hearty burst of laughter. The officers were still grinning, the Tribune of the Saracens shaping to tell the story of the ass and the murderess, when Calgacus ushered one of the Equites Singulares into the room. The cavalryman spoke quietly to his unit commander. It seemed it took a moment or two for the message to get through, but when it did Mucapor's bovine face darkened with anger.

'How bloody dare he . . . outrageous . . . teeth before tail, every fucking time.' Mucapor slammed his cup down and rose, none too steadily, to his feet. He addressed Ballista. 'A bloody outrage . . . my men are cavalry, fuck all use if their horses are fucked.'

'Whoa, whoa.' Ballista made soothing noises, exactly as he would to a horse. He smiled. 'Back up and try the fence again – I have no idea what you are talking about.'

'Gaius Acilius Glabrio has just ordered some of my men's mounts turned out of the barn I have stabled them in so that those fucking carts which carry his possessions can be sheltered.'

Ballista's smile was frozen for a moment. Then his face changed. 'Has he indeed.' The big northerner took a drink. The others were silent. There was expectation as well as alcohol in the intensity of their gaze. 'Calgacus, Demetrius, fetch torches.' Ballista smiled in the direction of Demetrius, although largely unseeing, his eyes glassy. 'We are going to form a *comus*.'

With a sinking heart, Demetrius went to do as he was told. It was seldom that anything good came of the Greek tradition that, at the end of a party, drunken revellers formed a torch-lit procession through the streets. The *comus* was nothing but trouble.

Ballista led them through the dark streets. Their progress was slow and noisy. One or two missed their step, even staggered a bit. Demetrius thought that they would be fortunate not to injure each other with the burning torches. In a strange mixing of cultures, they began to sing a marching song from the legions of Rome, one as old as Julius Caesar:

> Home we bring our bald whoremonger
> Romans, lock your wives away.
> All the bags of gold you sent him
> Went his Gallic whores to pay.

By the time they reached the barn they were being trailed by a crowd of the curious, civilians and soldiers alike. Ballista roared at a small group of soldiers to open the gates. They stopped staring incredulously and obeyed. The gates swung back, and there, polished wood softly gleaming, were Acilius Glabrio's wagons. Ballista asked one of the soldiers if they were unloaded. The man stammered that he thought so.

'Haul them out, boys.' Ballista's voice carried well. 'Haul

them out and push them together in the middle of the *agora*.'

Demetrius could feel the way that this was going. It was not well. The wagons, their shafts up in the air, were crammed up tight together in the centre of the open space. Ballista stepped forward from the gaggle of the *comus*. He called for oil. While he waited, he swung his burning torch through the air. The oil arrived. Ballista tossed his torch to Maximus, who had appeared from nowhere. Ballista sloshed the oil over the nearest wagon and threw the empty amphora into another, where it shattered into a hundred shards. He gestured to Maximus, who handed him back the torch.

'No one in this army disobeys orders.' Ballista swung back the torch and threw it overarm. It whooshed through the air towards the oil-soaked wagon. It landed, and instantly, with a crump, fire broke out. A cheer went up and the torches of the others were arcing through the air. The first thick, black coils of smoke went up into the clear night sky.

Demetrius sensed a movement in the crowd at the edge of the *agora*. Ballista and the officers around him were oblivious to it, passing a wineskin from hand to hand. Demetrius saw Gaius Acilius Glabrio, his face immobile, like that on a portrait bust in the atrium of a great house, watch his wagons catch and begin to burn.

Demetrius turned back to the crowd around Ballista. They had not noticed Acilius Glabrio. Ballista was laughing at something Aurelian was saying. There was much about his *kyrios* that reminded Demetrius of his boyhood hero Alexander the Great. There was the courage, the openness, the impulsive generosity, but there was also the darker side, the dangerous, often drink-fuelled, violence, seldom far from the surface. Today Ballista was not the good Alexander who had put the first torch into his own wagons to lighten the baggage train in distant Bactria. Instead he was the drunken Alexander torching the palace of the Persian kings at Persepolis at the suggestion of a whore.

Demetrius looked back at Gaius Acilius Glabrio. The young patrician was staring at Ballista with open loathing. Whether or not he was the young *eupatrid* who had set assassins on Ballista, there could be no doubt that Acilius Glabrio hated the big northerner. After a time, without a word, the nobleman turned and left.

Nothing good could come of this, thought Demetrius, nothing good at all.

IX

The army saw its first Persians at the Balissu River. There were three of them on the far bank. They sat on their horses, quietly watching the Roman army approach.

These were the first Persians that Gaius Acilius Glabrio had seen. Gods below, he had been waiting for this moment. Ever since that humiliating day in Caeciliana he had been waiting to see the Persians. Cold steel would show that bastard Ballista the difference between barbarian filth like him and a Roman patrician, the difference between mindless, brittle ferocity and *virtus*, the true, enduring courage of a Roman. What was it the Spartans had said in the old days? *If you think your sword is too short, take a step closer.*

And how long he had waited. First, seventeen interminable days training around Caeciliana, seventeen days of pointless drill and manoeuvres, the barbarian *Dux Ripae* fussing and fretting like an old woman. It was as if the northern barbarian were more interested in collecting boats and pack animals for the baggage than in fighting. It seemed that he was reluctant to march out and face the enemy. The young patrician had been only too aware of the sniggers and smiles behind his own back, of sordid plebs, barbarians even, laughing at a member of the Acilii Glabriones. In response, he had just trained his cavalrymen all the harder.

Finally, on the fifteenth day of February they had marched out. It was the day of the festival of the *Lupercalia* in Rome. Had he been in Rome, Gaius Acilius Glabrio would have been running with the other *lupercali*, everyone of them drawn from a leading family. He would have run naked except for a girdle cut from the skin of a freshly sacrificed goat, run through the streets striking out at passers-by with the goatskin thong. But he was not in Rome. He was hundreds of miles away on the Euphrates, desperate to meet the enemy, to prove himself in the terror of battle. They had marched out – and nothing had happened.

For fourteen days the army had crawled southward, the great Euphrates rolling along next to them. The army had been ordered by the timorous *Dux Ripae* into a ridiculous defensive formation, as if scared of meeting the Sassanid reptiles in open combat, and progress had been painfully slow. They had only marched in the mornings. By midday they would have halted and started to dig trenches and construct a fortified camp. At the well-fortified city of Soura, it had taken the army two days to cross the stone bridge to the eastern bank of the Euphrates. Two short days' march after that they had halted for three whole days at Leontopolis. And in all that time they had not seen a single Persian.

A few miles south-east of Leontopolis, the Balissu river ran into the Euphrates from the east. The Balissu was a small, insignificant watercourse, probably dry in the summer, but it was here that the first Persians showed themselves.

Acilius Glabrio, riding in the van of the army, as was only proper for a man of his status, peered intently at the three Persians on the other side of the stream. He could see them clearly. They were less than a hundred paces away. They sat on their horses placidly and watched the advancing Romans. They wore loose, brightly coloured, patterned tunics, baggy trousers, bushy beards and long hair. One wore a cap, the other two tied their black hair back with a band. They were slender men, dark-skinned. It was true what he had often been told: their eyebrows joined, and their eyes were like those of goats.

When the Romans had almost reached the Balissu, were little more than twenty paces away, the Persians languidly wheeled their horses and rode off. They saw no others for the rest of the day. The army forded the small stream and laboriously constructed its fortifications for the night.

At dawn the next day, as the Roman army, with Acilius Glabrio well to the fore, marched out of its camp, the Persians were back – or Persians who looked just the same as the ones of the previous day. For the rest of that day and the two that followed, as the army marched down in easy stages to Basileia, the Sassanid scouts hung about. Two or three at a time, never more than five or six, now always keeping well beyond bowshot, sometimes in the path of the army, sometimes off to the left flank. When the army was safely quartered for two days in the great fortress town of Basileia, the Persians could still be glimpsed here and there outside the walls, now down on the narrow ground by the river, sometimes up on the cliffs. Their constant presence incensed Acilius Glabrio. How he wanted to get at them. What he would do to them when he did. Their hanging about at a distance reinforced everything that he had ever learned about easterners – born cowards, they were simply too scared to come to close quarters. He began to worry that they would just melt away back to Persia, that the army would relieve Circesium without a blow struck, that he would never have a chance to strike at the reptiles.

It was still quite dark as the army marched out of Basileia. Gaius Acilius Glabrio stretched and yawned until his jaw cracked. He was tired. He settled back into his saddle, the creak of leather and wood lost in the general sound of the slowly moving cavalry. He was very tired. The barbarian *Dux* had summoned the *consilium* to meet four hours before dawn. By lamplight, the officers had been treated to the usual injunctions: hold the formation; keep the men closed up; above all, no one was to break ranks or to charge without express permission. As for what else they had been told, Acilius Glabrio wondered which of the officers were so stupid that they could not have seen for themselves that the road south of Basileia ran through a narrow gap between the Euphrates on the right and high cliffs on the left. Apparently, not far south, the road forded a watercourse, which ran from the hills into the Euphrates. The locals called it the canal of Semiramis. There had been reports of dust clouds to the south. The barbarian *Dux* had said it might signify that the Sassanids intended to make a stand there. Nonsense, thought Acilius Glabrio. The cowardly little easterners did not intend to make a stand there or anywhere else. The chance would be a fine thing. As for Semiramis, every ditch, wall and hillock out here was credited to the ancient Assyrian queen.

Beyond its fringe of reeds, the river shone, as water sometimes does in the darkness before dawn. An arrowhead of ducks flighted past, splashing down somewhere towards the tail of the army. The sky was lightening. A handful of high clouds could be made out. They were moving north. Down where the army of the barbarian *Dux Ripae* marched, there was no wind.

Barbarian *Dux Ripae* – the words did not fit properly together. It was, thought Gaius Acilius Glabrio, like saying 'sedentary Scythian' or 'virtuous whore'. Lulled by the motion of his horse, his thoughts ran on: 'short-haired Gaul', 'vegetarian nomad', 'trustworthy Carthaginian', 'taciturn Greek'. A darker line running through the gloom, running across the path of the army, interrupted his paradoxical ethnographic musing. He raised himself in the saddle and peered ahead. The cliffs off to the left made the dark of night linger longer down on the floodplain. Distances and heights were hard to judge in the murk. The dark line appeared to be about a hundred paces away and somewhat taller than a man. It seemed to move, to waver or sway. Was it a line of tamarisks such as you often found out here, along watercourses, moving gently in the early morning breeze, or even poplars?

Then Acilius Glabrio remembered: there was no wind down on the floodplain. A large, pale shape moved along the dark line. On it something seemed to glint in the half-light. A horse. A horse and rider. A cavalryman. The line was a line of Sassanid cavalrymen.

'Form line, form line on me,' Acilius Glabrio shouted, his voice loud and slightly cracked. After a second or so, there was a rising swell of noise as junior officers barked orders, armour and weapons jingled and clashed, and horses snorted. The three hundred men of Equites Primi Cata-fractarii Parthi began to manoeuvre from a column five abreast into a line five deep.

Whisp, whisp, whisp; something shot past his face. Something else struck the ground by his mount's near fore-leg and skittered away. Arrows! The reptiles were shooting arrows out of the near-darkness. The bastards!

'*Bucinator*, prepare to sound the charge.' Acilius Glabrio was pleased that, this time, his voice sounded less ragged.

'Wait, *Dominus*.' Out of the body of men, Niger, the prefect of the unit, drew his horse up alongside that of Acilius Glabrio. He leant over, speaking softly to avoid being much overheard. 'The *Dux* ordered us to hold the formation, not to charge.' The prefect's voice was clipped and urgent. 'We must halt. Find out what is facing us. Send a messenger to fetch the *Dux*. He will give us our orders.'

Us, thought Acilius Glabrio. *Us*, indeed. Since when had plebeians like this prefect seen themselves as equals of a patri-cian? Wait like a slave for orders from a northern barbarian? Never. A sudden thunder of drums made the young noble-man physically jump. It was followed by the braying of Sassanid trumpets. He turned his back on Niger. He could feel his heart pounding. *Carpe diem*: seize the day.

'*Bucinator*, sound the charge.' Acilius Glabrio saw the musician look past him to the prefect. To Hades with all of them. He kicked in his heels savagely, and his mount jumped forward. He felt an arrow fly past. Behind him the charge rang out. When his horse reached a steady canter, he looked back. It was all right. There was no formed line, rather a mob of men on horses. But it was all right. They were following him. *Carpe diem*. This was going to be his day. This would show the barbarian bastard that had left his brother to die, and that Danubian peasant Aurelian. This would show them all.

'Are you ready for war?' The young patrician's words were lost, snatched away over his shoulder, drowned by the pounding hooves, the ringing of weapons and armour.

He caught sight of the canal a moment before they were on it. His horse seemed to disappear from beneath him. Only the high horns at the rear of his saddle stopped him being thrown. The horse found its feet. Acilius Glabrio slammed painfully down into the saddle. It knocked the breath out of him. They splashed across the watercourse. The bed of the watercourse was smooth, the water no more than hock high. Acilius Glabrio heard himself sob as, hunched over in agony, he forced air back into his lungs.

The far bank was in front of him. Thank the gods it was not too steep. As his mount gathered itself, Acilius Glabrio looked up. A fierce, bearded face was gazing down at him. The Persian yelled something in their incomprehensible tongue, his teeth very white in the midst of his black beard. A long Sassanid cavalry blade glittered. Acilius Glabrio remembered he had not drawn his own sword. One hand clinging to the saddle, he wrestled it out of its scabbard as they scrambled up the slope.

His horse hauled them over the top of the bank into bright sunshine. The Persian was gone. All the Persians were gone. The nearest was twenty paces away, his bowcase banging against the flank of his mount, puffs of dust rising from under its hooves. They were running. All the reptiles were running.

'After them. Don't let them get away.' Acilius Glabrio kicked on. The reassuring sound of his men at his heels. *Carpe diem*. He was laughing out loud.

The Persians were light cavalry. They were riding hard. Unencumbered by armour, their bright clothes shining in the morning sun, they were pulling clear of the Roman heavy cavalry. Off to his right, down by the Euphrates, Acilius Glabrio saw tethered horses, Sassanids on foot milling around. He glanced over his shoulder. The *bucinator* was nowhere to be seen. But the standard bearer of Equites Primi was close. He waved for the man to follow and steered towards the riverbank. He did not look back again. He knew the troopers would follow the standard.

Down by the bank, Persians were throwing away pick-axes, cutting the tethers of their horses, throwing themselves into the saddle, spurring away. The gap closed quickly. Acilius Glabrio picked his man: a tall, thin Persian some way from his mount, running desperately. His baggy trousers flapped as he ran. As Acilius Glabrio came up with him, the man looked round. Acilius Glabrio leant out from the saddle, swinging his long blade in an arc. The Persian threw up an arm, screaming, his goat eyes wild with terror. The blade bit home. The impact wrenched Acilius Glabrio's shoulder, almost pulled the hilt from his grasp. The Persian fell, and his horse carried Acilius Glabrio past.

'After them. Don't let them get away.' Leaning forward in the saddle, Acilius Glabrio urged his mount on. The Persian light horse were getting away. He pushed his horse harder. The sound of a Roman *bucinator* playing recall cut into his consciousness. How dare the bastard, without orders? Acilius Glabrio looked around. The widely scattered

Roman *catafractarii* nearest to him were slowing down, reining in, coming to a stand. He stared after the Persians. Possibly it was for the best. The reptiles were outdistancing the pursuit. The south wind was blowing the dust of their passage into his face. He pulled up his own horse.

It was lame. He had not noticed. Now that he had, he did not care. He had another ten as good with the baggage train. He was sweating. His sword was slick with Sassanid blood. His heart was singing.

As the lame animal picked its way down to the riverbank, Acilius Glabrio counted six Persian corpses, the glorious colours of their clothes dimmed by dust and blood. One of them was his. He was not sure which. It did not matter. He had been the first to kill his man.

Puzzled, Acilius Glabrio looked at the pickaxes, shovels and other tools scattered by the riverbank. The Persians had been digging. Then he realized what they had been about. The shifty little easterners, too cowardly to face Roman steel, had been trying to enlist nature on their side. They had been digging through the embankment to flood the land between the Euphrates and the cliffs. Only a little longer and they would have succeeded. Well, he had put paid to that. Laughing out loud again, he kicked on his lame horse. *Carpe diem*. It was his day, his victory. A glorious victory. *If your sword is too short, take a step closer.*

X

Sunrise usually made Ballista happy. Today it did not. He was with the scouts, about a mile in front of the marching camp. He sat on Pale Horse, watching the sky over the cliffs turn a delicate lemon-yellow. A small hawk was hunting – a black, humped silhouette against the beautiful sky. None of it lightened his mood.

Gaius Acilius Glabrio was a fool, an insubordinate, arrogant fool. Yesterday he had disobeyed orders. His headstrong charge had scattered Equites I Parthi, worn out their horses – easy pickings had the Sassanids laid a trap. The charge had left the army in disarray, the van completely open if the Sassanids had been ready with an attack. He had courted utter disaster. But it had not happened. The Sassanids had not set a trap, had not been ready with a counter-attack. Not only had the fool got away with it, he had prevented the enemy sabotaging the levee and the irrigation sluices, prevented them from flooding the path that the Roman army must take. Had they done so, it would have stopped the army in its tracks, delayed them for days. The insufferable fool had returned a hero in his own eyes and even in the estimation of many of his men.

Angry as he had been, Ballista had somehow summoned

the restraint to wait until they were in the relative privacy of the his tent before upbraiding Acilius Glabrio. It had done no good whatsoever. Yesterday's stupidity had merely served to reinforce the young officer's patrician pride. Six dead Persians, and he had had the gall to speak of a glorious victory. Ballista doubted the widows of the four dead troopers from Equites I Parthi would see it in the same light. Patting his ridiculously coiffed curls, Acilius Glabrio had started to talk of the famed *celeritas* of Julius Caesar. Unwilling to listen to a lecture on the efficacy of speedy action from the young fool, Ballista had summarily dismissed him from his presence. If only he could equally summarily dismiss him from his command. But the general could not. Acilius Glabrio had been appointed personally by the emperor. The fool had to remain cavalry commander, and the worst of it was that, now, he had been reinforced in his insubordination, now he would be even less ready to obey Ballista's orders. It did not look good – an insubordinate, arrogant fool, and possibly a murderous one . . . Who better fitted the assassin's description of a young *eupatrid*? At least he had not made an attempt on Ballista's life since Antioch.

Angrily, Ballista tried to push the patrician out of his mind. He returned his attention from the skies to the terrain his army must cross. Here, the cliffs started to run away to the west, opening up a wide, largely featureless plain between themselves and the Euphrates. Ideal terrain for cavalry. Ideal for the Sassanids; bad for the Romans.

A brassy peal of trumpets announced that the army was breaking camp. Ballista turned in his saddle to watch. He wanted to study the order of march that he had prescribed

– to see it, as it were, from the outside, through the eyes of the enemy. Straight away, the four parallel columns that were the heart of the formation began to be apparent. First, out on the river, some one hundred boats of all shapes and sizes were being rowed, paddled and poled into position. Around the ungainly transports nipped five little one-banked galleys, chivvying like sheepdogs. Ballista was pleased that he had gone to the trouble of finding and requisitioning the galleys, partly crewing them with experienced boatmen from Legio IIII Scythica. He was even more pleased that he had bullied the military commander at Caeciliana into handing over five bolt-throwing *ballistae* to mount on the galleys. The galleys were manoeuvrable. The artillery on them had a far better range than any hand-held bow or sling. A Sassanid cavalry force was very unlikely to have any boats or artillery with it. The little improvised war galleys gave Ballista command of the Euphrates. And that secured one flank of his army.

Next, keeping as close to the riverbank as possible, came the land-based half of the baggage train – over three hundred indiscriminate beasts of burden: donkeys, mules, camels, horses and broad-shouldered slaves. Somewhere in that braying, surging mass were the ten spare mounts of Acilius Glabrio and the rest of his luxurious equipage. At least the latter was now carried on the backs of animals or men, not on lumbering wagons which got stuck at the merest hint of bad going. Ballista watched horsemen spurring up and down the column trying to instil some order. He was glad that he had not only seconded Turpio some legionaries for the galleys but twenty cavalrymen from the Equites Singulares. It was not just that they would help

Turpio control the awkward land column; if everything went wrong, he would have some good men at his back to help him cut his way out of the rout. Ballista pushed the thought away. He was irritated with himself for thinking such an ill-omened thing.

The *Dux Ripae* switched his attention from the tail to the teeth of his army. Parallel to the baggage rode the cavalry: eight hundred heavily armoured men in columns of fours. It was easy enough to spot Acilius Glabrio. One only needed to locate the standard of the lead unit, Equites Primi Catafractarii Parthi, and look just in front of it for the elegant figure in scarlet and gold who rode alone. Some way back, looming above the dust, was Ballista's own standard, the white *draco*. It marked the mid-point in the column where marched the Equites Singulares. The rear unit, the Equites Tertii Catafractarii Palmirenorum, was already completely obscured by the dust.

The fourth and final column was the tough outer carapace behind which the others sheltered. This was the column furthest from the river. Here was the infantry, Legio IIII Scythica followed by Legio III Felix: two thousand legionaries marching in a column four wide and five hundred deep. They were ordered just so, two paces between ranks to allow the bowmen, four hundred Armenians and four hundred Mesopotamians, to come and go. The tough, fiery Aurelian had taken his post at the centre of the column.

Finally, Ballista considered the three units that were not organized into the columns. Across the front and rear of the army were two thin lines of bowmen, turning the whole formation into a hollow square. But how very thin the line at the front looked – just two hundred Saracens. Ballista could not see them, but he knew that the line at the rear was little better, just three hundred Itureans. The last unit that made up the army was also lost in the dust. But somewhere between the columns of cavalry and infantry, the resourceful Sandario held his three hundred and fifty slingers ready to reinforce any part of the square.

It was quite good. Bits of it – the river flank and the infantry column – were very good. But there were undeniable problems. There was not enough heavy infantry. Another five hundred legionaries in the van and in the rear, and the square would have been nigh on impregnable – or rather it would have been nigh on impregnable if everyone obeyed orders and held their position.

As it was, Ballista was worried about the obedience of his command. It was not really the two columns of baggage under Turpio. Yes, the sardonic ex-centurion had been mired in corruption when the northerner had first met him. Turpio had sworn that he had been blackmailed into it. Ballista did not know what it was that had laid Turpio open to such coercion. Turpio claimed that it was resolved, that it could not happen again. But one never knew. Ballista tried to shrug all this away. Turpio had more than redeemed himself in action since then, and Ballista liked him. You had to trust your judgement. As for the infantry on the other wing under 'hand-to-steel' – Aurelian might be something of a hothead but, in a paradoxical way, he was also the personification of old-style *disciplina*. Ballista had no real worries there – unlike with the cavalry. It all came back to Acilius Glabrio.

How much damage could the young patrician do?

Ballista would take his position with the Equites Singulares. They should not be directly affected by any foolishness of Acilius Glabrio. The Equites Tertii Catafractarii Palmirenorum rode at the rear of the cavalry column. Ballista was between them and Acilius Glabrio. Their prefect, Albinus, was a sound man, a long-service career officer. They should be all right. Which left Equites Primi Catafractarii Parthi at the head of the column. Again, their prefect, Niger, was a sound man. Ballista had told Niger not to let his men follow Acilius Glabrio if he tried to do anything stupid. But would the men heed the sensible prefect or the glamorous patrician? Allfather, do not let that arrogant young fool lead them off in another mad charge. And what if he did? What would Ballista do then? Watch them become isolated, surrounded, cut down? Or try and rescue them – and run the risk of dragging the whole army down in bloody ruin?

Maximus rode between Ballista and the Roman army, breaking into his worries. 'Time to go.'

The Sassanid scouts were coming on at an easy, loose canter. There were more of them than before, maybe forty or fifty. They were strung out across the plain in no particular order. From time to time, as if on a whim, an individual horseman would turn, now angling towards the river, now the cliffs, then again heading straight for Ballista and his small party.

Some way behind the Persian scouts rose a large, whirling dust cloud. There was no breeze, and it rose straight and tall. Its base was some miles away. It was moving towards them.

'It could be onagers,' said Demetrius hopefully. 'Turpio

told me that when a herd of wild asses is attacked by lions, they come together in a dense pack to frustrate the predators. He said the dust was often mistaken for that raised by troops.' Keen for reassurance, the young Greek talked on. 'Turpio has been out here a long time. He knows what he is talking about, knows about these plains.'

'It could be onagers.' The flat tone of Ballista's reply showed that his mind was elsewhere.

'Time to go,' said Maximus again, more loudly. As if woken from a reverie, Ballista realized that the Sassanid outriders were coming into bowshot. He hurriedly made the signal, and turned Pale Horse. The Romans rode hard and straight for the safety of the army, only jinking around the occasional scrub of camel thorn. Behind them, the easterners swooped across the plain like swallows.

A couple of hours later, mid-morning, about the time when, in Rome, the courts stop sitting, even Demetrius could not cling to the idea that the dust was raised by onagers.

A fold in the plain hid the Sassanid army until it was quite close. The first things that could be seen quite clearly were the big standards: fierce beasts – lions, wolves, bears; and abstract, minimal designs – here a straight line, there a curve, something like the shape of a cup. They flashed bright in the sunshine, all colours: scarlet, yellow, violet. Strange, thought Ballista, how the abstract patterns were more threatening than the animals. A bear is just a bear, but who in the Roman army could tell what powers and horrors the minimal and totally alien designs symbolized?

The Sassanids were drawing closer. As their cavalry

breasted the slight rise, individuals could be easily made out. They were less than a thousand paces away now. Ballista looked carefully. He could just about determine that some wore pointed helmets and others domed caps, while the majority appeared bareheaded. Now they were less than seven hundred paces away, and advancing at a brisk canter. There were a lot of them. They filled the plain. The thunder of their coming preceded them.

'Steady, boys,' Ballista called as he rode along behind his front line. He had reinforced the two hundred Saracen archers led by Viridius with the three hundred and fifty slingers of Sandario, but the line still looked horribly thin. Light infantry will seldom stand a really determined charge by cavalry. It was a risk, but he did not want to weaken the rest of his formation. 'Steady, boys,' Ballista called again, as much to himself as anyone.

At five hundred paces he could pick out details of the Sassanid riders' accoutrements: flashes of colour, glints of metal, the paler smudges of their faces, the occasional white sock on a horse. The northerner felt a tentative sense of relief. He could see the riders' faces, see the legs of the horses. These were not the feared Sassanid *clibanarii*, the terrible, heavily armoured men on heavily armoured horses. Ballista's gamble with having only light infantry in his front line might work. These Sassanids were horse archers. These bowmen should have no intention of trying to charge home against an unbroken enemy.

'Hold the line, boys. They are just horse archers. They will never close with us.'

Ballista rode past Acilius Glabrio, to his left at the head of the central column of the army, the cavalry column.

'They will not charge home. Leave them to our infantry. Hold the line,' the northerner called. He did not notice any response from the patrician.

Ballista moved on, offering a few words of encouragement to the front line as he went. Now and then Demetrius would lean over and mutter in his ear, and then he would call out to junior officers and one or two men by name.

'No fear, *Dominus*. These easterners do not have the balls to face us,' shouted a grizzled slinger.

'True, *comilitio*, and they are only light cavalry – they are nothing close to the steel,' replied Ballista. He did not add, *But the* clibanarii, *the heavy cavalry, they are out there somewhere, hidden by the drifting dust cloud, waiting, long spears in hand and murder in their hearts, and they, fellow-soldier, they are something, something terrible close to the steel.*

Ballista pushed Pale Horse into a canter. The others followed: Maximus, Calgacus, Demetrius, the standard bearer called Bargas, a trumpeter and ten Equites Singulares. The great white *draco* hissed and snapped above their heads. Ballista had wanted to speak to Sandario, on the extreme left of the front line, before the attack came into range. Now it was obvious that was not going to happen.

Ballista was still some way short when he saw Sandario make the signal: the trumpets called, the slings whirred round and he half-glimpsed the slingshots fly towards the enemy. A moment or two later Roman trumpets rang out behind Ballista. He turned in his saddle and watched Viridius' men loose their bows. Archers on foot outrange those on horseback, and slingers outrange both. For a short time, the Romans were in the god-like position of being able to kill without the least danger of being killed. With a clear view over his own infantry, Ballista could see the effect on the Sassanids. Men were knocked from saddles, some horses went down in a maelstrom of thrashing hooves and dust. But far, far too few to stop the charge.

The bright day darkened and a storm of Persian arrows came slicing down. All around, men were roaring with fury, screaming in pain. Ballista felt an arrow tug at his cloak, saw the sparks as another ricocheted off Pale Horse's armour. He made a signal and turned his tiny column back the way it had come. Everyone feels better with their left, shielded side to the enemy. As if in confirmation of the thought, Ballista was knocked sideways in his saddle as an arrow punched into his shield. Pulling on the horns of his saddle, he hauled himself upright. The bright fletchings of the arrow nodded as he moved, its steel tip embedded in the thick linden boards.

Without conscious thought, Ballista had slipped into the altered state of almost complete calm that sometimes came on him in battle. At the centre of the storm, he looked out over the heads of his infantrymen and tried to work out how the fight was going. Men were falling on both sides. Neither side wore heavy armour. The Sassanids had the advantage of numbers, but the dust and movement made it impossible to judge by how much. On horseback the Sassanids were bigger targets, but then again they were moving.

As the northerner watched, the front rank of Sassanids, no more than thirty paces distant, turned to their right, spun round and headed away. As they retreated they aimed their arrows back over the rumps of their horses, employing the famous 'Parthian shot'. The next rank, and the one after that, and all those following repeated the manoeuvre. Arrows still rained down, but in next to no time the whole force was cantering away.

A great wave of confused noise hit Ballista. It came from up ahead, from near the centre of the Roman line. For a few seconds the northerner could not accept the evidence of his eyes. There was the scarlet and gold figure of Acilius Glabrio out in front of the line. The standard bearers and musicians were with him. Behind him, the column of cavalry surged forward. The heavy cavalry of Equites Primi Catafractarii Parthi were riding through, riding over the line of Roman light infantry. Slingers ran desperately out of the way. One or two, too slow, were bowled over, were either sent spinning like tops or, worse, disappeared beneath the plunging hooves. Acilius Glabrio, scarlet *paludamentum* flying, was leading his men out in a hell-for-leather charge after the Sassanid light cavalry.

You fool – they are not running, it is just their way. They will turn in a moment. Ballista was not sure if he shouted out loud or not. He found that he had put Pale Horse into a flat-out gallop towards the point where more and more armoured horsemen were pouring out of the Roman formation. Ballista turned in the saddle. His entourage were still with him: Maximus, Calgacus, Demetrius, the others. Good. He called for the trumpeter to sound recall. Towards the rear of the column some of the troopers began to rein in their horses.

Ballista angled his horse into the charging column of *catafractarii*. His knee crunched painfully into the armoured knee of a trooper. Highly strung for the charge, the trooper rounded on the man who had barged into him then, as he recognized his general, the fight drained out of him. Ballista seized the trooper's reins and pushed their mounts across the four-wide column, bringing those behind them to a skidding halt.

Rising in the saddle, Ballista looked round to take stock. He had managed to prevent about one hundred men of Equites I Parthi leaving the army. But the rest of the unit, some two hundred troopers, were streaming away across the plain.

'Bugger,' said Maximus eloquently. 'Bugger, bugger, bugger.'

Ballista summoned over a decurion. Demetrius quietly provided his name. 'Lappius, I am appointing you in temporary command of those of Equites I Parthi still here with the main body of the army. I want you to get them in order and form them up in close order, knee to knee, in a line two deep, with the right-hand men by the riverbank. Hold that position. On no account move without a direct order from me.' To give him credit, the decurion took this unexpected turn of events in his stride, saluting smartly and barking out orders to make things so.

Staring out across the plain, Ballista watched the rest of Equites I Parthi hurtle towards their fate. They were already some two hundred paces away. The Persians, of course, were giving way before them. But now some of the eastern horse archers were beginning to hang back to lap round their flanks. In a classic manoeuvre, the Persians were drawing the Romans on while flowing around them like water.

Ballista spoke fast but clearly to a messenger. 'Tell Mucapor to bring the Equites Singulares forward. I want them in a line one hundred across and two deep, in open order, a horse's length between each rider, the whole line cantered on me.'

The messenger clattered away. Ballista looked back out over the plain. The majority of the Equites I Parthi still galloped hard after Acilius Glabrio, though now they were strung out like the train of a meteor. Carrying their own heavy armour and their armoured riders, the horses must be nearly blown. Towards the rear, some troopers were slackening their pace. One or two had even stopped and were turning their mounts.

The jingle of equipment, the stamp of hooves, and the muted grunt of orders announced that his bodyguard, the Equites Singulares, were being deployed behind him, as Ballista wished. He did not turn around, he kept his eyes on the plain. The main group of Roman troopers had come to a halt. He could see the standards still flying above them. They were about four hundred paces away. And the Sassanids were closing around them. Across the plain were isolated Roman troopers. Sassanid light cavalry will fight hand to hand if the odds are well in their favour. One after another, the isolated Roman cavalrymen were dragged down, overwhelmed by sheer numbers as the trap closed. In a matter of moments the main body of Acilius Glabrio's men was surrounded. Arrows were flying at them from all directions.

Leave the bastard there. A small voice spoke in Ballista's mind. *The bastard hired someone to kill you. Leave the bastard to die. It is his own fault.*

Mucapor approached, saluted, and waited for orders.

But leave the bastard and you leave the rest of them to die . . .

Ballista returned the salute. 'Mucapor, you will take the right-hand hundred men of the bodyguard, and I will lead the left. We will advance separately, driving the Sassanid horse archers before us until we are on either side and just beyond where, as you can see, the Legate Acilius Glabrio has got his men trapped. Then, while the remnants of Equites I Parthi run back to the army, we will conduct a controlled withdrawal, one line withdrawing through the other so that there are always some troopers facing the enemy.' Ballista paused for questions. There were none. 'The river should help guard your right flank.' As it occurred to him, the general issued orders for Sandario to try to protect the left flank with his slingers.

Ballista indicated where the unit was to be divided. He and Mucapor trotted off in opposite directions to take up their positions in the centre and just in advance of their men. Once in position, Ballista wasted no time making the signal to advance.

They advanced slowly, a walk at first, never rising to more than the gentlest of canters. Ballista gave some of his attention to dressing the line of his men – it was vital they kept together – and some to the Persian horse archers ahead. But much, much more of his mind was directed to piercing the cloud of dust that hung over the plain. Somewhere behind that thick, swirling, red-brown cloud were the Sassanid *clibanarii*, the terrible heavy cavalry that could sweep over the tiny forces of his own cavalry in a matter of moments.

This is madness, thought Ballista. *I am risking the whole army on the off chance of saving a couple of hundred men and a man who probably paid an assassin to kill me.*

As was only natural, the Persian light horse withdrew before these new forces of Roman heavy cavalry. A few feinted towards them, loosed off an arrow or two, but then were gone. As Ballista made the signal to halt, he saw the surviving troopers of Acilius Glabrio's unit streaming towards the army. Some of them were on foot, discarding their weapons and armour as they ran. He could not see if the young patrician was still with them.

Ballista waited a few moments. The Persians were rallying just out of bowshot. He ordered the retreat to begin. The front line of the men with him turned to the right, passed through the line behind them, cantered for about fifty paces, then turned again and pulled up once more, facing the enemy. Then the other line turned and repeated the procedure. So it went, Ballista and his immediate entourage remaining always with the line nearest the enemy.

It seemed no time at all before the horse archers were back, snapping round the heels of Ballista's men, shooting innumerable arrows from but a few yards. Despite their heavy armour, men and horses of the Equites Singulares were being wounded, were falling. A rider crashed into Pale Horse. Ballista turned to curse him, then realized with a lurch that there was no point. The man was dead, held on his mount by the horns of his saddle. Two arrows protruded from his face. As the horse carried him away, the shafts seemed to dance in a grotesque parody of a set of Pan pipes.

Ballista looked back at the Roman army – still some three hundred paces away. They were going to be a very long three hundred paces. Then he looked south towards the Persians. For a moment, the dust cloud parted – and there was the sight that the northerner least wanted to see. Glinting and flashing in the sunlight, coming on like an army of living statues was a solid line of Sassanid heavy cavalry, the *clibanarii*.

The dust cloud covered them again. How far away had they been? Ballista was unsure. He had made out details of their surcoats. They must be within at least five hundred paces, probably much closer. This ordered retreat was not going to work. The *clibanarii* would overrun them before they reached the army and then, with no organized force at the front of the Roman columns, they would overrun the whole army.

Ballista gestured wildly for a messenger to attend him. 'Ride to the Legate Aurelian, who is with the infantry column. Ride as fast as ever you can. Tell him I want him to bring five hundred legionaries around to the front of the army. I want them set out in five blocks of one hundred. Enough space for our cavalry to pass between each block. As soon as my men have passed, he must have them ready for the rear ranks to come round to form an unbroken line. They must be ready to lock shields, ready to repel a cavalry charge. Got that? Good, now go.'

The messenger disappeared to the north, and Ballista's world slowed to an agonizing snail's pace. At his signal, the rank of cavalry nearest to the enemy turned and followed him as he cantered away. The Sassanids surged after them, yelling, howling. Their arrows, loosed at almost point-blank range, hissed at the riders' backs, at the horses' hind quarters. So many arrows, some had to find an unprotected spot or even punch clean through armour. Men and horses were screaming, falling, writhing in the dust. The Romans rode through their second line, and the Sassanids pulled back a little.

Ballista looked at the Roman army. There was no sign

yet of Aurelian's legionaries. He looked at the Sassanids. There was nothing to see except the myriad wheeling horse archers and the plumes of dust – no further sign of the dreaded *clibanarii*.

Again Ballista made the signal, and the line of cavalry nearest to the enemy turned and cantered away. Again the Sassanids swept forwards. Again the arrows flew, and men and beasts felt the sharp stab of pain and fell. There was a nightmarish quality to these awful repetitions, to this painfully slow flight from a terrifying menace you could not see but knew was coming.

An arrow punched into Ballista's shield. Its feathers were dyed scarlet. In fact, he was surprised to see, there were four arrows embedded in his shield. The earlier clarity of his battle-calm had slipped away, leaving him as if in a trance. He pulled himself together and looked at the army. At last. There they were. He could make out Aurelian's legionaries. They were about two hundred paces away, jogging across the front of the army.

Ballista turned to regard the Sassanids. There was nothing to see but horse archers and dust. He made the signal, and the front rank of the Equites Singulares followed him away. And something had changed. Arrows were still falling, but not so many and not released from so close. Ballista swivelled in the saddle. Still nothing in sight but horse archers and dust. Almost casually, he fended off an arrow with his shield. All the eastern riders were galloping away from the Euphrates, away to the east. Already there were none down by the riverbank. Absently, Ballista noted the little galleys out on the river, saw their torsion-powered artillery bolts speeding after the Persians. *I must remember to praise Turpio for his initiative* . . . Ballista waved the trumpeter and Bargas the standard bearer to his side . . . *If I get to see the bugger again.* He looked at the Roman army. It was about a hundred and fifty paces away. Aurelian's men were not yet quite in position. It could not be helped. It had to be now. He gave the order: all-out retreat, every man for himself.

It takes a little while for a heavily caparisoned horse to reach full speed. But fear communicates itself easily from man to mount. Soon, all the Equites Singulares, those under Mucapor as well as those with Ballista, were galloping flat out across the plain, riders leaning forward, horses with nostrils wide, ropes of saliva streaming back from gaping mouths, galloping straight and hard, only when essential jinking round a clump of camel thorn.

Ballista glanced over his shoulder. The horse archers were gone, cantering now off to the north-east to lap round the flank of the main body of the Roman army – and in their place were the *clibanarii*. No more than a hundred paces away, a solid wall of steel, bronze, leather and horn, as far as the eye could see. The earth trembled under their horses' hooves and the air above them was bright with banners, with flowing streamers – yellow, violet, red – and with wicked, glinting spearheads.

Ballista was riding hard, but not pushing Pale Horse near the gelding's limit. He was reasonably secure in his mind. The Sassanid *clibanarii* had to maintain their line. They could not ride at a full gallop like the fleeing Romans. It should be all right.

Pale Horse swerved around some thorn bushes. Beside and behind him Ballista heard a sound like a whimper.

Demetrius was half off his horse, clinging despairingly to its neck. No horseman, the boy must have been dislodged as his mount avoided the sharp camel thorn. As Ballista watched, the Greek youth's grip failed and he was rolling on the hard, dusty ground. Without thought, Ballista reined in, grabbed the bridle of Demetrius' mount and circled back. The boy was on his feet. He was babbling as the northerner led up his horse. The Greek youngster looked over his shoulder, saw the advancing *clibanarii* and leapt at his horse. He misjudged it entirely and slipped back to the ground.

'Plenty of time,' said Ballista reassuringly. He looked across the ever-diminishing no-man's-land. The steel visors and the mail hangings that covered all the face below the eyes made the *clibanarii* appear entirely inhuman.

Demetrius tried again. He got half up and stuck, wriggling. Then he started to slip again. 'Try again,' said Ballista. The *clibanarii* were close now. The northerner was struck by the cold, hard beauty of one steel visor which was sculpted like a human face. It reminded him of the horseman in the alley at Antioch. Here was a whole army of horsemen that wanted to kill him.

In a flurry of hooves and kicked-up dust, Maximus reined in. With typical economy of movement, he swung his right leg over his horse's neck and dropped to the ground like a cat. Gripping him by the scruff of the neck and his belt, he threw the Greek boy up into the saddle. In the twinkling of an eye, Maximus had remounted his own horse as it started to run. A heartbeat later all three were on their way.

They squeezed through the small gap in the line of legionaries and pulled up. Their horses stood, flanks heaving. They heard the big red shields of Legio IIII Scythica slam together. They heard the levelling of the spears of the legionaries. No cavalry on earth would charge into a formed line of close-order infantry. They were safe.

XI

Maximus stepped out of the dark shadow of the tent. The moon was big and bright – but often it is easy to follow a man without him being aware of it. A lot depends on the environment. An army camp is a good place: rows of tents, horse lines, piles of forage; at any hour, men wandering, some of them drunk. More depends on the followed man not thinking about being followed.

They were down near the river by now. The baggage boats, moored three deep, clanked together as the current tugged at them. Up ahead at the palisade, Maximus heard a sentry call the watchword – *disciplina* – then came the response – *gloria*. He waited for a short time, then followed. The call, *disciplina*; the response, *gloria*; and he was outside.

Outside, it was all different. Quiet and empty. The great plain ran away moon-washed and open for two or three miles until it met the twinkling lights of the Persian camp-fires. To Maximus' right was the river, its waters black and oily. Along the riverbank the undergrowth had been cut back for about fifty paces from the palisade. After that was a stand of trees, poplars with reeds fringing the waterline. The bright moonlight made the shadow under the trees very black.

Maximus walked quietly to the trees. He stopped just inside the gloom, letting his eyes adjust. He stilled his breathing. At first it was very quiet, but then he started to hear the normal night noises, the rustles and squeaks that marked the life and death of some small animals. Slowly, watching where he put his feet, watching for signs of the man, he moved deeper into the wood. He had gone no distance when he saw him – down by the water, motionless, sitting with his back to the trunk of a tree. Stepping ever so softly, Maximus began to circle around him, to put himself between the Sassanid camp and the man.

'Stop prancing about and come and sit down,' said Ballista.

Maximus jumped slightly then looked all around once, very carefully, and did as he was asked. He felt more than slightly foolish.

They sat in silence for a time, seeing the river flow past, hearing the whispering of the reeds.

'I have been thinking, sure, what would be sending the renowned *Dux Ripae* wandering alone in the dead of the night?' Maximus kept his eyes on the river. 'Certain, it would be another nocturnal visitation by the late and completely unlamented emperor Gaius Iulius Verus Maximinus Thrax.'

Maximus watched his *dominus* and friend stifle a move to look around, to check that no one was listening. Apart from Ballista, only three people – his wife Julia, his body servant Calgacus, and Maximus himself – knew that from time to time the *Dux Ripae* suffered the terrifying appearance in his sleeping quarters of the long-dead emperor known and hated as Maximinus the Thracian – the emperor who died long ago because a sixteen-year-old Ballista, having taken the *sacramentum*, the military oath to protect him, had instead assassinated him in his tent.'

'No, thank the gods below, I have not seen that big bastard since the night before the fall of Arete.'

They sat quiet again. Maximus was sure his friend was thinking back to that summer day all those years ago before the walls of Aquileia, thinking about the mutineers falling on the dead emperor, desecrating the corpse, denying it burial so that the daemon of Maximinus Thrax was condemned to walk the earth for ever in eternal misery, to walk the earth haunting the man who had killed him. Wordlessly, the Hibernian took a piece of air-dried beef from a pouch on his belt and passed it over. Ballista took it and began to chew.

'It could have gone worse yesterday.' Maximus received no reply, but continued anyway. 'Admittedly, your man Glabrio got about fifty of his own men killed and your Equites Singulares lost nearly as many rescuing the stupid bastard, but it could have been a lot worse. And it is good that Niger's wound is not serious – your young aristocrat might not have been able to even start his foolishness if the very first arrow had not taken the commander of Equites I Parthi in the arm.' He passed over some more dried beef and smiled. 'It was a fine stroke ordering officers to give up their spare horses to remount those troopers who had been dismounted – fine indeed.'

'Mmm,' grunted Ballista.

'And our young patrician has behaved well enough today. All day the reptiles were at it – galloping up like madmen, letting fly a few arrows, and running off again, and never a move from our handsome young nobleman.'

'Do you think he hired the assassin?' Ballista asked.

'Ah, but I doubt it. More likely would be one of the Macrianus boys, or even those Borani, who think so highly of you.' Actually, Maximus thought it quite probably was Acilius Glabrio but, like many in the army, he mistrusted what would happen if things came to a head between the big northerner and the Roman aristocrat.

They sat in silence some more. The smell of mud and decaying reeds was strong down by the water.

At length it was Maximus who spoke again. 'The letters – it must be something in the letters that is preying on your mind.' Early that afternoon, just as the army had begun to erect its marching camp, a small despatch boat had pulled in from Zeugma in the north. There had been no letters for Maximus, there never were – the few who might have wanted to send word to him could not write. With no pang of jealousy, the Hibernian had watched Ballista take charge of two bundles of post, one sealed with an eagle in imperial purple, the other with an Eros winding a piece of artillery.

'No,' replied Ballista. 'I have no objection to carrying out the instructions of Valerian Augustus, Pius, Felix, Pontifex Maximus, and ordering everyone in the army to sacrifice to the *natural* gods.' He held up a hand and cut off Maximus before he could speak. 'Of course,' continued Ballista, 'it is aimed at the Christians. Anyone who will not sacrifice is to be sent off to some unpleasant designated place of internal exile, and if when there they continue to hold assemblies or enter *the places known as cemeteries*, they are to be executed. Now who except the followers of the crucified god call a necropolis a cemetery?'

'That is not what I meant. I was . . .' Again Maximus was cut off.

'I doubt we have many Christians with us here in the army. What little I know about them suggests that military life would not be to their taste. Worshipping the standards every morning and all the other official sacrifices, *to Queen Juno a cow, to the Divine Hadrian an Ox* and all that – I believe a hard-line Christian could not be persuaded to do any of it. And there is the pacifism – their god has told them never to kill.'

'Bollocks, that cannot be true.'

'Well, I listened to one of them in Antioch – he was holding forth in that street known as the Jawbone, they seem to be thick as flies round there – and that seemed to be what he was on about, *Thou shalt not kill.*'

'*Thou shalt not kill*, my arse. That is a recipe for a religion with no future.' Maximus was glad Ballista was talking, even if quite deliberately avoiding what was bothering him.

'Even so, I think I will delay implementing the order until it is over with the Sassanid reptiles, one way or another. You never know, if directly ordered to sacrifice to the *natural* gods, some closet Christian soldiers might suddenly rediscover their principles. Have you noticed how it is with men who are given to bothering the gods – their principles come and go? And what about the arrogance of the bloody Romans? Their gods are just the *natural* ones.'

'It has to be said, they are a lot closer to the sort of gods you and I worshipped when we were young, a bloody sight closer than a criminal on a cross,' said Maximus.

'Well, Woden the Allfather did let himself hang on a tree in agony for nine days.'

'Actually, I was really talking about the other letter. The one from your wife.'

Ballista grinned, his teeth white in the gloom, but said nothing.

'Everything all right at home? The boy is all right?'

'Isangrim is fine.'

'And the *domina*?'

'She is fine too.'

'Gods below, man, you are not thinking there is another man's mule kicking in your stall?'

Ballista laughed quietly. 'A lovely turn of phrase, but no, it is not what I was thinking.'

For a time they sat in silence again, now a more companionable, a somewhat happier silence.

It was Ballista who spoke first this time. 'It is nothing specific. I suppose I just miss them. But then, when I start missing them, wanting to be with them, I start worrying where it is I want to be with them – in the villa in Sicily or back north in the halls of my people.'

'I do not pretend to understand. You have a marble home on a beautiful island under the southern sun, and you want to go back to living in a glorified mud hut in a bleak northern forest.' Maximus shook his head in mock sadness. 'The world is full of girls and women, all shapes and sizes, almost all of them willing, some ever so grateful, and the few reluctant ones just needing to be shown what they are missing, and you stick to just the one.'

From somewhere Maximus produced a flask. He drank and passed it over.

'It is not natural, and it is not good for you. But you will probably have the better time than me.'

Ballista, drinking, made a doubting noise.

'What do I have? Apart from the fighting, just the two things. One makes me feel like dying in the mornings and the other is finished in a quarter of an hour.'

Ballista laughed. 'A quarter of an hour?'

'I have got better.'

Both men laughed. Ballista passed the flask back and said they had better get some sleep. They got to their feet and walked back under the big moon.

Already, as the army snaked out of camp, Ballista could sense the coming heat of the day. Today would decide things one way or another. Ballista's mission was to raise the Sassanid siege of Circesium. Today, barring disaster, Ballista would reach Circesium. If he entered the town, the Sassanids would go away. Yet that was not enough. As soon as Ballista and his army left, the Sassanids would return and place Circesium under siege again. He had to defeat the easterners in battle. But it was difficult for an infantry-based army such as Ballista's to force a cavalry horde into battle. He had to trap them in unfavourable terrain. The only place where that might happen was before the walls of Circesium itself. The town was sited on a promontory at the junction of the Euphrates and a river called the Chaboras. The Euphrates ran north-west to south-east. The Chaboras flowed into it from the north-east. With his rear protected by the Euphrates and his right resting on the outskirts of Circesium, one all-or-nothing charge might catch the Persian cavalry in the narrow triangle of land leading up to the banks of the Chaboras.

Everything depended on timing and *disciplina*. Charge

too soon and all the Sassanids would escape, galloping away to the north-east. If Ballista's men did not all charge as one, most of the Sassanids would escape, streaming away through the gaps between the Roman units. One united all-or-nothing charge before the walls of Circesium.

It was the best that Ballista could come up with, but he knew it was not much of a plan. And for it to have any chance of working, the army had to reach Circesium in one piece. Any break in the line, any premature charge, would be fatal. And the line was painfully thin. After the near-disaster with Acilius Glabrio, he had reinforced both the front and rear of his column with five hundred legionaries of Legio IIII Scythica. It had left only a thousand legionaries of Legio III Felix guarding the left flank. And the line was becoming ever thinner. Casualties had mounted steadily.

It was the fifteenth day of March, the *ides*. How could any country be so hot in the springtime? He looked at the sky. There was no breeze down on the plain but, up there, high up there, clouds moved away to the north. He watched them retreating. Big, heavy clouds, full of rain. They could have made all the difference today: a sudden downpour dampening the bowstrings of the Persians, forcing them to give up their hit-and-run tactics and fight with spear and sword at close quarters, forcing them into his hands. He had prayed to the high god of his people – *Allfather, Grey Beard, Wand-Bearer, Fulfiller of Desire*. Woden-born though he was, the Allfather had ignored him. The rainclouds had swept on to the north. Behind them, the sky was an empty blue. Ballista shrugged. What could one expect of a god who started wars just because the fever was in his blood and he was bored?

A roll of drums brought Ballista's attention back to earth. The Sassanids were confident. Last night, for the first time, they had encamped barely a mile away. This morning, they had been up and about earlier than usual. While the dew still held the sand together, before the choking clouds of dust rose, they had come up from the south, spread out like a triumphal procession. The great line of *clibanarii* had taken station out in the desert to the east, spear tips flashing, standards glinting in the rising sun. Ballista had estimated the line about a thousand riders long and at least two deep: at least two thousand *clibanarii*. As was their way, the light horse archers had swooped and circled across the plain. It made their numbers hard to judge – maybe somewhere between five and ten thousand, maybe more. An army of between seven and twelve thousand riders, maybe more, maybe a lot more. It made little odds. Ballista had to bring them to battle today, had to get them to close quarters in the confined space before Circesium, and then sow panic in their ranks.

So far there was no sign that Pan or any other god had put fear in the hearts of the Sassanids. They looked and sounded confident. The horse archers had swept around the Roman army, enclosing it on every side except the west, where the river ran. Not far out of slingshot, they taunted the Romans, caracoling their horses, calling out insults. Now and then an individual would spur forward yelling a challenge. When no one stepped out to take it up, the Sassanid would make his mount rear, spin it round on its hind legs, and vanish back into the seething mass of horsemen.

The noise of the easterners rose up like a wall around the

Roman marching column – drums, trumpets, cymbals, the yells of men and the neighing of horses. Some lines of Homer drifted into Ballista's mind.

The Trojans came with cries and the din of war like wildfowl
When the hoarse cries of cranes sweep on against the sky.

As Ballista had ordered, the Romans trudged on in silence. It was not that he dismissed the value of noise. Only a fool who had not stood in hot battle would do that. Often you could judge the outcome before a weapon was cast by the volume and quality of the shouting. But his men were outnumbered. There was no point in getting into a contest you could not win. Sometimes an ominous, disciplined silence can also unsettle and demoralize.

. . . Achaea's armies
Came on strong in silence, breathing combat-fury,
Hearts ablaze to defend each other to the death.

Ballista's mouth was dry, gritty. He took the water flask that hung on a horn of his saddle, unstoppered it, rinsed his mouth, spat then drank. He replaced the flask and, without conscious thought, ran through his pre-battle ritual: pull the dagger on his right hip half out of its scabbard and snap it back, do the same with the sword hanging on his left, finally touch the healing stone tied to the scabbard of the sword.

The dust was rising high and straight in the still morning air, hiding the *clibanarii*. But they were there, somewhere beyond the horse archers, waiting for their chance, waiting for the moment of disorder, the gap in the line, the ill-considered charge. The noise of the light cavalry was swelling to a crescendo.

'Steady, boys, here they come.'

A high, ululating cry echoed through the Persian ranks. Allfather, they sounded confident. As one, the horse archers kicked their boots into the flanks of their mounts. They gathered pace quickly, eager to cross the short killing ground where the Roman slings and foot bows outranged them. Ballista heard Roman trumpets sound. Slings whirred, bows twanged. Some Persians went down, but the vast majority raced on at a breakneck gallop. At little more than a hundred paces, they drew and released. Eastern arrows sliced into the Roman column. The sounds of the incoming missiles echoed all around Ballista. Arrows thudded into the hard-packed ground, thumped into wooden shields, clanged off metal armour, and here and there came the awful knife-into-cabbage sound of metal penetrating flesh. Men were screaming. Ballista jerked his head back as an arrow flashed by his face. At about twenty paces, the Sassanids spun round and raced away, still plying their bows over their horses' quarters.

In moments they were gone out of range. They left a few crumpled bodies, their dark blood staining their bright clothes, draining away into the sand. Ballista watched a horse struggle to its feet. One of its front legs broken, it limped after the Persians. He looked around the Roman column. It was responding well. The legionaries were closing ranks. The light infantry ran around gathering spent missiles. Camp followers helped the wounded to the baggage train. The dead were left where they had fallen. If they were lucky, their *contubernales*, their mess-mates, would put a coin in their mouths, close their eyes, sprinkle a little soil on them. It was not what one would hope for, but it was better than nothing.

Out of range again, the Sassanids resumed their jeering and boasting. The first test of the day was passed. But it would be a brief respite. The easterners would come again within half an hour. Ballista idly wondered how many such attacks the column had weathered. It was the *ides* of March, the fifteenth day of the month. Six days counting inclusively, as everyone did, since Acilius Glabrio's nearly ruinous charge. Six days of marching under a hot sun with the spirits of death hovering close at hand. Six days with wave after wave of attacks.

As a heavy surf assaults some roaring coast
Piling breaker on breaker whipped by the West Wind
. . .
And in come more shouldering crests, arching up and
    breaking
Against some rocky spit, exploding salt foam to the skies –
So wave on wave they came . . .

'Here they come again,' called Maximus.

With a thunder of hooves, the Persian light horse surged forward. Their shadows flickered out far in front of them. The sun was still quite low. Allfather, it can only be the second hour of the day, thought Ballista. Again the storm of arrows burst over the Roman column. Again the inhuman noise, as wicked steel and bronze filled the air. Acting on instinct, Ballista caught an arrow on his shield, the impact jarring up his arm. He saw an arrowhead dink off Maximus' helmet. He looked around to check Calgacus and Demetrius were safe. He tried to smile reassuringly at the tense-faced Greek boy. With no warning, Albinus was in front of him.

'You had better come to the front of the column.'

Ballista nodded and waved for his immediate entourage to follow. As they cantered up between the columns of infantry and cavalry, Ballista wondered what could be important enough to make the commander of Equites III Palmirenorum seek him out himself. The pressure was always greater on the rear of the column than the front. So, every day, Ballista rotated the units at the two stations. In both places Albinus had shown himself calm and capable. Ballista had a far from good feeling about this.

When they reached the front of the column, Ballista peered out for a few seconds from behind his shield. He saw nothing unexpected: incoming arrows, Persians, dust. He ducked back then looked again. This time he saw it: Sassanids on foot, plying bows and slings.

'Bugger, infantry.'

Behind him he heard Demetrius ask Maximus why it mattered.

'It means there are a lot more of the bastards than we thought.' The Hibernian's voice was resigned. 'This is not a cavalry raiding force but a full-scale fucking army.'

I have to nip this in the bud, thought Ballista. Don't think, just act. He repeated the mantra to himself a couple of times then, putting his shield aside, braving the missiles his standard attracted, he raised himself in the saddle and called out to the nearest men. 'A few reptiles without horses

– who gives a fuck? Everyone knows they have the hearts of sheep. They do not have the bollocks to fight on foot. And their big, baggy trousers mean they cannot run. All the more for us to kill at Circesium. Remember: every one of them carries all his wealth sewn in his belt – rich cowards who cannot run!'

A thin cheer rippled away down the front line.

The arrow storm faltered and died as they rode back down the column. With Demetrius inconspicuously prompting him, Ballista called out to men by name as they passed. Already dust powdered the legs of the infantry white, like men on a threshing floor.

At the rear of the column they found Acilius Glabrio and Niger under the red standard of the Equites I Parthi. The young patrician had a nasty-looking gash on his cheek. They all saluted each other.

'We will do what is ordered, and at every command we will be ready, next time, you must let me lead the men out, just a short, controlled charge to drive the goat-eyed bastards away,' Acilius Glabrio said in one breath.

'No, we hold the line until Circesium.'

Unexpectedly, Niger joined in. 'The cavalry commander is right. The men will not take much more. The infantry are having to walk backwards, trying to defend themselves as they do. My cavalry are losing horses and men and have no way of striking back. No men can take that for ever.'

'No, I know it is hard, but it is not far to Circesium now. Then we will all charge as one. If we charge too soon, if we do not all charge together, we have no chance of smashing them and we risk disaster.' The northerner looked at their unconvinced faces. 'I know it is torture, but not for long.'

Then, again, using the saddle horns, he raised himself up and called out to the soldiers. 'The reptiles are only brave at a distance. Not far to Circesium now, and then you can kill to your hearts' content.' He paused. There was a less than convincing cheer. 'Remember: they are all as rich as Croesus. They carry all their gold in their belts, hidden in their clothes, maybe stuffed up their arses, for all we know. There will not be a poor man in our camp tonight.' This time the cheer was somewhat louder.

Ballista turned his horse. He looked steadily first at Acilius Glabrio, then Niger. 'Hold the line until my command: six blasts on the trumpet. Hold the line until Circesium.'

By the time Ballista and his entourage reached their station with the Equites Singulares in the centre of the cavalry column, the Persians had struck again. Now the dust hung so thick that you could not see further than a shepherd could throw a stick. The arrows scythed out of the murk before the horsemen could be seen. Again the air was full of horrible, inhuman sounds.

In the middle of the maelstrom Turpio calmly rode up to Ballista. As Turpio saluted, a gold bangle on his wrist flashed. It was his proudest possession. He had taken it in a daring night raid on the Persian camp outside Arete, taken it from the hastily vacated bed of Shapur, the Sassanid King of Kings himself.

Ballista and Turpio leant from their horses to embrace. 'How goes it with the baggage train?'

'Rather quieter than with you,' Turpio replied. 'But rather less well than it was going. There are marshes fringing the Euphrates here. They are getting wider. It is making it harder to ferry the wounded out to the boats. I am running out of porters and animals on shore to carry them and the supplies.'

Ballista looked over and stopped. He had grown so used to the dust and noise all around wherever he looked that it was a shock to be able to see all the way down to the water, across the river and to the sandy bluff opposite. It was, he noticed, a beautiful day, quiet and sunny. From this distance, the boats looked serene, bobbing on the turquoise waters.

'If it comes to it, abandon the supplies. If we win today, we can take all we want, and if we do not . . .' Ballista shrugged.

Turpio nodded. 'I am not going to ask for them, but I could do with some more of your Equites Singulares. The twenty you seconded to me are becoming overwhelmed by the number of malingerers trying to hide among the wounded and get out to the boats – the light infantry mainly, but some legionaries and cavalrymen too.'

'Do your best. As I keep saying, not long now.'

Turpio saluted and rode away. Ballista watched him go down to the riverbank. The dust raised by his horse streamed away to the north. Good, thought Ballista, the wind is getting down to the plain. Hopefully it will be strong enough to blow away some of this shit, and then we will be able to see what the fuck is going on.

The *ides* of March. An ill-omened day for Romans – the day Julius Caesar was assassinated. A day of bad memories for Ballista – a year ago, he had first encountered the Sassanids: they had ambushed him, chased him, and a big blond Batavian with the ridiculously Roman name of Romulus had paid with his life for the escape of Ballista and the others. Not a good day for a battle. But there was no choice.

Another wave of arrows swept through the Roman ranks. Ballista had not even noticed the previous attack end. At least now the wind was getting up you could see the bastards shooting at you. A slingshot clunked off the armour on Pale Horse's shoulder. Ballista pulled him out of line and circled him. He did not seem to be lame. The slingshot meant there were Sassanid infantry all around the army now. Was this the third or fourth attack of the morning? Ballista was not sure. His mind wandered. The *ides* of March. Julius Caesar was killed, stabbed to death in the senate house by fellow senators, by men he had pardoned, men whose careers he had advanced, men he had thought of as friends. But they could not be his friends, precisely because they and he were senators and he had advanced or even pardoned them. The *dignitas* of a Roman senator did not allow another senator to advance, let alone pardon him. Caesar himself had said his *dignitas* meant more to him than life itself. Times may have changed under the autocratic rule of the emperors, but *dignitas* still lay at the heart of a senator's being. *Dignitas* could still be a reason to kill. And whose wounded *dignitas* drove them to try and have me killed, Ballista thought sourly. That of Acilius Glabrio, a dead brother to avenge, the stain of obeying the man who abandoned him to wipe out? Or that of the sons of Macrianus the Lame? Quietus, who he had punched in the balls? Or Macrianus the Younger, who had been shown up in failing to help his brother? Macrianus himself? The *Comes Sacrarum Largitionum et Praefectus Annonae* was not often called a cunt to his face in the courtyard of the emperor's palace. Maybe more to the point, he was not a man who liked to be crossed when he had decided who should have a command on the Euphrates against the Persians. Perhaps it was nothing to do with the Romans at all. Perhaps it was something altogether simpler, something Ballista understood better: perhaps it was a straightforward northern bloodfeud between him and the Borani?

For some time, Ballista's eyes had been resting on the black smudge in the sky to the south beyond the head of the column. Now, with a hollow feeling inside, he began to realize what it might be. Without signalling to his entourage, he kicked his heels into his mount's flanks and set off towards the front of the army. He was only slightly aware of the sound of hooves behind him. His attention was focused on the blackness in the sky.

Infantry to the left, cavalry to the right, soldiers of his army flashed past. Some called out. He did not answer. Their voices vanished behind him. Missiles shot from left to right across the front of his face. He galloped on, almost oblivious, his thoughts concentrated on the black marks against the brilliant blue of the sky.

Arriving at the front of the column, Ballista skidded Pale Horse to a halt. He gazed out over the heads of the infantry. He vaguely noticed his followers pulling up in a clump behind him, Albinus trotting up next to him. The wind was getting up. It was shredding the curtain of dust – blowing it straight at the Romans. Ballista wiped his streaming eyes. He could see the Sassanids, horse and foot, about fifty paces away, shouting, edging closer. Squinting, he could see beyond them the road, running straight and dark through the desert. And, about two hundred paces away, he could see the first tombs of the necropolis on either side of the road and, spreading wide on either side of them, suburban gardens and orchards. And there, no more than four hundred paces off, were the walls: tall, crenellated, mud-brick, the same colour as the desert. Beyond the walls was the city of Circesium, but he could not see it. The billowing black smoke was getting in the way. The city was burning.

The city had fallen. Circesium, just like Arete, had fallen to the Sassanids. Ballista had failed again. They will have a field day in the *consilium*, was Ballista's first thought. Led by Acilius Glabrio, they would close in for the kill: negligence and sloth – how long wasted in unnecessary training upriver? – if not something worse – what do the reports of the *frumentarii* say?

'Fuck, oh fuck,' said Maximus.

The flow of lively obscenity put an end to Ballista's unhappy imaginings. What was the point of worrying about what people might say some time in the future when he had to find a way to stop them all dying here and now?

Ballista looked south. Not much more than a hundred and fifty paces to the first of the tombs, gardens and orchards. As soon as the head of the column reached there, he would order the charge – the walls, ditches, close-packed trees, and huts of the market gardens would shield the right wing of the army. Any sooner would mean throwing away the chance to trap the enemy, might even bring catastrophe. Just a few more moments of torment. Not long now.

A huge, swelling roar rolled up the line of the Roman march. Ballista could make out hundreds, thousands, of voices chanting, '*Ready, Ready, Ready.*' He could not hear who was shouting out the formulaic question – 'Are you ready for war?' – but he could guess. His heart sank. There was a great, rattling thunder as the soldiers beat their weapons on their shields.

Calling Maximus over and leaning on his shoulder, Ballista precariously stood on his saddle. He looked back to the north and saw what he expected to see. With the red *signum* fluttering above them, the two hundred or so remaining troopers of the Equites Primi Catafractarii Parthi were charging out to the east against the enemy. They were riding knee to knee in a tight-packed wedge. At their head was an elegant figure in scarlet and gold. *Too soon, you fool*, Ballista cursed, *too soon. Most of the reptiles will escape*. He watched for a few moments. The Sassanids turned to flee. Some were too slow. In their confidence, they had come too close. The first Sassanids, both horse and foot, were bowled over by the heavily mailed Roman cavalry, disappearing beneath the pounding hooves.

Ballista clambered down into the saddle. Thanks to Gaius Acilius Glabrio, the Romans were charging too soon, not all charging as one. Somehow Ballista had to try to retrieve the position. He rapped out a string of orders: Infantry, open ranks! Cavalry, prepare to charge! Light infantry to follow! Legionaries will then close ranks and remain halted! Aurelian commands until my return! Ballista signalled to the trumpeter. Six blasts rang out. The men roared. It was the moment for which everyone had been waiting, six long days of waiting. The die was cast.

'Albinus, I will ride with you.' Ballista then raised his voice. 'Equites Tertii Catafractarii Palmirenorum, good hunting.' The two hundred and fifty or so troopers made their way carefully between the ranks of infantry and re-formed beyond them. Ballista trotted a few paces forward to form the apex of the wedge, Maximus on his right, Albinus on his left, Calgacus just behind, his white *draco* and the unit's green *signum* following, hopefully Demetrius tucked in somewhere ostensibly safe towards the back.

Another roar drew Ballista's attention to the left. Mucapor at their head, the main body of the Equites Singulares was charging. It was a small, armoured wedge, not many more than a hundred horsemen, but the Sassanids were running from them. All along the line, the easterners were running. Damn, thought Ballista, it is all too soon, all fragmented, most of the bastards will escape.

Ballista put Pale Horse into a trot, rising gently to a canter. There were one hundred paces of bare desert to the backs of the nearest Sassanids. *Time to take charge*, thought Ballista, it is all or nothing now. He pushed on into a flat-out gallop. The distance between the horsemen and the running Persian foot soldiers closed quickly. Ballista unsheathed his long cavalry sword. He fixed his eyes on the point between the green-clad shoulder-blades of a running easterner. He held the sword out straight. At the last second, a glimpse of terrified, dark eyes, and the man hurled himself to the ground. The charge ran over him.

They were through the infantry. Ahead were the backs of the cavalry. Ballista angled the charge towards the right. The horsemen there were moving more slowly, were milling about. Ballista could feel himself starting to grin like an idiot. His plan might yet work. Despite Acilius Glabrio, it might yet work. The Persian cavalry in front of him realized the Romans were coming. The easterners began to push, to jostle each other. They came to blows. They were at a standstill, literally fighting to get to the lip of the bank, to have a chance to scramble down the steep banks of the Chaboras.

A *clibanarius* at the back of the mob sawed on the reins to bring his horse round to face Ballista. The horse's nostrils were wide, its mouth bloody. The man's surcoat was a delicate violet, covered in abstract swirls. His face was hidden behind a mail hanging. Even the eyes, in deep shade, could not be seen. The man must have thrown away his lance. He was tugging his sword out. Ballista aimed a vicious back-handed cut over Pale Horse's ears. Steel rang and sparks flew as the *clibanarius* parried the blow with his own blade. As his gelding drew level, Ballista reached out and with his left hand grabbed the mail aventail covering the Persian's face. It slipped up, blinding the warrior. The momentum of Pale Horse dragged the Persian half out of his saddle. Ballista smashed the pommel of his sword down into the hidden face of his opponent. There was a sickening sound like the carcass of a chicken breaking. Ballista pushed the man over the far side of his horse to the ground.

Another Persian came at Ballista from his left, heavy sword swinging down in a mighty overhand chop. The northerner took the blow on his shield. Splinters flew, and he heard the linden boards crack. Blindly, he thrust out under the damaged shield. The point of his sword slid off the Sassanid's armour. The press of horses and men crushed Ballista and his opponent together, too close to effectively use their swords. The Persian's left hand shot up, his mail-clad fingers clawing at Ballista's face, searching for his eyes. Swaying back, hot blood on his cheek, Ballista dropped his sword, feeling its weight tug at the wrist strap. He grabbed a streamer floating from the easterner's helmet. He yanked hard. The man began to topple backwards. Then the streamer tore. The Sassanid grinned savagely as he regained his balance. Their horses moved a little apart. Ballista punched the metal boss of his broken shield into the man's face. The man grunted with pain. He swayed in the saddle. Flicking the hilt of his sword back into his grasp, Ballista swung with his right fist. The Sassanid jerked his head aside. Ballista felt a scrunch of bones as at least one of his knuckles shattered on the steel of the man's helmet. A stab of white-hot agony shot up his arm. Bellowing with pain, Ballista smashed the edge of his shield across the easterner's face. The jagged wood sliced through flesh. Screaming, the man doubled up, his hands flying to his lacerated face. Bright blood matted his black beard. Ballista chopped the blade of his sword down into the back of the man's neck, one, two, three times. Ignoring the sharp bursts of pain from his broken hand, he finished the job.

The Sassanids were no cowards, but they had been caught unprepared, trapped between the impetus of the Romans and the steep slope down to the river. Panic spreads through an army like fire across a Mediterranean hillside in high summer. Soon the only Persians left on the stricken field were dead or helpless and soon to die. Ballista kept the Equites Tertii Catafractarii Palmirenorum close in hand. He did not let any of them descend the banks of the Chaboras, although after a time he let some dismount to throw rocks down into the tangled mass of horses and riders struggling in the stream. Any recruits in the ranks now knew that a river running red with blood was not just a literary conceit.

Here in the south where the Chaboras had impeded their flight, the slaughter of the Sassanids had been prodigious. Some easterners had also died in the north, those who had been too close to avoid the charge of Acilius Glabrio and Equites Primi Catafractarii Parthi. In the centre, all the Persian horsemen had got away into the desert to the east. Mucapor and the Equites Singulares had merely run down some poor infantrymen. Yet Ballista's plan had worked. Although Acilius Glabrio's premature charge had let the majority of the Sassanid army escape, it mattered little. The easterners were scattered, their morale was broken.

As Ballista slid from the saddle to relieve the weight on Pale Horse's back, a wave of depression broke over him. What did it signify? He had beaten this army. The Sassanids would send another. And another after that. This was a religious war. The easterners would not stop until they had lit the Bahram fires, the sacred fires of Mazda, throughout the whole world. A black thought struck Ballista – even if he defeated Shapur himself, even if he killed or captured the King of Kings, the eternal war between east and west would continue.

XII

The aftermath of any battle is hellish, and the battle of Circesium was no exception. Under a high sun, the flat, bright desert stretched away. The ground was covered with the detritus of warfare: discarded, broken weapons, dead horses, the half-naked, humped corpses of men, sweet-smelling piles of horse droppings, the foul stench of human guts.

'*Ave*, I give you joy of your victory.' Acilius Glabrio had taken off his helmet. His usually purposefully teased curls lay flat to his skull. Sweat was running down into his beard. He was beaming, very full of himself. Ballista noticed the cut on the young patrician's cheek was still open. '*Celeritas* and cold steel. Nothing a goat-eyed easterner can do about it.'

Ballista stepped very close to him. 'You insubordinate little prick. I ought to kill you now,' he hissed.

The smile stayed on Acilius Glabrio's face, but his eyes went cold. 'Be grateful, you jumped-up barbarian shit. I have just given us a great victory.'

'You have just given us half a victory, and thrown away the better part,' snapped Ballista. His right hand was swelling. It throbbed like hell. His temper was on a knife edge.

'You gutless barbarian bastard.' Acilius Glabrio's face was full of scorn. 'I have chased away the Sassanids you were so scared of, and now you can retake Circesium unopposed. A great victory. Enjoy it while you can. I have not forgotten what you did to my brother.'

Ballista struggled to control his fury. 'And what will you do about it? Hire another assassin?'

Acilius Glabrio's snort of laughter was genuine. 'You judge others by yourself. I would be as low as you if I stooped to such things.'

The cavalry prefects Niger and Albinus walked up. They said it was time to acknowledge the acclamations of the troops. Ballista, eyes still locked with those of Acilius Glabrio, stepped back. The terrible thing was, he believed him: the odious young patrician had not hired the assassin.

Bone-tired, Ballista hauled himself back into the saddle. Pale Horse's flanks were lathered in sweat, his head down. With his officers, Ballista slowly rode back towards the army's starting position. Everywhere was the frenzied looting of the dead. Many of the scavengers were civilians. There were far too many to have all come from the baggage train. Ballista had seen it on so many stricken fields that he did not wonder at it. No matter how remote a battlefield from human habitation, as soon as the fighting was over, the scavengers appeared. The skinny, furtive men and the hideous old crones, sharp knives in their hands and, always among them, always upsetting the northerner, the young children, far too young for that disgusting work.

Yet on the plain before Circesium, most of those despoiling the dead were soldiers. The Roman moralists were wrong. *Disciplina* was not a durable, inherent quality. On the contrary, it was terribly fragile. A victory could shatter it as easily as a crushing defeat. When the *milites* saw the cavalcade coming they stopped their searching. They drew their swords and, hunched over, chopped down, as many blows as it took. Then, as the horsemen drew near, they stood. They thrust out their right arms in a sort of salute, in their fists the severed Persian heads. One man had a head in each hand and the long black hair of a third gripped in his teeth. The gore ran up his arms, down the front of his mail shirt. As a Roman general should, Ballista inspected the grisly trophies, commended those holding them with a kind word or an affectionate look.

In the liberty of the moment, the soldiers called out whatever they pleased: praise, jokes, boasts. Small knots of men chanted the names of the officers. Ballista noted that more chanted for Acilius Glabrio than for himself. The northerner bitterly reflected how all his hard work, all his planning, counted for next to nothing in their eyes. One foolish, insubordinate charge – a charge which brought a half success and squandered total victory – had won the odious little patrician the hearts of the men.

'*Gaius Acilius Glabrio! Gaius Acilius Glabrio!*'

The chanted name rang through Ballista's angry thoughts. Acilius Glabrio was an arrogant, stupid, self-satisfied fool – but not a murderer. Ballista had been so convinced that he had hired the assassins. But there had been an honesty in the young nobleman's contemptuous retort – 'I would be as low as you, if I stooped to such things.' It had changed the northerner's mind.

'*Gaius Acilius Glabrio! Gaius Acilius Glabrio!*'

Ballista's thoughts scrabbled round like rats in a trap.

Not Acilius Glabrio . . . then who? Ballista had never really thought it was the Borani prince, Videric. This conclusion was not from any misty-eyed sentiment that northerners such as himself would not resort to such underhand methods. They did. Often. Bloodfeuds in Germania involved murder. It was more that various things did not seem right: the assassin in the clearing shouting, 'The young *eupatrid* sends you this,' the pantomime masks and cavalry parade helmet in the alley, the man himself in the silver mask calling Ballista a barbarian. But if it hadn't been Videric or Acilius Glabrio who had hired the assassin, it must be the sons of the sinister Count of the Largess, Macrianus the Lame. But which one? Quietus, who Ballista had punched in the balls? Macrianus the Younger, who had been shown to lack the courage to help his brother? Or was it both of them? And what of their powerful, devious father? Was Macrianus the Lame a part of it? If he was, Allfather help me, thought Ballista. Apart from the emperor, there could be no more dangerous enemy in the whole *imperium*.

Voices were raised in anger. A fight had broken out among some of the looters. Ballista ran his right hand over his face. He felt a stab of pain. At least one knuckle was broken and the hand was swelling fast. I must get a grip on things, he thought. He had to take charge before this army descended into chaos, laid itself open to a Sassanid counterattack.

Ballista called his officers to him. He rapped out orders. Niger and Albinus were to send out patrols. They were to report immediately if any still-formed bodies of Persian troops were to be found within five miles. Mucapor was to recall the Equites Singulares to the standard and have them fall in behind Ballista. Legio III, under its prefect, Rutillius Rufus, was to secure the town. Sandario was to use his slingers and any other light infantry he needed to bring the fires there under control. Turpio was to get the baggage train in order and, as soon as possible, quarter it safely within the walls. Acilius Glabrio was to disperse the looters, sending the troops among them back to their units on pain of death. Legio IIII was to remain formed on the road as a reserve under Castricius. Aurelian was to attend the *Dux Ripae*.

Some horsemen clattered away purposefully. Others remained, looking concerned. There was something unspoken in the air. Aurelian? Where was Aurelian?

Macapor edged his horse forward. 'He is hurt.'

'Badly?'

Mucapor shrugged.

'Everyone, carry out your orders. Mucapor, we will go to him.' Even in the extremity of his fear – this was no trick, no false alarm – Ballista did not push Pale Horse too hard. He forced himself to keep the gelding to the gentlest of canters, forced down the hollow feeling of panic.

There was a knot of men under the standards of Legio IIII. It parted as Ballista approached. Aurelian was lying on his back. His right leg was at an odd angle. An army doctor was on his knees, preparing to set the broken limb.

Ballista jumped down from the saddle. Aurelian's face was grey, and he was sweating. Through gritted teeth, he whispered, 'I give you joy of your victory.'

Ballista looked into his friend's eyes. 'Thank you.' Unable to say more, Ballista leant down and very gently squeezed

Aurelian's shoulder. Then he straightened up, turned away, and got on with what needed to be done.

The army had stayed at Circesium for thirteen days. It had been a busy time for Ballista. He had pushed cavalry patrols out further and further in all directions. There had been no sign of any Persians – or none that were still living. The premature charge of Acilius Glabrio had robbed him of the chance to destroy the Persian army, but it seemed the east-erners had withdrawn, at least for the time being.

There had been many, many burials to attend to. Aelius Spartianus, the tribune commanding the Roman forces in Circesium, who had fallen with almost all his men when the Sassanids took the town, was interred in a splendid sarcophagus in a fine tomb by the main road into town – admittedly, both sarcophagus and tomb were reused, but the local stonemason made a good job of the new inscrip-tions. The other Roman dead among the soldiers were buried in communal graves, but they were accorded all due respect: their eyes closed, a coin in each mouth, a newly sculpted monument on top of each grave.

Things had been different with the Sassanids. Their often mutilated remains were burned and the ashes thrown anyhow into pits. But this was not just casual contempt for the enemy. The Romans knew that the Sassanids were Zoroastrian fire-worshippers who exposed their dead to the birds of the air and the beasts of the field. They knew well that the Zoroastrians held that the mere touch of a corpse polluted the very sacredness of fire. A small voice at the back of Ballista's mind had whispered that this could only exacerbate the conflict between east and west, that it might even rebound personally on its perpetrator. The Sassanids would see it as an atrocity, a deliberate insult to their religion. They would, of course, be right. Yet there was little that Ballista had felt he could do. His men had suffered day after day at the hands of the easterners. They had wanted revenge even on the dead bodies of their tormentors.

Ballista had tried to set the defence of the town on a sounder footing. Across the Chaboras a tower was built to give early warning of any Sassanid forces advancing up the Euphrates. The walls and gates of Circesium itself had needed little work, as the town had fallen to a surprise attack rather than regular siege works. Ballista had arranged for supplies and materials of war to be transported by boat downriver from Zeugma. Two thousand inhabitants of Circesium had been conscripted to form a local militia. Legio III Felix and the Mesopotamian archers were to be left as a regular garrison. They would be supported by three of the small war galleys.

The whole was to be commanded by Rutillius Rufus, the prefect of Legio III. The gods knew it was a small force, but Rufus seemed solid enough. While having done nothing outstanding, he had performed creditably on the march and in the battle. Ballista had started to give him a lengthy lecture on the tactics and stratagems to be adopted in defending a town against the Sassanids. The northerner had stopped abruptly when he thought he detected a badly suppressed smile on the prefect's face. Ever since he had entered the *imperium* as a sixteen-year-old from *barbaricum*, Ballista had had a strong dread of being mocked. He knew he was still oversensitive about it. But there again, it had to be admitted that Arete, the only town Ballista had defended from the Sassanids, had fallen in a bloody sack. And now it seemed Acilius Glabrio had stolen much of the credit for the victory at Circesium.

The march back had initially retraced their steps, north to Basileia and Leontopolis, across the Euphrates by the wide stone bridge at Soura, and on to Barbalissus. It had been hot and tiring but, with no enemy in sight, it had been a stroll in a Persian *paradise* by comparison with the march south. At Barbalissus, Castricius had taken his leave, marching his *vexillatio* on up the Euphrates to the base of Legio IIII at Zeugma. Ballista had led the remainder of the army west, skirting the southern shores of the great lake of Garboula to the city of Chalcis ad Belum and on to the main road to Antioch.

As they approached the capital of the Roman east, they had passed through the small village of Meroe. It was strange how some unimportant places stuck in one's mind. Ballista could always picture the dingy, dust-covered, mud-brick houses which flanked the road, the cracked public fountain, the thin, straggly trees which passed for a sacred grove. He had been through the village four times, on his way to and from first Arete and then Circesium. Nothing of note had happened on any of these occasions. Yet he could summon it up exactly, down to the smell of the water evaporating in the sun as it leaked from the fountain.

For five days, the returning army had been camped outside the Beroea Gate. Finally, the emperor Valerian had given his gracious permission for them to enter. Ballista looked up and down the procession. Everything was nearly ready.

Turpio rode up and saluted, the gold bracelet he had taken from the Persian king's tent sparkling in the sun. All was ready. Ballista cast a last look down the line. The army made a brave show, standards flying, infantry in serried ranks, cavalry and officers on prancing horses. Acilius Glabrio looked particularly splendid on a glossy black charger. Aurelian, on account of his broken leg, was having to ride in a carriage. Ballista adjusted his helmet and made the signal to move off.

The crowds were waiting through the Beroea Gate. They lined the colonnades of the Street of Tiberius and Herod. They threw flowers and called out compliments. A few girls, surely prostitutes, lifted their skirts or pulled down their tunics, offering the troops tantalizing glimpses of flesh.

'Keep the line straight, boys,' exhorted Ballista. 'Plenty of time later.'

They turned off into the street that ran down to the second bridge over the Orontes. They made their way across the island, the *circus* and the imperial palace to their right, past the *Tetrapylon*, the four columns supporting statues of elephants where imperial orders were posted, through the district known as the Bull, and out over the far bridge to the suburbs. There were no crowds on the western bank of the river. Instead, at no great intervals, the heads of malefactors and those who had earned imperial disfavour rotted on their pikes. They reached the *campus martius* and drew up in front of the imperial tribunal.

Ballista played with Pale Horse's ears as they waited. Imperial ceremonies tended to involve waiting. Junior officers scurried about checking the men were standing properly squared off, their kit just so. The sand of the *campus martius* had been watered that morning. No one wanted the polished arms and armour coated in dust. The usual wind from the south-east that blew up the Orontes valley was getting up. Already it tugged fitfully at the purple hangings of the imperial tribunal. Ballista smiled to himself. Outside verse Panegyrics, the gods and not the emperors controlled the winds.

After a decently short amount of time, the imperial party arrived. Slowly, the aged emperor Valerian stepped down from his carriage. After him, equally slowly, emerged the *Comes Sacrarum Largitionum*. There were few higher honours in the *imperium* than the invitation to ride in the emperor's carriage. Macrianus the Lame looked as if he felt he belonged there.

Laboriously, the two old men climbed the steps. The other great officers of state followed them. When they were all in the position their rank dictated, Valerian alone moved to the front of the tribunal. He saluted the army. The army saluted back. The prearranged chants rang out: 'Hail, Valerian Augustus, may the gods preserve you!' – twenty times; 'Valerian Augustus, deliver us from the Persians!' – thirty times; 'Valerian Augustus, long may you live!' – forty times.

In the quiet that followed, the snap of the purple hangings in the wind echoed across the parade ground. Valerian filled his lungs, put his head back and began to speak.

'*Ave*, hail the victors of the battle of Circesium. *Ave*, hail the conquerors of the eastern barbarians!'

He had got no further when an exceptionally strong gust of wind tore one of the purple hangings from the front of the dais. It eddied for a moment. An imperial servant ran after it. A second gust sent it skidding along the ground, to come to rest where the injured Aurelian stood, leaning on a walking stick. The Danubian picked it up and handed it to the slave.

There was a slight stir at the back of the dais, but most of the men standing there had not risen high in the imperial service by exhibiting obvious interest in things that might be interpreted as dangerous omens. The emperor himself had paused, but he did not deign to look directly at the incident. Now the servant had retrieved the bit of cloth, Valerian continued.

'From the very earliest times, the west has been relentlessly attacked by the cruelty, avarice and lust of the east. First, duplicitous Phoenicians who sailed to Greece under the pretence of trade abducted Io, daughter of King Inachus of Argos. Since then, Mardonius, Xerxes, and now Shapur, in their pride have led innumerable Asiatic hordes against us.

'There have been times when oriental cunning and treachery have brought defeat to the west. The aged Roman general Crassus betrayed and beheaded at Carrhae. The agonies of hunger and fear suffered by Mark Antony and his men on the retreat from Phraata in Media. A few years ago, in the time of troubles, the defeat at Barbalissos, the sack of so many cities, including mighty Antioch herself. Last autumn, the fall of Arete.

'But there have been many, many victories won by open western courage and *disciplina*. From the Athenians of old burning Sardis to the Roman emperors Trajan and Septimius Severus sacking Ctesiphon, the capital of the oriental despot.

'And there will be more western victories. Make no

mistake, war is coming, all-out war. The insolence of Shapur, the so-called King of Kings, must be crushed once and for all. It will not be this year or next, there are many preparations to make, many things at home to set in order but, soon, your emperor at your head, we will march east and finish the Persian menace for ever.'

Valerian paused to allow for the required cheering. After a time he waved a hand to quieten the army. 'You, the victors of Circesium, must have your rewards.' The aged emperor had their attention now.

'After your labours, you deserve rest, a time of pleasure. Every man in the victorious army will receive five days' leave. Your valour deserves recognition. When you return to the standards you will each be issued with a new red military tunic.'

When the soldiers were sure the emperor had stopped, they cheered again, rather less enthusiastically.

'The officers – just as their duties are greater, so should be their honours. Each officer in command of a unit will be presented with a silver-ornamented swordbelt.' There was a most perfunctory cheer.

'Your commander, the *Dux Ripae*, Marcus Clodius Ballista, must be praised for the rigours of the army's train-ing, the dedication with which he kept order on the march down the Euphrates. To him will be presented a golden armlet weighing seven ounces, a gilded silver clasp, and four handkerchiefs from Sarepta.

'In every battle there is a time when all hangs in the balance. Our sacred majesty is well informed that, at Circe-sium, the moment was seized by one of the noblest of young Romans. With no thought for his own safety, on his own initiative the Legate Gaius Acilius Glabrio led a daring charge against overwhelming odds which shattered the Sassanid army. To our most dear Gaius Acilius Glabrio we will present a golden collar weighing one pound, a golden clasp with a Cyprian pin, and a white part-silk tunic ornamented with purple from Girba.'

As the old emperor, accompanied by Macrianus the Lame, made his way to his carriage, the army repeatedly chanted, 'Valerian Augustus, long may you live!'

The men in the ranks were chanting loud enough, but Ballista knew they were not happy. They had five days' leave, but no donative, no gift of money, in their hands to spend on drink and women. As for being given a military cloak, the *Comes Sacrorum Largitionum* was responsible for supplying clothes to the army. Several thousand new cloaks must be some scheme of Macrianus the Lame to further enrich himself. The majority of the officers also were unlikely to be thrilled. An ornamental sword belt seemed a tawdry reward.

At least one man in the army would be delighted, Ballista thought sourly. Despite disobeying orders, despite putting the entire army at risk and throwing away the chance to wipe out the Sassanid army, Gaius Acilius Glabrio, with his patrician glamour and excellent contacts at court, had somehow emerged as the hero of the battle of Circesium. Publicly honoured and flattered, there could be no doubt he stood high in imperial favour.

Equally, there was no doubt where Valerian's speech left Ballista himself. The inclusion of Arete in the list of western defeats, the faint praise for his training and ordering of the army, the lack of kind words and, above all, the demonstrable inferiority of his gifts compared with those of Acilius Glabrio, showed clearly that he had lost imperial favour. The gods alone knew how long it would be before he might get a chance to win it back – if ever.

'Valerian Augustus, long may you live!' As the imperial carriage left the *campus martius*, the chanting died away.

Vicarius Proconsularis

(Summer AD258 – Spring AD259)

'For it is written, "I shall destroy the wisdom of the wise, and bring to nothing the learning of the learned." Where is the wise man now? Where is the scribe? Where is the investigator of the present age?'

– Paul of Tarsus, I *Corinthians* 1. 19–21

XIII

The imperial summons came early on a July morning one thousand and ten years *ab urbe condita*, since the founding of Rome. It was over a year since Valerian had addressed the returning army of the *Dux Ripae*, over a year since Ballista had lost the favour of the emperor. In all that time, apart from being told to remain in Antioch, he had received no further orders, no command to attend the imperial *consilium*. He had been ignored.

At first Ballista had been happy enough in his unlooked-for freedom, away from the court and the poisonous intrigues that surrounded the vice-regent of the gods. He had money. Technically, he was still the *Dux Ripae*. His *stipendium* was still paid. He had peace. The sons of Macrianus the Lame made no new attempts on his life – the northerner was convinced they had been behind the assassin with the scar on his hand. Ballista had time to do all the things that made him happy. He had played with his son, made love with his wife, eaten a great deal of seafood, passed whole days reading.

True, the social life of a man cast out from the imperial circle was somewhat reduced. Not all want to be seen to be too close to such a man. Ballista had spent more than a usual amount of time in waterfront bars with Maximus. Yet Aurelian and the Danubian circle had not deserted him. He had gone drinking and, once Aurelian's injury had healed, hunting with them. They went searching for lion and tiger in the mountains. Sometimes they even took Julia and Isangrim with them. They found only fallow deer. However, there were always ostrich and humped ox out on the plains towards the lake.

But a year is a long time. Although he would hardly admit it to himself, Ballista had found that a life of unremitting *otium*, leisured peace, can begin to drag. There are only so many times you can eat your favourite fish dinner. Of course, he told himself, things would have been very different if he had been at home, either in Tauromenium in Sicily, or his birthplace in the far north.

The imperial summons, when it came, was a complete surprise. The emperor wished Marcus Clodius Ballista to attend him. He should bring his letter of appointment as *Dux Ripae*.

As Ballista walked into the great courtyard of the imperial palace, the water clock struck. Four golden spheres rested at the bottom of the stake, held by the gilded statue on top of the inner gate. At least he would not be late.

Something in the conviction of his stride conveyed itself to the throngs of petitioners, who moved out of the way. Near the inner gate, he had to check his pace as a party of northern barbarians were slow to step aside. For a few seconds, he suspected they might be Borani, but a sharp look revealed the striped clothes and elaborate hairstyles of northern Germania. It was just the habitual truculence of a group of Franks.

At the foot of the steps, the sight of the imperial codicil in his hand parted the ranks of the *silentarii*. The praetorians saluted and opened the doors. A eunuch appeared to lead him down the long peristyle. Their footfalls echoed. Statues of long-dead, deified emperors – Augustus, Claudius and Trajan among them – gazed down impassively as the heavy doors shut behind them.

Through the next doors, the warm, scented near-darkness of the imperial vestibule surrounded them. With the utmost politeness, the eunuch asked Ballista to wait and then disappeared into the gloom.

Ballista looked around. There were four other men waiting: three senators and another equestrian like himself. Ballista found an upright chair and sat down. He carefully arranged the formal folds of his toga and placed the imperial codicil on his lap. He nodded to the other men. They nodded back. One of the senators coughed. No one spoke.

Left alone, Ballista studied the ivory document case in his lap: the gold corners, the gold roundel in the middle with the portraits of the emperors Valerian and Gallienus. It was tangible proof of his office as *Dux Ripae*, the office which, now, certainly, would be taken away. Would it be replaced with anything?

A movement in the thick air rather than any sound indicated that someone was coming through the hangings from the audience chamber. All five seated men tried not to jump, tried not to stare. The long face of Cledonius, the *ab Admissionibus*, appeared through the curtains. He remained still for what seemed to the waiting men an improbably long time but was really only just long enough for his eyes to adjust to the gloom. He walked over to one of the senators and spoke softly. The senator almost leapt to his feet and, gathering his toga around himself, hurried after the *ab Admissionibus*. The heavy drapes fell behind them. The vestibule was quiet and still again. The remaining men stared into space, avoiding each others' eyes, hugging their *dignitas* close.

After what seemed an age, Cledonius reappeared. This time the *ab Admissionibus* went to the chair where the other equestrian sat. In a few moments the purple curtains closed behind them, too, and Ballista and the two remaining senators were left in the cloying near-darkness. Although both the other men were silent, their faces expressionless, Ballista could sense their annoyance. An image came into his mind of senators long ago waiting on the Italian mainland opposite Capri, forced to petition the sinister equestrian praetorian prefect Sejanus for permission to cross over to the island to see the emperor Tiberius. The rule of the emperors was difficult for senators. For centuries, while Rome was a Republic, they had been the masters. When the first emperor Augustus had reintroduced monarchy, things had changed. In the new order, the 'restored' Republic, the senators remained the highest social class, but now they had a master. Power now came with access to the emperor, and the emperor could call anyone he wished to his side. It was no longer to do just with the social hierarchy. Nowadays, senators sat in the gloom of the imperial vestibule and watched their social inferiors being admitted before themselves. Cledonius' face was now peering down at Ballista. Lost in his own thoughts, the northerner had not noticed him come back into the room. Cledonius was leaning close, softly saying something. Ballista did not hear the words. It did not matter, their meaning was plain – come with me. He scrutinized the other's face, trying to read it in the gloom. It was hopeless. The best-trained physiognomist in the empire would have learnt nothing. The *ab Admissionibus* presented the same inscrutable face to a man he was ushering in for the emperor to shower with gold and one he was leading to his death. As he stood up, Ballista wondered about the secret passages that must run from the imperial audience hall, down which the condemned would be manhandled. He stopped himself. It was always best not to think about what might happen down in the cellars of an imperial palace.

Cledonius turned away, expecting Ballista to follow. He did not instantly do so. Instead he put his commission down on his chair and used both hands to smooth out the voluminous folds of his toga. Picking up the codicil, he noticed the smear of his sweaty hands on the ivory and gold. Not quite as brave as you hoped, he thought to himself. He did not look at the two seated senators as he followed Cledonius across the vestibule. There was no need, he could feel their animosity pressing hard on his back: not just an equestrian, but a barbarian to boot.

Beyond the double hangings of heavy royal purple, the imperial audience chamber looked just as it had over a year earlier. Light blazed through the windows of the great apse. There was the emperor on his elevated throne, golden radiate crown glinting. Behind his left shoulder were the bank of secretaries, behind his right Successianus the Praetorian Prefect. At the foot of the steps, the sacred fire burned on its low altar. There were just four togate figures primly seated near the fire: a small, intimate *consilium*.

The ritual played out as all the times before: the long walk down the silent room, the introduction by the *ab Admissionibus*, Ballista's face close to the cool marble floor for the *proskynesis*, the hand with the heavy ring held out to be kissed, the taste of the jewel and metal, the cold, formal words of welcome from the gods' vice-regent on earth.

Ballista stood just by the sacred flame. Covertly, he checked the seated members of the *consilium*. There were the *Comes Largitionum* Macrianus the Lame and the *Princeps Peregrinorum* Censorinus, one in charge of imperial finances, the other the spymaster controlling the *frumentarii*. Both were sinister in their different ways. The other two were senators unknown to Ballista. While he recognized one of these senators from having been seated outside, there was no sign of the equestrian Cledonius had shown in.

At length, the prominent chin of the emperor lowered. He looked full at Ballista. The corners of the imperial mouth were up-turned, but Valerian was not smiling.

'Marcus Clodius Ballista, last year, five days before the *ides* of March, you received a written imperial order signed by me and addressed specifically to you, which ordered you to oversee that every soldier in the army you then commanded as *Dux Ripae* was to make sacrifice to the natural gods. You were ordered to implement this immediately on receipt of the order.'

'Yes, *Dominus*.'

'You did not see fit to administer this oath until the *kalends* of April, twenty-two days later.' Valerian paused as one of the senators began to cough. When the man did not stop, Valerian started to speak again, louder than before. 'During that interval there were . . .' he consulted a document '. . . some twenty soldiers who left the standards without permission. One of these deserters came into the hands of the *frumentarii*. After some . . . persuasion' – the emperor nodded benignly at Censorinus – 'this deserter confessed that the reason for his flight was that he was a Christian. Quite possibly the same reason motivated the others. Your dilatoriness allowed these enemies of the gods and man to escape.'

'*Dominus*, we were fighting for our lives then. It may be that these men ran to try to seek safety.'

'Are you a Christian?' The question was sharp and unexpected.

'No, *Dominus*.'

'Are you sympathetic towards Christians?'

'No, *Dominus*.'

'What do you know about this deadly superstition?'

'Very little, *Dominus*. What I can remember reading in Tacitus and the younger Pliny. Like the latter, I have never been present at the trial of one. All I know is that they lost your sacred majesty Arete, and your army many good men.'

Valerian paused. Ballista thought he saw the emperor's eyes flick towards Censorinus. The *Princeps Peregrinorum* did not respond. The senator's coughing had subsided. It was very quiet in the audience chamber.

A new voice spoke. '*Dominus*, if I may?' It was Macrianus. He rose carefully to his feet, favouring his lame leg. '*Dux Ripae*, what are your feelings towards this cult?'

'I think they are fools and traitors,' Ballista replied.

'Because some of them betrayed the city of Arete?'

'Yes.'

'What do you think about persecuting them?'

'It is a thoroughly good idea.'

'Would you be happy to persecute them yourself?'

'Delighted.' As Ballista spoke, Macrianus smiled a big smile and cumbrously sat down.

The emperor spoke. 'Your words please the *Comes Sacrarum Largitionum et Praefectus Annonae*, and they please our sacred majesty.' Valerian paused to allow time for Ballista to duck his head in acknowledgement of the imperial favour.

'This degraded and disgusting superstition, which preys on the weak and the ignorant – women, children, slaves and the feeble-minded – has spread like a plague through the *imperium*. And the reason, I am sad to say, has been the complacency and inertia of the emperors. Time and again, our loyal subjects have risen up and demanded the sacrilegious Christians be thrown to the beasts. Some have been, but not enough, not nearly enough. Persecution has been local and sporadic. Only our predecessor, the emperor Decius, attempted to stamp out these scum empire-wide. His untimely death, the death of a hero, sword in hand against the Goths at Abrittus, brought an end to his commendable initiative.'

Valerian sat brooding for some moments.

'Our edict of last year has been widely ignored or flouted. This cannot continue. Our patience is at an end.' The heavy face turned to survey the whole room. 'We have drafted a new edict. It will be imposed across all the *imperium*, both here in the east, and in the west, where my son Gallienus commands. It will have the full weight of the law and the swords of the army behind it. There are three areas especially where we are led to believe these evil-doers swarm like flies: Africa, Hispania, and the *Provincia* of Asia.

'That is why I am sending Galerius Maximus' – he pointed at the senator whom Ballista had seen outside, the one who had had the terrible coughing fit, 'to govern Africa Proconsularis.' Again, the imperial finger pointed, 'Aemilianus here will go to Hispania Citerior.

'The case is different in the *Provincia* of Asia. There, the proconsular governor, Nicomachus Julianus, already has much on his hands. Any day, the barbarians from the Black Sea – the Goths, the Borani, the Heruli, whatever the Scythians call themselves now – may strike again from the water. I have issued *mandata* ordering the governor to make it his especial duty to see to the safety of his province, to see to the defences of the coast, the islands, and the cities.' Again the imperial hand pointed. 'Which is why I am appointing you, Marcus Clodius Ballista, his deputy. Your brief is to travel to the provincial capital Ephesus and see to the rigorous – the most rigorous – persecution of the Christians. Of course it is an exceptional honour for an equestrian to act as *vicarius* to a proconsular governor, let alone that of the *Provincia* of Asia.' There was a carefully judged pause, just the right length to give Ballista time to bow his head in thanks.

'Let no one think that this is a matter of anything other than the greatest importance. The rapacious barbarians who surround us – Sassanids to the east, Moors and Blemmyes to the south, Goths, Sarmatians, Alamanni, Vandals, Franks, Saxons in the north – only pose a threat because of these sacrilegious Christians.' The imperial chin lifted, Valerian's voice rang out in fine oratorical style.

'What can a ferocious barbarian do on his own? He can kill and burn along the frontiers. But he can never strike at the heart of the *imperium*. And what is the heart of our *imperium*?' Valerian let the question hang. His gaze steadily traversed the chamber.

'*Pax Deorum* – the peace between gods and man – *Pax Deorum*. For over a thousand years we have done our duty by the gods. For over a thousand years the gods have held the *imperium* safe in their hands. All that has gone wrong in the last generation – the plagues, the usurpers, the mutinous troops, the endless inroads of the barbarians, the death of the emperor Decius, cut down by the savage blades of the Goths, above all, the insufferable arrogance of Shapur the Sassanid, who threatens our empire from the east – all of it has been caused by the sacrilege of these Christians. The arrogant fools claim that only their nameless god exists. The blind fools claim either that our gods do not exist or that they are mere evil daemons. No wonder the gods withdraw from us, turn their favour elsewhere, if we allow such things to be said. No more! The Christians will sacrifice or die!'

There was silence. The emperor's words seemed to echo back from the great beams of the roof.

After due time to deliberate the imperial words, Galerius Maximus, the most senior senator in the *consilium*, rose to his feet. With stately orotundity, he praised the emperor's piety and wisdom: success in war was in the hands of the gods. War loomed with the Sassanids; if the *imperium* did not end the Christian atheism, Syria, Egypt, Asia – maybe much more – would be lost to oriental despotism.

Ballista composed his face into what he hoped was a look

of reverend attention. In his mind were questions, questions. Why had Valerian chosen him to impose the persecution in Ephesus? True, Christians had betrayed Arete, so Ballista might be thought to have more reason than most to hate them. But why choose a military man with next to no experience of civil government? Why choose an equestrian of barbarian birth? A man who had been out of favour for more than a year? And, more disturbingly, why had Macrianus supported his appointment? The *Comes Sacrarum Largitionum* was said to be ever more influential with the elderly, ever more indecisive Valerian. Had Macrianus even instigated the appointment? Why? One or both of Macrianus' sons had tried to kill Ballista, he was sure of that. But even setting that aside, whether Macrianus was party to that or not, he had always been an opponent of Ballista at court. What dark, devious game was the sinister, lame one playing?

XIV

Lucius Calpurnius Piso Censorinus, *Princeps Peregrinorum*, commander of the *frumentarii* and hence one of the most feared men in the *imperium*, sighed and put down the children's book. He ran a hand over his face. He was tired, and it was not going well. He rose and went over to the window. Outside, the late-afternoon sun was slanting down through the fruit trees. A patrician Censorinus had been close to had once said to him that the true test of a man's *humanitas* was his appreciation of a garden. Censorinus made a positive effort to appreciate the patterns of light and shade as the zephyr moved through the orchard between the imperial palace and the *hippodrome*. He had a retentive memory. He had filed away that opinion and been grateful. Of course, it had not stopped him informing against the patrician.

There was a quiet knock at the door. Unhurriedly, Censorinus checked that the concealed door that led down to the cellars of the palace was shut. Then he returned to his desk, put some papers over the book he had been reading, and said, 'Enter.' The *frumentarius* who came in was wearing dark civilian clothes. He was an unexceptional-looking man – all the best *frumentarii* were.

'Marcus Clodius Ballista has chosen you to accompany him to Ephesus as a scribe.'

'Yesh, *Dominus*.'

'This will be the third time that you have served with him.'

'Yesh, *Dominus*.'

'I have looked at your reports.' Censorinus vaguely indicated the wall of overflowing pigeonholes behind his desk. 'Your reports from Arete were most uncomplimentary. But those from the Circesium campaign contained much praise.'

The *frumentarius*, who had been slouching in a commendably unmilitary fashion, drew himself up a little straighter. 'I report things as I shee them.' Censorinus noted that the *frumentarius* had still not been able to completely lose his North African accent, the occasional 's' still being pronounced as 'sh'.

'What more could one ask?' Censorinus ventured a brief smile. 'In the imperial *consilium* earlier today Ballista said he knew no more of Christians that what one finds in Tacitus and the younger Pliny.' The *Princeps Peregrinorum* spoke as if he were often in the habit of reading their works. 'A report indicates that he may have been somewhat economical with the truth. Last year, here in Antioch, he was seen listening to a Christian preacher in the street known as the Jawbone. We expect extra vigilance from you, Hannibal.'

'Yesh, *Dominus*.'

After the man had gone, Censorinus remained at his desk. His eyes unfocused, he let his thoughts probe at the appointment of the new *Vicarius* to the Proconsul of Asia. Although the young patrician Gaius Acilius Glabrio had taken almost all the credit, Ballista had done well at Circesium. The northerner was not without backers at court: the generals Tacitus and Aurelian were close friends of his; the *ab Admissionibus* Cledonius seemed well disposed; so, too, the praetorian prefect Successianus. But Ballista had been out of the emperor's favour for over a year. He had never before served in a purely civilian post. It had been a big surprise when Macrianus had strongly championed his appointment. Since the fracas in the courtyard on Ballista's return from Arete, the *Comes Largitionum* had consistently exerted his considerable influence to the detriment of the northerner. It was quite probable that Macrianus' sons, Quietus and Macrianus the Younger, had been behind the three attempts to assassinate Ballista. So why should Macrianus now want Ballista to persecute Christians in Ephesus?

Censorinus felt a small stab of pleasure as his thoughts scouted the mystery. Ferreting out secrets was something he was good at. It was a talent that had taken him a long way. He allowed himself a few moments of self-satisfaction. He had travelled a long path indeed from the dye works in Bononia where he had been brought up. He had escaped from the great stinking vats of stale urine to enlist as a legionary in Legio II Italica in Noricum, up on the Danube. Promotion had followed swiftly. He had quickly been made a *speculator*. Only four years in the scouts, and he had been commissioned a centurion in the *frumentarii*. Five years, and a well-timed act of betrayal had brought him command of the imperial secret service. He had no intention of stopping there. Had not the great Marcus Oclatinius Adventus, *Princeps Peregrinorum* under the divine Septimius Severus, been offered the throne after the murder of Caracalla? Of course, the fool had turned it down.

Yet, as with everything, Censorinus' meteoric rise had had its price. The glow of self-satisfaction died as he moved the papers and reached for the book he had been reading. In the exalted circles that he now inhabited, it was necessary to grasp any allusion to the poetry of Homer. Reluctantly opening the commentary on the *Iliad* for children, the *Princeps Peregrinorum* again began to painfully unpack the nearly 16,000 lines of arcane dactylic hexameter verse.

The early morning on-shore breeze had almost blown the smell of corruption from the port; almost, but not quite. It was getting on for three years since Ballista had been in Seleuceia in Pieria. He had passed through there on his way to Arete. Some things had changed since then. The collapsed jetty had been rebuilt. The naval ship sheds had been given a lick of paint. There were far more vessels, both warships and merchantmen. It was no longer a backwater. It had a bustle to it. Yet the presence of the imperial court just up the road at Antioch had not changed everything. The wide polygonal harbour was still full of decomposing rubbish. It bobbed and floated up against the docks, entangled the buoys. There was one dead dog there, and any number of deceased rats. Presumably, Ballista thought, the long, dog-legged canal that connected the manmade harbour to the Mediterranean prevented the sea getting in to cleanse it.

The two men were standing on the military dock next to the warship that would take them to Ephesus. She was called the *Venus* and, near her ram, boasted a well-rounded figurehead of the goddess, naked. The *Venus* was a *trireme*, a long, narrow galley rowed by nearly two hundred men seated on three levels. Crowded and uncomfortable, less than seaworthy in a storm, the *Venus* was designed with just one purpose in mind: to catch and sink other ships. She was ordered to cruise up the Aegean to Byzantium looking for pirates from the Black Sea – Goths, Borani, Heruli. On her way she was to deliver the new *vicarius* to the Governor of Asia to Ephesus. From the ship came intermittent barked orders and a steady undercurrent of swearing. Ballista watched the men swarming over her decks, stowing away spare oars, cordage and tackle, and generally getting her ready for sailing. Maximus ran his eye appraisingly over the figurehead.

A particularly florid burst of swearing, and a large, domed skull rose up the gangway. A moment later, Calgacus' thin, pinched face appeared. As usual, the Caledonian's muttering was perfectly audible. 'No, no . . . it's quite all right. You two just stand there and take it easy. No way I need a hand with all your kit and forty fucking attendants to get onboard.' Then, in a somewhat different tone but at exactly the same volume, 'One of the sea-chests is missing, but most of the attendants are in their quarters.'

'Well done,' said Ballista. 'You are not overdoing it, are you?'

Instead of answering, Calgacus gave Ballista a withering stare and turned to stump back on board. 'Ha, fucking ha,' floated behind him.

The Caledonian had been exaggerating wildly. Ballista had tried very hard to keep the numbers down. But Roman ideas of what was fitting had not let him get away with fewer attendants than he had possessed when he was *Dux*

Ripae. So there were six *viatores* to run messages, four *scribae*, two *praecones* to announce him and two *haruspices* to read the omens in the pecking of chickens and the livers of slaughtered animals. Fourteen in all. Two of them, the North African scribe and a messenger from Gaul, had been with him since he first left Italy for the east. As was his custom, he had appointed Demetrius *accensus*, to run his staff. Presumably that was where the Greek boy was now.

'Here they come,' said Maximus.

Ballista turned but did not see them. His eyes were drawn upward by the zigzagging alleys and staircases flanked by jumbled houses which climbed towards the acropolis and the stark Doric temple which dominated the city of Seleuceia. Behind were the scarred, grey-white slopes of Mount Pieria.

'No, over there,' said Maximus.

They were much nearer than Ballista had expected. The blue litter was flanked by the two ex-gladiators still employed as household guards. It was carried by eight porters. Ballista felt a flick of irritation. Possibly Julia was reverting to type – the senator's daughter who could not even walk the few minutes down from the house where they had stayed to the dock.

The porters grounded the litter. A hand pulled back the curtain. Ballista stepped over to give his wife a hand. Julia stumbled slightly as she got out. Steadying her, Ballista was surprised by her weight. It did not trouble him. He had always liked his women rounded. He reached in and lifted out his son. He was not in the least surprised by his weight as he swung him through the air. He was well aware that Isangrim was big for six. Ballista kissed him on the forehead and, with a slight grunt of effort, set him on his feet. *Allfather, how many more of these partings?* Ballista had asked permission for his family to accompany him to Ephesus. Denying it, Valerian had stated that women and children might be upset witnessing the rigours of a determined persecution.

Ballista still had no more idea why he had been chosen than he had had in the *consilium*. Julia, well-versed in the ways of the court, had not been able to find out either. Even Cledonius professed himself unsure. No one could fathom the warmth with which Macrianus had urged the appointment. Ballista had begun to mistrust the intimacy between his wife and the *ab Admissionibus* slightly. As they walked along the dock, he put the thought aside. Julia and Cledonius had a shared background, he was married to one of her many second cousins, and they understood the inner circles of the *imperium* in a way the big northerner knew that he never would.

They reached the ship. It was time to go. Ballista crouched down by his son and hugged him, burying his face in the blond curls. He breathed in the smell of clean skin and hair, willing himself to remember it. He whispered in the native tongue he had been so insistent Isangrim should learn. 'Be brave. Look after your mother.'

As Ballista went to stand, Isangrim held out a hand. The boy unclenched his small fist. Inside, rather crumpled, were two leaves. 'We can put them in our wallets.' His solemn blue eyes looked up at his father. 'We can look at them to remember.' Not trusting himself to speak, Ballista looked down and busied himself putting his leaf away safe.

Ballista drew Julia to him. He kissed her gently on the

lips. This time he spoke in Latin. 'Take care. I will be back as soon as I can.'

She leaned close. 'You take care.' Her lips were close to his ear. 'When you come back you will be a father again.'

Ballista felt the strange lurch that all men feel when told that. 'When?'

Julia smiled. 'Towards the end of the year.'

For a moment Ballista nearly said that he would kill the Christians quickly, but stifled the inappropriate and probably ill-omened words. He looked into her eyes. 'Good. Take care,' he said simply.

It was time to go. He turned and walked aboard the ship, his boots ringing hollowly on the gangplank.

XV

The theatre of Ephesus can be seen from miles out at sea. The *Venus* came out of the early morning mist and there it was, directly ahead, its marble cladding gleaming white, its geometrical simplicity drawing the eye from the architectural complexity that surrounded it.

It had been an unexceptional and unhurried voyage. As was the preferred way with oared warships, each night they had moored, for the crew to eat and sleep ashore. Only when crossing from mainland Syria to Cyprus, then later from that island to Rhodes, had they been forced to sail in cramped discomfort through the hours of darkness. They had lingered for several days in New Paphos, the provincial capital of Cyprus, and again in the decorous city of Rhodes.

Ballista was in no hurry to reach Ephesus. It was not that he had any grave doubts about the rightness of persecuting Christians. As Valerian had said, they were dangerous atheists, and their continued existence threatened Roman defeat in the coming war with the Sassanids. Ballista himself had found out that the members of the cult were not to be trusted. Yet it was not the same as a military command. To be a *vicarius*, deputizing for the governor of an unarmed province and chasing civilians, was a different matter entirely – no matter how vile and depraved the civilians, no matter how very deserving of persecution – from being a *Dux* on a wild frontier, commanding troops and facing a daring enemy in arms.

And there was what Julia had said. No matter how settled, how emotionally and financially capable, how ready one was, it took some getting used to the idea. Ballista wondered if he had the capacity to love another child as he loved Isangrim.

All in all, the northerner had been glad to be on the boat. It was a time out of time. Soothed by the ever repeated, hypnotic rhythms of life on a warship, he felt urgency, even responsibility itself, slip away. He was rather like a boy unexpectedly released from school.

Ballista had given out that their stay on Cyprus was in order to honour the senatorial governor – having taken his hospitality on the voyage east, it would be a terrible snub not to visit him on the return.

At least one member of Ballista's *familia* was delighted. All his young life Demetrius had wanted to see the ancient shrine of Aphrodite at Old Paphos. Although it was just down the coast from the seat of the Roman governor in the new city, the pressing urgency of their mission to Arete three years earlier – everyone continuously crying, 'No time to lose' – had prevented him up until now.

This time, Demetrius had had a whole day; more than enough time to ride there, study the antiquities, worship the goddess, consult her oracle, and return. Ballista had let himself be persuaded to go as well. Actually, the cloak of religion was welcome; the governor, although well meaning, was a crushing bore, much given to lengthy expositions on the genealogy of the Roman elite and the size and location of their land holdings – 'Your wife's family, my dear *Vicarius*, of course must be kinsmen of the Julii Liciniani, who have such broad estates in Cisalpine Gaul up near the lakes around Sermio.' The governor was far too well mannered to give any hint that he had noticed the barbarian origins of his guest, yet it had been a relief to escape from him.

Ballista and Demetrius had ridden alone, leaving Maximus and the others to their own devices. Cyprus was a quiet province, far from any enemies and with no great reputation for bandits, and it was almost two years since the three assassination attempts many miles away on the mainland at Antioch. Ballista was certain in the knowledge that his would-be killers had been hired by Quietus and Macrianus the Younger but still had no idea why they had not tried again. And, confusing matters further, he did not understand why their father, the powerful Macrianus the Lame had wanted him sent to Ephesus. Certainly he did not like the feeling of being an *ordinarius*, a pawn, in a game of *latrunculi*, robbers – moved here and there across the board with no idea of his role in the game.

The Cyprian plain sloping up from the sea to the parched-looking brown foothills was green even in August. The road east had been empty, the only sounds the clop of their horses' hooves and birdsong. 'Where Aphrodite treads,' Demetrius quoted, 'grasses and flowers spring up, doves and sparrows fly around her head.'

When they reached the sanctuary, Demetrius had loved everything about it: the cult object of the black stone fallen from heaven, the open-air altar on which no rain ever fell and where a sacred fire burned for ever, the glitter and antiquity of the many offerings. Demetrius happily paid his money and went to wait for a private oracle. Less keen on gods, even those he had grown up with, Ballista had found some shade and looked at the sun sparkling on the sea a couple of miles away.

When the Greek youth had returned, his mood had changed to one of anxious introspection. Ballista could recall clearly how their conversation had gone.

'Priests often misinterpret the will of the gods,' he had said.

'Not in this case,' the boy had replied glumly. 'The priests here are all descended from Cinyras who founded the sanctuary. Everyone knows their reputation. I paid for them to inspect the liver of a kid goat – expensive, but it ensures infallibility. A long time ago, they correctly foretold that Titus would accede to the throne.'

'I know. I also have read the *Histories* of Tacitus.'

'I am sorry, *Kyrios*. I did not mean to imply . . .'

'It is all right. I only wanted to make you less anxious about whatever the goddess had foretold of your future.'

'The answers to the questions about me were propitious. It was the answers about you – you and your friend Aurelian – which trouble me. They said the goddess promised both of you the highest glory, but that it would vanish in a moment.'

Ballista had laughed. 'Glory – and what do your beloved philosophers make of it? For most, it is no more than a threadbare cloak, the worthless shouts of the mob. It is better gone. Anyway, its loss does not have to mean exile or death. Think of our situation. It may mean no more than that the emperor will praise me for persecuting the

Christians of Ephesus, then his words will be quickly forgotten.'

On the ride back, Ballista had put himself out to cheer the youth, but it was not until they were approaching the suburbs of New Paphos and he told the story of the embarrassing incident in a backstreet in Massilia that had happened to Maximus a long time ago that Demetrius had brightened. It was a favourite story in the *familia*. Ballista told it well, with free addition of dialogue and anatomical detail. As they had crossed the breezy headland to the palace of the governor, Demetrius had begun to laugh.

With these memories turning in his mind, Ballista walked to the prow of the *trireme*. The *Venus* was nosing into the great harbour of Ephesus. Progress was slow. There was a great deal of traffic in the fairway, from massive merchantmen out of Alexandria and Ostia, down to minuscule local fishing boats. It was good that the fear of Gothic pirates out of the Black Sea had not strangled trade in the Aegean.

Behind him, Ballista could hear Maximus and Demetrius talking. The Hibernian was teasing the young Greek.

'And what makes the temple of Artemis here better than any of the other hundreds or thousands of temples of Artemis scattered all over the place?'

'Even a barbarian must know it is one of the seven wonders of the world? It is its size and beauty that makes it so. Its inviolable right of asylum. The power that comes from being the favourite dwelling on earth of the goddess.' The Greek boy's voice rang with the tones of a true believer.

'Sure, but in the back of my barbarian mind is there not a story that it once all burned down?'

'It is true. Long ago, a madman committed that terrible sacrilege. Great Artemis of the Ephesians had gone north to attend the birth of Alexander the Great.'

'Was that not terrible careless of her? It being her favourite place and all.'

The *Venus* lay motionless in the water, resting on her oars. Large mudflats had narrowed the entrance to the harbour. Many vessels were waiting to enter or leave. The military engineer in Ballista considered the difficulties of closing the harbour. There would be a serious problem putting a chain across, with the oozing reed beds providing no secure footing for the towers and winches necessary on either side. Dredging would be the only answer. Ruinously expensive and hideously time-consuming, but the only answer. As it was, with the port wide open and all the wealth bobbing about on board the moored ships and stored along the quays, if he were the leader of a Gothic pirate fleet, he would be sorely tempted. A moonless night. A quick raid. Cut out one or two of the richer-looking roundships. Be gone before dawn. But if the fleet were big enough, what then? What of the city itself, let alone the famed wealth of the temple of Artemis just beyond?

Flavius Damianus, the scribe to the Demos, stood waiting dutifully on the quay. He looked around him. It was the festival of the *Portunalia*, the dock-hands' holiday, but everything seemed in order. The retinue behind him was sober and quiet. It was of just the right number and quality – enough to show respect for rank but not so exalted as to give the man arriving ideas above his station. Flavius Damianus looked up at the harbour gate, with its triple arches flanked by tall Ionic columns. He surveyed the white marble quay curving away on either side. It was all good, possibly too good for a barbarian. Marcus Clodius Ballista: from his name you would not know he was a barbarian. The *praenomen* and *nomen* might indicate that he had been given Roman citizenship by Marcus Clodius Pupienus, one of the two emperors that had ruled for a few months after the killing of the tyrant Maximinus Thrax. The *cognomen*, Ballista, was a civilized name, if unusual.

The scribe to the Demos permitted himself a slight smile. Words can mislead. His own title might suggest that he was a minor functionary and that Ephesus was a democracy. Both impressions would be very wrong. Flavius Damianus was happy to avow publicly that his was the magistracy that carried the weightiest duties and thus, naturally, the highest honour in the city. As for Ephesus, of course it was a democracy in name, but it was one where there was a property qualification to attend the assembly and whose agenda was strictly controlled by the council, the *Boule*. There was a high joining fee to pay when elected to the *Boule*. Some four hundred and fifty men – rich men, men of prudence, men who served for life – controlled the politics of Ephesus, the city of Great Artemis. Flavius Damianus knew from his wide reading of the ancients that the well-ordered government of modern Ephesus was little like the *ochlocracy*, the mob rule, for which the Athenians had invented the term *democratia*, and of which they had been so proud in the days of Hellenic freedom long before the coming of Rome, before even the rise of Macedon under Alexander the Great and his father Philip.

The imperial *trireme* carrying the new *Vicarius* to the Proconsul of Asia had cleared the confusion at the harbour mouth and was coasting gently with a slow oar beat towards the quay. Flavius Damianus thought it was a pity that the hulk of a merchantman embedded in one of the ever-encroaching mudflats spoiled the approach to the quay. As the morning was well advanced, the onshore breeze had died. With its passing, the smell of decay from the reed beds and the odour of the fish market came to his delicate nostrils.

Possibly it was all to the good that Marcus Clodius Ballista was a barbarian. They were notorious for their savagery, barbarians from the north most of all. Certainly the utmost severity – it might be savagery itself – was needed for the task in hand. The pernicious cult of those who worshipped the crucified Jew was spreading. They tended to keep away from the educated, the wise, anyone sensible, but anyone ignorant, anyone stupid, anyone uneducated, children, them they drew up to boldly. They whispered their poison in the ears of the young: they should leave their father and their schoolmaster, and go along with the women and the little children to the cobbler's or the washerwoman's shop, that there they might learn perfection. Savagery was needed to wash Ephesus clean of the Christians – they were traitors to the emperors, traitors to the gods, atheists whose treachery could turn the gods against the *imperium* and bring it down in ruin in the coming war with the Sassanid King of Kings.

The *trireme* swung in a neat circle and backed oars to the quay. Sailors leaped ashore and secured the mooring ropes. A wide boarding ladder was run out. From the warship, a herald boomed out, 'Marcus Clodius Ballista, Knight of Rome, Deputy to the Proconsul of Asia.'

A large man appeared at the top of the boarding ladder. His shoulder-length blond hair betrayed his origins in Germania, but the folds of his toga were well arranged, the narrow purple stripe of his equestrian status gleaming against the dazzling white. He walked slowly down. At the bottom, he seemed to hesitate for a moment before very carefully stepping on to the quay.

Flavius Damianus stepped forward and made a formal speech of welcome. Great Artemis be praised that she had put it in the august mind of the most noble emperor Valerian to send to the favourite city of the goddess the glorious victor of the battle of Circesium. All the citizens were as one in rejoicing in the safe arrival of Marcus Clodius Ballista, warrior of Rome. Flavius Damianus kept it short and reasonably simple, but he felt that his ancestor and namesake, the famous sophist, would not have disapproved.

The object of this praise replied in almost unaccented Attic Greek. He thanked the gods, great Artemis first of all, for this day – all his life he had longed to gaze on the sacred city; the reality before his eyes exceeded his dreams. He would carry out his *mandata* from the emperors in the sure and certain knowledge that the gods were holding their hands over him. His was also a brief speech.

As the new *vicarius* was talking, his staff had disembarked and lined up behind him. Formal introductions were made on both sides of those significant enough to merit it.

The essential rituals conducted, Flavius Damianus turned and led everyone through the tall central arch of the gate and off up the long street that ran straight as an arrow to the heart of Ephesus. After receiving polite but rather unforthcoming replies to a couple of light conversational gambits, Flavius Damianus relapsed into silence. Clearly the new *vicarius* was not in the mood for idle chatter. The scribe of the Demos thus was very startled to be addressed by his *accensus*. The tone was extremely respectful, Demetrius' phrasing politeness itself, but Flavius Damianus was unaccustomed to being spoken to in public by slave boys, even attractive ones like this, unless he had spoken to them first. In fact, he was so thrown, that the youth had to repeat the question.

Once it had been confirmed to him that the buildings on their left, the Harbour Gymnasium, were where Apollonius of Tyana had been granted his divine vision, Demetrius began to tell the story to Ballista. Apollonius, the great philosopher and wonder worker, as usual ignoring the midday heat, had been lecturing, when things happened that had never happened before: Apollonius lowered his voice. He stumbled over his words. Finally, he looked at the ground and was silent. There was a large audience. Apollonius had converted many of the Ephesians from their love of frivolities – from dancers, pantomime artists, pipers, and such effeminate rascals – to a love of true *arete*, virtue. A whispering spread through the crowd. Apollonius looked up with a terrible, far-away look. The noise stopped. Apollonius strode forward three or four paces. He cried out. 'Strike the tyrant, strike him.' The crowd was confounded. Some of them thought him mad. Apollonius recovered himself, and in a normal voice explained that he had just then seen the tyrant Domitian struck down, stabbed to death far away in Rome. Sure enough, when messengers came from the eternal city, they confirmed the time and manner of the emperor's death, thus in turn confirming Apollonius' closeness to the divine.

As the Greek youth told the tale – and it had to be admitted that he told it in fine style – Flavius Damianus surreptitiously observed the new *vicarius*. The big northerner listened attentively, his eyes moving from the youth to the Harbour Gymnasium, a smile playing on his lips.

No sooner had the story ended than they passed the last of the famous fifty lanterns that lit the road and came to the statue of the boar. Immediately, the Greek youth began to tell his *kyrios* of the founding of Ephesus. Androclos, the son of king Kodros of Athens, had received an oracle. He was to found a colony 'where a fish will show and a boar will lead'. Moored one night, the would-be colonists were preparing their meal ashore when a fish and a piece of burning tinder fell from the fire. Some brushwood caught fire. From the thicket burst a wild boar. Grabbing his spear, Androclos pursued the beast through the hills. Where, eventually, he ran it down, he founded the city of Ephesus.

As the boy talked, the procession entered the square in front of the theatre. Wordlessly, Flavius Damianus led them to the right, into Marble Street. As ever, the main street in the city of about two hundred thousand was crowded. Auxiliary archers went ahead to clear a path through the throng. Flavius Damianus was still covertly watching the responses of the northerner. Marcus Clodius Ballista was nodding his head, now smiling broadly. Once he exchanged a quick grin with his bodyguard.

This was all very encouraging, thought the scribe to the Demos to himself. A hulking barbarian warrior enraptured by tales of the Hellenic past. Flavius Damianus required a *vicarius* who could be led to carry out the savage persecution the city of Ephesus needed, that the gods demanded, that was so necessary for the forthcoming war with Persia. And had he not had the signal honour of a private letter urging him to keep this Ballista up to the mark from no less a man than the *Comes Sacrarum Largitionum et Praefectus Annonae*, Macrianus the Lame himself? It should be child's play. Nothing was as malleable, as easily led, as a barbarian enamoured of culture.

XVI

The heavy purple curtains erected to make the walls of the court hung down motionless. Although it was still quite early, it was already hot. There was no hint of a breeze. It was going to be another stifling day. It was 27 August. Ballista had been in Ephesus since the seventeenth of the month. Comfortably lodged in the luxurious palace of the Proconsul, he had been in no hurry to begin his work. But the scribe to the Demos, the earnest Flavius Damianus, had been most pressing. The vaguely distasteful task could not be postponed for ever. If nothing else, the prisons were full.

Ballista shifted on his *curule* throne of office. The court functionaries appeared to have ceased their scurrying about. They must be satisfied. He looked around. The statues of the reigning emperors, the Augusti Valerian and Gallienus, accompanied by that of the latter's son, the Caesar Valerian, had been brought into the *Chalcidium*, the committee room at the east end of the *Stoa Basilica*, and set up in front of and below the permanent statues of the founder of the principate, Augustus and his wife Livia – both depicted seated, larger than life, and with severe expressions. In front, an altar had been placed on which a low fire burned, adding to the heat. The incense in the air was already cloying. All seemed ready.

'Bring in the first prisoner,' said Ballista.

The curtains parted, and a thin man flanked by two soldiers entered. His prominent eyes flicked round the room. He had a strange air of unstable hilarity, as if he had been celebrating a festival on his own.

'Name? Race? Slave or free?' Ballista rattled out the formula.

'I am a Christian,' the man replied.

'You may well be, but that is not one of the questions I asked you.'

'I am a Christ –' The man staggered forward to his knees as one of the soldiers hit him across the shoulders with a cudgel.

The *eirenarch*, chief of police, stepped forward. 'He is Appian son of Aristides, a Hellene from Miletus. He is of free birth.' The soldiers hauled the prisoner to his feet. The *eirenarch* continued, without needing to consult the notes in his hand. 'He was denounced last year, anonymously. That, of course, strictly speaking, is illegal, but in court he admitted he was a Christian, adding of his own volition that he was a priest of the cult, one they call a presbyter. He was exiled to the village of Kleimaka. There, in flagrant disobedience of last year's imperial edict – the terms of which were made clear to him – he openly attended cult meetings and travelled to one of their burial places that they call a cemetery.'

He stepped back as he finished. The *eirenarch*, Corvus, had a heavy, not unintelligent face. He flashed an odd look at Flavius Damianus. There is bad blood there, Ballista thought, before giving his mind back to the case.

The prisoner was grinning, although his eyes still slid nervously around the court.

'You were aware of the emperor's orders?' Ballista's words were as much a statement as a question.

'I do not know the orders. I am a Christian.' A quick gesture by Ballista stopped the soldiers knocking the prisoner down again.

'They have ordered you to worship the gods.'

'I worship the one God who made heaven and earth, the sea, and all that is in them.' The brave words were a little undercut by a nervous, high-pitched giggle.

'Do you know the gods exist?'

'No, I do not.'

'You might do soon.' Some of those in court smiled. 'If you return to your senses, you can obtain the pardon of the emperor. A pinch of incense in the fire on the altar, a small libation of wine and swear by the *genius* of our lord the emperor.'

'I do not recognize the empire of this world.' The man spoke out clearly, although his eyes never stopped moving.

'You are a presbyter?'

'Yes, I am.'

'You were.' Slightly irritated with himself for the cheap joke, Ballista turned to consult with his *consilium* of local worthies. The opinion of course was unanimous – death. Flavius Damianus recommended burning alive. The *eirenarch* Corvus pointed out that, as a freeborn citizen, the man should die by the sword. No, Flavius Damianus was adamant, an example must be made. The other worthies agreed. Ballista gestured to one of his staff, the scribe from

North Africa, who handed him a scroll. Turning back to the prisoner, Ballista unrolled the papyrus.

'Appian, son of Aristides' – Ballista looked in the man's face, then down to read from the scroll – 'you have persisted in your sacrilegious views and have joined to yourself many other vicious men in a conspiracy. You have set yourself up as an enemy of the gods of Rome and of our religious practices, and the pious and most sacred emperors Valerian and Gallienus Augusti and Valerian the most noble Caesar have not been able to bring you back to the observance of their sacred rites. Thus, since you have been caught as one of the instigators of a most atrocious crime, you will be an example to all those whom, in your wickedness, you have gathered to yourself. Discipline shall have its sanction in your blood.'

The man's eyes had stopped sliding around the court. Trembling, he stared at Ballista.

'Appian, son of Aristides, in the consulship of Tuscus and Bassus, six days before the *kalends* of September, you are sentenced to death. You will burn.'

The man's mouth opened and closed. Nothing audible emerged. Ballista signed for the soldiers to take him away.

The morning was devoted to the priests of the cult. Much to the disappointment of Flavius Damianus, no bishops had been caught in the round-up, but there were another five presbyters, no fewer than ten deacons, servants to the presbyters, and two slavewomen *ministrae*. Ballista never really ascertained the role of the latter in the cult. As slaves, they had been routinely tortured and, most probably, repeatedly raped. It seemed to have driven out what wits they may once have had. The only intelligible answers that were extracted from them were affirmations that they were Christians. Ballista's court condemned them to the beasts.

In the course of the whole morning, only two of the accused denied their faith. One presbyter hotly denied that he was a Christian. He claimed he had been falsely denounced by his neighbour, who was having an adulterous affair with his wife. He was eager to offer sacrifice to the imperial images and, unprompted, cursed the name of Christ. Ballista ordered him to be set free and the neighbour arrested on suspicion of a malicious accusation. One deacon hesitantly admitted that he had been a Christian, but he said that it had been a long time ago – it was years since he had returned to the rites of his ancestors. He too made sacrifice and went free.

After lunch, a solemn affair in the dining room of the *Prytaneion* a few paces from the *Chalcidium*, the afternoon was given over to the lay members of the cult. There were twenty of them. Two were imperial freedmen. Following the guidelines of the latest edict of Valerian, the possessions of the ex-slaves were seized by the imperial *fiscus* and the condemned were sent in chains to hard labour on the estates of the emperors. It was generally thought that, after a few years of that, they would wish they had been killed. The rate of apostasy was higher than the morning. Eight of the accused offered sacrifice and were released.

About midway through the afternoon, Ballista was presented with the case of one who did not renounce the cult which he found particularly disturbing. She had been denounced by her husband. Young, with a small baby on her hip, she stood straight and answered clearly: name, race, status – yes, she was a Christian. A breeze had got up and was gently moving the heavy curtains behind her. She looked Ballista in the eye.

Her father asked permission to reason with her. On his knees, taking her hands in his and kissing them, he gazed up at her. For a time, he could not speak, and his voice, when it came, was little more than a croak. 'Daughter, give up your pride. You will be the death of all of us.' There were tears in his eyes. 'Perform the sacrifice – have pity on your baby, my grandson.'

She looked sternly at him. 'I cannot be called anything other than what I am, a Christian.'

Ballista leant forward. 'Have pity on your father's grey head, have pity on your infant son, offer the sacrifice for the welfare of the emperors.'

Unnaturally calm, she looked at Ballista. 'I will not.'

'Have pity on your child.'

'God will have pity on him.'

'You would make your child motherless?'

Still she betrayed no emotion. 'If he, too, sees the light, we will be reunited in the hereafter.' There was an inhuman confidence in her tone.

The *consilium* was divided. As expected, Flavius Damianus argued vehemently for the severest measures. Free women must not think that their status and sex protected them. This one should be thrown to the beasts with the slave *ministrae*. Indeed, a harsher punishment was fitting. Until execution, she should be confined to a brothel, naked, available to all, on a diet of bread and water. The *eirenarch* Corvus, in far fewer words, and those evidently carefully chosen, pointed out that the law demanded none of this.

As he listened to the members of the *consilium*, and it was clear that the majority inclined to Flavius Damianus, for whatever reasons, Ballista looked at the woman and child. She was immobile. The child wriggled. He was a fine-looking boy. How old? Less than a year. Maybe about ten months. A good head of hair, serious, light-brown eyes. His podgy fists reached up to grasp the woman's necklace. She ignored him.

Flavius Damianus was finishing another impassioned speech. The members of this deadly cult threatened the very existence of the *imperium*. War was coming with Persia. If the Christians were not destroyed, the gods would desert Rome; Shapur would triumph. The emperors demanded the sternest measures against the Christians. Those closest to the emperors urged the same.

Ballista thanked the members of the *consilium*. He turned back to the woman. Expressionless, she returned his gaze. There was an expectant hush in the courtroom.

'It is my understanding of the edict of the emperor Valerian that a free matron convicted of being a Christian should have her property confiscated and she herself should be sent into exile.' He paused. 'You will return to jail until such time as I have determined your place of exile and the fate of your child.' He looked sharply at her, wondering what reaction his last words would provoke. There was none.

The curtains were parted for her to be led away. For a moment, Ballista had a glimpse down the long colonnade of the *Stoa Basilica*, bands of afternoon sunlight shining across it from the left, the backs of the auxiliary archers keeping the crowd at a small distance. He very much wished he were somewhere else.

The last prisoner of the day had caused the biggest stir in the city. Aulus Valerius Festus was a member of the *Boule* of Ephesus and held the rank of a Roman equestrian. He entered court dressed in a Greek tunic and cloak. He stood quietly. He was newly shaved, his thinning hair carefully combed back, hands clasped in front of himself in the pose seen in statues of the great antique orator Demosthenes. He looked for all the world a model of Hellenic civic responsibility.

Aulus answered the standard questions and, without fuss, averred that he was a Christian. Ballista wondered why he should have chosen to enter a Roman court in a Greek tunic and *himation* rather than a Roman toga with the narrow purple stripe to which he was entitled. It might be an unspoken rejection of the *imperium* of the Romans but, there again, there might be any number of more prosaic reasons. It was important not to overinterpret a man's every action.

'Tell me, Aulus Valerius Festus, why a man of your rank, one of the *honestiores*, should choose to associate with a cult composed of the unwashed, of the *humiliores*?' Ballista pitched his voice at an amiable, conversational level.

'It is easier for a camel to pass through the eye of a needle than for a rich man to enter the kingdom of Heaven.' Aulus intoned the poetic-sounding but mysterious words with assurance. Only a small fidgeting of the thumbs of his clasped hands betrayed any inner turmoil.

'The cult stands accused of cannibalism and incest.'

'It is a lie. We neither indulge in Oedipean marriages or Thyestes-like dinners. It would be sinful for us even to think of or speak about such things.' Aulus smiled. 'I doubt such things have ever happened among men at all.'

'You are an educated man. Most Christians are not.'

'It is written, "I shall destroy the wisdom of the wise, and bring to nothing the learning of the learned."'

Ballista decided to try a different approach. 'What is the name of your God?'

'God has no name as men have.'

'Who is the Christian god?' Ballista persevered.

'If you are worthy, you will know.' A low, angry muttering ran through the court. The *vicarius* might have barbarian origins, but in this courtroom Ballista was the embodiment of the majesty of the Roman people. The *maiestas* of Rome was not to be insulted.

Ballista silenced the courtroom with a gesture. He had had enough of this. 'The edict of the emperor is explicit concerning men of rank, concerning the *honestiores* – you will lose your status and property. The emperor's mercy, his *clementia*, allows you a chance to reconsider. You will remain in jail. If you persist in your evil, you will die.'

After Aulus had been led out, there was a shout from beyond the curtain.

'I am a Christian, and I want to die!'

'Who said that?' Ballista snapped. 'Bring him in.'

There was a scuffle, and two soldiers propelled a youth into the court. They pinioned his arms. He was already bleeding from a cut to the head.

'Name? Race? Slave or free?' Ballista could feel his grip on his temper slipping. This was degenerating into farce.

'I am a Christian, and I want to die!' The youth was wild-eyed, shouting.

'There are plenty of cliffs here, and I am sure ropes can be found down at the docks.' Ballista waited for the laughter to fade before repeating: 'Name? Race? Slave or free?'

The youth did not answer. Instead, he jerked forward and spat at the images of the emperors. 'The gods of the nations are daemons,' he yelled. 'It is better to die than worship stones!'

'Which?' Ballista said.

Confused, the youth glared defiance.

Ballista pointed to the imperial images. 'Which? Stones or daemons?'

The youth snorted his contempt. 'I wish to be with Christ!'

Ballista smiled a savage smile. 'I will send you to him directly.'

Laughter rang round the court. Ballista felt a strong wave of disgust; at the obstinate zealotry of the Christians, at the cruel, sycophantic laughter of the courtiers, at his own role in all this. 'Enough,' he shouted. 'Take him away!'

XVII

The palace of the Proconsul had the best site in Ephesus: facing west, high on the central mount, perched above the theatre. If the view did not inspire you, there was something wrong with your soul. To the left, the neighbouring mountain range curled round towards the sea, slanting down before rearing up in a last, solitary peak topped with a bastion. The red-tiled roofs of close-packed houses climbed the lower slopes; above, the hard, grey limestone poked through the brush. Ahead, your eye soared down dizzily over the steep bank of the theatre to the wide, column-lined road that ran ruler-straight to the curved harbour with its toy-sized ships and on to the glittering Aegean beyond. Off to the right meandered the mud-coloured Caystros, through the broad, flat plain the river's own silt had created, and, beyond, usually blue with distance, were more mountains.

The best site in the city but, Ballista thought, everything comes at a price. The path down was steep. A close-laid buttress wall to the left, a vertiginous drop to the right; to start, the path ran above the theatre. Gesturing at the tiered seating, the northerner said that, long ago, a Christian holy man and wonder worker had been tried there. Despite being both an ex-tax collector and a notorious troublemaker, somehow the man had got off. His name was Paul, Saul . . . or something like that.

Demetrius snorted with derision. For his own good, Ballista thought, I must give him his freedom soon, or rein him in.

'Christians to the lion,' said the Greek youth. 'A real holy man performed a genuine miracle there. No Christian trickery. There was plague in the town. The Ephesians begged Apollonius of Tyana to come to them and be the physician of their infirmity. He led them into the theatre. There was an old blind beggar sat there, squalid, clad in rags, a wallet with a scrap of bread by his side. Apollonius spoke to the men of Ephesus: "Pick up as many stones as you can and hurl them at this enemy of the gods." The Ephesians were shocked at the idea of murdering a stranger. The beggar was praying and pleading for mercy. But the man of Tyana urged them on. He was implacable. He cast the first stone himself. Soon, stones were flying. As the first ones hit, the beggar glared at them, his blindness gone. There was fire in his eyes. Then they recognized him for what he was – a daemon. He turned this way and that, but there was no escape. The stones flew thick and fast – so many they heaped a cairn over him. Apollonius told the Ephesians to remove the stones. With trembling hands, they did. And there lay a huge hound. It had the shape of a Molossian hunting mastiff, but it was the size of a lion. Pounded to a pulp, it was vomiting foam, as mad dogs do. The plague-bringer was no more.'

'Great stuff,' said Ballista. 'Although I do not remember the holy man casting the first stone in Philostratus' *Life of Apollonius*.'

'My rhetoric may have overcome me,' admitted Demetrius.

'I do not believe it,' said Maximus, 'a Greek getting carried away with his own words.'

'You know how it is.' Demetrius grinned.

'Me? Gods below, never in life,' the Hibernian answered.

As it neared the main thoroughfare, the path became so steep that it was cut into steps. The three men walked carefully, in single file. As they emerged on to the *Embolos*, the sacred way, Ballista looked to the left, towards the civic centre and the scene of his distasteful judicial duties of the day before. By one of those quirks that can happen even in the most populous of cities, there was not a soul in sight. Between its columns and honorific statues, the road ran away up the slope, broad and white, beneath a sky of intense blue.

Turning to the right to face downhill, Ballista now saw the people. Above their bobbing heads, just beyond where the *Embolos* appears to end but actually turns sharp right, was the library of Celsus. He and the others walked down to it and stopped in the square in front.

The library was not just a memorial to Tiberius Julius Celsus Polemaeanus, benefactor of Ephesus, magnate of nearby Sardis, consul of distant Rome, it was also his final resting place. His son, Aquila, had had it designed so that Celsus could be buried somewhere beneath it.

Ballista had never really studied it before. Now, between yesterday's unsettling task and the one he would soon have to undertake, he paused and studied the library-tomb. On either side of the steps were statues of Celsus on horseback. In one he was dressed as a Greek, in the other as a Roman. There were four standing statues on each level of the two-storey façade. Ballista moved closer and read the inscriptions on the lower ones. *Sophia, Arete, Ennoia* and *Episteme* – female personifications of wisdom, virtue, good sense and knowledge – all most suitable qualities for a member of the Greek elite. Craning his head back, Ballista looked at the upper storey. Up there were three more versions of Celsus, clad as a Roman general, a Roman magistrate and a Greek civic dignitary. The final statue was the dutiful son Aquila, also in the guise of a senior Roman military commander.

It was odd, thought Ballista, how these rich Greeks who prospered under Roman rule clung to their Greekness. Even those such as Celsus, who entered into the heart of the *imperium*, commanding Roman armies, holding the highest Roman offices, being counted a friend of emperors, wished to be remembered as much as a Greek as a Roman. Read in a certain way, the façade almost seemed to say that all the Roman worldly success of Celsus was underpinned by his possession of distinctively Greek attributes. Ballista smiled as he thought how all of them, Greeks and Romans alike, would have him forget his own northern roots – except, of course, when they wished to despise him for them.

At a right angle to the library was the southern gate of the *agora*, its stones light pink in the sunshine. Again, Ballista read the prominent inscriptions. They proudly boasted that the *agora* had been built by two freedmen of the imperial family of the first Roman emperor Augustus. They had been called Mazeus and Mithridates. Ballista wondered how the local Greek worthies would have reacted to its construction. Here was the new order in stone. Right in the heart of an ancient Greek city was a monument dedicated to the glory of the house of the Roman autocrat, paid for by two ex-slaves, whose very names revealed their eastern origins. Being Greek under Rome seemed always to involve many, necessary compromises.

A thought struck Ballista. He turned round. There, on the other side of the square, was a grandiose monument to a Roman victory over Parthia, the eastern power that had preceded the Sassanid Persians. The Parthians were sculpted to look suitably barbaric, the Roman warriors rather like Greeks. Perhaps if you were Greek, there were always ways to make yourself feel better about reality.

Ballista walked through the gate. They followed the course of the sun round the *agora*, walking in the cool of the shady porticos. Everything you could imagine appeared to be available for hard currency. Apart from the usual foods, oil and wine, both essential and luxurious, the Ephesian *agora* seemed to specialize in colourful clothing transported from Hierapolis and Laodikeia and locally produced perfumes and silverware.

As they passed a line of shops, each with a silversmith on a stool outside industriously tapping out souvenirs of Great Artemis of the Ephesians, Ballista thought he recognized another shopper. The man – his clothes proclaimed him a local notable – took one look at Ballista and hurried off diagonally across the *agora*. In moments he was lost from view behind the equestrian statue of the emperor Claudius which stood in the middle of the open space.

It was odd behaviour. Why had the man scurried away? It was most unlikely the man was a Christian. The zeal of the scribe to the Demos, Flavius Damianus, would not have left a prominent citizen who belonged to the cult free to stroll the *agora*. Flavius Damianus – there was a man with a fire for persecution. Then Ballista half-remembered something. What was it that Flavius Damianus had said in court? The emperors demanded the sternest measures; those around them urged the same. *Those around them?* Who could it mean except Macrianus, the *Comes Sacrarum Largitionum et Praefectus Annonae*? Macrianus must have communicated with Flavius Damianus. Why? Ballista had publicly insulted Macrianus. He had hit one of his sons. Then the sons had three times tried to kill him. Macrianus was a powerful man who, on any count, should be numbered an enemy. Why had he urged that Ballista be sent to Ephesus in the first place? And now it seemed that Macrianus was communicating with the most important magistrate in Ephesus. What deep and sinister game was Macrianus the Lame playing? Again, Ballista felt like an *ordinarius* in a game of *latrunculi* – picked up and dropped by an unseen hand.

In the north-east corner of the *agora*, beyond the temporary wooden livestock pens, were permanent stone cells for the instruments with voices. Ballista's enjoyment of the colour and bustle of markets was always tainted by this area, but something always forced him to go there, always forced him to do what he was about to do.

Men with broad faces and brutal eyes lounged about. They watched Ballista and his companions approach. One of the men stepped forward.

'Good day, *Kyrios*,' he said, in heavily accented Greek. 'What are you looking for – a girl, a boy?'

Ballista looked at him, the disgust rising in his throat. Behind him, he sensed Demetrius' fear and Maximus' hostility.

Realizing he was on the wrong tack, the slave dealer flashed an oily smile. 'A maid for your wife maybe? Very clean, very trustworthy? Or another well-educated Greek boy to keep your books? Another pair of strong arms to guard your treasures?'

'I will know what I want if I see it,' said Ballista.

'Of course, of course.' The slave dealer grinned ingratiatingly. 'It is always an honour to serve a *kyrios* of discrimination, a man who knows his own mind. Please feel free to inspect the goods.'

Ballista stepped past him and regarded the huddled, downtrodden humanity there. Then, in a voice pitched to carry, he called out in his native tongue. 'Are there any Angles here?'

Faces pinched with misery looked at him with blank incomprehension. Ballista felt a wave of relief and turned to go. Corvus was striding purposefully towards him. The *eirenarch* of Ephesus was followed by a couple of burly Men of the Watch carrying clubs. Between them was a skinny old man in rags. Not another fucking Christian, thought Ballista. They brought it on themselves, but he had not realised until yesterday just how distasteful it was to act as a persecutor.

'*Vicarius*, we need a word with you in private.' Corvus led them to the centre of the *agora*. The few people promenading there gave the Watch a wide berth. Corvus stopped under the equestrian statue of Claudius. Cast in bronze, the emperor looked nothing like the slobbering, twitching simpleton described by Suetonius.

'This is Aratos.' Corvus indicated the man in rags. 'He is a fisherman from out of town. Has his hut on Pigeon Island. It is in a bay not far south of here.' The *eirenarch* turned to the fisherman. 'Tell the *vicarius* what you saw.'

Ballista realized that the fisherman was on the verge of tears. 'I was out in the boat last night – a good catch, plenty of . . .' Corvus gestured without impatience for him to get to the point. 'Sorry, *Kyrios*. I was bringing the boat in at first light. I knew something was wrong. My wife . . .' He paused, fighting down the tears. 'My wife is always down by the water waiting. She worries. We live on our own on the island. She was not there. I saw them in time. Took the boat out again. Barbarians. Lots of fucking northern barbarians. My wife, my children . . .' Now he cried.

Ballista gently put his hand on the man's shoulder. 'How many boats?'

The fisherman mastered himself. 'Just one – a big long-boat, about fifty rowing benches.'

'Does anyone else know they are there?'

The man wiped his nose on the sleeve of his tunic. 'Their boat was almost out of sight up under the trees. We keep to ourselves. I should not think so.' The fisherman dropped to his knees and clasped Ballista's legs, the classic pose of a suppliant. '*Kyrios*, my wife, my children . . .'

'We will help.' Disengaging himself, Ballista indicated for Corvus to step out of earshot with him. 'Is he reliable?' Corvus shrugged. 'You are the local man,' Ballista continued. 'What do you think?'

'I have not spoken to him before. I think he is telling the truth.'

Ballista considered this for a moment. 'Are there any warships in harbour?'

'No.'

'How many troops are there in Ephesus?'

'Just a detatchment of about a hundred auxiliary spearmen and fifty bowmen.'

'How many Men of the Watch do you have under your command?'

'Fifty.'

'It will have to be tonight. If they are still there. We do not have much time. We need a plan.'

The lantern at the top of the mast swung gently against the night sky. Ballista watched it from where he lay, next to Maximus, in the bottom of the small fishing boat. Both men were completely naked but it was a warm August night, and they had thought to bring blankets. Apart from the strong stench of fish, Ballista was quite comfortable.

Above them, Corvus, the old fisherman and an auxiliary soldier, all clad in rags, worked the boat. To give an air of normality, they talked quietly in Greek as they fished. The little boat edged south into the bay towards Pigeon Island. Corvus sat down on a bench next to Ballista's head. 'Not far now,' he said, 'about half an hour.'

The old fisherman had sketched a map of Pigeon Island. It was roughly oval, with two tiny bays to the south. All its coasts were rocky, except the eastern, where there was a narrow band of sand. The barbarians had beached their vessel at the extreme southern end of the sand, drawing it up the few yards to the tree line. Careful observation from the fishing boat had revealed a large campfire up on the highest point of the island and a smaller one halfway up the slope from the longboat.

The plan was straightforward. Ballista and Maximus were to swim ashore with short swords and combustibles in waterproof packs strapped to their backs, kill any sentries and fire the longboat. Once it was well ablaze, they would swim to safety on the southern headland of the bay. The mainland here was only a couple of hundred paces away to the south. With luck, as the barbarians rushed to fight the fire, they would be slow to notice the two large merchant galleys, crammed with one hundred and fifty soldiers, bearing down on the beach. The galleys were a worry. Coming down from the north, there was no headland close enough for them to hide behind. Now they were lying with no lights aboard about a mile off in the open water. To lessen the chance of a barbarian spotting them, Ballista had arranged for another half-dozen fishing boats with bright lanterns to ply their nets between the galleys and the island.

All depended on the barbarians being unsuspecting. Local pirates would have had contacts ashore who may have warned them of the preparations. It was unlikely anyone in Ephesus would want to aid the barbarians – although, to be on the safe side, Corvus' Men of the Watch had been stopping any unauthorized person leaving the city by land or sea since midday.

Corvus had argued vehemently that it was madness for Ballista to swim ashore – let a couple of the auxiliaries do it. Overruling him, Ballista had pointed out that it might be necessary to lull the suspicions of barbarian sentries, and none of the soldiers spoke the language of Germania. But now, as he lay in the boat, he knew the real reason he had insisted on going himself: the excitement that for a time would free him from thinking about his unpleasant task as a persecutor.

Almost as if reading his thoughts, Corvus spoke. 'Great Artemis, this is better than grubbing about at the beck and call of Flavius Damianus.'

'You do not like him?' Ballista's words were barely a question.

Corvus smiled in the gloom. 'I became *eirenarch* of Ephesus to chase savage bandits over wild hillsides, not to pursue Christians through slums.'

'I had the impression there was ill feeling between the two of you.'

Corvus smiled again. 'Oh, there is. Our beloved scribe to the Demos – how many times has he told you that he is the descendant of the famous sophist? – Flavius Damianus thinks I showed less than commendable zeal a few years ago during the persecution instituted by the emperor Decius.' Sensing Ballista's interest, he continued. 'Seven young men of respectable families were informed against. Of course, I arrested them. Put them in the prison off the civic *agora*, ordered them to have the best cell, by the door. They escaped. The jailor vanished. I assume they bribed him to disappear. The *imperium* is big enough. Anyway, Flavius Damianus considers I did not put enough manpower into searching for them.'

'Did you?'

'I detailed a couple of men to it. There were many things to do.'

Ballista thought for a moment. 'You do not approve of the persecution of Christians?'

'It was not why I became an *eirenarch*. Yes, I understand the logic of it. The open atheism of the Christians may well anger the gods. If the gods are angered they may well turn against us and, as everyone is now saying, the coming war with the Sassanids may end in disaster. But there is something inhuman about the persecution. Most of the Christians are merely foolish, like those young men. There is something disgusting about tearing families apart, torturing and killing the weak and misguided. Anyway, I incline to an Epicurean view – the gods are far away and take no notice of mere mortals.'

Ballista was surprised at the man's candour. 'I have imperial *mandata* to persecute the Christians. Should you be talking to me like this?'

Corvus opened a wineflask and drank. 'You will not inform on me. Your face in court yesterday was a picture. You hate it as much as I do or, if not yet, you soon will.'

'My feelings do not come into it.' Ballista took a deep breath. 'I have my *mandata*. I will do my duty.'

Corvus just smiled and passed down the wineflask. 'There is a ludicrous rumour that the young men who escaped went into one of the caves outside the city, lay down and went to sleep. The Christians say the sleepers will wake when the emperor is a Christian.'

Ballista grinned. 'They might have a long sleep.'

'And would the world be a better place when they woke up?' Corvus took the wineflask back. 'You two had better get ready. We are almost in position.'

The old fisherman brought the boat broadside to the

island. He used the spritsail to shield the far side of the boat. Ballista and Maximus rose to their feet. They were blackened from head to toe with a dye they were assured would not wash off in the sea. Ballista had tied his long fair hair in a strip of black material. Maximus had daubed an extra dollup of the tarry mixture on to the white scar where the end of his nose was missing. Corvus and the soldier helped them strap the packs on their backs. Ballista clasped hands with Corvus and, as quietly as he could, lowered himself over the side.

The water was shockingly cold. Ballista bit his lip to stop himself gasping. But once you were in the water, it felt fine. With just his fingertips on the gunwale of the boat, Ballista looked round to find his bearings. On the mainland, in the far south-east of the bay, he could see one or two chinks of light from the village of Phygela. From there, the dark line of the hills ran round to the west. They ended in a large independent hill like an upturned bowl. He knew it was directly south of the island.

Maximus joined him in the water with a sharp intake of breath. The fisherman angled the spritsail to catch the faint offshore breeze, the boat pulled away and, there, to the west, was their target. Pigeon Island was a dark outline in the moonlight. It was steep, heavily wooded. It reminded Ballista of the boss of a shield or one of those fancy cakes the Greeks offer to the gods. Near the summit, the large campfire blazed. The smaller one flickered about halfway down. The island was about two hundred and fifty paces away. Aiming to the left of the fires, Ballista started to swim.

There was just the gentle offshore breeze and a faint swell; otherwise, it was a flat calm with a clear, moonlit sky above.

Ballista and Maximus swam with slow, even strokes, not wanting to stir up phosphorescence in the very still waters. Pumped up with anticipation, in no time Ballista sensed the seabed shelving up. Hardly swimming now at all, just the occasional slow stroke, he drifted until there was sand beneath him. Maximus came to a halt a few paces to his left.

They lay full length, just their heads out, the water lapping up to their noses. The beach here was about twenty paces wide. At first Ballista could see nothing but the black tree line beyond. Then he made out the shape of the long-boat, just off to the right, its stern sticking out from the trees. He lay motionless, searching for sentries.

Now and then, voices floated down from higher up the island. Ballista did not look up towards the campfires; he did not want to ruin his night vision. He scanned the trees around the longship until his sight blurred and his eyes ached. Nothing. When he had almost decided the ship was unguarded, he heard a voice, much nearer, to the right of the boat.

At night the trick is not to look directly at something. Look to the side or above it. After a time, Ballista made out the shapes of two men to the right of the longship. They were sitting with their backs to a tree.

Gently bringing his hand out of the water, Ballista indicated to Maximus that they should go up by the left side of the boat. Quietly pulling himself up, Ballista set off. The sand was very white in the moonlight, horribly exposed. Crouched over, Ballista moved up the beach. At every step he expected a shout from the sentries. None came. He reached the lee of the boat. Maximus dropped down next to him. The Hibernian was grinning. Thy shrugged off their packs and drew their swords.

Ballista touched Maximus on the shoulder and indicated that they should go up the left side of the boat and work their way round through the trees and come up to the guards from behind. Maximus gestured that he understood. Leaving the packs behind, they set off.

The trees gave good cover, the slope not too steep. They had sighted the guards and were creeping down on them, when one of the men stood up. Ballista froze. The sentry was about thirty paces away. He walked some distance into the trees. He stumbled slightly. Maybe he had been drinking. He stopped in front of a tree and began to fumble with his trousers. Ballista moved to get between him and the other man.

Ballista came up silently behind him. The man was swaying slightly, one hand braced against the tree as he urinated. Ballista's left hand covered his mouth and, in a flash, the sword in his right found the man's throat. There was a spray of blood, black in the moonlight. The man's body shook violently as Ballista held him close. There was an unpleasant stench as the dying man's bowels opened.

Ballista lowered the corpse to the ground and looked about him. Maximus was crouched in the shade of a tree. There was no sound from below. Working quickly but quietly, Ballista stripped the cloak from his victim. It was fouled. Ballista turned it inside out and draped it round his own shoulders.

Walking with no attempt at concealment, deliberately finding the odd twig to step on, Ballista went down to the tree line.

'Feeling better?' The south German accent startled Ballista. The speaker was one of the Borani, the tribe who had a bloodfeud with Ballista. Wherever you go, old enemies will find you.

'Much better,' Ballista mumbled. The man looked up as Ballista walked round the trunk of the tree. His eyes widened, but he had no time to scream as the sword cut into his face. A horrible gurgling sound came from his smashed mouth and jaw. He doubled forward, hands to his face. Ballista chopped the edge of his blade into the back of the Borani warrior's neck. The man did not move any more.

Shrugging off the cloak, Ballista ran to where they had left the packs. He swung up into the longboat, searching about. He found the furled sail, dragged it out and turned it over so the side unexposed to the dew was uppermost. Maximus passed up the first of the packs. Ballista drew out the containers of naptha, unstoppered them and sloshed the contents over the sail. Maximus passed up the other pack.

As Ballista removed the kindling, his heart sank. It was sodden. The pack had leaked. Nevertheless, he heaped it up over the naptha-soaked sail. Taking the flints, he struck them against each other.

Sparks showered down. Nothing. The kindling was too wet to catch. Cursing inwardly, he worked the stones feverishly. Nothing. A vicious stab of pain as he skinned his thumb. He worked on. Still nothing. This was not going to work.

Ballista jumped out of the longboat. He leant close to Maximus. 'We are going to have to fetch a brand from the small campfire up above.' Maximus just nodded.

Ignoring the path that zigzagged up the island, Ballista led them straight up through the trees. The slope became steeper. Sometimes they were moving on their hands and knees. When he needed to look at the small campfire to get his bearings, Ballista closed one eye, again wanting to keep his night vision as much as possible.

They came out on the edge of the path, just above the little campfire. There were half a dozen Borani around it. Huddled in blankets, they were asleep. Ballista and Maximus lay watching them, getting their breath back. Although the fire was low, the crackle and hiss of burning wood was loud in the silent night. Now and then, a voice could be heard from above. Some of the warriors up there were still awake.

There was no point in waiting. 'Grab a brand, and straight down,' Ballista whispered. They got to their feet. Drawing a deep breath, Ballista counted to three and set off down the path.

The warriors stirred as the two naked black figures burst into the clearing. Ballista selected a good-looking brand. He turned to go. A Borani was getting to his feet, blinking the sleep from his eyes, reaching for his weapon, blocking the way. As Ballista swerved past, he arced his sword down into the man's shoulder. The blade stuck. Ballista had to stop and use his foot to push the injured man off the blade.

Ballista and Maximus launched themselves down the hillside; behind them, a confused, angry babble of voices – then the unmistakable sounds of pursuit. The hillside here was steep. Stumbling. Sliding. Every step threatened a fall. A branch whipped Ballista's face, bringing tears to his eyes. He felt hot blood on his cheek. The crashing pursuit was close behind.

'I will draw them off,' Maximus shouted, and turned to the right. There was no time to answer. Ballista plunged on down the hill.

It was bright on the beach after the trees. His chest burning, Ballista ran to the longboat. Dropping his sword, he used his right hand to swing himself up level with the gunwales. He brought his left hand over and dropped the burning brand on to the naptha-saturated sail.

Ballista landed back on the sand. He scooped up his sword. He turned to face his pursuers. There were just two of them. Ballista stepped forward, carving figure of eights with his sword. The steel hummed through the air. The Borani skidded to a halt.

Time's arrow seemed to have stopped as the three armed men faced each other on the moonwashed beach. The Borani started to spread out, to come at him from two sides. Ballista stepped to his right. The Borani stopped. Behind him, Ballista heard a fizz as the naptha caught. Slowly, slowly, he moved backwards. Out of the corner of his eye he saw a blue flame lick over the side of the ship. The Borani both exclaimed. Ballista did not catch the words.

With a loud yell Ballista feinted forward. Automatically, the warriors facing him gave ground. Again Ballista backed away. Now there were big streamers of fire lifting up from the boat. Ballista turned and ran.

When he reached the water, Ballista swung round, braced for an attack. There was none. One of the Borani was climbing the side of the ship, the other racing back to bring help.

The stern of the longship was burning fiercely. Only the gods could save it now.

Ballista waded out. When the water reached his middle, he gripped the sword in his teeth and struck out from the shore. After a time he took the sword in his left hand and swam one-handed, slowly moving west, parallel to the southern shore of the island.

The moon shone on the water. In front of him, Ballista could see the promontory which jutted out, making the end of the bay. At its extremity was a humped rock. The outline reminded him of the silhouette of a whale. He floated on his back. To his right, Pigeon Island was in uproar. The longship was burning bright. Men were rushing down the path towards it. Ballista wondered if the Borani chasing Maximus had given up. He could not see any torches moving west. What had happened to that sodding Hibernian? Without further thought, Ballista swam back towards the island.

It was rocky where he came ashore. Again gripping the sword in his teeth, he hauled himself over great slabs of stone, then clambered through a belt of rough grass and shrubs, feeling sharp thorns scratching his exposed flesh. When he reached the wooded slopes, he stopped a little way in and calmed himself. The trees here were quite widely spaced – palms, firs, wild olives – with little undergrowth. Bars of moonlight shone between the black trunks. There was a great deal of shouting from out of sight at the eastern end of the island; near at hand, nothing but the breeze moving quietly through the foliage.

Walking on the balls of his feet, feeling for twigs and dry leaves as his weight came down, he moved up towards the big campfire on the summit. Every few paces, he stopped and listened and sniffed the air. Moving silently through a forest at night was second nature to him. Following the custom of Germania, as a youth he had gone to learn his warcraft with his uncle's tribe. His mother's brother was one of the leading warriors of the Harii. Their fame as nightfighters spread even into the *imperium* of the Romans.

Ballista had not gone far when he smelled something: a faint odour of fish and tar. He waited, immobile. Soon enough, a ghostly, dark figure appeared, slipping from the shade of one tree to another. Ballista let the apparition pass him, then called softly, 'Muirtagh of the Long Road, you are out late.'

Maximus whirled in a fighting crouch. His blade glittered in the moonlight. 'Ballista, is that you?'

'And who else on this island knows your original name and speaks your native tongue?' Grinning, Ballista stepped out and hugged his friend.

As they crept upwards, almost at the summit, a new series of sounds came to their ears from below: the ring of steel, the disjointed shouts of men in combat. The galleys had arrived. Men were fighting and dying down on the beach.

The big campfire was not quite deserted. In one corner of the firelight, a woman was sobbing. In her arms, she held her daughter. Her young son crouched behind her. When the two naked, blackened men stepped out into the light, all three shrank away and began to wail. Ballista put his finger to his lips in the universal gesture for silence. They continued to wail, a thin, keening sound. Ballista walked over. The girl's clothes were torn. There was blood on her thighs. He spoke to the mother in Greek. 'There is nothing to fear from us, Mother, we have come to kill them.' The girl continued to cry. The others stopped. The boy was about ten. Ballista hoped that nothing very bad had happened to him. Ballista spoke to the boy. 'You must know the woods of your island well. Take your mother and sister to your best place to hide. It will be over soon. When you hear men talking Greek or Latin, come out.' The boy nodded seriously. With that, Ballista and Maximus turned and went towards the sound of the fighting.

From the tree line, the scene down on the beach was spread out as if at a theatre. The burning longship illuminated it as if it were day. Ballista and Maximus could see every detail. At the bottom of the bare, rocky slope, the Borani stood in a ragged shieldwall of about thirty men. Facing them across twenty paces of beach was a line of about double that number of Roman auxiliaries. More were wading to join them from the two beached galleys. A score or more bodies lay on the sand. Borani or Roman, it was hard to tell. One corpse can look much like another on a battlefield.

Ballista gestured for Maximus to follow, and they jogged back towards the summit. When they reached the big campfire, the family had gone. There was a sudden noise. Both men spun round. Corvus, the fisherman and the auxiliary from the boat stepped out into the light.

'Corvus, you bastard. You nearly made us die of fright.' Ballista laughed. 'What on earth are you doing here?'

'The old fisherman could not stand the waiting. Needs to know what has happened to his family. We anchored the boat just off to the north. Swam ashore. Thought we would see what was going on.'

Ballista turned to the fisherman. 'Your son has taken your wife and daughter to his favourite hiding place.'

'I know where he will have gone. Thank the gods they are alive. Are they . . .'

Before he could put his fears in words, Ballista told him to go. When he had left, Ballista told the others to each take a burning brand from the fire and follow him.

Alone, Ballista stepped clear of the trees. Down the slope, the Borani were about thirty paces below him. They had their backs to him. The Romans facing him saw him first. Soldiers pointed. Then one or two of the Borani looked over their shoulders and saw the unearthly figure up on the rocks. Then more and more looked up at the naked, blackened man with a torch in one hand and a blade in the other. Shouts of consternation came up from the barbarians. The shieldwall began to waver. Ballista gestured with his torch and, at well-spaced intervals, Maximus, Corvus and the soldier stepped out of cover. Ballista called a command over his shoulder: 'Troops halt!'

The Borani shieldwall was in confusion. Warriors pushed and jostled. None knew which way to face. Ballista called over their heads to the Roman auxiliaries on the water's edge. 'Are you ready for war?'

A full-throated roar came back. 'Ready!'

Three times the question. At the third answer they surged forward. Ballista turned and yelled, 'Charge!' to his imaginary troops in the trees. Screaming at the top of their voices, he and the other three set off down the rocks.

The one thing all troops fear above all else is to be

surrounded. The Borani broke. Throwing away weapons, shields, anything that might hinder their flight, they streamed away up and down the beach. The battle was over. Now all that remained was a night of the wildest hunting of all – the hunting of men.

XVIII

In the extreme north-east of the city of Ephesus, hard by the Koressian Gate, across the street from the Gymnasium of Vedius or, as it was often called, the Gymnasium in the Koressos district, was the stadium. It was not what it had been. The old Greek running track had been altered after the coming of Rome. Its eastern end had been rebuilt. Stone walls and seats had been constructed, circumscribing a circle – a killing circle.

Ballista sat in the box reserved for the presiding magistrate and his entourage, but his thoughts were miles away, back down on the beach at Pigeon Island a month ago, revisiting the fierce exultation of victory, the almost sexual thrill of violence overcome, the heightened awareness of being alive. There had been much to do: getting the auxiliaries in hand, organizing a sweep of the island, putting some of the men back in the galleys – one to intercept Borani trying to swim to the mainland, the other to protect the village of Phygela from any barbarians who made it across. He had been dog-tired, but even the muttering ministrations when Calgacus appeared from out of the ships and started to tend his cuts had not dampened his spirits.

A blare of trumpets brought Ballista back to the present.

He shifted in his seat. Apart from a couple of trips to relieve himself, he had been sitting there all morning. The morning had been fine. Ballista had nothing against wild beast hunts – although it did strike him as ironic that Greeks and Romans sneered at Persians for the supposed effeminacy of hunting in enclosed parks, the famous *paradises*, when the nearest most inhabitants of the *imperium* came to hunting was to sit in complete safety, in seats made comfortable by cushions, to watch professional huntsmen kill animals in very much smaller enclosures. Still, it was true there was a certain amount of skill and courage on display.

The afternoon would be fine as well. Ballista knew that Romans argued that watching gladiators in mortal combat instilled moral fibre in the viewers. If slaves and outcasts did not flinch when close to the steel, how much more was expected of free men should Roman citizens be called to fight? With the way the *imperium* was going, the latter was no longer such a remote possibility.

It was neither the morning nor the afternoon that troubled Ballista, but the lunchtime entertainment.

There was another blare of trumpets. Then the water organ struck up a deep marching tune. The music swirled round the stadium, a rousing march. The gates swung back and the religious procession entered, a statue of Artemis of the Ephesians at its head. It was 28 September, four days before the *kalends* of October, the sixth day of the month of *Thargelion* in the local calendar – the birthday of Great Artemis. Flavius Damianus, who had asked Ballista for the privilege of organizing the ceremonies, could not think of a better day to kill atheists publicly in inventive ways.

The statue of Artemis took her place, flanked by other deities, including past and present members of the imperial family, in a box opposite Ballista. The priests and *ephebes*, the upper-class young men of Ephesus, filed up to their places in the stands. With heavy rumbling and sharp squeals of wood, in were wheeled the cages containing the beasts. From one of them came a low, throaty roar which raised the hair on Ballista's neck.

The music stopped and there was an expectant hush. All eyes were trained on the gates. An auxiliary archer stood at Ballista's right hand. The northerner looked around him, at Flavius Damianus. The scribe to the Demos was leaning forward eagerly in his seat, his face rapt. Ballista wondered if Flavius Damianus had always been so fervent in his worship of the traditional gods, or if the intransigence of the Christian atheists had caused it; if fanaticism called forth an equal and opposed fanaticism.

The music welled up again, and a line of seven prisoners was driven into the stadium. They were dressed in simple tunics, and barefoot. There was a placard around the neck of each. The first read, 'This is Appian the Christian.' Ballista looked at the man. The Christian's protuberant eyes flicked here and there. He was trembling. Ballista noticed that Appian's mouth was opening and closing. So were those of the others. It took Ballista a few moments to realize that they were chanting or singing. Their song was drowned by the music.

Flavius Damianus leant over and said, 'I thought it best there should only be seven. We need enough for other festivals, and having too many executions at once spoils the spectacle, dulls the senses.'

'Mmm.' Ballista made a noise that could be taken as affirmative.

The Christians were nearing the gladiators. Now they would have to run the line. The thick, knotted leather whip swung and hit Appian hard across the shoulders. It sliced through his tunic. He staggered forward. The next whip struck. Appian fell to his knees. The following Christian moved to help him but was felled by the first gladiator. Appian struggled to his feet. The third gladiator plied his whip. There were ten gladiators. By the time Appian reached the end his tunic hung in shreds. His back was a bloody mess. Ballista saw with disgust that the final Christian was one of the slave women *ministrae*.

The Christians were herded out again, except for one, the wild-eyed young man who had shouted that he was a Christian and that he wanted to die. His hands were tied together, a chain played out from his bonds. A gladiator on either side of him, he stood, swaying. He was speaking, but his words did not carry. Most likely he was praying.

One of the cages was opened, and four gladiators emerged, manhandling a wild boar. The beast was furious, its coat bristling, its wicked tusks flashing this way and that. The end of the Christian's chain was fixed to the boar's collar.

As the gladiators stepped back, the boar lunged. A tusk caught one of its tormentors, opening his thigh to the bone. As the blood poured forth and the gladiator's companions dragged him away, the young Christian raised his eyes to the heavens and crowed with laughter. There was a threatening roar from the crowd.

Its immediate vengeance exacted, the boar stood still, its head turning from side to side, its piggy little eyes alive with malice. It looked at the Christian. The young man stared back, still praying. They were separated by about ten paces' length of chain.

Without warning, the boar turned and ran. The chain snapped tight. The young man was jerked off his feet. As the boar ran, it dragged the youth along, face down through the sand. The crowd laughed, shouted with delight.

Either the new noise or the weight on the chain made the boar stop. It turned. The youth got to his knees. The boar charged. The youth was smashed backwards. Blood sprayed into the air. The crowd hooted their approval. '*Salvum lotum, salvum lotum,*' they yelled, the traditional Roman greeting at the baths: 'Well washed, well washed.' The boar stood over the ruined body of the young man.

The next execution frankly failed as entertainment. Again, a lone Christian was brought forth, another lay member of the cult. He was left unbound. Matched against him was a sleek black fighting bull with splendid, razor-sharp horns. The idea must have been that the unfettered Christian would provide a good comedy turn, that he would run and his doomed scampering about would delight the audience. The Christian did not run. The bull did not charge. It stood facing him.

After a time, a team of trained bullfighters had to be sent in. They pricked and goaded the animal, working him round the arena, trying to get his blood up. The bullfighters were skilful. They showed the grace of pantomime dancers, but this was not the right time. It was not what the crowd wanted to see. There was an ugly murmuring and one or two cushions and pieces of fruit were thrown.

Eventually, a bullfighter led the beast to charge the

Christian. It tossed him, perfunctorily gored him, then trotted away. The Christian was still alive, groaning, making small, agonized movements. The bull was corralled. The attendants, dressed as deities of the underworld, started to drag the Christian away to the usual place of despatch, out of sight behind the stands. The crowd shouted their disapproval. 'No, no. Here and now. Blood on the sand.'

The audience was imploring Ballista as the presiding magistrate to intervene. Smothering a feeling of pity, Ballista indicated for the death blow to be administered at once. The crowd could turn very ugly at any moment – there was always the possibility that a volatile mob would riot – and what difference could it make to the poor bastard anyway, he thought.

The Christian was pulled up on to his knees. His head was wrenched back. A gladiator unsheathed his sword. It flashed in the sunlight. The gladiator steadied himself, took aim and plunged the sword down into the Christian's exposed throat. The blow was not good. The blade struck bone. The Christian screamed. Hastily, the gladiator withdrew the sword and struck again. The Christian died. The gladiator's arms and chest were slick with blood. The audience hooted derisively as he walked to the gate.

'A pity,' said Flavius Damianus, 'but the rest of the spectacle will restore their good humour.' He was eating a chicken leg. All around, people were tucking into their picnics or food bought from vendors. There was a plate of food by Ballista's elbow. He took a swig of watered wine. He had no appetite.

The music had stopped. A deep, coughing roar from the cages told Ballista what would come next. The rank smell of the beast caught in the back of his throat. He had faced a lion once. Faced it and killed it. But he had been armed with a stout spear. He had not just been brutally whipped. And he had had no time to dwell on what was to come, no time to become really frightened.

The Christian was a third layman. Ballista assumed that Flavius Damianus was saving the priests for the finale. The Christian had to be beaten to get him to move out into the circle. The gladiators left. The gates were shut. The Christian turned this way and that, hopelessly.

The door of the cage slid open. The lion padded out. He was an elderly male, enormous but shabby, blind in one eye, slightly lame in one front paw. His great nostrils sniffed the air. They caught the scent of blood. His one good eye focused on the Christian. Something like recognition seemed to pass across the beast's face.

With no preliminaries, the lion accelerated. The Christian screamed, a thin, desperate wail. Three bounds, and the lion gathered itself and sprang. The Christian turned to flee. It was far too late.

The lion used its bulk to knock the man to the ground. Its widespread front paws with their long claws pinned the Christian down. With a feline delicacy, the lion tore out the man's throat.

The beast raised its bloody muzzle and roared a great roar. Truly it was the king of beasts. The crowd yelled their recognition of its majesty.

As the lion was recaptured and the remains of the Christian removed, Flavius Damianus spoke. 'See' – he had to raise his voice to be heard – 'now they are happy again. The next will be something special, something fitting.'

Ballista felt an unease in the pit of his stomach as one of the *ministrae* was led forth. She was quite young and, despite her ordeal, she was still attractive. She looked bewildered. Her tunic hung in rags off her back. The crowd whistled, called out obscenities.

A bellowing and frantic pounding of hooves came from the last of the cages. The door was opened, and a maddened heifer burst into the arena. It ran in circles, butting at thin air.

The audience laughed. The auxiliary archer to Ballista's right stood impassively at attention. Flavius Damianus leant round him to speak to Ballista. 'They see the joke – one mad cow chasing another.'

The slave girl ran towards the wall of the enclosure. The movement caught the attention of the animal. It thundered after her. The girl jinked to one side. Travelling too fast, the beast crashed into the wall with an impact that seemed to shake the entire stadium. The crowd bawled with delight. Ballista wanted to look away, but found he could not.

The beast stood stunned. Then it shook its head and pursued her. The girl was not running freely. Ballista could see the marks of the whips on her back. He felt sick.

The cow caught up with the girl. It lowered its head and butted. She fell on her back, her ripped tunic riding up to expose her thighs. Something in the animal's addled thoughts sent it careering to the other side of the arena.

The slave girl sat up painfully. Her hair had come loose and fell wildly over her shoulders. She looked around vacantly. Then, with strangely everyday gestures, she rearranged her tunic to cover her thighs and started to pin up her hair.

Ballista was on his feet. He held up his right hand for silence. The eyes of everyone in the stadium were on him. He filled his lungs with air and, in a voice trained to carry on the field of battle, ordered the animal restrained and the girl led out through the *Porta Sanavivaria*, the Gate of Life.

As Ballista sat down, the crowd bayed their disapproval. He saw Flavius Damianus suppress a look of fury.

No sooner had the girl and cow been removed than the carpenters appeared. This was the finale, the bit Ballista had been especially dreading. As the hammering echoed around the stadium, he sat white-knuckled on his *curule*, lost in the darkest thoughts. All his adult life he had been haunted by the reek of burning flesh. Uncontrollably, the memories came back – Persians before the walls of Arete, Goths on the plains at Novae, his own men at the foot of the ladders at Aquileia. Again and again the ghastly, thick stench, the discoloured, peeling skin, the hideous sight of unnaturally exposed pink flesh.

The hammering ceased. The three crosses reared up, stark and awful. At the last moment before entering the stadium, Ballista had issued a couple of orders. He had done what he could to ease the suffering. But it was going to be bad.

The condemned were brought in. The presbyter, Appian, son of Aristides, walked quite normally. Behind him came another presbyter and a deacon. Unlike Appian, they were stumbling and staggering. One fell and had to be set on his feet by the other two.

The Christians were led to the crosses. Ropes were produced and the men were tied to the wood. There was some muttering from the stands, a few catcalls. A voice called out, 'What is wrong with nails?' Ballista ignored a sharp look from Flavius Damianus.

There was a breathing space as attendants piled kindling around the base of the crosses. Two of the condemned lolled in their bonds, mouths slack. Appian looked around him. His prominent eyes lighted on the divine statues.

'The emperor Valerian,' Appian shouted, 'the *theos*, god, Valerian.'

Everyone stopped. Everyone gazed at him. Even the men on the other two crosses seemed to raise their heads and regard him. Was he about to recant, about to acknowledge the divinity of the emperor? If so, he must be released. Ballista, much surprised at Appian's composure, hoped he was.

'*Theos* in name but not in nature,' Appian yelled. 'Valerian was given a mouth uttering boasts and blasphemy. He was given authority and forty-two months.' There was a shocked silence. There was no way back now. This was treason. Even to inquire into the length of the emperor's reign brought the death penalty. There could be no pardon from publicly predicting his death. Forty-two months. Three and a half years. Ballista did some rapid calculations. Valerian had been on the throne for five years. The Christian must mean that the emperor had forty-two months to live. Whatever, he would not be around to see if his prediction came true.

Appian was not finished. He tipped his head back and addressed the heavens. 'Behind Valerian, whispering in his ear like a teacher of evil, stands the magician, the cripple, the lame Macrianus – leading him on to perform devilish rites, loathsome tricks and unholy sacrifices, to cut the throats of wretched boys, use the children of distraught parents as sacrificial victims, to tear out the intestines of newborn babies, cutting and mincing God's handiwork, as if these things would bring them happiness . . .'

Ballista signalled Maximus to come close. 'You got them to use ropes not nails, but why did that one not get the drugged wine?'

'He would not drink it,' whispered Maximus. 'Some religious reason, said it was a Friday or something.'

'A pity.'

'Sure, it is for him.'

Appian raved on. 'I see plague, earthquakes, the Euphrates running with blood. I see the mighty of the *imperium* grovelling in the dust by the hooves of the barbarians' horses.'

Attendants put lit torches to the kindling. Some accelerant must have been used, as tongues of flame shot upwards immediately. One Christian was still comatose. The third opened his mouth in a silent scream.

Above the sound of the fire Appian shouted. 'I will burn now. You will all burn for eternity in hellfire.'

Ballista forced himself to release the arms of his *curule*. His palms were wet with sweat, there were livid marks where he had gripped the ivory. He wiped his hands on his thighs. He had his *mandata*. He would do his duty. The Christians would be persecuted. But this, the burning, he could not stand.

Smoke billowed into the stands. It carried the revolting sweet smell, so close to roasting pork. All three Christians were screaming now.

Ballista stood up. The auxiliary archer was well disciplined.

He betrayed no surprise when Ballista ordered him to hand over his bow. Ballista took three arrows from the soldier's quiver. Carefully, he placed two of them on the parapet of the box. He notched the third and drew the bow.

Closing his mind to the smell and the noise, Ballista focused on the sinew, bone and wood in the belly of the bow. He aimed. He released.

The arrow thumped into the Christian's chest. Appian's body arched, went into spasm, was still. Twice more Ballista notched an arrow, drew, aimed and released.

All three Christians hung limp in their ropes. They had died quickly. The fires raged on, consuming their bodies. Maybe their souls now were seated at the right hand of their Christ. And maybe not.

The north African *frumentarius* known as Hannibal stretched luxuriously. One of the better things about working for Ballista was the privacy. The barbarian always insisted on the smallest possible staff and the palace where they were lodged in Ephesus was designed for the entourage of a proconsul, so everyone, down to a humble scribe such as himself, had a room of their own. As soon as the spectacles at the stadium were over, he had hurried to his quarters, locked the door and set to work. Now it was done. He looked out of the window at the dark, moonless night. He flexed the fingers of his writing hand and reread the central part of the letter to his spymaster, Censorinus.

I will attempt, Dominus, *to answer all the questions in your last letter as fully and truthfully as I am able.*
With regard to the schemes of the Comes Sacrarum

Largitionum et Praefectus Anonnae *Marcus Fulvius Macrianus, it is true that so far I have uncovered no hard evidence. However, there is much that raises disquiet.*

On three occasions I have managed to overhear private conversations between Marcus Clodius Ballista and members of his familia. It is worth noting that, as one might expect from a northern barbarian, Ballista never confides in any of his official staff or indeed in any free citizen. As you well know, he only opens his mind to his own sort, the two slaves from the barbarian north called Calgacus and Maximus. An exception to this circle of northerners is Ballista's slave-secretary, a Greek boy called Demetrius. This slave is well educated, but obsessed with religion and the supernatural. I have feigned similar interests and, over time, in these last years have become familiar with him and I think to some degree to have won his trust. It was he who unwittingly gave me the opportunities to eavesdrop.

Ballista continues to be puzzled and deeply concerned as to why Macrianus, 'that devious lame bastard,' as he customarily refers to him, should have supported if not engineered his appointment to persecute the Christians in Ephesus. The northerner and his familia have no answer, but they are convinced that is a part of some deep plot on the part of Macrianus. Similarly, the familia are convinced that Macrianus has been in clandestine communication with the leading magistrate in Ephesus, the scribe to the Demos, Flavius Damianus, but for what nefarious reason they do not know.

Today, one of the Christians executed, one Appian, son of Aristides of Miletus, uttered terrible words against our sacred emperor, including the treasonous prediction that the noble Valerian had but forty-two months to live. The atheist did not say who or what would kill our noble emperor, but three rumours run round Ephesus: the perpetrator will be Shapur the Sassanid, a high-placed Roman, or, which cannot be true, the gods themselves. Appian went on to claim that the emperor had been led into impiety, namely the persecution of the Christians and the performing of human sacrifice on newborn babies, by none other than Macrianus.

To turn to the actions of Ballista himself. Since he arrived in Ephesus, he has carried out his duties quite commendably overall.

In the area of public security, he has performed outstandingly. When, a month ago, a boatload of Borani pirates were reported to be hiding on a small island south of Ephesus, he took prompt and decisive action. Thirty-two were killed and twelve enslaved and sold in the agora. While it is thought a few may have escaped to the mainland, it is most likely that these have subsequently been hunted down by the locals. The operation was carried out at the cost of just four auxiliaries dead and five wounded.

As far as the persecution of the Christians goes, Ballista has applied himself reasonably diligently, if with some seeming reluctance, until today. To celebrate the birthday of Great Artemis, Flavius Damianus had organized a splendid spectacle. Yet as it came to its climax, the burning alive of three notorious Christians, Ballista seized a bow from one of his guards and shot the criminals dead with his own hand. This extraordinary act cannot be interpreted other than as a shameless attempt to win favour with the mob.

That would do. Hannibal sealed the letter with his *frumentarius* seal: *MILES ARCANUS*. By next morning it would be on its way to Censorinus' office in the imperial palace at Antioch, winging its way along the *cursus publicus* at some fifty miles a day.

There was no moon, but the silver coins glinted in the starlight as they were counted out. There were a lot of them. There needed to be.

'It is enough.' The centurion did not try to keep the contempt out of his voice. 'Wait here. I heard something over by the Gymnasium of Vedius. I will take my boys to investigate. Half an hour – if you are still here when we return, you will not leave.'

The twelve men waited, crouched in the darkness under the wall of the stadium. There should have been fifteen of them, but three had lost their nerve. Torchlight flared out from the gate. The distinctive sounds of soldiers marching – the scrape of metal-studded boots, the jingle of equipment and ornaments – echoed in the still of the night. The *contubernium* of ten auxiliaries emerged and were led away by the centurion.

The men rose to their feet and picked up the full wineskins. They looked at each other, waiting for someone to take the lead. The priests were all taken, or fled into hiding. Eventually, one man started towards the gate, and the others followed.

The killing circle smelled of woodsmoke and burnt humanity. In the dim light, it seemed enormous, the sand stretching away. In the centre, the pyres shimmered silver; the air around them shivered.

It took courage for the first man to step out on to the open, exposed sand. The rest hurried after. When they had come within a few paces, they could feel the heat on their faces. They slung the wineskins down from their shoulders, fumbling with nerves as they opened them.

At first, they all crowded round the central pyre, each trying to pour the liquid that would cool the ash that hid the remains of the blessed martyr Appian. Harsh, even unchristian, words were hissed. Three or four reluctantly moved to the other two pyres.

The hot ashes hissed, and steam rose up as the wine splashed down. Suddenly, a man leant forward and, ignoring the singeing hairs on his forearm, clasped the shrivelled left hand of Appian. Another man grabbed the martyr's right hand. Both men snapped at each other. Neither would let go. There was a tussle. Both men pulled. With a horrible wrenching sound, Appian's corpse came apart like an overcooked joint of meat. The men from the other pyres came running. Everyone wanted his own relic, and a vicious fight broke out.

XIX

It was snug and comfortable in the private study of the proconsul. The thick glass of the windows and a glowing brazier kept the autumnal air at bay. It was Ballista's favourite room in the palace. The windows looked south at the jagged crest of the mountain wall. There was a fine mosaic on the floor, orientated to be viewed from the window seat. In the lowest register, a couple of huntsmen set out with their dogs to hunt hares. Above them, a lion killed a deer and a panther leapt at a wild boar. In the middle, two well-equipped, mounted huntsmen were on the point of despatching a tiger. Towards the top, three men were outnumbered by four wild animals. Two of the beasts were wounded or dead, but one of the hunters had only a split second to shoot an arrow and save his companion from the ravening lion which was about to pounce on his back.

Ballista wondered if there was any sort of narrative or message here. Maybe, as one progressed through the mosaic, from near to far, things became ever more threatening. You set out on something that appears to be safe, but it turns out otherwise. It is a dangerous world out there. He turned back to the three letters spread on the desk.

Julia's had been delivered personally that morning by

one of her endless cousins, who had been on his way back to Italy. Ballista read through it again. First, there was much news of Isangrim, his humour and strong will, above all the wonderful progress in his riding lessons. Then a little about her pregnancy: she was bigger than she had been the first time, moved like a beached whale. After the domestic, came the public news. To the east, the Sassanids had been active. A raiding force had appeared before Nisibis in north-east Mesopotamia. Their horsemen had ridden west to beneath the walls of Carrhae, before moving down the Chaboras to Circesium. They had enacted religious ceremonies there on the field of battle, before disappearing south. Out in the deep desert, other raiders had taken caravans bound for Palmyra. In Antioch, Julia had talked to Cledonius and his wife, her distant relative. Neither they nor anyone else could yet suggest a reason that Macrianus the Lame had wanted Ballista appointed to the persecution in Ephesus. But the influence the *Comes Largitionum* had over the emperor was ever growing. As always, Julia ended her letter with a simple sentence that she loved and missed him.

Ballista looked at his reply. First, the pregnancy: expressions of sympathy for her discomfort, prayers for a happy outcome. That was tactful, before moving on to fulsome praise of Isangrim and requests for ever more news. In response to her public information, he merely stated that he was carrying out his *mandata* in Ephesus and hoped he would be returned soon. He, too, ended with a simple statement that he loved and missed her.

Ballista knew that his wife understood Roman imperial politics better than he did. He had always relied on her insight. But there was a huge difference between accepting that a woman knew about politics and wanting her to become actively involved. When she was heavily pregnant, it was especially unthinkable. Ballista picked up the letter he had written to Cledonius.

After the usual expressions of politeness to the *ab Admissionibus*, Ballista launched straight into the persecution in Ephesus. Ballista was doing his duty. As his official reports to the emperor must have made clear, he was following his *mandata*. Although a Christian had betrayed him at Arete, it was a distasteful task, one for which he was unsuited – taking an Epicurean view, was it likely that the gods really cared what these humble, misguided atheists believed? He had heard that the Sassanids were raiding in Mesopotamia. A man of his background would be of far more use there. Would Cledonius petition the emperor for Ballista to be reassigned to a military post on the eastern frontier? And there was another thing that the *ab Admissionibus* should raise with Valerian. On the point of death, one of the Christians had denounced the malign and ever-increasing influence which Macrianus wielded over the emperor. Letters to Ballista from Antioch confirmed this. Neither Macrianus the Lame nor his sons were to be trusted. Cledonius should warn Valerian – or should Ballista write directly to the emperor himself? Whichever Cledonius thought best; Ballista would do nothing until he had his advice.

Ballista sealed the two letters. He called for Calgacus.

'Never a moment's peace, for fuck's sake.' The Caledonian actually did not look in the least put out. 'What now?'

'Are Demetrius or Maximus about?'

'No, the Greek boy is out and the Hibernian is' – a horrible leer crept over Calgacus' face – 'entertaining a friend.'

'Allfather, it would not do to interrupt that,' Ballista said, deadpan. 'Send a boy down to the docks with these. Tell him to find a ship heading for Seleuceia in Pieria and pay the captain to make sure they are delivered in Antioch.'

With only a minor string of muttered complaints, Calgacus left. Once he had gone, Ballista picked up one of the confiscated writings.

And the beast was given a mouth, uttering haughty and blasphemous words, and it was allowed to exercise authority for forty-two months; it opened its mouth to utter blasphemies against God, blaspheming his name and his dwelling, that is, those who dwell in heaven. Also it was allowed to make war on the saints and to conquer them.

Religion, thought Demetrius, is dangerous. Like strong drink, wild music, the juice of the poppy, it makes people do strange things. He knew what *he* was going to do. He knew he should not – apart from its sordid nature, it was illegal. It was very, very dangerous. Yet something irrational was making him do it.

Those with any claims to philosophy should not give way to irrational impulses. All the philosophical schools stressed that. Following an eclectic line, melding the doctrines of the various schools, as Demetrius himself did, was no excuse. But, still, he could not help himself.

Demetrius walked up through the city towards the Magnesian Gate. It was still raining hard, so he walked in the cover of the colonnade on the north side of the Sacred Way. Wrapped up in anticipation, he did not give the market stalls outside the East Gymnasium a glance. He stopped and looked around. The colonnade was busy, but there was no one he recognized. Everyone seemed preoccupied with keeping out of the downpour.

Demetrius waited for a gap in the line of slow-moving traffic, then crossed the rainswept road, nearly turning his ankle in one of the deep ruts cut into the stone by generations of heavy wagons. With a final furtive glance about him, he entered an alleyway. Although not blessed with a great sense of direction, he turned left and right, navigating easily through the potters' quarter. The alleys became narrower and dirtier. Mud soaked into his sandals.

He stopped at an inconspicuous door in a blank wall of peeling plaster. He knocked. As he waited, the rain ran down his neck. The door opened a crack.

'Ah, it is you again.'

The door creaked wide.

'Come in, come in.' The old man spoke in strangely accented Latin. There was no particular warmth in his voice. 'Shut the door, and leave your sandals there. I do not want mud all through my home.'

Demetrius removed his sodden footwear and followed the old man down the shabby corridor. It smelled of damp and other, harder-to-identify things. There was no light except from the cheap clay lamp the old man carried. They turned into a small room. Apart from a pile of things hidden by a cloth in one corner, it was completely bare. There was a small trench cut in the packed earth of the floor, bird droppings around it.

'*Ave*, Dio, son of Pasicrates.' As the old man spoke, he turned his back and lit a second lamp, which he placed on a ledge. 'What do you want this time?' He looked back, the flickering light making hollows of his sunken cheeks. He smiled a knowing smile. 'Chickens. You will want the chickens again. Each of those devoted to the dark things has his own preferred method. The chickens are infallible.'

The old man did not wait for an answer but rummaged under the cloth and produced a large wooden board. He placed it in the centre of the floor. Squares were marked on the board, in each a letter of the Latin alphabet. The old man went back to the corner and returned with a cloth bag. From it he took a handful of wheat. He placed one grain on each square and carefully tipped the remainder back into the bag. He went out, shutting the door behind him.

Left on his own in the dim light, Demetrius wondered what in his soul demanded such dangerous, guilty pleasures. He was frightened, very frightened. He had consulted the Etruscan magician before, but he had no proof the old man was trustworthy. He always gave the false name but, if he were denounced, almost certainly the *frumentarii* would discover his real identity. His heart was beating fast. He could ask a different, a safer question. Or, there was nothing stopping him from just leaving.

The old man returned, in one hand carrying two black cockerels by their feet. 'What question would you have the shades of the underworld reveal?'

Demetrius fumbled the usual fee from the wallet at his belt. The coins in his hand were slick with sweat. Almost against his will, he found himself asking the question.

A strange look passed over the face of the aged Etruscan. Fear, excitement, greed – Demetrius could not tell.

'It is a terrible thing you ask. You place us both in great danger – not just from the powers in this world. It will be three times the normal fee.' The old man held out his free hand, waiting until Demetrius had crossed his palm with the correct amount of silver. 'I will bar the front door.'

Alone again, Demetrius looked round the dark, dingy room. There were no windows, just the one door. No other means of escape. He looked at his bare feet, standing on an earth floor spotted with chicken shit. He thought he must be mad, or possessed by some evil daemon. But something inside him sang with the deep thrill of it all.

The old man came back. He trussed up one of the cockerels in a corner of the room. He held the other in his right hand. Signalling Demetrius to remain silent, he stood gazing down into the trench. His lips moved. At first it was inaudible, but then he began to mutter and finally chant in some rusty archaic language.

Demetrius could hardly breathe. It was 8 November, a day when the *mundus*, the gate to the underworld, stood open. The spirits of the dead hovered thick all around him, desperate, thirsty for blood.

A knife appeared in the magician's left hand. With a deft sweep, he cut the throat of the cockerel. Its blood spurted down into the trench. The old man's eyes became glazed. He chanted louder, in the tongue of his distant ancestors. The cockerel's body twitched. Blood dripped from the knife. The spirits feasted.

Abruptly, the old man dropped the carcass of the cockerel. The knife vanished. He turned and untied the other bird and held it near the board. As he let it free, he asked, in Latin now, the treasonous question:

'Spirits of the underworld – what is the fate of Valerian, emperor of the Romans?'

As the words faded, there was a terrible stillness. The black cockerel tipped its head on one side and regarded Demetrius with a glittering eye. It stretched its clipped wings. It made a low, crooning sound and gave its attention to the board. With a delicate, high action it stepped on to it. Its head darted from side to side, choosing which grain, the spirits guiding the selection.

The cockerel's head snapped down, then up. The square with the letter P was empty. The bird ate, regarding first one then the other of the men with suspicion. It struck again, three times in rapid succession – E, R, F. Again it paused, ruffling its feathers. It took another grain – I.

The bird was motionless. Its feathers gleamed black in the lamplight. There was perfect silence in the room. Suddenly, the cockerel flew up, scattering grains across the board, and the two men jumped as there was a loud knocking on the door of the house.

With a speed which belied his age, the Etruscan swept the board and the body of the sacrificed bird under the cloth. He grabbed the live bird with one hand and Demetrius' arm with the other. He hauled the Greek youth out of the room.

The knocking had stopped. They stood for a moment in the corridor. Someone pounded again on the front door. The old man dragged Demetrius down the passageway, the thunderous sound pursuing them.

For a moment, Demetrius thought the passage was a dead end. Someone shouted outside the house. The hammering on the door increased. The magician manhandled Demetrius through a low doorway and across a pitch-black room. The young Greek barked his shin on something hard then piled into the back of the other, who had stopped abruptly.

As the Etruscan fumbled with something in the darkness, several voices could be heard, raucous voices demanding admittance: 'Open up, you old bastard, or it will be the worse for you.'

Without warning, the grey light of an overcast day flooded in as the little side door opened. Demetrius felt a strong push in the small of his back, and he was outside, his feet sliding in the mud. The door was slammed behind him. The rain was still sheeting down.

Not pausing to think, Demetrius started to run down the side alley, away from the noise. He ran without direction, through wider and narrower alleys, splashing through the puddles and the refuse, turning right and left at random.

He ran until he thought his chest would explode then stopped, bent over, shaking. He looked about him. He had no idea where he was. The rain beat down harder. He heard a noise: men shouting. He could not tell which of the innumerable alleys it came from. Hopelessly, he turned, scouting in each direction. The noise was getting louder now. A stray dog came round a corner. It snarled at him. He ran away from it. Again, he plunged down alley after alley. The stray dropped back, gave up. Demetrius ran on.

At last, unable to go any further, he skidded around a corner and came to a stop. Doubled up, painfully he sucked air into his lungs. The rain beat on his back. When he had regained some control over his breathing, he listened. There was nothing but the sound of the rain. Nothing to indicate pursuit.

There was a small balcony projecting from the wall on

the other side of the alley. He went and huddled under it. Outside his makeshift shelter, the rain fell like a curtain.

He was lost. He was frightened. From his bare feet to his thighs, he was covered in mud and worse. He wanted to cry. Never again. He had lost his sandals. He had lost a serious sum of money. He thought of Calgacus, of the proverbial parsimony of the Caledonian. He started to laugh, a high, slightly unhinged giggle. He wanted to be back safe in his *familia*, back in the solid, reassuring presence of the three barbarians who now were the nearest he had to a real family: Ballista, Maximus and Calgacus, each in their different ways so capable, so good in a crisis.

Never again. The awful physical risk just run, the looming danger of denunciation – and for what? What had he learned? Five letters: P–E–R–F–I. What did they mean? It did not help that Latin was not his first language. Perfi– . . . *perficio*? To bring to an end, to finish? A possibly even darker word struck him: *perfixus*, pierced through.

The rain showed no sign of easing. The fear of being pursued was rising up again in Demetrius. He had to find his way home. Stepping out into the downpour, he set off down the alley, the mud and semi-liquid rubbish oozing through his toes. Then he stopped, stock-still in the rain. As he stood there, the water running into his eyes, he knew. It came to him as a divine revelation: *perfidia* – treachery.

XX

The head gaoler shut the door behind them. The air was close and fetid. Ballista could feel it catching in his throat, could sense the prison stench seeping into his clothes.

'You are not a soldier, and they are not your brothers!' The voice was raised in anger.

As they were in the large, outermost cell, it was only gloomy rather than completely dark. There was a slit window high up on the front wall and, by its light, Ballista could see the two men quite clearly. They were a few paces away, in front of a partition made of an old cloak, a couple of blankets and a shirt. The men were standing face to face. They looked almost identical. The intensity of their dispute had prevented them noticing the new arrivals.

'You are mistaken, Gaius. Like all Christians, I am a soldier of Christ. We will not serve in the armies of the emperor here on earth, but we pray for him. Now we pray for Valerian to revert to his previous mild and gentle nature, to cast off the evil advice of the lame serpent Macrianus.'

The other snorted with derision. 'You are a fool. You are the one who has listened to evil advice. These Christians are not our sort. They are ignorant, unwashed hoi polloi. They are not your brothers. Think of your real family. I am your brother. You will lose your equestrian status. You will die. The imperial *fiscus* will take your estate. Will you leave your wife and children destitute – the widow and orphans of a convicted traitor?' The speaker thrust his face forward aggressively.

Ballista knew who the two men were now: Aulus Valerius Festus, the Christian of equestrian rank whom he had tried and remanded in prison; the other, now revealed as the Christian's brother, the mysterious man from the *agora*, the one Ballista had thought he recognized, who had hurried away.

'We have a saying of our Lord Jesus Christ: "He who loves his father or his mother or his wife or his children or his brothers or his family more than me is not worthy of me."'

It was the last straw. Gaius Valerius Festus punched his brother savagely in the face. The Christian sat down hard on his arse. His brother loomed over him. Ballista stepped forward and caught his arm. He swung round angrily. A momentary look of confusion crossed his face, then he spat, 'This is no brother of mine. Burn him with the slaves and illiterates he loves so much.' He shook off the northerner's hand and stormed out.

Maximus and Demetrius helped the Christian to his feet. 'Your brother has a forceful line in argument,' said Ballista.

Aulus looked Ballista in the eye. 'My brother has always been the victim of strong passions. I pray for him, that he will see the true light. I pray for you all.'

As the Christian held his gaze, a sudden realization struck Ballista. Among his people in the far north, it was thought right that a freeman should look another in the eye, no matter what their respective status. Clearly, these Christians thought something similar. It was not the way of the Romans; with them, the inferior should quickly look down or away. When he had first arrived in the *imperium*, Ballista had inadvertently caused offence on several occasions, but these Christians had all been born within the *imperium*. It was as if they deliberately courted a charge of insolence.

'*Malus, perversus, maleficus* . . . the stars of heaven are swept down to earth by the dragon's tale.'

Ballista was not alone in jumping at the words. They came from under a bundle of rags in one of the far corners. '*Kakos, kakoskelos malista* Macrianus . . . the vine which the right hand of God planted is ravaged by the solitary, well-horned stag.' A closer look revealed an elderly, unkempt man.

'Forgive my brother in Christ,' said Aulus. 'The spirit of the Lord is in him. He talks in tongues.'

The old man raved on. 'I see a sideways-walking goat . . . Come! And I saw, and behold, a pale horse, and its rider's name was Death.'

'The spirit will soon leave him,' Aulus said. 'He has fasted for two days and nights, not a mouthful of food, not a drop to drink. He has little strength. His devout soul nourishes itself by continuous prayer.' Indeed, the old man's voice had already fallen to little more than a whisper as he, it seemed, listed a number of angels who would blow trumpets and relished the ghastly things that humanity would suffer in the aftermath.

'He is an inspiration to us all,' Aulus continued reverently. 'He has nearly attained sixty years and never once lapsed from bodily continence.'

'A sixty-year-old virgin,' exclaimed Maximus. 'No wonder he is off his head.' He shook his head in wonder. 'I cannot see this religion catching on at all with *my* countrymen.'

The mumbling of the aged Christian dropped into inaudibility.

'I came to see you,' said Ballista. He looked for somewhere to sit. There was just one bed. He remained standing. The cell was moderately filthy. He really could not believe the accusation of Flavius Damianus that Christian sympathizers came to the prison to have sex with the condemned.

'As you see, I have leisure to talk,' said Aulus with a smile.

'Aulus Valerius Festus,' began Ballista with some formality, 'when you were brought before me, I gave you time to reconsider. You have had –'

'Three months and seventeen days,' supplied Demetrius.

'Ample time,' Ballista continued. 'You are one of the *honestiores*, an educated man from one of the leading families of Ephesus, a member of the *Boule* of the city, an equestrian of Rome. Will you not renounce this treasonous cult of slaves and the *humiliores*?'

'I am a Christian. We do nothing treasonous. Night and day we pray for the emperor and the *imperium*.'

If your first tactic does not bring down the wall, try another, thought Ballista. 'You meet before dawn and after sunset, secretly, in the dark, like conspirators. You remind the educated of Catiline and his band in the monograph of Sallust: meeting at midnight to swear foul oaths, drink human blood and plot the fall of Rome.'

'We do nothing of the sort. We merely remove ourselves from the prying eyes of our neighbours and those in our families who might inform against us.'

'The authorities say you reject their power. Do you deny you call a meeting of your cult an *ecclesia*, an assembly?'

'It is just a word.' Aulus spread his hands wide. 'Our Lord ordered us "to render unto Caesar that which is Caesar's".'

'I have been talking to those who have returned to the traditional gods and reading some of your books.' Ballista was pleased to see the Christian's annoying calm somewhat disturbed by this. 'Your holy man Paul told you to ignore Roman judges and take your disputes to the priests you call Bishops.'

The Christian was silent for a time. Then he burst out, '"Answer not a fool according to his folly!"'

In the long silence that followed, the mutterings of the aged Christian could again be heard: seals, dragons, horns; woe, misery, unhappiness. Flies buzzed somewhere in the distance. Near at hand, someone moved behind the partition.

'I will give you one last chance. If you do not take it, I will have to order your execution,' snapped Ballista. 'Just offer a pinch of incense and a prayer to Zeus, and you can go free.'

'I will not. I am a Christian. "He who sacrifices to the gods, and not to God, shall be destroyed."' Aulus' voice was loud, sonorous, implacable.

'Can you not say the words and believe what you like in your heart?'

'Never! What would you have me be? One of the Helkesaites? A follower of heretics like Basilides or Heracleon?' He glared with self-righteousness.

'I have no idea what you are talking about,' said Ballista.

'You mean there is more than one type of Christian?'

'Never! There is but one holy church. The ones I named are cursed heretics. And they will burn for ever in hellfire!' He laughed a strange laugh. 'You have already released several of these heretics. They think themselves clever. They think themselves Christians. Fools! They will discover different on judgement day.'

A thought struck Ballista. 'Do you know anything of the Christian priest Theodotus who betrayed Arete?'

'He was no Christian, but a foul heretic, a follower of the Phrygian whores, a Montanist – even now his pitch-black soul is tormented in Hell,' thundered Aulus. 'Any true son of the Catholic Church knows the Apocalypse will not fall for at least another two hundred years.'

Before Ballista could pursue Aulus' mysterious statements, the makeshift curtain parted and the young Christian mother who had appeared before Ballista on trial looked through. She addressed herself to Ballista. 'I have just got my child to sleep. Can you be quiet?' She spoke with the icy self-possession the northerner remembered.

'Of course.' Somewhat taken aback, Ballista spoke quickly to her. 'I will decide your place of exile soon. I should have done so sooner. In the meantime, I hope you are not too uncomfortable? I see you have a curtain for some privacy.'

'It is not for privacy,' interjected Aulus. 'I erected it myself. She is another heretic, a follower of Apollos, a long-damned local heresiarch. The curtain is to prevent her spreading contagion to those of the true church confined here.'

Behind the curtain the child started to cry. The woman

went to soothe it. Aulus laughed. Anger rising in him, Ballista turned on his heel and left.

Back in the civic *agora*, standing outside in the fresh air by the *Bouleuterion*, Ballista called the head gaoler over. The anger hot in him, Ballista spat out orders. No visitors were to be admitted to the Christians. No one was to take in food, drink, lamps, clothes, bedding; above all, no books. Let them live on prison fare, nourish themselves with prayer. Any gaoler found breaking these orders, found taking a bribe, would be treated as a Christian suspect. He would find himself on the rack, heading for the arena. The cells were to be searched; any luxuries, anything treasonous, was to be confiscated. Aulus Valerius Festus and the old fool who talked in tongues were to be thrown in the deepest dungeon.

Ballista paced furiously back and forth across the *Stoa Basilica*. The old man would probably die in there. Maybe the equestrian would too. Perhaps they all would. Good. Most likely it was what they wanted anyway. Fuck them. The Christian woman? Fuck her too. Fuck them all. Christians to the lions.

But the woman had a child. The boy must be what? About a year old. Two days earlier, news had reached Ballista from Antioch: he had a second son. Born five days before the *kalends* of December, the boy was healthy, the mother doing well. Imagine if the fates had been different. What if Julia and the boy were imprisoned? What – a more horrible thought than any – if Isangrim were in the dark hell of an imperial gaol?

'Wait!' Ballista looked away, beyond the civic *agora*, beyond the red-roofed houses climbing the slopes. He looked up to the bare mountainside above, where the grey slabs of rock thrust through the greenery. It was nothing like his homelands in the north, but it *was* untouched by the *imperium*. It was wild and free. It was clean. That bastard Corvus was right: Ballista hated this. It was not even as if the people he was persecuting seemed to belong to the same sect as the bastard who had betrayed him in Arete. He was caught between Scylla and Charybdis: on the one hand, the self-righteous intransigence of the Christians; on the other, the implacably cruel imperial orders and the inhuman gloating of the pagan mob. What was Ballista doing to these Christians? What was he doing to himself?

As he rescinded his orders, Ballista made a vow to himself. That very day, he would send the woman and child to a comfortable place of exile, one as safe as he could find. Then he made another vow to himself, a much more dangerous one: the persecution in Ephesus would stop. He could not order it. But there must be a way to make the process fail, to bring it grinding to a halt.

Ballista thought of the volatile crowd in the stadium at Ephesus. He thought of the riot in the *hippodrome* in Antioch. Yes, there was a way. The first duty of a governor was public order. He was the *vicarius* to a governor. Therefore, his first duty must be public order. He knew the sophistry would not save him if he were caught. It was ridiculously dangerous. But a man has to have a code to live by. A man has to live with himself.

It was an upmarket brothel, just across from the library of Celsus in the centre of town. Maximus had chosen it. He had been there once or twice, not enough to be a regular. The high prices meant it was seldom very full, and he had wanted somewhere quiet to talk to Calgacus about the very dangerous thing they would do the next day.

'Do you know what she said to me?' Maximus beamed.

'No, I do not.' Calgacus' tone and demeanour showed a supreme lack of interest.

'She said' – Maximus drew himself up to his full height – 'she said I was the best she ever had.' He raised his arms from his sides, spread them wide. He half turned, first one way then the other; a victorious gladiator basking in the applause, waiting for the palm of victory.

'Interesting – her only speaking Aramaic, and you not knowing a word of that language.'

Maximus grinned. 'Oh, brother, I could tell – that is what she was trying to say in her funny lingo.'

When there was no response, Maximus dropped his trousers and undergarment to his ankles. Lifting his tunic, he took the next seat to Calgacus in the communal lavatory.

The brothel really was upmarket – it had running water. Maximus leant forward and picked up the sponge on a stick from the trough in front of him. He fidgeted with it. 'Sure, but I have almost got used to the Roman habit of having company when you shit.'

'I cannot tell you how happy that makes me,' Calgacus replied.

Although they were the only two in the privy, Maximus looked all round in an unconscious parody of shiftiness. Reassured that there was no one else there, he bent over to Calgacus and spoke quietly. 'Did you see your man?'

'Aye.'

'And . . . ?'

'It was good.'

Maximus replaced the sponge. 'I still say it is a mistake of the *Dominus* to involve one of the *factiones* from the theatre.' He held up his hand to forestall an interruption from Calgacus that did not come. 'I grant you, the theatre gangs have the organization to get the numbers out. They are always up for trouble. There is never a riot in any city in the *imperium* and them not behind it – although why they usually get so worked up about some mincing dancers who have probably been taking it up the arse since they could crawl I cannot see. No, your problem is that they are too well known. Everyone knows who is the head of each *factio*. It makes an easy trail. The *frumentarii* find your man. He leads them to you. Then you lead them to Ballista. And then I am next to the pair of you in the palace cellars with someone dancing on my bollocks.'

'Aye, all life is a risk.'

'Until just now, only you, me and Ballista knew the plan. Not even Demetrius knew. Now, half the idlers in Ephesus must know.' He picked up the sponge again. 'And if we were going to a *factio*,' Maximus continued, 'it should have been me that talked to the head man.'

There was a horrible grating, wheezing sound. Calgacus was laughing. 'Wonderful, a half-witted Hibernian with the end of his nose missing – what could be more inconspicuous?'

Maximus bridled. 'And what about you, you old fucker? An ugly old Caledonian with a face that could turn milk at a hundred paces, fucking great dome of a head.'

'I wore a hat,' Calgacus said simply. 'Anyway, when do

I get to leave the proconsul's palace? Next to no one in Ephesus knows me. My man has been well paid. How did you get on?'

With an instantaneous change of mood that even the briefest acquaintance revealed as quite customary, Maximus grinned again. 'As you would expect from a man of my qualities – wonderful. Five wild boys from Isauria. They would cut their own mothers' throats for a few coins. And, the best of it is, they sail with the evening breeze tomorrow.'

'If they are still alive and the *frumentarii* have not got them.'

'Brother, your cup is always half empty.'

'Maybe so, but as we may well not be able to tomorrow – you know, us being dead or on the rack – tonight I am going to have a few drinks and a lively-looking girl.'

They both got up and began to clean themselves with two of the sponges.

'Poor girl, but sure, you have the right of it. And tomorrow is *Saturnalia*. Back when I was a gladiator, I always enjoyed myself the night before a fight.' Maximus tossed his sponge back into the trough of running water. 'I think I am ready for another – that plump little Syrian. It is good of you to offer to pay.'

'I did not.'

As they adjusted their clothing, Maximus spoke softly again. 'Just so it is fixed in my mind, when do we start?'

'How many times do you have to be told? When they bring Aulus Valerius Festus, the Christian with equestrian status, into the arena.'

XXI

It was the seventeenth day of December, the first day of the festival of the *Saturnalia*. It was the best of days for the slaves of Ephesus, but the free men were not going to be left out. The afternoon before, they had exchanged small presents: perhaps a jar of wine, a hare or a plump bird, maybe the traditional candles and clay dolls; sometimes, among the less well to do, just a garland of wild flowers. That morning many groups of friends and colleagues had thrown dice to determine which of their number would be their King of the *Saturnalia*, the one whose every command, no matter how ridiculous or embarrassing, must be obeyed. Most, slave as well as free, hoped to dine on suckling pig that evening. And that was just the start. There were seven days of hard drinking and partying to be done. But the crowd gathered in the stadium for the spectacles, for the *munera*, did not seem particularly happy.

Up in the presiding magistrate's box, standing behind the right shoulder of his *kyrios*, Demetrius hardly noticed the mood of the crowd. He wished he had been given a day's leave, like Maximus and Calgacus. He loathed everything about the *munera*. The beast fights in the morning, the spectacular executions at noon, the sweaty, overfed gladiators huffing and puffing in the afternoon: he despised them all. It was difficult to number the reasons for his dislike. The *munera* were not Hellenic. The stadium had been built for something worthy, for athletics, for free citizens to run, perfect in their nakedness, competing for honour. Now, its very structure altered, it hosted slaves and criminals, worse than the savage animals, screaming, bleeding, pleading for their lives. The *munera* were not a thing of Hellas. They were a disgusting import; one of the very worst things that had come with the disaster of Roman rule. The *munera* were not only barbaric, they appealed to the basest appetites of the sordid hoi polloi. Again and again, they chanted, '*Blood on the sand,*' as if no Hellene had ever made offerings before an altar dedicated to *Pity*.

Of course, there was something far worse than all this. Worst of all, the *munera* were a dangerous threat to every individual spectator. The excitement, the power of the spectacle, was hard to keep out. An unguarded moment, and in it slipped by the eyes and ears and, there, insidiously in the soul of a man, its raw emotion undermined self-control, attempted to overthrow the very rationality that made a man what he was: a man, not a beast.

A loud jeering from the crowd brought Demetrius back to his surroundings. Near the magistrate's box, a King of the *Saturnalia* had ordered one of his group to strip and sing. The elected man stood unhappily naked in the keen north wind. His tormentor, face blackened, threadbare imitation of royal robes flapping, hopped around him, miming the castration of the victim with a ceremonial scythe. The singer's barbaric Greek, an up-country accent from Cappadocia or Isauria, was drowned by boos and catcalls. It crossed Demetrius' mind to wonder what this King did when it was not *Saturnalia*. There was something very familiar about the capering figure under the tawdry get-up.

Demetrius' thoughts wandered anxiously down a well-trodden path. It was over a month since he had been nearly trapped in the lair of the Etruscan; forty days, to be precise. Demetrius wondered if he had got away with it. If the men hammering at the door had been policemen sent by the local *eirenarch* Corvus or, worse, imperial *frumentarii*, they would have tracked him down by now – if the old man had talked. Demetrius had not been back. Surely the magician would not have confessed to the treasonous question? But even now he might be in prison, cunning torturers probing him as his aged body lay tormented on the rack. Demetrius felt sick with fear. The terrible risks he had run. And what had he learned? P–E–R–F–I . . . Perfidia. But whose treachery would bring down the emperor Valerian? A traitor at court? The natural perfidy of easterners such as Shapur? Demetrius had risked so much, to find out so little. Sometimes he disgusted himself.

A chorus of disapproval swelled up from the stands. It was led by a group on the far side of the arena. 'Bears! We want bears! Cruel, cruel bears!' The rhythmic chants and clapping indicated that they were one of the theatre factions. They and the rest of the crowd had reason to be disappointed. It was lunchtime. The morning's *venationes* had been very uninspiring. A few deer and wild asses had been hunted, and a couple of bulls had fought. The only fanged animals despatched had been three mangy-looking leopards. There had been little fight in them. They had come from no further than the nearby province of Cilicia. Some ostriches were the only animals to have been transported from overseas. Even though they had stood stock still, as if drugged, the bow-armed *bestiarii* had managed to miss them several times.

So far, the lunchtime executions had been no better. Ballista had taken over the running of the show himself. Yet he had done nothing but stage a watered-down version of what Flavius Damianus had organized back in September. The same wild boar, bull and lion had reappeared, each quickly killing a Christian of no consequence. The mad cow had not been seen. It was *Saturnalia*. The crowd expected better. There was a bitter north wind. They were not happy.

Demetrius looked at the back of his *kyrios*. Ballista's shoulders were set in a mulish hunch. Over the last few days, Demetrius had realized that he was not the only one in the *familia* that was preoccupied. Ballista, Calgacus, even Maximus, each in his different way had seemed under strain. The young Greek suspected that the three barbarians were keeping something from him. If he had not been so wrapped in fear and self-loathing, he would have been more hurt.

A squad of gladiators escorted Aulus Valerius Festus into the ring. He was not shackled and there was no placard around his neck. A herald stepped forward and announced him. The equestrian atheist would die by the sword, as befitted his rank.

Like surf beating on the shore, the crowd thundered their disapproval: 'Nail him up!', 'Burn him!', 'Bring out the bears!', 'Make the bastard dance!' Cushions, pieces of fruit, half-eaten sausages were thrown into the arena. Before the first projectiles landed on the sand, as if on cue, Ballista summoned the herald back to his side. He spoke briefly, so low that Demetrius could not hear him over the din.

The herald stepped to the front rail. He held up his arms. The missiles ceased. Apart from the odd whistle and yell, the crowd quietened.

'Silence,' boomed the herald, 'that is what the *vicarius* wants: *Silence!*'

For a few heartbeats, there was indeed silence, a shocked silence as the crowd digested the insufferable arrogance of this barbarian *vicarius. How dare the northern bastard ignore their wishes? Was it not* Saturnalia, *when all is permitted? Who did he think he was to deny their pleasures? Was he the emperor? Would they take this, even from an emperor? Fuck him!*

The thunderous clamour rang out again. More missiles flew. This time, they were sharp and hard: stones, coins, things that could hurt, even kill. They were hurled into the arena at the Christian. Some in the crowd began to turn their aim on the magistrate's box. A rock whipped past Demetrius' ear. The secretary gazed at the back of his *kyrios.* Ballista sat immobile.

On the far side of the sand, the theatre faction that had been chanting for bears was pushing forward. The foremost of them were climbing the wall, dropping down into the ring, scuffling with the attendants. A figure with an outsize *pileus,* the cap of freedom, pulled low down, almost over his face, balanced on the wall, waving them on. Near at hand, around the Saturnalian king with the blackened face, a fight had broken out. Still the *kyrios* did nothing. Missiles were landing around him. The scribe Demetrius liked, the one from North Africa, was doubled up in pain. *Send in the troops*, Demetrius silently begged. *At least have the bucinator blow a threatening note on his instrument*. Still Ballista did nothing.

Without an order, the auxiliary archers in the magistrate's box closed rank around the *vicarius* and his party. Missiles rattled off their small shields, helmets and armour. Down on the sand, the gladiators were hauling the Christian out of the ring. He was bleeding freely from a head wound. Fighting was becoming general. The situation was slipping out of control. It was turning into a full-scale riot.

Suddenly, Ballista stood up. He turned and said it was time to leave. He swept past Demetrius. The young Greek could not understand it. He was sure he saw the big northerner briefly grin, as if he were perfectly happy with the way things had worked out.

The old man was sitting by the side of the mountain track. He was waiting. In his hand was a roll of papyrus. Oh no, thought Ballista, not even out here.

It was three days since Ballista had posted the notice suspending executions of Christians as a threat to public order. Four days since the riot in the stadium. He had ridden out that morning with the *eirenarch* Corvus, just to get out of the palace, as much for some peace and companionship as for the hunting.

They had left the Magnesian Gate at dawn. Two mounted huntsmen in embroidered coats with four Celtic hounds on long leashes had followed them. They had turned south and followed paths up Mount Prion in the general direction of the sanctuary of Ortygia. It was a beautiful midwinter day, hardly a cloud in the sky, and the cold, hard sunshine illuminated every bare branch and rock. In the morning the hounds had coursed a couple of hares, but they had got away. They had stopped for lunch and lit a fire. That was when the boar had emerged from the thicket. It regarded them with keen malevolence in its small eyes, then turned and made off, its short legs jerking out fore and aft. The hounds were slipped. All four men threw themselves into the saddle. The fire was well made, and it was winter. It would not spread. The boar gave them a good chase, scrambling fast up and down the slopes, its trotters kicking out showers of stones, before going to ground in a thick tangle of dead undergrowth. No sooner had the hounds gone in than the boar charged. The men were still swinging down from their mounts, unslinging their spears. The beast made straight for Corvus. There was no time, nothing Ballista or the huntsmen could do. At the last moment, the *eirenarch* levelled the blade. The impact drove him back two or three steps. The boar impaled itself ever deeper as its fury drove it, snapping up the shaft. When it reached the crossbar, with a foot and a half of steel inside it, the beast died. There was a drop of blood like a tear in each of its eyes.

They ate lunch. Then Ballista and Corvus watched the huntsmen remove the tusks, skin the beast and butcher the meat. Time was passing, and they had set off back. That was when they came across the old man.

Petitioners were the bane of anyone with power in the *imperium*. They cropped up wherever you went. You were expected to give them a hearing. There was a story that the emperor Hadrian had been out riding one day when an old woman approached him with a petition. Hadrian said he was too busy. She called out after him, 'Then stop being emperor.' Dutifully, he turned back and gave her a hearing. Ballista preferred the story of Mark Antony. Bothered by several petitioners under similar circumstances, he turned and held out the folds of his toga to catch their petitions. Then he walked to the nearest bridge and threw them all in the river.

Indicating for the huntsmen to carry on, Ballista and Corvus reined in. The old man got stiffly to his feet. From under his broad-brimmed hat, he mumbled in up-country Greek that he wished to speak to the *kyrios* alone. Both Ballista and Corvus looked all around, scanning the hillside. When they were sure the old man was alone, the *eirenarch* walked his horse on.

The aged petitioner did not speak immediately. He waited until Corvus was well out of earshot. Then he tipped back his hat. He was not nearly as old as Ballista had thought; he was actually quite a young man. He smiled and spoke quietly in good Latin. '*Ave*, Marcus Clodius Ballista. My *dominus* the *ab Admissionibus* Cledonius sends his greetings. He requests that if you must write to him about political matters, you do so only in the most oblique way and that, in future, you only send a letter by the most reliable of carriers. Macrianus has spies everywhere. If they do not intercept the letter, Censorinus' *frumentarii* probably will. There are fears that the *Comes Largitionum* and the *Princeps Peregrinorum* are drawing ever closer. My *dominus* regrets that he thinks it would be unwise to talk to the emperor about transferring you to the eastern front and that it would be tantamount to suicide to try to denounce

Macrianus. He begs that you try nothing of the sort. Valerian comes to trust and rely more and more on the lame
one.'

The man stopped. He looked along the road to where
Corvus sat on his horse, waiting. 'Here, you had better take
this.' He handed over the papyrus roll and turned to go.
Ballista untied and unrolled it. It was blank. He looked
after the man. The hillside was bare; the messenger had
vanished. Ballista studied the slope carefully. There the man
was, moving inconspicuously up a narrow gully. He was
good at fieldcraft. But not that good.

Alone in his room in the palace, the North African scribe
began to write.

> *To Lucius Calpurnius Piso Censorinus*, Princeps Peregri-
> norum, *Commander of the* Frumentarii.
>
> *Written at Ephesus, ten days before the ides of March, the
> anniversary of the accession of the divine emperors Marcus
> Antoninus and Lucius Verus, in the Consulship of Aemil-
> ianus and Bassus.*
>
> Dominus, *I write to inform you of the lamentable state of
> affairs in Ephesus.*
>   *With regard to the schemes of Macrianus, rumours
> abound. But it is true that still no hard evidence has
> emerged.*
>   *As for Marcus Clodius Ballista himself, I have informed
> you how at first he applied himself diligently to the appre-
> hension and trial of the atheists, and how at the original*

336

executions he even went so far as to seize a bow from one of his guards and shoot three of the criminals dead with his own hand. Happily, this despicable demagoguery failed to bring him the popular acclaim he sought.

Ballista ordered another round of executions to be held at the munera *which marked the opening day of the* Saturnalia. *Organized by the* vicarius *himself, from the outset it was the poorest of spectacles. In the morning there were few beasts, next to none exotic. At lunchtime, only three Christians had been killed, in the most uninventive ways, when an atheist of equestrian rank called Aulus Valerius Festus was brought into the arena. The crowd democratically clamoured for this arch-criminal to suffer exemplary punishment. The answer Ballista gave via a herald was so haughty as to befit an emperor. When the first stones flew, he was at a loss, not knowing what to do. When a riot erupted, he fled the stadium, his face twitching with terror. The latter I can swear to; I was standing behind him and I saw him clearly as he passed. Back in the palace, sunk in a barbarian stupor, it was two hours before he ordered in the troops. By then the majority of the rioters had dispersed. Those that remained easily avoided the auxiliary archers, except for a handful too drunk to run. None of the ringleaders was apprehended.*

The next day, the vicarius *posted an edict suspending the execution of Christians as a threat to public order. At the same time he sent reports to the emperor and to the Governor of Asia justifying this measure. Since then, he has discouraged any attempts to seek out more members of this revolting sect. He has postponed the trial of those already in custody. The persecution has come to a halt.*

There is no obvious explanation for the change in the attitude of Ballista. It goes without saying that northern barbarians are incapable of any consistency. One moment buoyed up with false pride and confidence, they think they can take on the world. The next they are sunk in the deepest despair and will attempt nothing.

It is noteworthy that Ballista now shuns the zealous Flavius Damianus, instead heeding the dilatory local police chief, the eirenarch Corvus. There is a story that the latter was censured by the then governor some years ago for letting seven well-known young Christian men of Ephesus disappear as if the earth had swallowed them alive during the glorious persecution under the divine emperor Decius.

It is on record that Ballista entered the prison just off the civic agora *only accompanied by two of his slaves, and there he talked most amicably with some of the Christian prisoners. What they said is not known.*

For the last two months, Ballista has largely withdrawn from the sight of the public. He ventures out of the palace only to hunt — animals rather than atheists — or, in the fashion of Nero, he goes down to the docks dressed as a labourer to drink with common men in low bars, with only his bodyguard Maximus for company. Men of quality are seldom invited to his table, and likewise it is most infrequent that he dines in the houses of the well born.

It is my sad duty to report that Ballista is neglecting, indeed has failed in the sacred mission entrusted to him by our most noble emperor Valerian. Dominus, if I may be so bold as to make a recommendation? Ballista must be removed from the office of vicarius.

Dominus, you write that over the years my reports on

Marcus Clodius Ballista have blown hot and cold – I can only repeat rather than try to rival the appositeness of your allusion to the divine poetry of Homer: indeed, sometimes I have praised him as the blind poet did Diomedes and sometimes execrated him as Thersites was in the Iliad. *In answer I would remind you of what I said when you were gracious enough to grant me an interview in Antioch before this mission. Consistency must take second place to truthfulness. My loyalty to you and to the emperors means that I must always seek to inform you correctly, even if at times I appear to change my song.*

As the ink dried, the *frumentarius* known as Hannibal read the letter over. Unthinkingly, he rubbed his ribcage, where the rock had hit him during the riot. It might be he had again slightly overdone the northern barbarian references but, overall, he was happy with it. Suggesting a course of action was a risk. *Frumentarii* were merely meant to report. But Censorinus was said to be a man who rewarded initiative. Had not the *Princeps Peregrinorum* himself once been a humble *frumentarius*? The right words at the right moment could lift a man high.

The North African signed the report. He reached for his seal: *MILES ARCANUS.* He would post this report *most urgent.* It should travel along the *cursus publicus* at over a hundred miles a day, twice the normal speed. Marcus Clodius Ballista's days as the *Vicarius* of the Governor of Asia was numbered.

XXII

I keep my vows, thought Ballista. He had kept the vows he had made outside that filthy prison.

He had done the best he could for the Christian woman. Her property, of course, had been confiscated, so Ballista had arranged for she and her son to live on a small, out-of-the-way estate owned by her estranged husband on the island of Samos. Her pagan husband had not been keen on the arrangement – he had wanted his son removed from the atheist influence of the mother – but Ballista had persuaded him: a very young boy needed his mother, and the enmity of a man such as Ballista was not to be entered into lightly.

And the bigger vow – he had kept that too. Maximus and Calgacus had organized the riot to perfection. There were no loose ends. The toughs that Maximus had hired to play the entourage to his Saturnalian king were long gone back to Isauria. The head of the theatre *factio* had no idea that the ugly old man who had paid him so much money was in the *familia* of Ballista. The riot and the threat to public order had provided the excuse needed to suspend the execution of Christians. Corvus had not been part of the plot, but he had needed no persuasion that his Men of the Watch would be better employed guarding against the increasing threat of northern pirates such as the Borani.

Ballista had kept his vows, but it had come at a price. For nearly four months, Ballista had felt like a prisoner himself. Every time he stepped out of the palace he had been assailed by demands from the pagan populace to bring out the Christians – 'Throw them to the lion!', 'Nail the atheists up!', 'Burn them!' Ballista could have ignored that but, on one of his first trips out after posting up the edict suspending the executions, something else had happened. The northerner had been walking down to the Harbour Gymnasium when three more wild-eyed young men had rushed at him. As one, they had yelled, 'I am a Christian and I want to die.' He had had no choice but to arrest them. Now they were languishing in the most unsalubrious gaol near the stadium. Since then, apart from the occasional unavoidable official duty, he had only ventured out of the palace to go hunting up-country with Corvus or, heavily disguised, to go drinking in waterfront bars with Maximus.

Ballista had kept his vows, had put himself and his friends at terrible risk, but for what? What good would it do in the long run? It did not change anything. If anything, his successor would be all the keener to press the persecution with the utmost cruelty. Still, a man has to have a code to live by. And Ballista was not quite finished in Ephesus yet.

He was standing in the shade on the terrace of the palace of the proconsul. The view which usually made his soul sing – the mountains, the sea, the river and the plain, and the mountains again – was completely ignored. Far, far below him was a ship. It looked smaller than one of

Isangrim's toys. It was blue. The distance was much too great to make out the figurehead, but he knew it was the imperial *trireme* the *Providentia*. For five days, since the message had been delivered overland by the *cursus publicus*, he had been waiting for it and the man it carried. At sunrise, he had watched the morning sea breeze waft it into the port of Ephesus.

At moments like this, Ballista thought that his whole life, all thirty-seven winters of it, could be measured by moments waiting to meet someone he did not want to meet: time running too fast in the hall of his father, waiting for the Roman centurion who would escort him as a hostage into the *imperium*; time dragging, Ballista desperate for it to be over, in the camp before Aquileia, before the fatal interview with the emperor Maximinus Thrax; the hurried moments that preceded him being dragged before the man who would have been High King of Hibernia . . .

'A creaking bow, a yawning wolf, a croaking raven' – the words of Calgacus broke into Ballista's recollections – 'the tide on the ebb, new ice, a coiled snake, a bride's pillow talk.'

'My thoughts entirely,' Ballista said dryly.

The old Caledonian gave him a sharp glance. 'You know what I mean. Do not be a fool.'

'I know what you mean.' Ballista smiled. 'A sword with a hairline, a playful bear, the sons of kings – I have not forgotten the words of the Allfather, the things that should not be trusted. Woden knows, as a child I had to listen to you recite them often enough.'

Calgacus leaned on the balustrade next to him. 'More fucking use than that Latin your father had you learn.'

'Maybe.'

'Are you sure you want to do this last thing?'

Ballista nodded.

'It makes the riot look like child's play. If we are caught, it is a *maiestas* trial for us. The family and friends of a convicted traitor suffer too.'

'When I was a child, you taught me a man must have a code to live by,' said Ballista.

'You have heart, boy, I will always give you that.'

'Then you taught me well.'

'Oh aye. You are as stubborn as your father. Anyway, Demetrius has paid off your official staff.' Calgacus smiled. 'He seemed upset to be parted from that North African, Hannibal, the one he is always talking to about the gods. Anyway, all the staff stay here in the palace. They do not know a thing. If it all works out, the others will meet us tonight at the fountain opposite the entrance to the Harbour Baths.'

'Good,' said Ballista. 'Is the man here yet?'

'Aye. Now, remember: say nothing, or as little as you can. "Three angry words are three too many if spoken to a bad man."' Calgacus continued quietly, 'Whatever he says, keep your temper – no matter what he says. Do that and it will be fine.'

'Where is he?'

'I left him to wait a little outside.' Calgacus straightened up. 'Ready?'

'Ready.'

'As I said, keep your temper and it will be fine.' Calgacus left.

The easy, confident step of Quietus paradoxically

343

reminded Ballista of the lameness of the young man's father, Macrianus the elder: the sinister click of the walking stick, the drag of the withered leg, the firm step of the sound one, click, drag, step. Quietus halted about five paces from Ballista. Belatedly, Quietus' entourage scurried out and took up station behind him. In the front rank, Flavius Damianus did not try to hide his delight. The faces of both the *eirenarch* Corvus and Gaius Valerius Festus, the brother of the Christian prisoner Aulus, were inscrutable.

Quietus half turned to assure himself that his audience was in place. Then he turned back to Ballista.

'A sword with a hairline, a playful bear, the sons of kings' – things not to trust, thought Ballista.

'Marcus Clodius Ballista, it is with the utmost sadness that I have to inform you that your term as *Vicarius* to the Proconsul of Asia is over.' From a fold in his elegant toga, Quietus produced a purple, sealed document. 'I have here your orders to return without delay to the imperial palace at Antioch. His sacred majesty Valerian wishes to speak to you.' There was a significant pause. 'No doubt he wishes personally to see that you receive your just recompense for the way you carried out his instructions to purge Ephesus of the atheists.'

'We will do what is ordered, and at every command we will be ready.' Ballista intoned the ritual words without emphasis.

Quietus smiled and produced another document. He flourished it above his head. The ivory and gold case caught in a shaft of spring sunshine. 'Our sacred emperors Valerian and Gallienus and the noble Caesar Saloninus have seen fit to honour me with the post of *Vicarius*. It is with humility and some trepidation that now I take the burden from your shoulders.' Everything about Quietus belied his words.

'We will do what is ordered, and at every command we will be ready,' Ballista repeated.

Again turning to his entourage, Quietus spoke with what he imagined was patrician amiability. 'My friends, it is fitting that Marcus Clodius Ballista and I speak alone, if you allow.' There was an almost unseemly rush to clear the terrace. In moments, only Calgacus remained, standing by the door. A minute nod from Ballista, and the Caledonian followed the others.

Quietus stepped over to Ballista, next to the balustrade. He looked down the steep slope to the theatre, savouring the moment. Then he swung round, bringing his face very close to Ballista's. He spoke fast and angrily. 'You arrogant barbarian piece of shit. Did you really think something like you could attack me, insult my father, in the court-yard of the imperial palace? Demean the *dignitas* of our family in front of a hundred witnesses? Did you think we might forget or forgive? To a true Roman, *dignitas* is more than life itself. We always attain *ultio*, revenge. It is our birthright.'

When Ballista said nothing, Quietus turned, this time letting his gaze roam over the city of Ephesus spread out below them, the city over which he now had power of life and death. Ballista watched him. With one finger, Quietus smoothed his hair. A ring bearing an image of Alexander the Great flashed.

Not deigning to look at the northerner, Quietus contin-ued in a calmer voice. 'My father was annoyed when he discovered I had hired that assassin in Antioch. He said

345

you would be more use to us alive than dead.' He smirked. 'I admit that when my father first told me how he intended to use you in Ephesus, I thought that, for once, he might be mistaken. If there is one thing you northern barbarians are said to be good at, it is massacring women and children, those who cannot resist. I thought you might do well persecuting the Christian scum.' He smiled; a self-satisfied smile. 'But my father is a deep thinker. He knew you had delayed implementing the oath to your army before Circesium so that the Christians in the ranks could escape. He had you followed in Antioch. You were seen in the Street of the Jawbone listening to their weak and treasonous drivel of "Thou shalt not kill."'

Quietus laughed. 'You see, my father realized that, while your sort can kill in hot blood, in the irrational fury of the moment, you could never understand the cold, slow process of true Roman *severitas*. No matter that you dress in a toga, learn Latin, marry a Roman wife, no matter what civilized titles you are given, you will never be a Roman. You will always remain what you were – an ignorant herdsman from the forests of *barbaricum*; a northern barbarian weakened by an irrational sentimentality.'

Leaning back against the balustrade, Quietus again looked into Ballista's eyes. 'My father was right. You did not have the stomach for persecution, you lacked the *disciplina*. Despite doing all you could to hinder the investigations of that useful fool Flavius Damianus, the prisons are full of Christians. Yet you could not bring yourself to kill them. My father sent you here to fail, and you have. Your failure opened the way for my appointment.'

Quietus turned the ring bearing Alexander's likeness on

346

his finger. 'I will not fail. The cells will be empty soon enough. I will kill the Christians in droves, and in the most diverting ways. While I triumph here in Ephesus, you must run back to Antioch in disgrace, like a dog with its tail between its legs, dreading the beating you will surely get.'

Complacently, the young Roman turned in his hands the gilded ivory of his letter of appointment. 'If I were you, I would run back as fast as you can to Antioch. Now that hot-looking wife of yours has whelped another half-breed barbarian bastard, she looks more than ready for fucking again. I am sure the whore will find any number of men to fill her cunt while you are away. If I were there myself . . .'

Forcing himself not to move, anger choking his words, Ballista stared at Quietus – at his weak chin, the pouched eyes, the lascivious mouth. Momentarily, the northerner had a vision – grabbing the voluminous folds of that fucking Roman toga, heaving the venomous little bastard off his feet; one heave and he was over the balustrade, pouched little eyes wide in realization and fear, filthy little mouth open in a despairing scream, arms and legs flailing hopelessly as he scrapped and smashed down the rocky slope and on to the hard, unforgiving stone seats of the theatre.

Ballista mastered himself. *Three angry words are three too many if spoken to a bad man.* Lose control now and it would be the end – of him, of his *familia*, and of the last bold stroke he would pull as he left Ephesus.

Ballista stepped very close. His voice was very low. 'One day, not today, maybe not soon, but one day, I will kill you.'

Involuntarily, Quietus took a step back. Then his fury

brought him up sharp. 'Oh no, you barbarian bastard, one day *I* will kill *you*,' he spat. 'When my father decides your usefulness is at an end. Then I will kill you. I will not need assassins. I will just order your death.'

Ballista laughed in his face.

Quietus' face flushed with rage. 'Laugh while you can, you barbarian cunt. Our beloved emperor Valerian is old. He is a fool. He relies on my father. Valerian's life hangs by a thread. And when that is cut . . .'

Ballista laughed again. 'Valerian has a son. No one would follow a cripple like your father if he seized the throne.'

Now Quietus laughed. 'Gallienus is far away on the Rhine. The east will welcome the dawn of a new golden age when my brother and I are invested in the purple.'

Ballista was shocked. 'Your father is malevolent, but you are mad. When I tell . . .'

'Tell who you like,' Quietus crowed. 'No one will believe you.'

A couple of things surprised the *telones* as he stood in the lamplight outside the customs house on the quay. But it did not show. A customs official of the city of Ephesus, beloved home of great Artemis, had to deploy tact when dealing with the coming and going of the officials of the *imperium*.

It was not in the least surprising that the ex-*vicarius* should sneak away like a thief in the night, and on the very day his successor arrived. He had not done well. Not one incestuous atheist had been burnt for months. Soft-hearted, some said. Barbarians were like women or children, soft-hearted, not fit for man's work. Others whispered worse

348

things. Conversion. The big barbarian had been seen going into the prisons, talking to the atheists alone. It was all too easy to imagine – there, in the gloom, the Christian preachers whispering their seductive, empty platitudes into the witless, childlike ears of a barbarian. Was it not always the children and the women they preyed on first? Whatever, the ex-*vicarius* had not done well. He had not even managed to punish anyone for that disgraceful riot in the stadium, and that breaking out at the *Saturnalia* too.

No, what the *telones* found worthy of comment lay in two other, lesser areas. He had a prosaic mind, filled as it was day to day with bills of landing and counting *amphorae*. This ship, the aptly named *Tyche, The Fortune*. It must have cost an emperor's ransom to hire the big 400-tonner. She was enormous. Gods below, when she had come in laden with grain from Egypt, there had barely been enough water under her keel at the jetty. Why squander money when the ex-*vicarius* could have travelled overland for free with the *cursus publicus*? Still, there was no explaining the whims of rich barbarians, or high Roman officials either, come to that.

And then there was the staff. The *telones* had been on duty that day last year when the ex-*vicarius* had arrived. Seventeenth day of August it had been, the festival of the *Portunalia*. And a serious nuisance too, him turning up on the day of the dock-hands' traditional holiday. The *telones* had a good memory, it was vital in his line of work. Not like most of the young men these days, hardly remember their own names, buggered if they were going to work on the *Portunalia*. But he had been there that night, keeping the drunks away from the official reception, standing at a respectful distance, listening to what he could hear of the speeches. Flavius Damianus, now there was a proper *eupatrid*: loved his *Polis*, openhanded, honoured the gods, could make a fine speech, maybe not as fluent as they said his ancestor the great sophist had been, but he had been on form that night, the high Attic pouring out of him like wine from a jug. The *telones* remembered it like yesterday. And what had struck him was that the big barbarian travelled light, no more than fifteen, twenty at most staff and *familia* lined up behind him. But watching them go on board just now, hoods up, muffled against the chill of a spring evening, there must have been at least twice as many. It was odd, since rumour had it that, in the seven months he had been in Ephesus, the ex-*vicarius* had not bought so much as one bum boy.

The *telones* watched as the *Tyche* slipped her mooring. He had said nothing when the ex-*vicarius* had come to hand over the customary tip, just wished him a safe voyage. Only a fool got mixed up in the doings of those connected to the imperial court. This Ballista might be under a cloud now, but who could tell what the future held? Like Ixion bound to his wheel, one moment these people were down in the depths of disgrace, the next they were carried aloft on the emperors' favour. If you thought about it, the whole story of Ixion was a warning not to stick your prick where it was not wanted. Ixion had been eating at the table of the king of the gods himself, then he tried to fuck Zeus' wife and, before he knew it, he was spending eternity bound to a fiery wheel. No, the *telones* had not said anything then, and he was not going to in the future.

* * *

It was a fine night: a bite to the air, a myriad stars wheeling overhead. Ballista watched as Maximus made his way to the stern of the *Tyche*. In the near dark, the tip of the Hibernian's bitten-off nose was strangely white against the deep tan of his face. They stood together in silence for a time, looking at the famous fifty lamps of Ephesus that lit the road up from the docks to the theatre slip away astern.

'The gaoler?' Ballista asked.

'Safely on a ship bound for Ostia, a big purse of our money at his belt, dreaming happy dreams of a new life in the eternal city. Sure, no one will ever find him in Rome. It is a city of strangers.'

The *Tyche* was nearing the harbour mouth. Ballista looked to his right. Mimicking the stars above, there were lights from thousands of houses climbing the lower slopes of the mountain higher up, the dark outcrops of limestone loomed.

'Still, it's all a horrible risk, even worse than organizing a riot,' said Maximus.

'Yes, but what can you do?'

'Maybe not feel you have to play the hero all the time.'

'Only partly the hero. It is only the gaol by the civic *agora*.'

'Gods below, don't you start brooding about the others.'

The sailors shipped the huge sweeps that had propelled the *Tyche* out of the harbour. The sails were sheeted home, and the great roundship heeled as they filled. Soon the water was singing down her side and a phosphorescent wake stretching behind.

Ballista took a last look at Ephesus and turned to Maximus. 'You might as well tell them they can come back on deck. Remind them: if they talk to the crew they are pilgrims going to worship at the famous shrine of Helios on Rhodes.'

'You always had a bad sense of humour. The equestrian one was saying he wanted to talk to you.'

'Oh, good,' said Ballista.

Aulus Valerius Festus, member of the *Boule* of Ephesus, knight of Rome and condemned Christian, was not a natural sailor. Gripping one hand hold after another, he stumbled precariously across the sloping deck to Ballista.

'On behalf of my brothers and sisters in Christ, I wish to thank you.'

'"I am a Christian, and I want to die,"' said Ballista. 'You do not seem to share that view.'

'It is written in the Gospels that our Lord Jesus Christ said, 'When they persecute you in one town, flee you into another.''

'The ones who volunteered for martyrdom must have missed that passage.' Ballista gave no time for a reply. 'We will drop you in Rhodes. It is a busy port. You and the others can take passage from there where you will.'

'One of our priests, a most learned and holy man called Origen – he joined Christ in paradise not long ago, during the persecution of the late emperor Decius – wrote that those pagans in authority who help Christians might not be irrevocably damned to hell. He considered the prayers of the faithful might rescue them. I will pray for you.'

Ballista rounded on him, eyes flashing. 'I do not need your prayers. I did not do it for you. I did not do it for your Christians from that gaol.'

Involuntarily, Aulus took a step back, and grabbed a rope to recover his balance. 'Then . . . why?'

'I do not know; something compelled me. Maybe it was *hubris*, that vice of the Greeks, a pride that expresses itself in humbling others. Maybe I wanted to prove to myself that I am a better man than you and your Christians, or the emperor and his courtiers.'

Aulus looked doubly shocked.

Ballista laughed at his discomfort. He looked up at the expanse of pale canvas and the stars above. 'Maybe *philanthropia*, love of mankind. My wife gave birth to my second son at the end of last year. I have not seen him yet. I hope there is enough love in my heart to love him as I love his brother. When I see him, I am sure I will.'

'I am sure you will.'

Ballista looked at Aulus as if surprised to find him still there. 'And how do you know my soul?'

'I can tell you are a good man.'

Ballista reached out to touch the backstay of the ship. It was taut. The Egyptian sailing master of the *Tyche* knew what he was about. 'If I became a Christian, and a man such as I was until today, a man with *imperium*, arrested me, tortured me, confiscated my property, and burned me, what would become of my sons?'

'God's love would provide for them. And I am sure the local Christian community would help. We are commanded to give to the needy.' Aulus' words were charged with an unlikely hope.

'You think it would be right for me to put my love of your unnamed and unknowable god above my natural love for my sons, my wife, family and friends?'

'The love of God must be above all. If you cared, I could instruct you in the ways of the Lord. I could help you on the path to conversion.'

Ballista laughed, a short, mocking laugh. 'You do not understand. Any religion that demands its followers love a distant, probably imaginary god more than those they should love – their family, friends; above all, their children – is cruel and inhuman. So, you see, I do not think I am the sort to convert to your crucified god. As far as I can tell, the ideal adherent of your cult is an ill-educated, half-starved virgin, not much given to independent thought but especially keen on self-harm.'

'I will pray for you.'

'If, as you say, your god is all-knowing, why would he need guidance from you? But do as you want. I suppose it cannot do any harm. Now, if you would not mind leaving me. There is a long journey ahead, but I want to think about my return home.'

XXIII

The baby was lying on the threshold of the house. Ballista was not surprised. There had been a message waiting for him when he landed at Seleuceia. In it, Julia had told him what she intended. The small figure lying there did not surprise him, but he still felt deeply shocked. It looked so much as if the child had been abandoned, left to die. Ballista had never got used to the custom of the Romans, and the Greeks, too, of exposing unwanted children. Wherever you went in the *imperium*, all too often you saw them – on the steps of temples, at crossroads, even on dung heaps, the pathetic little bundles of humanity wailing for a mother and father who would not return. It was not the way of Ballista's people. In Germania, all children were raised. *And they have the audacity to call us barbarians*, thought the northerner.

As Ballista walked across, the baby kicked its feet in the air before thumping its tiny heels down on the mat. Good. Julia had at least respected his instructions that the child was not to be swaddled. Ballista remembered the epic struggle when he had said that Isangrim was not to be swaddled. Julia had been horrified. All Roman infants were tightly wrapped. It was the way to ensure they grew straight and true. But Ballista had been adamant. In Germania, children were not constricted. Nobleman or slave, they started naked and free on the same floor. How else did his people develop the strength of limb and tall stature which even the Romans admired? No son of his would be swaddled. Eventually, Julia had given way on this. But on feeding at the breast she was immovable. A wet nurse had been hired for Isangrim as now one had been for the new child. It was the custom of the Roman elite, and it was her body. Ballista had found no answer to her double argument.

The big northerner went down on one knee and looked into the face of his new son. Huge, dark-blue eyes looked back. Long, black eyelashes. The first, light-blond curls. The tiny boy gurgled quietly. Ballista found himself softly cooing back. He felt a strange hollowness in his chest. He went to pick up his new son, then stopped. It was ridiculous. Isangrim was only seven, but Ballista was struggling to remember how to hold a baby. You had to support the head. Gently, very gently, he slid his large, scarred right hand beneath the boy, spreading his fingers to hold the head and shoulders. His left hand under the boy's bottom, Ballista rose to his feet and raised the innocent child in his man-killing hands. The baby wriggled, not unhappily. Ballista kissed the top of his head, smelling that distinctive, clean-baby smell.

Ballista looked up. He took in the laurel wreaths on the door, the benches in the street laden with food, the crowd of onlookers.

'This is my son, Lucius Clodius Dernhelm.'

There was applause. Then three men emerged from the

crowd and walked to the house. The door was shut. The first man carried an axe. He lifted it above his head. He struck the door. Wood splintered. He freed the axe and stepped back. The second man carried a pestle. He, too, struck the door. There was a dull thud. The third man had a broom. Ceremoniously, he swept the threshold.

After Isangrim's birth, Ballista had asked the meaning of this ritual. He had received various answers. It was the stages of first life: cutting the umbilical, checking for soundness, cleansing. It was to scare away evil daemons. Ballista suspected the Romans had no real notion. It was just something they did.

Demetrius was next to Ballista. He handed over a golden pendant containing a protective amulet. Ballista slipped the cord around Dernhelm's neck. Fat little fists closed on the *bulla*. Ballista smiled as the boy tried to cram the thing into his mouth and eat it.

As was only right, the friends of the new father approached in order of status to pay their respects. Solemnly, the General Tacitus intoned a prayer of thanks to the goddesses of childbirth, Juno Lucina and Diana Lucifera, for bringing the boy safely into the light. The close-cropped head of Aurelian bent over the infant. He prayed for Sol Invictus to hold his hands over the child. Straightening up a little unsteadily, he announced that the boy looked tough; he would make his father proud when he came to take his place in the battle line. Turpio asked to take the boy. For once, his smile was not sardonic. His ostentatious Persian bracelet flashing, Turpio held the boy up and began to recite in Greek.

As your first little gifts, child, nature herself
Will give trailing ivy, berries,
Lilies of the Nile mixed with bright acanthus.
At milking time the goats will troop home on their own,
The herds will not fear the majesty of the lion;
Your cradle itself will grow flowers to gentle you.

There were fewer well-wishers than there might have been. It was common knowledge that Ballista's mission to Ephesus had not worked out well. Not everyone around the imperial court wished to be too closely associated with a man who might be out of favour with the emperor. This part of the proceedings was soon over.

Julia came forward and, as a Roman *matrona* should, formally welcomed the return of her husband. By her side was Isangrim. His face was reserved. As he clearly had been schooled to do, he equally formally greeted his *dominus*. Ballista felt a stab of irritation. He had never liked the way senatorial families such as his wife's wanted sons to refer to their fathers as *Dominus*.

Ballista handed his new son to Julia. He knelt down and opened his arms for Isangrim to embrace him. With a quick glance at his mother and only the slightest hesitation, the boy stepped forward and let his father hug him. Ballista buried his face in the boy's blond curls, breathing in the smell he loved so much.

After a time, Ballista leaned back. Isangrim regarded him steadily. Ballista took a purse from his belt. He opened it and showed the contents to the boy. It contained the dried, crumbled remains of a leaf. Isangrim made no reaction. Ballista reached behind himself, and Demetrius placed a package in his hand. Ballista gave it to his son. Isangrim unwrapped it, and his face split into an enormous smile. He lunged forward and hugged his father close. Laughing with unalloyed pleasure, he thanked his papa for the best present ever. He disengaged himself and drew the miniature sword. He swung it this way and that through the air, only pausing to admire the sunlight playing on the colours in the steel.

Ballista took Dernhelm back from Julia and nestled him on his shoulder. Standing on the threshold, he gave his permission for the feast to begin. There was a cheer. The majority of the crowd surged forward to the benches. Soon, stable boys jostled with gardeners and all types of tradesmen rubbed elbows with porters in a good-natured crush to get their hands on the rare treat of cooked meats and honey cakes, to drink the health of the new child in free wine.

Ballista led the invited into the house. In the *atrium*, a couch was set for the gods of infants, Picumnus and Pilumnus, choice foods on a table close at hand. Near the *lectisternium*, a small fire burned on a portable altar. It was all well done, yet Ballista thought it was eccentric of Julia not only to have combined the ceremonies of the raising of the infant and the naming but to have postponed both until his return. She had not even registered Dernhelm's birth and, strictly speaking, in legal terms that should have been done within thirty days of the birth. Still, it was typical of her. She had always been strong-willed, with a streak of unconventionality. He thought they were probably useful attributes for a senator's daughter married off to a man of his barbarian origins.

The human guests were distributed around the two

dining rooms opening on to the *atrium*. With Julia and his two sons, Ballista toured the tables, passing a few polite words with the man on each couch. That done, they took their places, and the food and drink were produced.

Julia sat on an upright chair next to Ballista's couch. She looked the very model of old-fashioned, wifely decorum: polite and attentive, but distant. Barely a drop of wine passed her lips. Ballista made much of his sons. He talked to the chief guests. As ever, Tacitus ate little, nibbling at morsels of bread sprinkled with salt or the odd lettuce leaf. He drank even less. Aurelian made up for him. A whole pheasant was washed down with heroic quantities of red wine. Turpio also ate well, but with more refinement. For a man risen from the ranks, he had exquisite manners. He enlivened his conversation with apt quotations from the more recent poets. Unconsciously, he toyed with the golden ornament on his wrist.

The feast ran on. Looking over at Julia, so very close yet so very far away, Ballista wished it was over. In the end, it was.

Together, the husband and wife said goodbye to their guests. Julia sent the children off with their nurses and dismissed the servants. Then she took Ballista's hand and led him to their bedroom. They made love as they had when they first met.

Afterwards, Julia got up and poured them another drink. Naked in the lamplight, she brought the cups to their bed. A demure Roman wife would have extinguished the lamps. Yes: there was much to be said for her unconventionality.

Propped on one elbow, Ballista told her what had happened to him in Ephesus and what he had done. He told it without elaboration: how he had come to hate the persecution; how he had organized the riot which provided him with the excuse of public order to suspend the executions; how he had arranged the escape of the Christians from the prison by the state *agora*. As exactly as he could remember them, he told her the treasonous words of Quietus. He told her how he intended to go to Valerian and tell him of the plot of Macrianus.

She listened without interrupting. She remained silent when he had finished. For a moment he thought it would be all right.

'You fool!' Her face was tight with anger. 'You stupid, barbarian fool!'

Ballista said nothing.

'What are these Christians to you? Ignorant, superstitious atheists! You would endanger my sons to help undeserving filth like that? If you were found guilty of treason, your family would suffer. At best, the *familia* of a man convicted of *maiestas* is reduced to poverty, and at worst . . .' She let the words hang, then again snapped, 'Barbarian fool!'

Ballista felt his anger rising. These fucking Romans. Always ready with the 'barbarian' insult. Even Julia. Well, the emperor Pupienus had given Ballista Roman citizenship for killing a tyrant while, all those three hundred or so years ago, Julius Caesar had given Julia's distant ancestor Gaius Julius Volcatius Gallicanus the same for helping enslave his fellow Gauls. Volcatius Gallicanus – the man from the Volcae Arecomici tribe of Gaul. The founder of Julia's noble house had been a long-haired barbarian from the north. The thought calmed Ballista.

'What should I do about Macrianus' plot to elevate his sons to the purple?' Ballista hoped the change of subject would divert her anger. It did not.

'What plot? It is just the stupid words of a stupid, pampered youth. There is no plot.'

'I think it is real. I must warn Valerian.'

Julia snorted with derision. 'And do you think you will just walk up to the palace, see Valerian on his own, and convince him his most trusted friend, his *Comes Sacrarum Largitionum*, is plotting to overthrow him? After all these years, how can even a northern barbarian be so naive? No one gets to see the emperor without Macrianus' permission.'

'I think it is real. I must do something.'

Julia swept her hand dismissively. The cup, forgotten in her grip, slopped wine on to the coverlet. 'You can do nothing. If you were out of Valerian's favour after Circesium, now you will be in deep disgrace for your complete failure in Ephesus – even if no one comes forward to inform against you.' She stood up, put down the cup and pulled a robe round herself. She walked to the door. She turned. 'I will go to the palace tomorrow and register the birth of our son. If I were you, I would keep well out of the way of the emperor and his court. And well out of mine.' She left.

Ballista did not move. What was it that old Republican senator had said? *Given the nature of women, the married state is almost intolerable, but being a bachelor is worse –* something on those lines. If it was not for the boys . . . But Ballista's anger was not deep, little more than a reaction to Julia's. It was slipping away already.

Clearly, no one was going to believe that Macrianus was

plotting for his sons to take the throne. Equally, just going uninvited to Valerian and telling him his most trusted friend was going to betray him was not a good idea. Ballista took a drink. He looked at the crumpled bed. He wondered how long Julia's anger would last.

Comes Augusti

(Spring AD 260)

'Who is this with the white crest that leads the army's van?'

– Julian, *De Caesaribus* 313B; quoting
Euripides, *Phoenissae* 120

XXIV

As everyone was ignoring him, Ballista studied the swan. It had been caught down by the river a couple of months earlier, just after the long-awaited announcement of the Persian expedition. The swan had been brought up to the temple of Zeus in the main *agora* of Antioch. Although its wings had not been clipped, it had not flown away. Instead, it passed its days strutting around the sacred precinct. Zeus had changed into a swan to seduce Leda. That a bird so associated with the king of the gods should make its home in his temple was generally taken as a good omen for the forthcoming war.

Certainly, a good omen was welcome. There had been others; they had all been bad. Up at Daphne, from a clear sky a violent wind had torn down several of the sacred cypress trees – the trees, thought Ballista, which Isangrim had said he would chop down. Although he had not been present, the northerner had been told that, during the last meeting of the emperor's *consilium*, the huge beams of cedar that supported the palace roof had groaned like souls in torment. At the same moment, in the outer hall, the statue of the deified emperor Trajan, that great conqueror of the east, had dropped the orb which signified mastery of the world.

Among the superstitious, there was talk of the birth of a horribly deformed child.

Undoubtedly, the swan was welcome. It was a fine-looking bird. Ballista sadly thought of farmers in the *imperium* sowing shut the eyelids of swans so that, in their darkness, they would fatten better. As the number of men in the precinct increased, the majestic bird removed itself to behind the open-air altar.

A hand touched Ballista's elbow. He turned to see the close-cropped head of Aurelian. Beyond him was the sardonic face of Turpio. It was good that not everyone had disowned him. It had been a bad nine months since he came back from Ephesus. Until today, no summons had come from the imperial palace. Instead, after a few days, a praetorian had hammered on the door demanding Ballista hand over his letter of appointment as *Vicarius* to the Governor of Asia. After that, Ballista had been ignored. Julia had persuaded her husband that he should not petition the emperor for permission to leave Antioch and return to their home in Sicily. It was best to keep the lowest of profiles. Following her outburst on his return, Julia's temper had cooled, her practical nature reasserting itself, but a slight strain remained. The worst of it was that she still did not believe that Macrianus the Lame was plotting against Valerian. None of the few that Ballista had told did: not Aurelian nor Turpio, not even Maximus or Calgacus. They all readily accepted what Quietus had said, but they all put it down to the wild temper of a petulant youth. Just as no one would allow a cripple such as Macrianus on the throne, so no one would follow two spoilt brats such as his sons Quietus and Macrianus the Younger if they seized the purple. Besides, Julia added, their father was of the basest origins.

Ballista watched the courtyard filling up with the good and great of the *imperium*, the high commanders who would travel with Valerian to the east. He wondered why he had been recalled. His friends and *familia* argued that, at such a time, an experienced commander who had faced the Sassanids in the field was not to be overlooked. He was not so sure. What was it Quietus had said? 'When my father decides your usefulness is at an end, then I will kill you.' Silently, Ballista made a vow. Far from being useful to Macrianus the Lame, he would do everything he could to put a stop to the plot of the sinister *Comes Largitionum*. The northerner had no great love for Valerian, but he would not stand by and watch the elderly emperor overthrown. There had been too many coups, too many insurrections; they weakened the very fabric of the *imperium*. And, one day – maybe not on this campaign, maybe not even soon, but one day – he would kill Macrianus' repulsive son Quietus. *Allfather, Woden-born as I am, hear my vow.*

The booming voice of a herald announced the most sacred Augustus Publius Licinius Valerian, Pontifex Maximus, Pater Patriae, Germanicus Maximus, Invictus, Restitutor Orbis. As the sonorous titles rang out, every man in the precinct performed *proskynesis*. Stretched out on the ground, Ballista watched the small procession. Valerian looked old, his step infirm. As ever in public these days, he was flanked not just by Successianus, the praetorian prefect, but also by the *Comes Largitionum*. Click went Macrianus' walking stick; his lame foot dragged; his sound one took a step. Click, drag, step; click, drag, step.

The imperial fire on its small altar was ceremoniously placed in front of the great altar of Zeus. The audience got to their feet. Out of sight, the swan hissed.

Valerian intoned a prayer to Zeus, let the king of the gods look favourably on the expedition, let him hold his hands over the army. The emperor's voice was high, reedy. At one point he seemed to lose his way. He looked to Macrianus. The *Comes Largitionum* nodded and smiled encouragingly, as one would to a child.

As priests brought fire to the great altar, the swan emerged. Its little black eyes regarded them with suspicion. Then it began to run, its wide wings beating. It took to the air. The front row of dignitaries cowered as it swept over their heads, the wind of its passing ruffling their hair and the folds of their togas.

The swan soared up to the height of the cornice of the temple. Then, stretching out its long neck, it circled the sacred building. As it flew, it sang, a low, mournful warble. After its third circuit, it climbed higher. The spring sunshine played through the feathers at the back of its huge wings. It turned and, following the line of the main street, flew out over the Beroea Gate and away to the east.

As everyone silently watched the dwindling shape, Macrianus seized the moment. He pointed after the swan with his walking stick. 'Behold,' he shouted, his voice resolute, 'a sign! The piety of our beloved emperor is rewarded. The gods approve. Zeus himself leads the way!'

Men cheered. They shook back their togas and applauded. Some prostrated themselves. Others literally jumped for joy. 'Zeus leads the way!' 'Zeus leads the way!'

Amidst the jubilant throng, Ballista stood silent. For sure

it looked like a sign from the gods. But a sign of what? The swan, the bird from Zeus' precinct, had flown without them. Of its own choice, it had flown away to the east, away towards Shapur, the King of Kings.

Turpio, newly raised to equestrian rank and appointed *Praefectus Castrorum* of the imperial field army, sat on his horse and looked at his special area of responsibility. The baggage train stretched for miles. On paper, the army was seventy thousand strong, fighting men drawn from all over the *imperium*. How big the baggage train was, no one knew. Turpio guessed it was at least half as big again. It contained every type of wagon and cart, every breed of draught animal – horses, mules, donkeys, camels – slaves, numberless merchants offering all sorts of goods: drink, food, weapons, glimpses of the future, their own bodies or those of others.

The unwieldy tail of the army straggled about in no sort of order. Turpio had been given just one unit of Dalmatian cavalry, nominally five hundred men, in reality not much over three hundred, to keep them in line.

Still, the journey so far had gone reasonably well. They had marched in easy stages from Antioch, via Hagioupolis and Regia, to reach the Euphrates at Zeugma. Now they were moving north, the mighty river off to their right, up to Samosata. Until they arrived there, they should be safe enough within the borders of the *imperium*.

When they crossed the Euphrates at Samosata, things would be very different. Then they would face the eastern horde. Shapur had taken the field in early spring. The King of Kings had divided his army and was besieging the towns of Edessa and Carrhae in Mesopotamia. The Roman plan was very simple. A detachment under the ex-consul Valens had remained in Zeugma to prevent any Sassanid attempt to move west and invade the provinces of Syria. Another sizable detachment, under the *Comes Largitionum* Macrianus, would stay in Samosata to likewise block the road north to the provinces of Asia Minor. The remainder of the field army, the aged emperor Valerian at its head, would advance south-east from Samosata. If Shapur wished to take Edessa and Carrhae, he must stand and fight.

The plan was straightforward, but Turpio did not think it was good. Carrhae was not a good place for Romans. Long ago, the army of Crassus had been annihilated there; thousands of legionaries were left dead, thousands more marched off to end their days in oriental captivity. Old Crassus himself had been decapitated, his head used as a stage prop in a production of Euripides' *Bacchae*. Much more recently, in Turpio's childhood, the emperor Caracalla had been killed near there. Riding to the temple of Sin, the moon god, he had dismounted to relieve himself. He had been crouched, trousers round his ankles, when the assassins had come for him. An inglorious death.

And it was more than just the ill-omened name of Carrhae that gave Turpio pause for thought. The army was in little better order than its baggage train. Valerian seemed to lack the will to impose *disciplina*. There were no regular roll calls, no athletic competitions for the men, no training manoeuvres for the units. If the silver-haired emperor did not impose better order by the time the army marched out of Samosata, disaster beckoned.

From his position on the edge of the bluff, Turpio surveyed the line of march. Below and in front of him, the road crossed the river Marsyas, a tributary of the Euphrates. There was a fine stone bridge. It was wide enough for ten men abreast, but it was a bottleneck for an army of this size. It had taken three days for the majority of the fighting men to cross. The gods alone knew how long it would take the bloated baggage train. As he looked, Turpio saw the huge, purple, sail-like flags that marked the personal baggage of the emperor edging through the crush towards the lip of the bridge. Off to the left, just in front of a stand of eucalyptus trees, a group of Arab nomads watched. Wherever you went in this part of the world, the tent-dwellers appeared from nowhere. They would stand and watch, completely impassive. Usually, they had their herds with them, children running about. But these were just a dozen or so men, standing still, watching.

As Turpio tiredly ran a hand over his face, the gold ring, the symbol of his new membership of the equestrian order, flashed. He turned it this way and that, noting how well it matched the golden bangle he had taken from Shapur's tent, taking pleasure in both of them. He had risen far from being a humble legionary. But he was not going to let it go to his head. Worldly success was transient. A poem came into his head:

> For mortals, mortal things. And all things leave us.
> Or if they do not, then we leave them.

Nice lines, fitting. Their author, Lucian, had been born in Samosata.

Down by the bridge, Turpio could make out the big figure of Ballista. Turpio felt intensely sorry for his friend.

Nine months in the wilderness, then recalled to the standards and given the humiliating post of deputy to the *Praefectus Castrorum*, deputy to his own ex-subordinate. Turpio thought Ballista may well be right that it was a deliberate slight engineered by Macrianus the elder. Not that Turpio believed the northerner's theory that the *Comes Sacrorum Largitionum* was plotting to overthrow Valerian. Whatever Quietus had shouted in Ephesus was just the juvenile outburst of a spoilt brat. The oily Quietus may have returned to court in something approaching triumph after his inventive massacring of Christians, but no one would stand him or his pampered brother on the throne of the Caesars any more than they would stand the old cripple of a father. Turpio knew that Ballista was hurt that even those closest to him did not give his theory any credence. Still, the northerner was bearing everything stoically. Turpio would do everything he could to make his position as least embarrassing as possible. Worldly success was transient.

Movement to the left of the bridge caught Turpio's eye. More Arabs were coming out of the trees. They were mounted, leading more horses. Those standing were swinging up into the saddle. They were all kicking on towards the bridge. They had spears and bows. There were at least twenty of them. Gods below, the camel-fuckers were raiding the baggage.

Turpio gathered his cloak in one hand and held it above his head, the army signal for enemy in sight. He roared a warning. No one in the jostling throng by the bridge noticed.

*   *   *

Although it was a mild spring day, Ballista was sweating heavily. His voice was hoarse from shouting orders. Which was the more bone-headedly recalcitrant, a camel or an imperial porter?

'Get those fucking wagons in line astern.'

Faces looked at him with incomprehension or dumb insolence. So this was what it had come to: the son of the warleader of the Angles, a Roman *Dux*, reduced to little better than a porter himself. Ballista realized his post as deputy to the *Praefectus Castrorum* was a deliberate slight. Still, if Macrianus thought injured pride would cause Ballista to slip up, he was mistaken.

'You there, with the emperor's charger, go next. You, with the imperial chariot, hold back here near me. The rest of you, with the wagons, wait over there where you are. There is only width on the bridge for one of you at a time.' His voice was almost lost in the braying of animals and shouting of men. The nearest wagon driver was not paying the least attention. He was looking over the northerner's head. Ballista filled his lungs to curse him. The man dived over the far side of the wagon. Something thumped into the wood next to Ballista. Shrill yells filled the air.

Ballista turned. An arrow was coming straight at him. He leapt sideways. The arrow missed by a hand's breadth. There were about twenty Arabs, mounted, armed, closing fast. He looked around. Chaos everywhere. Baggage handlers screaming, running, some trying to hide under wagons, others throwing themselves over the parapet of the bridge. A couple of Dalmatian cavalrymen, dismounted like himself, were nearby, standing open-mouthed. He roared at them to form up on him. They shuffled either side of him. The three men were without helmets, armour or shields. Ballista drew his sword and wrapped his black cloak around his left arm. He missed Maximus at his side. Typical of the Hibernian to choose this moment to go and see to their horses.

The tent-dwellers sheered off to either side. They had no intention of fighting armed men if they were not forced. They were intent on plunder and the easy pleasure of killing the unresisting. Just to Ballista's right, by the columns that marked the start of the bridge, half a dozen raiders surrounded the purple, gem-encrusted chariot and its four almost snow-white horses. The groom who had been too slow to flee was cut down. One of the Arabs jumped into the chariot. He was gathering the reins.

Calling for the Dalmatians to follow, Ballista ran to the chariot. An Arab spun his horse, jabbed his spear. Ballista sidestepped, caught the shaft in his left hand and tugged. The rider was yanked forward, half out of the saddle. Ballista brought his sword down on his skull. It cracked like the shell of a snail. Blood and brains splashed hot in Ballista's face.

Ducking under the hooves of the rearing horse, Ballista vaulted up into the chariot. Wrestling with the reins, the Arab did not see him coming. Ballista thrust the point of his sword into the driver's back. He twisted the blade, withdrew it, the man screamed and toppled out sideways. The battle-trained pale grey horses stood motionless.

Ballista turned. He was alone. The Dalmatian cavalrymen were gone, swallowed up in the melee. The northerner was surrounded by four mounted raiders. They would fight now. They wanted revenge for their slaughtered kinsmen.

For a few moments, the five men and eight horses were a still point in the eye of the storm.

Ballista sensed as much as saw the Arab over his left shoulder throw his spear. He swivelled and, gripping his sword two-handed, batted the missile away, inches from his face. He spun through 360 degrees. The other three did not move.

The one who had thrown his spear unslung his bow. He pulled an arrow from his quiver. He grinned. The others were grinning, their teeth very white in their long, dark beards. The bowman notched the arrow. He drew the bow. One of the others laughed.

Out of the confusion, a Dalmatian soldier launched himself at the bow-armed Arab. With no fuss, the raider shot him through the chest. The soldier staggered back. Hands clutching uselessly at the black-feathered shaft, he fell.

There was a surge of noise. Another tent-dweller galloped up. In a high, urgent voice, he yelled at the men facing Ballista. They hesitated. The newcomer yelled again, turning his own horse back the way they had come. Reluctantly, the others booted their mounts and, shouting over their shoulders what were threats in any language, raced after him.

A small body of cavalry headed by Turpio appeared from the left and thundered after the raiders. There was little likelihood it would catch them.

All around Ballista was utter chaos: dead and dying men and beasts; clouds of dust; deafening noise. Up on the bridge proper, Valerian's war horse was rearing and plunging. The groom hanging on its back was incapable of controlling the maddened stallion. There was a vicious crimson gash along the animal's flank. A stable lad ran to try to grab its bridle. With a wild eye, the charger span away on its hind legs. It bucked. Reared up again. And then, almost too quickly to be comprehended, it jumped clean over the parapet.

With a resounding splash, horse and groom vanished beneath the waters of the Marsyas.

XXV

Almost all the men arriving at the imperial headquarters in Samosata had either neatly sewn little bags of herbs or perfume-drenched rolls of material wedged in their ears and pushed up their noses. They were very frightened. Some of those invited to the emperor's *consilium* actually rattled, they wore so many protective amulets.

Turpio had been no more concerned than most when it started. A couple of days after the army had crossed the Marsyas river, the camp dogs had started dying. No one had given it much thought. As they marched north, the turquoise waters of the Euphrates on their right, the strangely flat-topped grey cliffs to their left and again on the other side of the river, it spread to the baggage animals. By the time they were following the great river to the east, some of the Moorish light cavalry were complaining of an eye infection. Within twenty-four hours, those affected were so disorientated they seemed not to recognize their closest companions. They began to vomit and suffer uncontrollable diarrhoea. Then the dreadful pustules appeared. Men from other units began to be struck down, too. The line of march was marked by hastily dug graves. By the time the army reached Samosata, no one talked of anything else. Plague is a terrible thing. The first part of the prediction of Appian, the Christian martyr of Ephesus, had come true.

Turpio paused for a moment to get his breath back after the steep climb to the citadel. In front of him was the residence of the Roman governor of the province of Commagene, which Valerian had taken over as his campaign headquarters. Once, it had been the palace of the independent kings of Commagene. It was a strange building, made of diamond-patterned small blocks of limestone. Over the gate was a newly cut inscription: 'Phoebus, the unshorn god, keep off the plague's dark onset.'

Turpio took a deep breath and moved on. His nose and ears were unplugged, but that was not because he was unafraid. Coming up through the town, he had hurriedly walked a block out of his way when he heard the bells of the *libitinarii*, the carriers-out of the dead, in the street ahead. He was very scared. But he had always had a particularly acute sense of smell. Strong-smelling herbs or perfume in his nostrils, or even in his ears, would have been insufferable.

The throne and dais at the end of the basilica were unoccupied so far. Below them, the *consilium* was filling up. One man was standing with a space around him. Turpio hesitated. A man of prudence might not choose to stand with Ballista. The loss of the imperial charger under the waters of the Marsyas had deepened the impression that the northerner was out of imperial favour.

Turpio walked over and stood next to Ballista. They nodded to each other. Now the plague had struck, no one embraced. Turpio ignored the covert glances of the others.

When Turpio and Ballista first met, the northerner could have had him executed for corruption. Instead, Ballista had promoted him, had given him his trust. Now Turpio knew it was his turn to show *fides*, good faith. Besides, Turpio liked the man. The big northerner had never asked how it was that Turpio had come to be blackmailed. Not that Turpio would have told him; that secret would go to the grave with him. But it was good of the man not to ask.

The basilica was hung everywhere with swags of laurel, that sure preventative of plague. Its pervasive odour formed the base to a riot of other scents. Turpio felt slightly nauseous. The Danubian Aurelian joined Turpio and Ballista. Since Tacitus had been posted to the west, they were the only two that stood with the northerner.

A herald announced the emperor Valerian. The *principes*, the leading men of the *imperium*, dipped their faces to the floor in respect. Turpio noticed that the floor had not been properly swept. There were no charms or sweet-smelling prophylactics on the person of Valerian. His courage had never been in question. But he looked old and frail. As he made his way down the aisle, he held the arm of Macrianus. Click-drag-step. Click-drag-step. It would take little imagination, thought Turpio, to see it as an omen: the aged seeking support from the infirm.

When the imperial party had ascended the dais, the members of the *consilium* rose to their feet and shouted ritual acclamations of good health that went on a long time.

Eventually, Valerian cleared his throat and began to speak in a voice that seemed to struggle for breath. 'Far-shooting Phoebus Apollo has sent his plague arrows amongst us. Rumours run through the camp. Some talk of the past. A hundred years ago. A shadowy temple in Babylonia. A golden casket wrenched open by Roman soldiers. An evil released on the *imperium*. Superstitious nonsense!' He paused. 'Some talk of the present. Criminals at dead of night. Flitting through the dark. Poisoned needles in hand. Bringing death to the unsuspecting. All nonsense! Superstitious nonsense!

'The real explanation of this evil is at hand.' The old emperor looked fondly, almost devotedly, at Macrianus. 'Christians! Our orders for persecution have not been implemented with true religious zeal. The gods punish us, Phoebus Apollo unleashes his arrows on us, because still we let many of these atheists live.' Valerian's voice began to fill out with an almost youthful vigour.

'All this will change tomorrow. Through the piety of our devoted friend Macrianus and the diligence of the head of the *frumentarii*, Censorinus, those disgusting atheists here in Samosata have been apprehended. There are many of them. Men and women. Tomorrow they will burn. Their ashes will be scattered to the four winds.'

A wistful look came into the emperor's eyes. 'All will be well. Long-haired Apollo will turn aside his bow. The kindly gods will hold their hands over us again. Our subjects will behold in the broad plains the crops already ripe with waving ears of corn, the meadows brilliant with plants and flowers, the weather temperate and mild. The strength of our arms will return. The Persian reptiles will flee before us. United we will conquer. Let us rejoice. Through our piety, through our sacrifices and veneration, the natural gods, the most powerful gods, will have been propitiated. The gods will smile on our endeavours. Let us rejoice!'

As the basilica echoed to the acclamations of his piety

and wisdom, the silver-haired emperor slumped back on to his throne as if exhausted. After the thirty-fifth 'Valerian, happy are you in your piety, safe are you in the love of the gods, safe are you in our love,' it was quiet. Macrianus came forward to the edge of the dais. He leaned on his walking stick topped with the silver effigy of Alexander the Great. '*Comites Augusti*, Companions of the Augustus, our noble emperor desires your advice on how to proceed against the Persians. He commands you to speak freely.'

Several hands shot up. Macrianus indicated that his own *amicus*, Maeonius Astyanax, should speak. 'There can be no doubt that the sagacity and piety of the emperor will avert the displeasure of the gods and sweep away the plague. But some five thousand fighting men have died, many more are sick. Just as it does with a man, it takes an army time to recover from illness. We are in no condition to campaign. We must stay here in Samosata and convalesce. An embassy must be sent to the Sassanids to negotiate a truce. The envoys should take rich gifts, the sort of luxuries that turn the head of an avaricious barbarian such as Shapur.'

There was a general rumble of approval. As Macrianus gave Pomponius Bassus the right to speak, it occurred to Turpio that the lame courtier had usurped the role of the *ab Admissionibus*. That functionary stood impotently at the back of the dais. Cledonius appeared to be fuming.

Striking an oratorical pose, Pomponius Bassus began. 'There is a time for war and a time for peace. A time for tears and a time for rejoicing.' Turpio heard Ballista exhale with irritation as the nobleman's sententious phrases rolled out. 'A time for love and a time to hate.'

Four more of the *comites* had spoken in favour of the

proposal when Ballista raised his hand. Turpio was surprised, and even more so when Macrianus gave the northerner permission to speak. Out of the corner of his eye, Turpio thought he saw the sons of Macrianus smirking.

'With all due respect, I do not agree.' There was silence at Ballista's words. 'To open negotiations is to show weakness, never more so than in time of war. It will only serve to encourage the *superbia* of the eastern barbarians. To initiate diplomacy is not the Roman way. Embassies come to the emperor. He does not send them. Has not emperor after emperor interpreted embassies from the Indies and beyond as tokens of submission?'

A hostile muttering ran through the basilica. Ballista ploughed on. 'We should not remain in Samosata. Plague comes to armies that remain in camp. We should take the field. If we impose strict *disciplina* on the march to Edessa, issue rigorous orders for hygiene and the digging of latrines, the plague is more likely to abate.' One or two of the *comites*, led by Quietus, sniggered.

Macrianus gave Piso Frugi permission to have the floor. Another of Macrianus' creatures, thought Turpio. 'While I will bow to Ballista's knowledge of barbarians and latrines' – he paused for laughter – 'I think none of us here need his advice on the ways of the Romans.' There was more laughter. 'The previous speakers were right. We must buy time with glittering trinkets.'

Amid the roar of approval, Macrianus turned and smiled encouragingly at the emperor. The hubbub died as Valerian laboriously got to his feet. 'We have heard your opinions. We thank you for them. Free speech is the heart of *libertas*. We have made up our mind. An embassy will be sent to

Shapur. It will take costly gifts. It will speak soft words. It will make a truce. It is the Roman way to send young men, those not yet of the highest rank, to deal with barbarians. The ambassadors will be the son of our beloved *Comes Sacrarum Largitionum* Titus Fulvius Iunius Quietus, the fierce young fighter from the Danube Lucius Domitius Aurelian and Marcus Clodius Ballista.' As soon as he had stopped talking, Valerian reached for the arm of Macrianus and left.

Both Ballista and Aurelian looked utterly dumbfounded. Quietus, however, appeared merely pleased.

Outside, Turpio stood waiting for other members of the *consilium* to finish congratulating Aurelian and Ballista. Fair-weather friends, he thought. From the town stretched out below him came the bells of the *libitinarii*, accompanying the carrying out of more of the dead.

Turpio really could not believe Ballista's claim that Macrianus was plotting to overthrow Valerian. But, every day, the *Comes Sacrarum Largitionum* seemed to have more control over the aged emperor. The *consilium* had been carefully orchestrated. It did seem that the lame one could do whatever he wished. Turpio wondered why Macrianus had chosen to have his son Quietus accompanied on the embassy by Aurelian and Ballista. Certainly the hateful courtier did nothing without a reason. Turpio played some lines of poetry over in his mind.

> May the earth cover
> your corpse lightly,
> loathsome Macrianus,
> so that the dogs
> have less trouble digging you up.

Across the river from Samosata, the road to Edessa ran over high plains and rolling hills. It was a dry landscape. Already in April the yellow-grey, sometimes reddish, soil was powdered and dusty. Sometimes, away from the road, the hills bunched up into real mountains, bare and closely folded, but Ballista was surprised by the general openness of the terrain. He was not pleased. He had thought the countryside would be more rugged, unsuitable for large numbers of horsemen. He had thought that, when the infantry-based army of the Romans finally marched, it would be reasonably sheltered, at least as far as Edessa, from the cavalry horde of the Sassanids. Now he knew that would not be the case.

The embassy was moving very slowly. Each of the three ambassadors had brought their servants; just a few for Aurelian and Ballista himself, a glittering cavalcade for Quietus. There were six interpreters and thirty packhorses carrying the diplomatic gifts, with half as many men again to look after them. There were twenty Dalmatian troopers to protect them from the nomadic tent-dwellers. But it was none of these that were slowing the pace, it was the garlanded ox that was being driven ponderously along at the front of the caravan. Quietus never missed an opportunity to sneer at its presence. But Ballista had insisted on it. Long ago, he had learned from Bagoas, the Persian slave boy he had owned, that it was a sign the Sassanids used to show they had accepted peace terms. Another was the bags of salt that he had ordered tied to the standards. To be sure, there was a Roman herald, complete with diplomatic wand, up front with the ox. But the symbols of one culture might mean something else or nothing at all in another. First contact with the enemy would be a dangerous moment. He did not want all his men riddled with Persian arrows before they had a chance to explain they were envoys who came in peace.

As he ambled along on Pale Horse, Ballista wondered for the umpteenth time why he had been chosen as an ambassador. On the one hand, he could speak Persian but, on the other, the embassy had been given a surfeit of interpreters. Ballista had been out of imperial favour for a long time. His advice against making these overtures of peace had been rejected. It was widely thought at court that the man who had frustrated Shapur for so long before the walls of Arete, who had killed so many of his warriors, the general who had ordered the burning of the enemy bodies after the battle of Circesium, would be far from welcome to the Zoroastrian, fire-worshipping Sassanid King of Kings.

Ballista's eyes followed a stork flying south-east, roughly parallel to them. His thoughts rolled on. Macrianus had run the *consilium* like a well-trained chorus in the theatre. The northerner now understood why Tacitus had been posted back to the west and the ex-consul Valens had been left behind to command the troops at Zeugma. Two less influential voices in the *consilium* to contest the growing influence of the *Comes Largitionum*. It galled Ballista that no one, not even those closest to him, accepted that that lame bastard was plotting to betray the frail old emperor who regarded him as his most loyal friend. Cledonius would no longer even see Ballista. The northerner had ceased to talk about it at all. It was doing no good and, even among *amici*, there was the ever-present danger of *frumentarii* spying. Still, as Ballista watched the stork disappear over a range of hills, he tried to comfort himself with the thought that surely even Macrianus would not send his younger son on a mission that would lead to his death.

A shout brought Ballista back to his surroundings. The Dalmatian on point duty was holding his cloak in one hand above his head. The trooper pointed to the hills in the east. Ballista scanned the bare, undulating skyline. A few stunted wild olive trees, twisted by the wind. And there among them men on horses. Six or seven. Then more and more. Fifty, a hundred, more.

Ballista ordered the caravan to halt. Automatically, the Dalmatian cavalry took up their positions around the column. Ballista took his helmet from the horn of his saddle. Inconsequentially, he noticed the marks of the repairs from the ambush at the Horns of Ammon. He settled the thing on his head.

Beside him, the northerner heard the rasp of steel as Quietus drew his sword.

'Put that away.'

Quietus bridled. 'Why should I take orders from you?' The young man's lip was trembling, his eyes wide with fear. For a split second Ballista wondered if his opportunity had come. Aurelian was the only witness of rank. Should he cut Quietus down now? But the moment passed. One day Ballista would kill him. Not today.

'Put it away.' Sulkily, his hands fumbling, Quietus sheathed his sword. Ballista raised his voice. 'No one touch a weapon. Those with bows, make sure they are unstrung. Do as I do.'

Ballista watched the Sassanid cavalry descend the hillside. Dark shapes against the yellow-grey dust they raised. There were at least two hundred of them. As they reached the level ground their line split, fanning out to surround the Roman column. *Allfather, Hooded One, Grey Beard, watch over me now.* Ballista forced himself to be calm. When the easterners were about two hundred paces away, Ballista pulled the bow from the quiver hanging from his saddle. He held it high above his head. From the shape of the composite bow, it was obviously unstrung.

The Sassanids came on fast, horsemen jinking round thickets of brushwood, streamers flying out behind them, loose eastern clothing snapping. They broke into high, ululating cries. The bows in their hands were strung, arrows notched. With a thunder of hooves, they crossed the front and rear of the Roman column, galloping round to encircle it. Quietus was whimpering. Behind him, Ballista could hear Demetrius praying.

A stone's throw away, they reined in, horses breathing hard, tossing their heads. Hostile, dark eyes stared from behind drawn bows. After the pounding hooves and the wailing, the quiet was ominous. Out of the corner of his eye, Ballista saw Quietus' hand moving to the hilt of his sword. Aurelian leaned across and stopped him. Their every move was tracked by Persian arrowheads. The tension was nearly unbearable.

A Persian detached himself from the line. His face, framed by long, black hair, was a picture of disdain. 'We have been expecting you, waiting for this invasion of the territory of the divine, powerful Shapur King of Kings.'

Ballista moved Pale Horse out of the line. 'We are not invaders. We are ambassadors from the pious Valerian, King of the Romans, to his brother, the virtuous, peace-loving

Shapur King of Kings. We bring gifts and a letter of peace.'

If the Sassanid was surprised that Ballista spoke in Persian, he gave no sign of it. His handsome face sneered. 'Shapur does not have a non-Aryan brother. He has non-Aryan slaves. The only King of the Romans he knows is the one who by his mercy sits on a lower throne at his own court, the one called Mariades.'

Ballista sensed a stir in the Romans behind him as, among the foreign words, they recognized the name of Mariades, the fugitive brigand from Syria set up by Shapur as a pretender to the throne of the Caesars. Ballista ignored it. 'The benefactor of mankind, the peace-loving Shapur King of Kings, beloved of Ahuramazda, would not smile on a man who harmed ambassadors.'

A look of suspicion appeared on the Persian's face. He brought his horse closer. He studied Ballista. 'The word that was given to me was true. I know you. I am Vardan, son of Nashbad.'

A distant memory struggled to surface in Ballista's mind. He did not move.

With no warning, the Persian drew his sword and thrust the long blade within inches of the northerner's face. The memory came back. A dark night in the south ravine below the walls of Arete. Vardan's sword at his throat, as it was now. The Persian smiled. 'I see you remember. You tricked me once. I said then that I would seek you out, that there would be a reckoning.'

Ballista fought down his fear. The blade at his throat did not waver. Vardan spoke. 'Tell your men to throw down their weapons.' Ballista gave the order, and Persians sprang forward to gather them up.

With a fluid movement, Vardan's blade sliced through the air. He sheathed it.

'If Shapur does not recognize your status as an ambassador, I will ask him to hand you over to me. The ungodly man who defiled the sacred fire of Ahuramazda after Circesium will not die quickly.' Vardan laughed with anticipation. 'We will camp here tonight. Tomorrow, I will take you to the King of Kings.'

Wherever you go, thought Ballista, old enemies will find you.

XXVI

The next day, Ballista and the others were marched down to the Sassanid camp on the plains before the walls of Edessa. As Vardan the night before had ordered the garlanded ox killed and eaten, he had been able to force a fast pace. It was a little after midday when they reached the crest of the last hill. The siege had been spread out below them like a scene in the theatre. Off to their right was the white-walled city of Edessa, nestled against the western hills. In front of them and to their left were the besiegers. Troops of cavalry wheeled across the plain. The camp itself stretched away into the distance. A cloud of blue smoke from innumerable fires of dried dung hung over it. The pungent smell carried all the way to the northern hills. There was an enormous, roughly circular palisade, but the camp had outgrown it. Thousands of tents and hundreds of horse lines were laid out in no discernible order, except at the very heart of the camp, where a series of huge purple pavilions marked the temporary home of the King of Kings.

Any idea that they were being hurried into the presence of Shapur had been quickly dispelled when the Roman party had ridden into the encampment. Vardan had brusquely ordered them to pitch their tents at the eastern extremity of the camp, between the elephant lines and one of the main latrines. Sassanid guards were posted. The Roman envoys were told to await the royal summons. There they had remained for fourteen days. The smell was appalling. The food provided was barley bread, chickpeas, lentils and raisins – the food of the local poor. The wine brought in was thin and sour. Every night, they were kept awake by the singing of the guards. And, if final proof had been needed of the deliberate contempt that was being displayed, it came when the guards mockingly recounted how envoys from Velenus, the king of an obscure people called the Cardusii, who lived far away by the shores of the Caspian Sea, had just been most hospitably received by Shapur as soon as they arrived.

Aurelian had paced about, fuming at the disrespect being exhibited to the *maiestas* of the Roman people. Quietus took it all with surprising equanimity. Ballista, as nothing could be done, had settled down to wait. He was rereading the *Anabasis* of Xenophon, the classic text about fighting easterners, when out of the blue the summons finally came. Aurelian was all for making Shapur wait, paying him back in kind. Both Ballista and Quietus thought it unwise.

After hurriedly changing into their best uniforms and getting the diplomatic gifts together, they were led out of camp towards a place on the bank of the Scirtos river where parasols shaded a high, elaborate throne, from which the King of Kings could survey the siege.

As he trudged across the plain, Ballista studied the scene. Edessa was in a good state of defence. The orchards and inns outside the city had been torn down to deny cover to the attackers. A dry wadi fronted well-built double walls.

To the south was a high citadel topped with the columns of a temple or palace. Rush mats to deaden the impact of missiles hung from the walls. The gates had been blocked with large stones. Where the Scirtos river emerged from the town, the watergates were protected by solid-looking metalwork.

Ballista knew there were ample springs of fresh water within the walls. But the attackers had to depend on the river, and that ran through the town. If he had been in charge, he would have found a way to poison the water before it flowed out to the camp of the enemy on the plain. Again, he would not have sealed the gates, making it impossible to sally out. He thought the situation demonstrated a lack of initiative on the part of the defenders. But, looking outside the walls, he saw no artillery and no evidence of a siege mound or mines. The attackers appeared to be no more active than the besieged. The whole affair had more the feel of a blockade than a closely pressed siege.

'Who comes before the divine, virtuous, powerful Shapur, King of Aryans and non-Aryans, King of Kings?' At the herald's question the Romans performed *proskynesis*, full length in the dust and, possibly carefully placed, horse droppings.

Ballista stood. He spoke in Persian. 'We are envoys from the virtuous, peace-loving Valerian, emperor of the Romans. This is Lucius Domitius Aurelian and Titus Fulvius Iunius Quietus. I am Marcus Clodius Ballista.'

As the silence lengthened, Ballista looked at the tableau in front of him. He had seen Shapur many times at Arete, but never this close. The Sassanid king was a tall, powerfully built man in vigorous middle age. He had a full, black beard and wore the dress of a horseman: short, purple tunic and white trousers. On his head was a high golden crown. Huge pearls hung from his ears. His eyes were lined with kohl. Across his lap lay a strung bow.

The King of Kings was flanked on one side by the great men of his empire. Tall, armed men, bright, embroidered surcoats over gleaming armour, each had a long, straight cavalry sword at his left hip. The men on the other side were equally gorgeously costumed but unarmed. These were the magi, the priests of Mazda. High above them all floated the Drafsh-i-Kavyan, the battle standard of the house of Sasan. A line of ten terrifyingly big elephants, carrying turrets full of armed men, formed the backdrop.

Suddenly, first one then another, Ballista recognized two of the men flanking Shapur. Among the warriors, dressed in Persian fashion, was a man with a long face with eyes that were too wide, and which matched the turned-down corners of his mouth. Ballista had last seen that distinctive face at the Horns of Ammon. It was no great surprise that Anamu, sometime leading man of the city of Arete and consummate survivor, had risen high in the service of the Sassanid king.

The other man was a total surprise. Ballista looked carefully: the tall, thin figure; the bushy beard and hair; the dark eyes that regarded him with no evident recognition. No, he was not mistaken. There, among the high priests of the Sassanid empire, stood the Persian boy who had once gone by the name of Bagoas and had once been the slave of Ballista, bought in the marketplace of Delos. At times, the northerner thought, it is a very small world – small, complicated and dangerous.

Another group of envoys was ushered forward. They were clad in eastern costume. They stopped next to the Romans and performed *proskynesis*. Again, the herald demanded identification.

'I am Verodes. I am the envoy of Odenathus, Lord of Tadmor, King of Palmyra.'

Shapur plucked the string of his bow. He had an air of supreme indifference. He looked at the Romans, then turned to the newcomer. 'What does Odenathus want?'

The envoy from Palmyra smiled a courtly smile. 'My Lord wants for nothing except to be admitted into the warmth of the friendship of the King of Kings. He brings gifts suitable to your majesty.' Verodes clapped his hands, and servants came forward. First, bales of silk were spread then piles of spices heaped. Finally, a magnificent white stallion was led forth. The mingled scent of spices and horse filled the air.

With no emotion, Shapur took an arrow from the quiver that hung from his throne. No one moved. Shapur notched it, drew and aimed straight at the chest of the envoy from Palmyra. As he released, he altered the angle of the arrow. The bright feathers on its shaft quivered in the neck of the horse. The stallion threw up its head. It started to rear. Its legs gave way, and it collapsed. Its muscles trembled for some moments, and it was still. The dark blood pooled out.

Shapur pointed with the bow at the other gifts. 'Throw these baubles in the river.' Men rushed to do his bidding. 'Tell Odenaethus that if he wishes the King of Kings to smile on him, to send no more slaves with trinkets suitable to win the favours of a whore but to come with his hands in chains, throw himself at our feet, let him prostrate himself and beg for our mercy. Now go!'

With all the dignity they could muster, Verodes and the other Palmyrenes hurriedly performed *proskynesis* and left.

Ballista could feel the anger radiating off Aurelian. The northerner himself was not angry – if anything, he felt a grudging admiration at the way it had been stage-managed. The Roman ambassadors had been kept waiting to witness one of Rome's chief allies in the east trying to change sides. In a superb display of power, Shapur had rejected the offer. He had neatly undermined all trust between Odenathus and the Romans and at the same time demonstrated the supreme confidence he felt in his own power.

Shapur pointed the bow at Ballista. 'And you?' He spoke now in Greek. 'What does your *kyrios* want?'

'He wants a truce, *Kyrios*.'

Shapur smiled. 'Does he? Even as we speak, Mazda strikes down the ungodly. Plague rages through the Roman army in Samosata. Why should we grant a truce?'

'My lord, the fortune of war is unknowable. Many have found war against the emperors of the Romans a terrible thing.'

Shapur laughed. 'The house of Sasan has always found it a thing of unalloyed joy, a bringer of exquisite pleasure.' He gestured, and a short, fat man dressed in an approximation of the martial costume of a Roman emperor scurried forth. Shapur clicked his fingers and Mariades, his tame pretender to the throne of the Caesars, dropped on all fours. Shapur swung his boots on to the back of his living footstool.

'I take it you bring tribute? The usual gold and silver plate finely embossed with lying images of easterners grovelling at the feet of Romans?'

Aurelian drew in breath. Ballista put a hand on his arm to stop him saying anything. As Ballista indicated for the gifts to be presented, it occurred to him again that his friend 'hand-to-steel' was far from an ideal ambassador.

'Delightful,' Shapur said as he casually inspected the cunningly wrought precious metals. 'I always admire the way Roman diplomacy is blind to irony.' He kicked Mariades none too gently, and he scrambled away. 'I will accept this tribute.'

Before Ballista could stop him, Aurelian snapped angrily, 'Gifts! Rome pays tribute to no one!'

In the terrible silence that followed, Shapur thrummed the string of his bow. Then he smiled. 'I have been told about you. You are the great killer of Sarmatians and Franks. I admire spirit in an opponent. To you, I will give suitable gifts.' At his gesture, a servant handed Aurelian a sacrificial saucer engraved with an image of the sun god. 'I thought you might find it suitable,' said Shapur. 'And, possibly, also this.' There was a loud trumpeting. The ground shook. An enormous elephant swayed into view. 'He is called *Peroz*, Victory. I give him to you. His mahout as well.'

As Aurelian stared, open-mouthed, Shapur turned to Quietus. 'To each his deserts. For you, this sack of gold.' Quietus started to stammer what might have been thanks. Shapur cut him off.

The Sassanid gestured at Ballista with the bow. 'But to you, the ungodly defiler of fire at Circesium, I give nothing. You are an envoy. But if we meet again when you are not protected by that status, it will not be good for you.'

Shapur rose. Everyone hurried to prostrate themselves. 'Tell Valerian there will be no truce. I long to test the strength of my arm against his. There will be only war. You will return to Samosata tomorrow.'

The torches along the *via principalis*, the main thorough-fare, of the first Roman marching camp south of the Euphrates guttered and flared in the remains of the storm. The south wind threw gusts of rain into Ballista's face, tugged at his cloak. The foul weather matched his mood as he splashed through the puddles to the imperial head-quarters.

The plague had abated. The pious put it down to the sagacious immolation of fifty-three Christians. But if the gods had been pleased, they had given no other sign today as the expedition moved out. At dawn, during the ceremony of purification on the citadel of Samosata, the slimy, grey ropes of sacrificial intestines had slithered slowly and irre-trievably out of the hands of the emperor. Valerian had done what he could to dissipate the omen: 'This is what comes of being old, but I can hold my sword tightly enough.' His words had elicited a half-hearted cheer. As the emperor went to leave, a servant had draped a black cloak around his shoulders. It had been some moments before Valerian had realized and called for the correct, purple one.

As the last of the army crossed the river, the storm hit: thunder, lightning, driving rain. A savage gust had torn free one of the rafts of the pontoon bridge. 'Be of good cheer,' Valerian had shouted. 'None of us will come back this way again.' His words were received in silence as the rain beat down.

Just before Ballista had left his tent, the first rations of the campaign had been delivered: lentils and salt – the food of mourning, offerings to the dead. Ballista suspected a malign hand. The *Comes Sacrarum Largitionum* was responsible for the imperial wardrobe; the *Praefectus Annonae* was in charge of provisions – but Macrianus could not be blamed for the trembling of the aged hands of the emperor or the fury of the elements.

Ballista stepped aside to let a troop of Equites Singulares pass. The cavalrymen were hunched in cloaks dark with the rain. Their horses' heads drooped, their sides ran with water.

Ballista would have one less friend at the *consilium* now Aurelian was gone. The failure of the embassy had done neither of them any good. Ballista knew it had been designed to fail. The northerner himself was unwelcome to the Zoroastrian Sassanids as the man who had burned their dead at Circesium. Aurelian was renowned for his lack of tact and short temper. Presumably, Quietus had been included to keep an eye on them. It had been a cunning move on the part of the Persian king to send no gifts to Valerian but to hand regal ones to Aurelian. As soon as they had returned to Samosata, the Danubian had presented the elephant to Valerian. But the suspicion had been sown. It could be no coincidence that Aurelian had been precipitously posted away to the court of Gallienus in the far west.

There was something else about the embassy that worried Ballista. When they first met the Persians, Vardan had said something like 'We have been expecting you.' And there were the words of Shapur himself as he gave the sacrificial saucer engraved with an image of the sun god to its devotee Aurelian: 'I thought you might find it suitable.' Was Macrianus actually in touch with the enemy? Had the evil, lame bastard hoped that the Sassanid king would not respect Ballista's diplomatic immunity, hoped that the northerner would not return at all but die a horrible death of eastern refinement?

Cold and wet, Ballista walked on. At least this would be the last council of war which Macrianus would attend, as he was remaining in Samosata, safe. Surely his creature Maeonius Astyanax and his repulsive son Quietus could not exercise the same control over Valerian? And while Macrianus might be plotting the overthrow of the aged emperor, even he could not want to bring about the destruction of the whole army. Not with his son in its ranks.

The praetorians outside the imperial pavilion came to attention smartly. A *silentarius* escorted Ballista into the vestibule. The rain lashed at the material of the roof. The *ab Admissionibus* appeared. 'Cledonius, a word in private,' said Ballista.

The long, thin face peered around. 'No. We have nothing to say to each other.' The big eyes looked hunted. 'Nothing at all,' Cledonius said loudly, and turned to lead Ballista into the inner sanctum.

Inside, Ballista dropped to his knees and kissed the ring the emperor proffered. Valerian did not look at him. Ballista rose and stepped back. It was a small, intimate *consilium*; not much above a dozen men. As custom dictated, the praetorian prefect was at the emperor's right hand. As was now normal, Macrianus was leaning on a walking stick at his left. Ballista froze at the sight of the man beyond Macrianus: the receding hairline, the turned-down eyes matching the turned-down mouth, the yellow-on-blue four-petal-flower embroidery – what in all the names of the Allfather was Anamu doing here?

Valerian nodded fondly at Macrianus, who began to speak. 'The wisdom of the emperor's pious actions against the atheists who worship the crucified Jew have made the gods smile on us again. The plague is gone. Now we have further proof of divine love. A loyal friend has returned to us. You all know how bravely Anamu fought at Arete. After the fall of that town, the Sassanids captured his wife and family. They threatened them with unspeakable tortures if he did not serve their vainglorious king. Despite this, Marcus Clodius Ballista can confirm how Anamu turned the Persians away at the Horns of Ammon.'

Thrown, Ballista muttered that Anamu had run with the Sassanids.

Macrianus continued. 'Now Anamu has put his love for Rome and love for our sacred emperor even above that for his family and has come covertly to tell us the secrets of the enemy.' He gestured Anamu forward.

'Most noble Valerian, *Comites Augusti*, I bring you good news. Shapur's siege of Edessa is in disarray. Every day the inhabitants sally out with swords in hand. The Persians die in droves. They do not know which way to turn. Their beds bring them no rest from fear and danger. Now is the moment for Rome to strike. The road between Samosata and Edessa is rough and rocky. The Sassanid cavalry cannot operate there. They cannot stop us reaching the plains before Edessa and, when we come there, they will run like sheep.'

Ballista took a deep breath and stepped forward. 'It is

not true. I was at Edessa but twelve days ago. The inhabitants did not stir. The gates were blocked with stones. They could not venture out. And the country between us and Edessa is not as rocky as men say. Over most of it, cavalry can manoeuvre with ease.'

Smiling, Quietus raised his hand. 'I was also at Edessa. While it is true that the northern and eastern gates were blocked then, they may well be clear now. And Ballista cannot deny that we ambassadors were given no opportunity to inspect the western and southern gates. As for the road to Edessa, I fear the habitual caution of Ballista makes it easier for the Sassanid cavalry than is the case.'

Eagerly, Anamu joined in. 'Nothing is needed but quick hands and feet to catch the reptiles before they flee to the east, to Scythia or Hyrcania. As your Latin poets say, "*Carpe diem*" – you must seize the day.'

Valerian raised his hand for silence. 'It is decided. This very night, our trusty and beloved Anamu will return to the camp of our enemies to keep us informed of their plans. His courage will be richly rewarded. At dawn, we will march. We will chase Shapur and his horde of goat-eyed easterners back to his capital at Ctesiphon. With the gods as our companions, we will pursue him to Bactria, India, the outer Ocean – wherever he may flee. Let those remaining atheists lurking in their holes witness the impotence of their false god, let them witness the power and the glory of the true gods!'

Valerian laboriously stood up. The *consilium* was over.

The night had not improved. The rain still fell. Thunder rolled around the hills across the river to the north. That was good: few men would venture out on such a night.

Deep in the dark of the overhang of a tent, Ballista and Maximus waited for the watch to pass. Then, faces blackened, dark clad, they slipped like ghosts on the *Lemuria*, the festival of the dead, from one tent to another.

Things became more dangerous as they drew nearer to the imperial pavilion. The tents of the courtiers had guards in front of them.

A dog sensed their approach. Hackles up, it came closer. It barked once. Maximus produced some of the air-dried beef he always seemed to have on him. He tossed a piece to the dog, who sniffed it with profound suspicion, then ate it. It came closer. The Hibernian fed it again. He fussed its ears. He threw another piece of meat out into the rain. The dog trotted after it. The two men moved on.

In the lee of the emperor's quarters, they came to the right tent. There was a praetorian sheltering under the entrance. Hands and knees in the mud, they slipped under the guy ropes and worked their way around to the back.

They waited, listening. Nothing could be heard but the falling rain, the distant thunder. Ballista unsheathed a knife. About two feet up, he pushed it through the taut side of the tent. He stopped to listen. Nothing. He slit the material down to the ground. Then, holding where he had cut, he made another slit parallel to the ground. He pulled back the flap. He put his head through into the darkness and listened. Nothing but the rain on the canvas – then, below that, the sound of a man snoring.

Gripping the blade in his teeth, Ballista wriggled into the tent. From outside, Maximus pulled the flap shut. Ballista waited, stilling his breathing. A little light shone through the inner wall from a lamp in the outer chamber. Gradually, Ballista began to make out his surroundings: a campaign chest, a folding chair, a stand for armour and, in the centre of the room, a bed.

Slowly, slowly, feeling with a hand for anything on the floor, he crept across to the bed. The man in it stirred in his sleep. Ballista stood motionless. The rain beat down on the roof. The man coughed, then began to snore again.

Ballista rose up. There was the white blur of a face against the pillow. Ballista put one hand over the man's mouth. With the other he brought up the knife. As the man woke, big eyes wide with fright, Ballista showed him the knife. Automatically, the man tried to lurch upwards. Ballista pushed him down, then put the point of the knife to his throat.

'Shout for the guard and you die.'

The man lay still. Ballista could feel the other's heart beating. 'I just need to talk. I am going to take my hand away. Do not shout or I will kill you.'

The man nodded slightly. Ballista uncovered his mouth.

Cledonius sucked in air. 'What the fuck are you doing? Creeping in here like a fucking ghost. I nearly died of fright.' There was an edge of panic in the hissing, whispered voice of the *ab Admissionibus*.

'Quietly, *amicus*.' Ballista smiled. 'You seemed reluctant to talk to me earlier.' If anything, the asymmetrical face on the pillow looked more frightened. Ballista conspicuously did not sheathe the knife.

'Macrianus is leading the army into a trap. He intends to depose Valerian and replace him on the throne with his own sons.' Ballista talked low and fast. 'You have the right of admission to the emperor. You must talk to him, warn him.'

Cledonius rubbed a hand over his jaw. 'The gods know you may well be right, but there is no proof. Anyway, even if there were, it would do no good. Valerian relies on Macrianus in everything. And now it is far too dangerous. Macrianus has completely won over Censorinus. If any of the few loyal men left near the emperor – me, Successianus, the young Italian Aurelian, who commands the Equites Singulares – if any of us try to warn the emperor, Censorinus will unleash the *frumentarii* on us and we will be killed on a trumped-up charge of *maiestas*.'

Ballista put the knife away. He leaned forward. 'Let me talk to the emperor. All you need do is get me in to see him on my own. I have served him for a long time. Seven years ago I fought for him at Spoletium when he crushed the rebel Aemilianus and took the throne. Valerian trusted me once. Maybe he will listen now.'

Cledonius smiled sadly. 'It would do no good. You would be killed, then the rest of the loyal men. We would all die for nothing.'

'Then what can we do?'

Cledonius grimaced. 'Do our duty. Watch and wait. Pray to the gods for salvation. Hope Macrianus makes a mistake.'

'Allfather, this is not right,' Ballista said vehemently. 'We are being led like lambs to the slaughter. There must be something we can do.'

'Watch and wait.'

'Doing nothing goes against the grain. But if there is nothing else?'

'Nothing else.'

Ballista walked back the way he had come. 'I am sorry I woke you like that.'

'I would rather this than you spoke to me in public.'

Ballista slipped out into the wet night.

XXVII

By midday, it was as if the equinoctial storm had never happened. The south wind had pushed away the clouds, leaving a perfect blue sky. Every puddle had been swallowed by the parched, yellow-grey soil. With the sun and wind, soon the high plain before them would be as dry and dusty as before.

Ballista and Turpio sat side by side on the ground, watching the last of the baggage train emerge from the marching camp. It had been a hectic day so far. At dawn, Valerian had ordered the army to march light: all except essential baggage was to be left in camp to be taken back over the remaining bridges and be left safely in Samosata with the forces still there under the *Comes Sacrarum Largitionum*, Macrianus. All morning, Ballista and Turpio had worked, deciding what was to go and what stay, their deliberations continually interrupted by messengers from officers demanding that their own possessions must travel with the field army.

'This is madness,' said Ballista. Turpio, toying with his Persian bracelet, gave an eloquent shrug, as if to say, *What else can one expect in this world?* 'Not to march in a hollow square' – Ballista shook his head – 'it invites disaster.' Convinced by Anamu and Quietus that the way to Edessa was unsuitable for the Sassanid cavalry, who anyway were on the verge of retreat, Valerian had commanded the army to advance in column. At the head rode half the cavalry, under Pomponius Bassus. The infantry came next, under Valerian himself, with Quietus close to his side. They were followed by the other half of the cavalry, under Maeonius Astyanax. The baggage brought up the rear.

'Time to go,' Turpio said. Ballista, whose clandestine nocturnal visit to Cledonius had left him no time to sleep, climbed wearily into the saddle. His *familia* – Maximus, Calgacus and Demetrius – fell in behind. They cantered down to take up again the frustrating task of trying to keep the non-combatants in order.

Valerian, no doubt urged on by Quietus, from the outset pushed the army hard. Soon the baggage train was moving down a road flanked by stragglers from the fighting units. From the rear, the way back to the north was seen to be already dotted with deserters from the standards heading back to the Euphrates. Worryingly, no orders had been given to post guards to stop them.

After about two hours' hard marching, word was passed down for the army to halt, for an overdue meal. In keeping with the feverish sense of urgency emanating from the emperor's staff, the men were ordered not to leave their posts but to eat and drink standing by the banks of a small, nameless stream. Even so, the command to move on came before most had finished.

Another hour *en route*, and horsemen galloped back down the column. They had cloaks bunched in their fists and were waving them above their heads. Enemy in sight! Enemy in sight!

Ballista's heart sank. They had barely set off, and the easterners were on them already. For some reason, he found himself thinking about the deaths of emperors: about Gordian III, mortally wounded by the Sassanids at the battle of Meshike; about Decius, cut down by the Goths in the marshes at Abrittus. In both cases, there were stories of a Roman betrayer. They were untrue. Ballista was certain it was untrue in the case of the latter. He had been at the side of the general Gallus, the supposed traitor, throughout the battle. But the idea of betraying a Roman emperor to the barbarians was in the minds of many men.

Trumpets blared. Executing its pre-planned manoeuvre, the Roman army, one unit after another, turned and marched to the right. When they were strung out in line across the plain, they halted. Then, as one, each unit turned to the left. To be fair, the manoeuvre was carried out reasonably smartly. In under half an hour, the Romans had moved from order of march to line of battle. Now, the cavalry of Pomponius Bassus formed the right wing; the infantry, with the emperor, the centre; the cavalry of Maeonius Astyanax formed the left wing. In theory, forty thousand armed men, ten thousand of them mounted, faced the enemy. Yet, even before the plague, many of the units had been vastly under strength. In reality, not many over twenty thousand soldiers of Rome waited for the onslaught.

Following orders, Ballista and Turpio brought the baggage train close up behind the infantry but kept it in line, strung out along the road. When it was in place, they took themselves and a few followers off to the left, to a low eminence from which they could see over the serried ranks of the infantry.

Across the high, rolling plain was the enemy. There looked to be roughly five to six thousand of them. Unusually for Sassanid cavalry, there were no bright colours on view. Instead, the cavalry had a drab, ochre appearance. They milled about, circling their horses just out of bowshot.

A huge kettledrum thundered. A high cry like that of cranes on the wing drifted down the south wind. The Sassanids came on.

Roman trumpets sounded. Officers bawled orders. At about a hundred and fifty paces, the Roman light troops shot. Arrows and slingshots whooshed away. Some of the enemy went down. Moments later, the easterners released. Arrows rattled off Roman shields and armour. Some struck home. Men and horses screamed.

Then the Sassanids were turning, spurring away. They rode hard, not even shooting back over their horses' quarters.

A sharp trumpet call rang from the centre of the Roman line. It was picked up and repeated by *bucinator* after *bucinator* up and down the army.

'Fucking Hades,' muttered Ballista.

'Indeed,' said Turpio. 'Not exactly what one would have hoped for.'

As the musicians continued to sound the general advance, the whole Roman line surged forward. Within moments, the cavalry wings were pulling away from the infantry.

Ballista looked at Turpio. Before the question was asked, Turpio gave the answer: 'Yes, go and try to make him see sense.' The northerner spurred away, with Maximus, Calgacus and Demetrius following. Watching them, Turpio spoke out loud, although to himself rather than to the handful of Dalmatian troopers around him. 'Not that it will do any good. The old fool will not listen. The eye of Cronus is on us. Some god wills our destruction.'

At a flat gallop, Ballista raced after the charging army. He set his course for the huge imperial purple standard that was snapping in the wind above a cluster of lesser standards towards the rear of the infantry. He let Pale Horse pick his own way through the dead and wounded, the clumps of partially trampled undergrowth. On the wings, the cavalry were rapidly disappearing out of sight. In the centre, wide gaps were opening between the infantry units. The men were no longer in neat files but in loose clumps around their standards. Without a blow struck hand to hand, the army was fast disintegrating as an organized fighting force.

Four Equites Singulares blocked the way. Furious, Ballista reined in. The commander of the imperial horse guards, the young Italian Aurelian, rode up. 'I have orders not to let you approach his imperial majesty.'

Mastering his anger, Ballista spoke urgently. 'You are a good and competent soldier, Aurelian. You can see what is happening. Someone has to try and reason with him.'

The young tribune hesitated.

'If he does not countermand this order, we are all dead.'

Still the Italian wavered between *disciplina* and his own judgement.

'Remember the fate of the men with Crassus at Carrhae.' Ballista laughed bitterly. 'Valerian at Edessa – it will be the same.'

Reluctantly, the young officer waved his men aside.

Ballista clapped him on the shoulder. 'Do not worry. Most likely we will all dine in Hades tomorrow.' Or, he thought as he kicked on, with luck I will dine in Valhalla; an infinitely better place, by all accounts.

For once, the emperor Valerian turned to Ballista with a broad smile. 'They are running. The reptiles are running.' He laughed; a senile laugh. 'We will chase the goat-eyed cowards to Babylon, to Ctesiphon ... ha, ha ... to Hyrcania, to Bactria.'

'*Dominus*, that is not their main force. They are a few light cavalry luring us into a trap. Their main army, the terrible, mailed *clibanarii*, are hidden over one of these rises, waiting.'

The emperor was not listening. '. . . to the Indies, the Seres, the outer Ocean.'

Ballista leaned over and grabbed the bridle of the emperor's horse. 'Caesar, pay attention to me.' The surrounding Equites Singulares put their hands to their sword hilts. Ballista ignored them. 'Caesar, look about you. This premature charge is destroying your army.'

'Premature charge? What would you know of that?' Quietus pushed his horse up on the other side of the emperor. '*Dominus*, do not listen to this timid barbarian. If Gaius Acilius Glabrio had not ignored his orders and charged at Circesium, there would have been no victory.'

The aged emperor was startled out of his dream of eastern conquests. He glowered at Ballista. 'Unhand my mount.'

Quietus pointed ahead. 'See, *Dominus*, our cavalry return victorious.'

A large mass of horsemen was riding up from the south.

Sunlight glittered on arms and armour. Even at a distance, they shone – yellow, red, lilac – gorgeous in the clear, spring light. Above their heads flew bright banners: wolves, serpents, stranger beasts and abstract designs.

'Gods preserve us,' said the emperor.

The massed Sassanid *clibanarii* advanced like a wall of steel. On their flanks rode clouds of light horse, their numbers beyond reckoning.

'What should we do?' Valerian looked around beseech-ingly.

'A truce, *Dominus*, we must ask Shapur for a truce,' said Quietus. 'I will go myself, arrange a safe conduct for you to talk to him.'

'No,' shouted Ballista. 'They will not listen now. They will ride him down, then the rest of us. Sound the recall now. Form square. It may not be too late.'

The Praetorian Prefect, Successianus, spoke up. 'Ballista is right, *Dominus*. Quickly, give the order to form square, prepare to repel cavalry.'

Emboldened, first Cledonius, then Aurelian of the Equites Singulares added their voices.

With an unreadable expression, Valerian looked first at Quietus then at Ballista. Eventually, the emperor's heavy, old face nodded. 'Successianus, make it so.'

The Praetorian Prefect rapped out the necessary orders. Trumpets sounded, standards waved, junior officers roared themselves hoarse.

Across the plain, the Roman infantry units stopped moving. Soldiers ran back to the standards. Centurions shoved men into place.

The Sassanids swept on, narrowing the distance. The

ground shook under the beat of their hooves. Five hundred paces. Four hundred.

Slowly, slowly, the Roman infantry wheeled and marched into position. Successianus had the praetorians face about the way they had come. The front and back of the square were in line. At an agonizing pace, the flank units marched back to form the sides of the square. An unbroken line is everything when facing a cavalry charge.

The *clibanarii* were closing. Sunlight flashed off spear points. Three hundred paces. Two hundred.

The Roman light infantry was running in no order, flocking together into the potential safety of the centre of the sluggishly forming square. The legionaries on the flanks were coming together, shuffling this way and that, closing the gaps between units, locking shields together.

The square was made.

Sassanid light horse swooped along each flank. Arrows arced down, finding ready targets among the close-packed Romans.

Cledonius spoke to the emperor. '*Dominus*, you should dismount. Let a squad of praetorians form a *testudo* around you.'

Valerian looked coldly at his *ab Admissionibus*. 'You give me bad advice, *amicus*. Would you have me believe that an emperor should hide while his men die for him?' For a moment, the silver-haired man looked like his old self. 'Together we will endure the storm.'

The Persian *clibanarii* had pulled up some fifty paces short. Those with bows, evidently a high proportion, were using them with a will. More – far more – arrows were tearing in from the flanks. At the rear, the Sassanid light horse were closing in on the baggage train, surrounding the Roman force, severing the way home. A confused roar of men and animals *in extremis* swelled.

Allfather, thought Ballista, the baggage train – Turpio! With mounting apprehension, the northerner scanned the chaos along the road. Where was he? Where was the bastard? There! A wedge of light-blue tunics. Some of the Dalmatian cavalry. At their head, a gold bracelet flashed as its owner wielded his sword. Left and right it flickered, as Turpio desperately tried to cut a way through to the infantry square. The cavalry was moving. But slowly, so very slowly.

An eddy of dark-haired easterners blocked the way. The momentum of the light-blue tunics decelerated even further. They came to a standstill. Sassanid horse swarmed around them. A Persian grabbed the arm with the bracelet. Turpio was being hauled from the saddle. It was all over.

There was the quick strike of a Dalmatian blade. The Persian fell. Turpio pulled himself upright. The golden bracelet rose and fell, rose and fell. The Romans were moving, initially barely, then gathering pace. They burst through the last enemy. They were clear, galloping flat out. In parade-ground fashion, the praetorians opened ranks. The Dalmatians thundered in. The praetorians closed the lane.

Turpio rode up to the imperial party. His helmet was gone. The front of his tunic was covered in blood. Grinning, he saluted. '*Dominus*, I am afraid we seem to have lost our dinner.' Despite the arrows whipping past, most of the men around the emperor laughed.

'*Dominus*.' Quietus was not laughing. His face was grey

with fear. '*Dominus*, we must send a herald, arrange a truce. It is our only hope.'

'No!' Valerian thundered, his voice dispelling his years. 'I will hear no more talk of truces today.' Then, seeing who spoke to him, the heavy face softened. 'My boy, I know it is only the love that you, like your father, feel for me that makes you suggest it. It is not for today. Their blood is up. Today there is no choice. We must fight.'

The emperor looked at Ballista. 'How far to Edessa?'

'Twenty miles.'

Valerian glanced at the sun. 'Several hours of daylight.' He turned back to Ballista. 'Is there water ahead?'

'A stream, four or five miles ahead.'

Valerian nodded. 'We will march in square. We should reach the stream long before dark, but we will camp there under arms for the night. Gods willing, the Sassanids will withdraw for the hours of darkness. At first light, we will march on. The easterners will be waiting. But if we hold our positions, keep our *disciplina*, hold fast to our *virtus*, and if the gods favour us, we will win through to Edessa.' He looked at the Praetorian Prefect. 'Make the orders.'

Successianus issued instructions and messengers hared off to all corners of the square. The *Comites Augusti*, with a subtlety intended to preserve the emperor's *virtus*, closed ranks around Valerian, placing their shields and bodies between the Persian arrows and the old man's body.

Quietus wormed his way between Ballista and Valerian. The young man leaned over, his face close. The smell of fear was rank on his breath. He hissed with venom, 'You barbarian shit, your usefulness is at an end.'

*   *   *

The march to Edessa was hard. Many died. Many were wounded. But it fell out as Valerian had predicted. At dusk, at the stream, the Persians melted away. The Romans passed a hungry, sleepless night in formation. At least they had water and, crucially, they still had *disciplina*. At dawn they marched, and the Sassanids were on them, circling like fighting dogs, mastiffs with their hackles up, snapping at their heels, feinting charge after charge, and ever the *whisp, whisp, whisp* of the incoming arrows, ever the screams of pain.

Fifteen long, agonizing miles, and the Roman field army of the east reached the white-walled city of Edessa. They found that the north gate, the Gate of Hours, had already been unblocked to admit the Roman cavalry. Inside, they located Pomponius Bassus and Maeonius Astyanax with their troopers.

They had made it. They had not left a wounded man behind. But, as Turpio whispered to Ballista as they rode in, they had marched and fought and died for two days to be trapped in a besieged city.

XXVIII

On 17 May in the consulships of Saecularis and Donatus, each for the second time, the one thousand and twelfth year since the founding of Rome, eight days after the arrival of the bloodied imperial eastern field army, the inhabitants of Edessa, despite the siege, were intent on celebrating the *Maiuma*.

Moralists of all persuasions – Roman, Christian and other – were as one in their condemnation of the *Maiuma*, the festival of lights, if in nothing else. For all their impassioned oratory, for all their long beards and evident earnestness, they were fighting a losing battle. Unless there was to be a seismic shift in morality – say something insane like a Christian becoming emperor – the spring festival would continue. It was everywhere in the east. Under one name or another, it was celebrated by most cities between Byzantium and the Tigris. It was hard to pin down. Many in Edessa thought it in honour of the deities manifest as the evening and morning stars, but others held the honorand to be Sin, the moon god, or Atargatis, the Syrian goddess, or none other than the lord of the heavens himself, mighty Ba'alshamin. The greatest stumbling block to the moralists was that the *Maiuma*, just like the *Saturnalia*, was a lot of fun.

In the afternoon, the gates and streets of Edessa were adorned with cloths of many colours, and lamps and candles were suspended from cords from the porticoes and trees. When the evening star came out, it was joined by the citizens, dressed in white linen. The men had turbans on their heads, the women tall headdresses from which hung silk veils. To the horror of those with stern morals, there was not a belt to be seen. Both sexes walked out with their garments loose or, as a moralist might put it, with their loins ungirt.

A flower in one hand, a candle in the other, the men and women processed down to the river. Soon the banks of the Scirtos were lined with thousands of tiny lights, from the west where it flowed into the city near the Gate of Arches, to the eastern Water Gates by which it left. Incense was offered to the 'Leaping River'. The flowers were cast on to the glittering, azure waters. Then men and women alike walked the streets of the city; singing, shouting, eating, drinking. Everywhere, there was music and dance. Everywhere, kohl-lined eyes flashed above silk. In the soft spring night, assignations were made. The *Maiuma* really was a lot of fun.

This year, Ballista thought, there was an additional reason for the citizens of Edessa to celebrate. It was common knowledge that the imperial field army was leaving. It was a terrible irony that, after two hellish days of fighting on the march to get there, Valerian's men had not been hailed as saviours but received as a considerable nuisance.

The siege had not been lying heavily on Edessa. The walls were sound. The garrison was big enough, both regulars and local levies. There was plenty of fresh water, and an ample supply of siege engines. The governor, Aurelius Dasius, was a popular and capable man.

Now, the imperial field army was within the walls. Soldiers were camped in every portico and open space. Others were billeted in private houses. Soldiers being what they are, free-born women and boys were roughly accosted not just in the streets but even in their homes; some were raped. It was not the gentle, once-a-year wooing of the *Maiuma*. And there was the looming problem of provisions. The supplies that had been got in for the garrison and the citizens now had to stretch to accommodate nearly twenty thousand more men and five thousand cavalry horses. But most worrying was the change in the strategic circumstances. While there had been a Roman army in the field, the Sassanids had remained ready to face it; they had not pressed the siege. With no likelihood of intervention, the easterners would sooner or later bring all the arsenal of scientific siege craft – mines, ramps, stone-throwing artillery, rams and mobile towers – against the walls.

It was no wonder, thought Ballista, that the citizens of Edessa were glad to know the field army would march out on the next moonless night, in seven days' time. He threw some bread into the sacred pool. The big carp came to the surface, a seething mass of bodies. There were so many, it looked as if you could walk on them.

Unhappily, he thought back over recent events. Out on the battlefield, when the *clibanarii* had appeared, for a few moments Valerian had been like his old self. But any optimism Ballista had then felt had been crushed at the next council of war.

Somehow, Anamu had reappeared. The untrustworthy Arab had joined with the creatures of Macrianus – the cavalry commanders Pomponius Bassus and Maeonius Astyanax, and his son Quietus – to persuade the aged emperor that a night march was the best way to start the retreat north to Samosata. Their arguments had been specious. Anamu knew a shortcut. The easterners did not care for fighting in the dark. They would get clean away. It would be as easy as a stroll in the Campanian countryside.

It was as clear as day to Ballista that if the citizens of Edessa knew when the army was marching, so did the Persians. He was sure the Sassanids would overcome any inherited prejudices against night fighting. They would be waiting. Ballista smiled grimly as he remembered his own intervention: 'Only a fool would follow an Arab on a short cut to Hades.' Night marches brought chaos. Attacked in the dark, armies disintegrate. Ballista had noticed how counterproductive his blunt words had been. As soon as he had stopped speaking, Valerian had announced he would follow the sagacious advice of the *amici* of his beloved Macrianus.

'Fuck it,' Ballista said out loud. A line of one of Turpio's favourite poems came into his mind: 'Weep for those who dread to die.' He threw the last of the bread into the pool.

Turpio walked out with the others: Ballista, Maximus, pretty, young Demetrius and ugly, old Calgacus. They passed a skin of unwatered wine from hand to hand. They had gone to see a pantomime in the grounds of the Summer Palace. They had chosen a performance to appeal to Maximus: Aphrodite, goddess of love, caught in adultery.

The dancer had been good. In his own body he had brought the story before their eyes: the passion of Aphrodite and Ares, their discovery by Helius, the forging of the bronze net by the lame cuckold Hephaestus, the entanglement of the lovers, the lascivious gaze of the other gods.

'Sure, that was very fine,' said Maximus. He threw the wineskin to Turpio. 'But I always say that a god-fearing man should heed what the deities show him. Now, brothers, will be the time for us to be putting on our own pantomime.'

'I know a place,' said Demetrius. 'It is a local speciality.'

They followed the young Greek across a small bridge over the Scirtos, the myriad lights reflected in the waters on either side, past the winter baths and up a side street. Turpio remembered a morning a long time ago when Demetrius had sent Maximus and him cross-quartering the city of Emesa on a wild-goose chase for upper-class girls supposedly waiting to fulfil their duty to the local god by letting strangers take their virginity. Gods below, Maximus had been angry when he realized he had been tricked. But, still, the Hibernian had found them some girls in the end, although very far from virgins.

They reached the end of another alley. Demetrius spoke to two burly men on the door, money changed hands, and they were admitted to a dimly lit courtyard. Surrounded by other men, they sat on cushions and were served wine. One lamp burned at the front of an open space backed by a blank wall. The scents of incense, wine and the audience's perfumes were strong in Turpio's nostrils. Suddenly, all the other lights were dimmed. There was a flash of steel in the near-darkness.

As their eyes became accustomed to the gloom, they

could see the figure of a youth lying on the ground behind the lamp. The sword was by his side. He appeared to be asleep.

A loud drumbeat made everyone jump. The youth woke and grabbed the sword. High, ululating singing, eerie to their western ears, came from somewhere. Tap, tap – drums began an anxious rhythm. Gracefully, the youth rose to his feet. He mimed searching for a hidden foe. He lit two candles from the lamp. With the sword balanced on his head, he looked high and low. Just three points of light, one fixed and two moving. As he turned, the sword flashed like the *pharos* that guides ships to port.

The drums thundered. The candles vanished from the hands of the youth. The sword arced through the air. Jagged chords were struck from stringed instruments as the youth leapt, twisting and turning as he fought off unseen assailants. Faster and faster the sword flickered. Smooth, brown, oiled flesh in the lamplight, muscles flexing; the sword moving too fast to see, just glimpses of light on the blade, the blur of a scarlet tassel on its hilt.

Then the sword was out of his hand, skittering across the stone floor. The youth was overpowered. He sank to the ground, face down. The music stopped. He lay still. Then, slowly at first, the music started again. The youth began to move. His hips rose and fell to the rhythm, faster and faster to the climax. A cymbal clashed. He lay still again. The lights came up. It was over.

There was an audible sigh from the audience, then they applauded. The youth sat up.

'Not bad,' said Maximus, 'but I will not be jumping the fence.' He finished his drink. 'Brothers, I think we should be continuing our search for earthly pleasures. I will be finding us a place.'

Demetrius was smiling at the youth, who was smiling back. 'I think I will stay here.'

'Of course you will,' said Maximus, rising to his feet. 'Just be careful what he does with that sword.' He ruffled the Greek's hair.

Outside, Turpio and the other two followed Maximus north past the basilica. True to his word, the Hibernian found a place soon enough. It was a broad, well-lit courtyard. Tables and couches, men and women, serving girls. In no time at all, they had a corner table. They were served rounds of thin bread topped with spicy lamb and strong local wine.

Turpio noticed Ballista was taking more than usual care eating and drinking. It was a sure sign that the big man was feeling the effects of the drink. Certainly, they had consumed enough.

Turpio leaned on his elbow and surveyed the courtyard; there were a few soldiers, but mainly locals. Four respectable women were at a nearby table. One of them looked back. Her eyes smiled above her veil. He turned to the other men. 'It is an odd thing,' he said. 'According to the laws of the Edessenes, not only is an adulterous wife killed, but even one suspected of adultery. And then, once a year, there is the *Maiuma*.' He raised his eyebrows.

'Not that strange at all, *amicus*,' said Maximus. 'There is no end to the strangeness of people. The other night, I was talking to a most philosophical local – huge beard he had, you should have seen it, a most impressive thing – and he was telling me that, away to the east, among the Seres, there is not a fornicator to be found. Now, among the Indians, while your Brahmans will not be indulging in the pleasures of the flesh – no, not even if Venus were in conjunction with Mars at the moment of their birth – the rest are at it like knives. Whereas, among the Bactrians, who are called Kushanians, the women dress like men and consider it the height of hospitality to fuck any stranger who comes to their country.' He paused for a drink. 'And, brothers, you are wondering what is the moral of this story?'

'Actually, no, I am not,' said Ballista.

Maximus ignored him. 'The moral is an important one for any man. It would be a sad thing to be born a Brahman or a Seres, but the height of good fortune is to be on the road to Bactria.'

A horrible wheezing sound rattled around the table. Calgacus stopped laughing long enough to say, 'Your philosophy for life – wherever you are, pretend to be a stranger in Bactria. You should write your memoirs: *A Stranger in Bactria*. A great title, far better than Marcus Aurelius' *To Himself*.'

Over the laughter, Ballista asked, 'Did it not cross your mind that this bearded local might have been less than serious?'

Maximus held up his hand. 'Not for a moment. I have never heard a man in greater earnestness.' A sly look came across his face. 'And let me tell you, he knew a thing or two. For example, did you know that, among the peoples of Germania, among whom I believe your own people, the Angles, stand very high, the men will be taking the handsome boys for wives, with a proper wedding feast and no shame at all?'

'Bugger,' said Ballista. 'I thought we had managed to keep that quiet.'

Maximus stretched. 'Anyway, all this talk of physical passion is, as Demetrius might say, threatening to undermine the rational part of my soul.' He got up, only a little unsteadily, and went off to strike a deal with a serving girl.

'I am for my bed. I cannot take the drink any more,' Ballista said. After they had stood to bid him goodbye, Turpio and Calgacus exchanged a look.

'It is a fetish that has grown on him the last few years,' said Calgacus. 'The idea that, the next time he is in combat, he will die if he fucks another woman.'

'Well, that woman of his is a likely-looking piece.' At Calgacus' sharp glance, Turpio went on, 'Oh, do not come on like Maximus. I am only talking. Drink talking.' As Calgacus' thin mouth twisted into what was probably intended as a smile, Turpio got up. 'It is the *Maiuma*. If you do not mind holding the table, I hear the irrational part of my soul calling too. Do not worry – as many women have told me, I do not take long at all.'

Afterwards, Turpio rearranged his clothing. He slapped the girl on the arse and gave her a small tip. The actual fee had been paid downstairs, to the owner. Leaving the narrow room, Turpio stood for a moment or two leaning on the rail of the first-floor gallery. Below, he could see Maximus gesticulating as he explained something to Calgacus.

The Hibernian was still talking when Turpio reached the table. 'Clitoris like a slingshot, I tell you.'

'That is me done. I am going back.' After saying goodnight to the other men, Turpio left.

Outside in the alley, it was quieter than before. It was getting late. Strange, he thought, how not only Ballista but his two slaves had become close friends. Still, they had all been through a lot together. A turn of the stars, and who knew what you would be. '*A Stranger in Bactria.*' He smiled and realized he was quite drunk.

Turpio had no trouble in retracing his steps. Crossing the Scirtos, he saw that most of the lights on the banks had gone out. After passing the fish ponds, he gathered his strength for the steep climb up the northern face of the citadel to their quarters in the Winter Palace of the old Kings of Osrhoene.

When he reached the entrance to the courtyard, he stopped to get his breath back. Immediately he knew something was wrong. The waning moon lit the empty space. There was no sentry at the foot of the stairs. Turpio looked around. Nothing. There was no sound. Suddenly, he felt very sober.

The sentry might have just gone to relieve himself. Turpio half thought he had heard footsteps as he approached. He wondered whether to draw his sword. He would look foolish if the sentry wandered back. Turpio drew his sword anyway. It came free with a rasp that sounded loud to him in the quiet building. As silently as he could, he crossed the cobbles to the stairs that ran up the inner wall of the courtyard. He stopped to look and listen. Nothing at all out of the ordinary. Along the first-floor veranda, bars of golden light gleamed out from behind the shuttered windows where the night lamps burned in the outer rooms of their sleeping quarters.

Placing his feet quietly, carefully keeping the blade away

from the stonework, Turpio went up the stairs. At the top he stopped again. Still nothing. Immobile, he probed the night with all his senses. He half thought he caught an unusual smell, but it was too faint. He could not tell. He waited, fully alert.

There! An extra chink of light. One of the doors was a tiny bit ajar – the door to Ballista's quarters. Without thought or hesitation, Turpio glided along the veranda. At the window, he ducked down and peered between the slats of the shutter. The outer room appeared to be empty.

Straightening up quickly, Turpio moved to the door. Sword ready, he pushed it open. The outer room was empty. There was a strong smell of waxed canvas. The door to the bedroom was half open. In three steps, Turpio was there. He kicked it open and dropped into a fighting crouch.

The big man in the hooded cloak dominated the small room. He was standing over the still figure on the bed. The blade in his hand shone in the lamplight.

Yelling incoherently, Turpio lunged. The hooded man whirled around. Sparks flew as he drove Turpio's blade wide. Instinctively, Turpio ducked, and the riposte whistled just over his head.

The combatants drew back for a second. Turpio could not see the man's face under the high hood. On the bed, still Ballista did not move.

The hooded man feinted low then thrust high. Jerking his head out of the way, Turpio neatly stepped forwards and to the right. Holding the hilt with two hands, he rammed the point of his sword at his opponent's stomach. The man's own momentum did the rest. Impaled on the steel, face to face with Turpio, the man shook and gasped out his life. The room was filled with the slaughter-house smell of violent death.

Bracing his right hand against the dead man's chest, Turpio used his left to withdraw his blade. It came free with a horrible sucking sound and a rush of blood. The body crumpled, and Turpio pushed it away. As the corpse hit the floor, its hood fell back, revealing a swarthy face.

Turpio looked at his friend. Ballista was alive. Unmoving, the northerner stared wide-eyed at the corpse.

'You all right?'

Ballista swallowed. He tried to speak. No sound came out.

'He tried to kill you, but it is all right now. He is dead.'

Still Ballista could not speak. Eventually he nodded.

Uncertain in the face of his friend's fear, Turpio looked away. His sword was dripping blood on the rug. He bent down, flicked back the dead man's cloak, found an unsoiled piece of tunic and cleaned his blade.

Ballista pulled back the covers and swung his legs off the bed. He sat staring at the corpse. The northerner was naked. The hair on his chest and legs was so damp he could have come from the baths. After a time, he spoke softly. 'I thought it was someone else.'

'Who?'

Ballista continued to look at the dead man. When at last he spoke it was in a monotone. 'A long time ago, at the siege of Aquileia, I killed Maximinus Thrax. I had little choice. If I had not killed the emperor, either I would have been executed by him or murdered by the conspirators. But I had taken the *sacramentum*, the military oath that I would protect him. In Germania, when you swear an oath

430

to a warleader, if he falls, you do not leave the field. And I killed him. Stabbed him in the throat with a stylus.'

For a time Ballista relapsed into silence. Turpio said nothing, waiting.

'They cut his head off, sent it to Rome. They mutilated his body,' Ballista continued. 'They denied him burial, condemned his daemon to walk the earth for ever. At times, at night, the daemon comes to me. It speaks. It always says the same thing – 'I will see you again at Aquileia' – sometimes it laughs.'

Ballista looked up and grinned shakily. He was regaining his self-control. 'In death, as in life, the emperor Maximinus Thrax favours a big, hooded cloak.'

Turpio smiled.

'Only Julia, Calgacus and Maximus know,' Ballista said. 'I would like to keep it a secret.'

'Of course.'

Ballista stood up, walked over and embraced his friend. He leaned back, looked into Turpio's eyes. 'Thank you.'

XXIX

It was a moonless night. At least that was part of the plan.
The hinges of the Gate of Hours had been oiled. Quite
pointless, thought Ballista. It was not possible to assemble
an army that still numbered over fifteen thousand men in
a besieged city and the attackers not be aware. Anyway, as
even the lowest water-seller in the *agora* had known for
several days when the field army would march, it was
impossible the Sassanids had not been forewarned.

Ballista stood, holding Pale Horse's bridle, at the edge of
the imperial entourage. Turpio was beside him. There no
longer was a baggage train for them to command. Orders
had been issued that a new one was not to be created.
Obviously, an exception was made for the *impedimenta*
necessary to maintain the *maiestas* of a Roman emperor.
The imperial possessions, on the backs of fifty or so packhorses, would travel in the notional safety between the
praetorians and the horse guards. Ballista and Turpio, with
the dozen of their Dalmatian troopers who had survived,
would join the Equites Singulares.

Ballista looked to where the aged emperor sat on a quiet
but magnificent grey horse. Valerian was taking last-
moment instructions from the creatures of Macrianus. They

432

leaned forward, speaking earnestly: Quietus, Maeonius Astyanax, Pomponius Bassus and Censorinus. Even the Arab Anamu, exotic in baggy blue trousers sewn with yellow four-petal flowers, was joining in. The tail wagging the dog, Ballista thought in his native tongue. The loyal men, the Praetorian Prefect Successianus, the *ab Admissionibus* Cledonius, waited at an appreciable distance.

The order came down the line; no trumpets were sounded: prepare to march. Torches were extinguished. The cavalry who were to march in the van mounted up. Pomponius Bassus and Maeonius Astyanax took station at their head. They were joined by Anamu, and half a dozen other supposedly loyal guides who would lead them all over the high country to the Euphrates, and safety in Samosata.

The gates swung back with barely a murmur. Then, hooves ringing, horses snorting, equipment jingling, the cavalry moved out. The arch was wide enough for five mounted men abreast. Rank after rank, they passed. It took a long time for a thousand ranks to clear the gate.

Finally, the backs of the last of the troopers disappeared through the gate. The first of the infantry marched out. Some had not reported to the standards, they had slipped away into the back alleys. It was little wonder that standing siege behind the well-founded walls of Edessa might seem preferable to a march of at least two days through unknown, hostile country. Even so, there were over ten thousand armed men on foot. The emperor, surrounded by the Equites Singulares, would take his place in the middle of them. The praetorians would be right behind the horse guards.

The word came down. There was a gap in the infantry. Those who were not already mounted in the imperial entourage swung up into the saddle. The Equites Singulares set off, its commander, Aurelian the Italian, at the head; Valerian in the midst; Ballista and his *familia*, Turpio and the Dalmatians at the rear. Immediately behind came the packhorses, led by praetorians, then the main body of the guard. The rest of the infantry would follow.

Outside the gate, it was lighter. A clear night; thousands of stars burning in the heavens. A chill wind was blowing from the south. Away to the south-east, a myriad campfires twinkling, the Sassanid camp lay spread out across the plain like a carpet. On the dark outline of the hills to the north was nothing; not a single watch fire – on this night of all nights. Only a fool, thought Ballista, could think they were not there. They know we are coming. They have put out the fires, maybe even withdrawn the pickets. They want us to march north. They are luring us out – out on to the high plateau, where their cavalry can kill us.

Allfather, Grey Beard, Deep Hood, watch over me this night. Let me see daylight again. Let me see Julia, my beloved sons Isangrim and Dernhelm again. In the dark, Ballista ran through his pre-battle ritual: pull dagger on right hip half out of sheath, snap it back, pull sword on left a couple of inches free, snap it back, touch the healing stone tied to the scabbard. Maximus, Calgacus and Demetrius rode behind him. He was as ready as he could be.

They had not ridden more than two hundred paces when they were brought to a halt by the backs of the infantry in front. A night march always brings confusion. Inexplicably, the column stops. Units run into each other, become entangled. Then, equally inexplicably, the way ahead is clear. Units surge forward. Stragglers lose their standards. Gaps open in the column. Whole units go astray.

Gods below, thought Ballista, this has all the makings of a disaster. He thought about taking a drink, but decided against it. Who knew when he would get a chance to refill the water flasks that festooned Pale Horse's saddle. Maximus passed over a piece of air-dried meat. Ballista chewed on that instead.

The troopers in front moved off. Ballista and those around him followed. Off to the flanks, shadowy figures flitted here and there through the starlight. Ballista tensed, hand on hilt, peering into the dark. He relaxed. The shapes were moving away from the column – deserters sliding away into the illusory safety of the night. Fools. He wondered how many of them would be found the next morning, beheaded or staked out and disembowelled, in the path of the army.

At night it is hard to judge distances. It is especially difficult to estimate how far you have travelled if you are in a column of armed men. All most see are the backs of the men in front. If you are at one edge of the column you can look out. But not many do. There are few landmarks in the dark. They are indistinct and soon drop behind. If you stare at them too long, they start to move, to become sinister – rocks and bushes change into enemy fighters. Better to keep one's eyes on the reassuring back to your front. He is your comrade. He is leading you out of the fearful night to safety. Best not let him get too far ahead. Ballista had known whole armies fall apart as everyone rushed faster and faster into the darkness, terrified of being left behind.

A burst of noise from behind. Voices raised in shock and anger. The clash of steel. It was coming from the praetorians leading the packhorses.

Telling those with him to follow, Ballista pulled Pale Horse out of the line and cantered back down the column.

As they came alongside, four or five men could just be seen running away. In moments they were lost in the darkness. One of the praetorians detailed to lead the packhorses was down. Several others were gathered around him. More than one were holding wounds. Ballista dismounted.

'Bastard legionaries,' a praetorian said. Obviously, the lure of the thinly guarded imperial treasures had been too much for the *disciplina* of some.

Ballista examined the man on the ground. He was dying, a deep sword thrust in his chest. There was no time for compassion. The packhorses were holding up the rear of the column. The front had not halted. A gap was opening in the middle of the army. The northerner spoke to one of the man's companions. 'Do the right thing. Then get moving again.' He remounted. He heard a blade drawn, a slicing sound, a death rattle.

Riding back into position, it struck Ballista that he had just assumed command of their tiny detachment. Turpio had followed his orders without complaint. The quizzical-faced bastard was a good man. Did not stand on his *dignitas* like most Romans. Starlight glittered on that ridiculously ornate Persian bracelet he always wore. Now was not the moment, surrounded by others, but Ballista would apologize and thank Turpio later – as if over the last few days he had not thanked him enough both for saving his life and for then keeping quiet about Maximinus Thrax.

Anamu was leading the army to the right of the first outcrop of the hills, to the north-east. The road to Samosata that Ballista had travelled before ran to the north-west. They were marching into country he did not know, country he suspected next to no one in the army would know. Off to his right, he noticed a large, solitary rock with an outline vaguely like a crouching lion.

With more and more frequent halts, they marched on through the night. The trail rose, twisting this way and that, until they were up in the rolling highlands, the black shapes of mountains all around.

'Prepare to receive cavalry!' The shouts rolled back down the column. No trumpets, but enough noise to wake the dead.

'Which direction?' a dozen or more officers called out.

'Right!'

'Left!'

The answers came back indiscriminately out of the dark.

Ballista made the best disposition he could, Turpio and eight troopers facing left; Ballista himself, Maximus, Calgacus, Demetrius and the remaining four troopers facing right.

Shouts continued to ring out: 'Over there!' 'Enemy in sight!' 'Stand down!' 'No, hold your position!'

Ballista heard the rattle of hooves. He drew his sword. Into his vision thundered a solitary horse. It was a white stallion, riderless, running free. It carried no saddle or bridle; no tack at all. It was indescribably beautiful. It galloped back down along the column the way they had come. In moments it was gone.

There was a strange hush after it had passed. One or two men laughed nervously.

'Resume line of march.'

From the head of the column, two riders spurred back towards where the imperial standard flew. Even at a little distance in the dark, Ballista recognized the baggy trousers of Anamu. The other was a Roman officer. Telling Turpio to keep the boys in line, Ballista edged forward up the side of the column.

Drawing closer, Ballista recognized the officer as Camillus, the tribune commanding Legio VI Gallicana, the Danubian Aurelian's old legion, transferred from Mogontiacum on the Rhine. Ballista had met him several times, and knew him for a sound man.

'No, *Dominus*, I am afraid there is no doubt,' Camillus was saying. 'My legion marches at the head of the infantry. My eyes have not played a trick on me. When we stopped for that loose horse, they carried on. The cavalry have gone. All of them.' Camillus added under his breath, 'Again.'

'What is to be done?' Valerian asked plaintively.

'No cause for alarm, *Dominus*,' said Quietus. 'See, Anamu is here.'

The old emperor looked at the Arab like a lost child recognizing its parent.

Anamu's long face smiled. 'They have some of my guides with them, *Dominus*. They know the route. When they realize we have lost touch, they will halt and wait for us. No cause for alarm in the Achaean camp before Troy. We have left the easterners far behind. There is not a Sassanid for miles.'

'I would not be so sure,' said Camillus. 'I have heard men on horses shadowing our march.'

'Wild talk which lowers morale,' the *Princeps Peregrinorum*, Censorinus, interjected softly. 'It cannot be allowed.' Camillus fell silent. When the head of the *frumentarii* made a veiled threat, most men fell silent. The tribune of Legio VI Gallicana was no exception.

Valerian seemed not to notice the interchange. 'Then we just continue the march?' It was more a question than a statement.

'As ever, *Dominus*, you make the wisest decision.' Anamu kissed his fingertips and bowed towards the emperor. 'With your permission, *Dominus*, I will return to the head of the column.' He turned to Camillus. 'Perhaps the tribune will ride with me?'

Camillus saluted Valerian, shot an unhappy look at Ballista, and turned his horse to follow.

As inconspicuously as possible, Ballista moved back to his place in the column. As they moved forward again, he told Turpio what he had heard.

'A loose horse. The cavalry vanish. But not Anamu. Quietus and Censorinus to hand,' Turpio mused. 'An odd accident.'

'No accident at all?' asked Ballista.

'Maybe not.'

'Still,' said Ballista, 'it was a beautiful horse.'

'Very,' said Turpio.

They rode on through the night, over the dark, rolling hills. They halted, set off, halted again. They skirted the black, folded mountains, turning west then east. Sometimes they doubled back on themselves. Once, off to the left, Ballista saw a solitary rock with the profile of a crouching lion. He checked the stars to make sure they were not back near where they had started, marching south. No, at that point they were heading north.

Tired, lulled by the rhythmic creak of leather and the hypnotic tread of Pale Horse, Ballista's thoughts wandered. A man had tried to kill him. A few days earlier, Quietus had said the northerner's usefulness was at an end. If there had been any doubts in Ballista's mind, the behaviour of Censorinus had dispelled them. Two years ago, in Antioch, the head of the *frumentarii* had worked hard to try to discover who the northerner's would-be killers were. This time, he had not even gone through the motions. Two years ago, Censorinus had not been a close *amicus* of Macrianus the Lame.

With a jolt, Ballista wondered if Macrianus might be right. The army was stumbling to disaster. Had the gods deserted them because they had not eradicated the atheist Christians? Had Ballista contributed to the divine displeasure by freeing the Christians from the prison by the state *agora* in Ephesus?

But, on the other hand, was it just possible the Christians were right? Only one previous emperor had ordered an empire-wide persecution. Soon after, Decius had been cut down by the Goths. Valerian had commanded the second, and now he looked likely to share a similar fate at the hands of the Persians. *Was* there one all-powerful, vengeful god who was not to be mocked?

It was inherently unlikely. All the different peoples – the Romans, the Persians, the chaste Seres, the adulterous Bactrians – how could one god fulfil their different needs, enforce their different moralities? If there was one all-powerful god, why had he made such a bad job of making his presence known to the majority of mankind? No, a god of compassion could never have a son who would say that a man who loved his father or his mother or his children more than the by-blow of divinity was unworthy.

Ballista thought about his family. He did not want to die here in the dark on this lonely plateau swept by a cold south wind. He wanted to see his family again: Julia's dark eyes, her strangely self-controlled smile; the line of Isangrim's cheekbone, his blue eyes, the perfection of his mouth; Dernhelm's round baby face beaming with triumph as he stood unaided for a few seconds before thumping down on his bottom again.

'There is something out there, to our right – troops, I think.' Maximus' words brought Ballista back. He listened. The scrunch of gravel under the horses' hooves. The rattle of equipment. The breathing of men and animals. He could hear nothing beyond his immediate environment.

'There,' whispered Maximus. Ballista pulled Pale Horse out of the line. He took off his helmet, cupped a hand to his ear and turned his head slowly, scanning through 180 degrees to the right. Still nothing. Then, from far away, he heard the call of an owl. Many cultures considered it a bad omen. Ballista could not see why. He had always found it a homely, comforting sound. He listened for the reply of another owl. It never came.

A clink of metal on rock. The Hibernian was right. From out of sight in the darkness, not far behind where they rode, came the sounds of armed men. Ballista strained to hear. Was it the missing Roman cavalry? Was it the Sassanids?

Just then came a confused series of shouts from the praetorians. 'Enemy to the right!' 'Halt!' 'Form to the right!'

'Javelins ready!' Shields slammed together. Weapons rattled. The sounds seemed to echo back from the night. The outline of a close-packed body of troops loomed out of the dark.

'*Halt! Hold the line!*' Then, a nervous praetorian centurion yelled the command for his men to throw. The command was repeated up and down the line. In no great order, each century acting on its own, the front rank ran three, four paces and hurled their weapons. They flew into blackness. Men screamed out there. Shouts echoed back.

For a few heartbeats, nothing. Then the whistle of incoming missiles. Heavy javelins sliced down among the praetorians. They thumped into shields, clanged off helmets and armour. Now, men close by screamed.

Ballista's small party was in no immediate danger. The incoming missiles were falling to their rear, beyond the packhorses. Asking Turpio to hold the men where they were, and telling Maximus to follow, Ballista wheeled Pale Horse off to the left. They cantered down behind the imperial baggage and the backs of the praetorians. No incoming arrows, just javelins. No sound of horses, just foot soldiers. Not the missing cavalry? Not Sassanids? A javelin overshot the praetorians. It skidded along in front of Pale Horse. Even in the gloom, Ballista knew it was not an eastern weapon.

'Cease shooting! Form *testudo* by centuries!' Ballista was on horseback. He had a voice accustomed to issuing commands. The praetorians hurried to obey this unknown officer who had appeared behind them. The ragged line resolved itself into small clumps of men, roofed over with shields fitted together like tiles. Javelins continued to scythe in out of the darkness. Maximus swore as one flew far too close.

'Cease shooting!' Ballista bellowed at the outline in the dark. '*Pietas*!' – he roared the night's watchword. One or two more javelins fell. Then they stopped.

Nothing moved . . . but there was a chest constricting tension in the stillness. Ballista moved Pale Horse to one of the gaps between the praetorian centuries. The darkness stretched in front of him. A rocky ground. An indistinct outline at the limit of his vision. He walked Pale Horse out into no-man's land. Suddenly, it was very quiet, just a few men moaning in the distance and the sound of the gelding's hooves on the hard ground. Ballista felt very exposed. '*Pietas*!' he called again.

'*Pax Deorum*!' came the correct answer. Ballista exhaled with relief, but he kept Pale Horse to a very slow walk. Men on both sides were jumpy.

'Identify youself.'

An officer on foot detached himself from the mass and walked to meet Ballista. 'Marcus Accius, tribune commanding the third cohort of Celts. And you?'

'Marcus Clodius Ballista. The men behind me are the Praetorian Guard.'

There were shouts and catcalls from the dark. The praetorians were detested as pampered parade-ground soldiers by both auxiliaries and legionaries. 'Silence!' Accius roared over his shoulder.

Ballista swung down from the saddle. Accius stepped up angrily. 'Why did those praetorians start shooting at us? I have men down. It is their fault.'

'They are nervous' – Ballista spoke calmly – 'but you are out of position. The blame is shared. Now gather your wounded and fall in behind the praetorians. We still have a long way to go tonight.'

XXX

The day came almost unannounced to the tired men of the army. One moment, all was black, the next there was a broad band of brilliant blue on the horizon. Above it, the dark of the night, now tinged purple, stretched away up over their heads and off to the west. The sun would be up soon.

The army was halted. Ballista had taken the weight off Pale Horse's back. He was giving the gelding a drink and a small tub of mash. Maximus touched his arm and pointed. Camillus was riding back down towards the imperial party. Handing his mount over, Ballista walked up alongside the Equites Singulares until he was in earshot.

'*Dominus.*' Camillus sketched a salute to Valerian. The tribune of VI Gallicana looked exhausted. 'Anamu has gone.'

'Most likely,' Quietus said quickly, 'he is merely scouting ahead.'

'No, he has gone,' Camillus snapped.

'How can –'

'*Dominus,*' the Praetorian Prefect interrupted, 'we have a more pressing matter.' Successianus pointed to the east.

The sun was rising over the crest of the hill. The skyline

seemed to waver, to be moving. Speechless, the Romans watched in horror. The sun rose higher, silhouetting the solid black mass of Sassanid cavalry. The horsemen filled the horizon. Golden rays glinted on their spear points and helmets. Bright colours flashed from the banners above their heads.

'Gods below,' muttered Valerian.

Everyone looked around. The Roman army was in a broad upland valley, somewhere between the city of Edessa and the Euphrates river. No one knew where. After the chaos of the night march, they were totally lost. The floor of the valley was bare except for patches of thorny scrub. It was ringed with hills.

A single trumpet rang out from the eastern hill. Its clear notes echoed back and forth in the still, early-morning air. Then, with a sickening inevitability, it was answered. Once, twice, three times. From the south, the west, the north, trumpets rang out. On all the surrounding hills appeared rank after rank of the enemy. A murmur of dismay ran through the Roman army.

'What have we done for the gods to desert us?' Valerian sounded old, defeated.

'*Dominus*' – Quietus' voice was wheedling – 'you must parley with them.'

The heavy silver head of the emperor continued to regard the easterners. His face became set. He squared his shoulders. 'An *imperator* under arms does not parley. Successianus, have the light infantry flank our column. *Comites*, we march north.'

Ballista ran back to his men. As he checked Pale Horse's girths, a thin screen of Mesopotamian archers got into position on either side. He mounted up and they moved off.

The tired men of the beleaguered field army trudged on. They did not have long to wait. The terrible, familiar drums thundered, resounding around the valley. The easterners gave voice, calling on Mazda to grant them victory. Thousands of Sassanid horse bowmen raced down the slopes. Their mounts ate up the ground. Quickly, they were on the Romans.

The air was filled with the ghastly sound of thousands of razor-sharp arrowheads. Ballista saw them fall like hail among the Equites Singulares in front. Horses reared and plunged. Men toppled from saddles. Pale Horse shied as a missile whipped past his nose. Ballista calmed him and concentrated on using his shield to keep the points away from his beloved animal. To the northerner's right, Maximus, holding his shield in his right hand, was doing the same with his mount.

Arrowheads thumped into the linden wood of Ballista's big round shield. He glanced back at Demetrius. 'Not long – they will soon run out of arrows.' The young Greek smiled back. Thump – an arrowhead punched half through Ballista's shield. Its point clinked off the gold arm ring he had been given on his return from Circesium. He snapped the shaft.

The Roman light infantry were doing what they could, but they were hopelessly outnumbered. Soon Pale Horse was stepping over or around the dead and wounded. A centurion lay by the side of the path; an arrow had pinned his thighs together. He held up his money belt, offering it to anyone who would help him, tears running down his face, pleading. No one even dropped out of line to kill and rob him.

The rain of arrows slackened. The Persians were cantering back uphill. A feeble cheer started in the Roman ranks, then faltered and gave way to a groan. There on the skyline were the unmistakable silhouettes of laden camels. Even Demetrius must have known what was happening as the Sassanids rode up to them, grabbed a bundle and spurred back at the Romans. The easterners would not run out of arrows. The foresight of the King of Kings had seen to that. Again the arrow storm howled down.

On they trudged through the valley of tears. Time lost all meaning. Sharp thorns in the brushwood lacerated their legs, pierced their horses' hooves. Blood on the sand. The cries of the wounded were pitiful in the Romans' ears. They were tired, hungry, their mouths as bitter as aloes. The sun was high in the sky. Clouds of dust wheeled up to obscure it. The heat was overpowering.

Here and there, individuals maddened beyond endurance ran out at the enemy. The Sassanids drew back. Let them run, raving, then shot them down, a dozen shafts quivering in their bodies.

It could not go on. *Disciplina* and desperation could not hold the remains of the army together much longer. Word was passed back to make for a lone hill to the right. They would make a stand there.

The Roman units wheeled, stumbled across the plain. The Sassanids redoubled their efforts. They rode close, very close, shooting from point-blank range, cutting down stragglers with their long, straight swords.

Somehow, the Romans reached the hill. Despite their

suffering, so far, the *disciplina* of the majority just about held. They formed a perimeter, shields locked together. It brought no relief. The Persians did pull back a little way, but the Romans on the hill were set out like men in the tiers of a theatre. Closer packed than on the march, they were hard to miss. The Roman light infantry had long run out of missiles. Only a few of them had enough fight left to scurry around picking up the incoming arrows.

A little way up the hill, Ballista stood holding Pale Horse's bridle. He had turned the gelding to face the enemy and protected both their heads with his shield. Four of the twelve Dalmatians were gone but, of the rest, only old Calgacus had a wound of any account: an ugly gash on his arm.

Tired, thirsty, despairing, most of the Romans had sunk to their knees. Ballista glanced over to where the imperial standard still flew. The huge purple flag snapped in the strong south wind with an ironic jauntiness. Under it, ringed by praetorian shields, Valerian sat with his head in his hands.

A groan rose up from the hillside, like that when a favourite chariot team crashes in the *circus*. The arrow storm seemed to have slackened. Ballista peeked out from behind his shield. A small unit of legionaries was cut off on the plain. There were probably about two hundred of them. They were huddled in *testudo*, completely surrounded by Persian light horse. Shot from the closest range, arrows were smashing through shields. Men were falling fast. The legionaries were pushing and dragging their dead to form a low barricade at their feet.

The tempo of the drums changed. The light horse trotted away. A wide space opened around the trapped unit. A wasteland of low thorn bushes, spent missiles, discarded equipment, isolated bodies. All the drums fell silent. A hush descended over the plain, then all eyes were pulled to the far hillside, where one drum began to beat.

Above the skyline appeared a huge, rectangular banner. It was yellow, red and violet and topped by a golden globe: the Drafsh-i-Kavyan, the battle standard of the house of Sasan. A lone horseman, clad in purple and white, mounted on a white horse, rode up beneath the banner. The King of Kings had come to oversee his triumph.

The drum changed to a double beat. Through the dust that hung down on the plain, a solid block of horsemen walked slowly towards the isolated Roman unit. These were no light cavalry; these were the feared *clibanarii*. Armoured in mail and steel plate, riding knee to knee, a dense array of long pikes above, men and horses appeared one solid mass. The outline changed as the pikes came down. The knights of Mazda quickened to a trot. The ground trembled beneath their horses' hooves.

Cracks opened in the *testudo* facing the *clibanarii*. Heads popped out to stare in horror, then ducked back. It would have been almost funny had it not been so tragic. The *clibanarii* moved to a canter. The first Roman threw away his shield, turned and ran. Another then another followed. The *testudo* began to lose shape. The Sassanids were galloping. The *testudo* disintegrated. All bar one tiny knot of legionaries ran. It was three hundred or more paces to the main army on the hill. They did not have a chance.

The wave of *clibanarii* broke around the handful of legionaries still holding their ground. They spurred on in pursuit of the fugitives.

As he watched, a half-remembered line from Plato came to Ballista: War was the highest – or was it the worst? – form of hunting.

Across the plain, the great pikes dipped and struck. The sharp steel pierced the fleeing backs of their foes. The armoured faces of the *clibanarii* were as cold and emotionless as statues.

It was over in moments. A new trail of corpses stretched out. The *clibanarii* walked back to surround the tiny clump of legionaries still under arms.

A tall, slim figure with gorgeous silks over his armour emerged from the re-forming ranks of the *clibanarii*. He was followed by a standard bearer carrying a bright banner with the symbol of a wild beast, a tiger or some other big cat. Ballista had seen him before. The Persian boy Bagoas had pointed him out at the siege of Arete. He was one of the sons of Shapur. Ballista could not remember which.

The Sassanid prince did not stop until he was little more than a sword thrust from the huddle of legionaries. He bowed in the saddle, touched his fingers to his lips and blew a kiss. Then he gestured. The ranks of the *clibanarii* opened. A lane appeared, running to the Roman army on the hill. The lone horseman motioned the legionaries to go.

After a hesitation, the tiny band of survivors began to move. There were no more than twenty unwounded. They dragged maybe another dozen of the not mortally wounded. They carried their weapons. Above them was the eagle of the legion.

Low at first, then swelling, the Sassanids started to sing as the Romans passed through their ranks. Some of the *clibanarii* pushed back their face masks, the better to be heard.

'Gods below,' Demetrius muttered in Ballista's ear. 'What cruel oriental trick is this?'

'No trick. They are praising the bravery of those men. They sing that they are warriors, the sons of warriors.'

The survivors reached the Roman line. The shieldwall opened. Ballista was pleased to see Camillus, the tribune, lead in all that was left of Legio VI Gallicana.

The big drum on the hill thundered. Throughout the valley, the others took up the beat. The Sassanids, *clibanarii* and light horse, turned and trotted away.

Demetrius grabbed Ballista's arm. 'Is that it? Is it over? Are they going to spare us?' The young Greek could not keep the desperate hope from his voice.

Ballista patted him on the shoulder. 'I am afraid not. They are going to have lunch.'

Unfortunately, Ballista was only partly right. A large group of Sassanid light horse rode off to the south of the hill and dismounted. Soon, the first coils of smoke rose up from the dry brushwood. The easterners got back in the saddle and spurred away. The strong south wind drove the line of fire towards the Romans.

Leaving the injured Calgacus, Demetrius and two of the Dalmatian troopers to guard their horses, Ballista led the others, stumbling down the hill and out in front of the line of shields. He called to the nearby centurions to lend a hand. They ignored him.

The brushwood was dry and tough. It was hard to cut with swords. The thorns shredded Ballista's soft leather riding gloves, cut his hands, lacerated his bare forearms.

Looking up, he was relieved to see Camillus had brought out some of his remaining men. Squads of others were being chivvied by officers to join in.

The smoke was rolling towards them, the dry bushes crackling, the fire drawing closer. The work was slow and painful. Ballista's back ached like hell. The hilt of his sword was slippery with blood. He could feel the heat of the fire on his face.

'Enough.' Maximus' hand was on Ballista's arm. The fire was only a few paces away, but there was a narrow firebreak. The northerner followed the others back.

For the Romans, the midday meal was a miserable affair. They sat on the ground. Many had no food or drink at all. Maximus passed round some air-dried meat. Ballista's mouth was too dry to chew it. They shared out the last of their water. Apart from one gulp, which he held in his mouth for as long as possible, Ballista gave his to Pale Horse. Then he forced himself to eat the tough shreds of meat. Smuts drifted down, further dirtying already grimy Roman clothes and armour. The smoke blew into their faces, gritting eyes, choking breathing. Men stamped and beat where glowing embers carried on the wind had sparked small fires. The remaining horses shifted unhappily.

The Sassanids were having an altogether better time. On the hills, there was music, dancing even. They sang – not paeans of praise, but drinking songs. Some of them taunted the Romans, waving skins of drink, bread and meat.

At length, as the easterners saw to their horses, a lone horseman left the group under the Drafsh-i-Kavyan. He picked his way down the opposite slope. When he reached the floor of the valley, he kicked on into a gallop. Coloured streamers floated behind him. This man Ballista recognized from the siege of Arete. It was the Lord Suren.

Asking Turpio if he would mind staying with the men, Ballista walked across the hillside to stand behind Valerian. Slowly, the *Comites Augusti* assembled. Quietus was last, until the very final moment whispering urgently with some centurions.

The Suren held an unstrung bow over his head. When he was a stone's throw from the Roman line, he caracoled his mount to a halt. He took off his helmet and hung it on the horn of his saddle. He wore make-up, his face shone with a clean, almost feminine beauty but, when he spoke, his voice was masculine, that of a warrior.

'Shapur, King of Kings, lord of all he surveys, would speak with Valerian.' The Suren spoke in Greek. 'Shapur will ride down to meet Valerian in the open between the armies. Each will be accompanied by five men. None shall be armed.'

There was a breathless hush on the hillside. Squaring his shoulders, Valerian stepped forward. 'A Roman *imperator* does not come running when a barbarian calls.'

There was a murmur from the troops around the emperor. Then soldiers started to bang weapons on their shields. The first shouts came. 'Meet him.' 'You expect us to fight him, but you dare not even talk to him.' 'Old coward, meet him.' Officers barked orders, took names. It did no good. The core of the shouting came from those with whom Quietus had been whispering. *Meet him. Meet him.*

Valerian looked around coldly at the mutineers. In truth, the old man had never been a coward. He tried to stare them down. It did not work. *Meet him. Meet him.*

The silver-haired emperor turned back to the Persian envoy. He answered in Latin. 'Tell your *dominus* it shall be as he asks. I will meet him in half an hour between the armies.' Valerian turned away. Calling just Censorinus and Quietus to him, he abruptly dismissed the rest of the *Comites Augusti*.

XXXI

Ballista was walking back to Turpio and the others when he heard the horses coming up behind him. He stopped and turned. Quietus skidded his horse to a halt, so close that Ballista had to step back hurriedly or be knocked over. The other three riders encircled the northerner. They were Arabs. They carried short spears at the ready. All wore the yellow-on-blue four-petal-flower symbol of Anamu. They effectively screened Ballista from the surrounding troops on the hillside.

'Get your horse. You have the honour of being one of the five *Comites* who will ride with the Augustus. Your *amicus* Turpio goes too.' The little pouchy eyes of Quietus shone with malicious triumph.

Ballista stepped closer. The Arabs raised their spears. Ballista stopped. He flatly intoned, 'We will do what is ordered, and at every command we will be ready.'

Visibly angered by the northerner's lack of emotion, Quietus leaned forward. '*At every command we will be ready,*' he mocked. 'You ignorant piece of barbarian shit. The weakness and arrogance of your kind have led you to be always ready to carry out every command of my father. Although you did not know it, you have done his will as if you were his most loyal slave.'

Ballista said nothing.

Quietus' pride and loathing for the northerner made his words run on. 'You did what he wished back in Ephesus. Your weakness unmanned you, stopped you killing the Christian scum, opened the way for my appointment.'

Still Ballista did not respond.

'Did you not wonder why you were recalled for this expedition? My father knew that your arrogance would always make you speak out against his advice in the emperor's *consilium*. And what could be better at swinging that old fool Valerian to follow the wise words of his most trusted friend, the *Comes Sacrarum Largitionum*, than a disgraced, possibly disloyal barbarian arguing the opposite? Every time you spoke you were fitting the lid on Valerian's sarcophagus a little tighter.' Quietus snorted with humourless laughter. 'If, of course, Shapur does not use his head as a stage prop and throw his body to the dogs.'

'Your father and his creatures have manoeuvred the emperor and the army to disaster.' Ballista held his voice level. 'It is a consolation that you will go down with us.'

Now Quietus' laugh was genuine. 'Oh, you are misinformed, as ever, my barbarian *amicus*. Just now, Censorinus and I received the most sagacious emperor's orders to ride to Samosata and inform my father how things stand with the army in the field.'

'The Persians will kill you both before you get out of the valley.'

'Oh dear, again you are misinformed. It has all been arranged by these men's master. Even among Arabs, Anamu is splendidly resourceful. During Valerian's talk with Shapur, a mere shout of *Perez-Shapur* and the Sassanid patrols will fall back and allow a small troupe of horsemen from the Roman army to go on its way unhindered. We should be in Samosata in time for breakfast.'

'No one will accept you and your brother as emperors. Valerian's son Gallienus has the western army, good generals. He will kill both of you, and your scheming father.'

Quietus shrugged. 'With the Franks, Goths and the rest of your hairy kinsmen rampaging across the northern borders, I imagine he will be rather busy. Now, although I am deriving great pleasure from our conversation, I really have to leave. Breakfast in Samosata. I wonder what prisoners get in the Persian camp?'

'I go as an envoy.'

'Hmm, yes, it saved you last time. I wonder if it will again? The King of Kings might be thought to have little love for a man who burned the corpses of his devout Zoroastrians at Circesium. Now I am rather glad that the assassin I hired in Edessa was as inept as the one in Antioch. Anyway, I really must be off.' Quietus half-turned his horse. 'When I get back to Antioch I will give my love to your wife.'

Before the northerner could move, the spear points of the Arabs were at his chest.

Ballista called after the retreating Quietus. 'One day, maybe not soon, but one day, I will kill you.'

Quietus did not respond. When he was at some distance the Arabs trotted after him.

Ballista turned and ran the other way.

*   *   *

Ballista reached his men. Not wanting to be conspicuous, he had slowed to a walk. They gathered round. 'Saddle up, boys, we are leaving. Do it quietly. We don't want to draw any attention to ourselves.

As the eight remaining Dalmatian troopers went to assemble their kit, Ballista indicated Turpio and his *familia* to remain. 'Turpio, you and I have the unfortunate honour of riding with Valerian to the parley. We go disarmed.'

Turpio looked at the northerner, expressionless for a moment, then nodded and turned away.

'Maximus, you have never cared for that mount of yours. You will take Pale Horse.'

The Hibernian said nothing. Nor did Calgacus or Demetrius. They tacked up in silence. Having double-checked the girths on Maximus' horse, Ballista rummaged in his saddle bags. He found a document case. Gesturing the others close, he spoke so that his voice would not carry beyond them. 'Calgacus, you will be in charge. As Turpio and I go to Valerian, you will lead the boys to the southern end of the hill. Do it with as little fuss as possible. When you see the imperial party set off for the meet, cross the perimeter. I doubt anyone will try and stop you. If they do, you will have to think of something. Say you have secret orders. Once out of the line, make your way around the far side of the hill. Ride north for the Euphrates. The Sassanid patrols have orders to let pass a small party of Roman horse who give the password, *Peroz-Shapur*. They are only expecting one group of riders, so you may have to talk your way through. But Maximus speaks Persian, and he is Hibernian.' No one smiled at the attempted joke.

'If all goes well, you should get to Samosata some time tonight.'

'You think the parley with Shapur is a trap,' said Calgacus.

Ballista nodded.

'You must tell the emperor,' Demetrius said.

'I may well, but it will do no good. He will not listen to me.'

Maximus looked puzzled. 'Then you must ride with us. We have cut our way out of bad places before.'

'Not this time. The emperor is expecting me. If I do not appear, they will search. None of us will get away. It may be all right with me, if they do not execute us straight away. I speak good Persian. I may yet be useful to the King of Kings.'

Ballista opened the document case. He took out three sealed papyrus rolls and handed one to each man. 'Manumission papers. Completely legal. I had them drawn up a long time ago in Antioch. Your freedom.'

Demetrius could not contain himself. He fell to his knees, took Ballista's hand and kissed it. 'Thank you. Thank you, *Kyrios*.'

Ballista raised him up, kissed him on both cheeks, hugged him. 'Don't get too carried away. As my freedman, the Romans would consider you still owe me all sorts of duties.'

Neither of the other men had moved. 'Time to go,' Ballista said.

Maximus threw his papyrus to the ground. 'I am not taking this, and I am not leaving you.' He looked very angry.

Ballista picked up the papyrus. He pushed it down the

neck of the Hibernian's mailshirt. 'You are taking this, and you are leaving.'

'The fuck I am.'

'The fuck you are.' Ballista pulled Maximus close. He whispered in his ear. 'The boys. They need you more than me. When you get to Samosata, make your way to Antioch. Look after Isangrim and Dernhelm as you have looked after me.'

Maximus was crying. He could not speak. He nodded. Ballista felt the tears in his own eyes. He squeezed the Hibernian tight, kissed him, then pushed him to arm's length. 'And look after Pale Horse. I love that animal. If anything happens to him, I will fucking kill you.'

'I will die before I let anyone harm your boys.'

'I know it.'

Ballista turned to Calgacus. He unbuckled his sword belt and handed it over, then they embraced. 'Get a message to my father in the north,' Ballista said. 'I will try to get back.'

The ugly old face twisted into a gentle smile. 'Of course you will get back. Like a counterfeit coin, you always do.'

Turpio led up his horse. 'Time to go.'

Ballista and Turpio rode in silence across the scorched hillside. Publius Licinius Valerian, Pius, Felix, emperor of the Romans, sat on his quiet horse. Bare-headed, the old man looked out at the enemy. The others were waiting behind him.

'*Dominus*,' said Ballista. The aged emperor regarded him with little recognition. '*Dominus*, I fought for you at Spoletium when you won the throne. I have served you for nearly seven years.'

The heavy, old face looked at Ballista. 'You did not do well in Ephesus.'

'*Dominus*, this parley is a trap.'

Wearily, Valerian drew a hand across his face. 'It may well be. But what else is there? The army cannot march — the Sassanids will massacre us down on the plain. It cannot stay here with no water or food.'

'*Dominus*, if we hold out until nightfall, we can try to break out to the north.'

Valerian shook his head. 'The men will not stand for it.'

'You still have over a hundred mounted men, the remains of the Equites Singulares, a few others. We could try and cut our way out.'

'We would never reach the river.' The old man laughed bitterly. 'My men might mutiny, but I will not desert them. Besides, that dear boy Quietus tells me Shapur is a civilized man for a barbarian — a great lover of Euripides. We must talk to him. We may be able to negotiate a safe passage for the army. There is nothing else for it. Let us go.'

Ballista said no more. There was nothing to say.

They rode in columns of twos, Valerian flanked by the Praetorian Prefect Successianus, then the *ab Admissionibus* Cledonius and the commander of the Equites Singulares Aurelian. Turpio and Ballista brought up the rear.

The valley floor seemed very wide and very empty. They had not gone far when a cheer rolled across from the hillside in front where the Sassanids waited. Behind them was silence.

Half a dozen horsemen detached themselves from the Persian horde and cantered down the slope. In the centre was the unmistakable figure in purple and white, streamers flying out behind, high gold crown on his head – the glorious son of the house of Sasan, the King of Kings in all his majesty.

The eastern horsemen crossed the distance in no time. Shapur reined in his Nisaean stallion in front of Valerian. The other Persians spread out around the Romans.

No one spoke. There was silence. The wind was getting up again. It brought the smell of burning. Little dust devils swirled beneath the horses' hooves.

Shapur's dark, kohl-lined eyes studied the silver-haired Valerian. At length, the King of Kings smiled, almost pleasantly. 'Who is this with the white crest that leads the army's van?' He spoke in Greek. 'You are just as they told me you would be.'

Ballista nudged his horse towards the emperor. His way was blocked by the Lord Suren, on another great black Nisaean stallion.

'Shapur, son of Ardashir,' said Valerian, also in Greek, 'this is an auspicious day.'

'Rather more for me than you, I suspect.' Shapur's laugh seemed one of genuine amusement.

'The first meeting of an emperor of Rome and a king of the house of Sasan. There is much to discuss.'

Shapur shook his head, the pearls he wore in his ears swinging. 'I must tell you, the time for words is past, old man.'

The Nisaean stallion surged forward. With the grace of a natural horseman, Shapur leaned across and seized both Valerian's wrists. He pulled them skywards, half hauling the old emperor up out of the saddle.

Ballista kicked his heels in. Frightened of the Suren's

huge mount blocking its way, the northerner's horse refused. Ballista was thrown forward, off balance. The Suren's mail-clad fingers dug into his throat. Desperately, Ballista's fingers sought the Persian's face. They grasped his beard. He pulled. Locked together, the two men struggled.

Shapur's voice rang out over the din. 'Valerian, emperor of Rome, with my own hands I take you prisoner.'

Over the Suren's shoulder, Ballista could see the Sassanid cavalry pouring down towards them. A horse reared near by. Successianus was thrown to the ground, among the stamping hooves.

The fingers at his throat were choking Ballista. He could not breathe. His vision was dimming. The Persian cavalry were surging all around them.

'Surrender, my children' – there was a catch in Valerian's voice – 'surrender.'

Ballista ceased to struggle. The Lord Suren released the grip on his throat. The northerner looked up. The emperor caught his eye. Valerian shook his head slightly and spoke with infinite sadness. 'I have been a fool. I doubted your loyalty and ignored your advice. And now it has come to this.'

The Sassanids had erected a raised golden throne on the hill opposite the remnants of the Roman army. Seated there, Shapur was shaded by a parasol. The mighty lords of the Sassanid empire flanked him. They were tall men. They stood proud, make-up immaculate, hands resting on the hilts of their long cavalry swords. Above them all, the Drafsh-i-Kavyan cracked in the breeze.

The six Romans stood, dirty, hands bound, waiting under

the pitiless sun. Among the nobles, close to the throne, Ballista recognized the Lord Suren. Further away, the jaunty blue clothes, embroidered with delicate four-petal flowers in yellow, of the traitor Anamu. Off to one side stood the Magi and the sacred fires. Ballista noticed with trepidation that the priests of Mazda had set pots to bubble over the flames. The memory of the fate of Roman prisoners at Arete was strong in him. Boiling olive oil tipped into the eyes: a hideous way to die. The northerner fought down a rising feeling of panic.

Shapur held a strung bow in his hands. He pointed it at Valerian. Two *clibanarii* pushed the old man forward, threw him face down in the dirt, then yanked him to his knees.

'Valerian, once emperor of the Romans, now slave of the house of Sasan, will you tell the remnants of your army cowering on the hill over there to surrender?'

'I will not.'

'A pity. It would spare much suffering.' Shapur spoke reflectively. 'Earlier today, my son, Prince Valash, the joy of Shapur, gave a noble example of the mercy of the house of Sasan when he let depart those who had fought bravely among the legion he had trapped and destroyed. Now, it seems, a different example is needed. That of exemplary cruelty; a sight of what will befall them if they do not come down from the hill.'

Shapur indicated the other prisoners be brought forward. One by one, they were thrown to the ground and their names and rank called out: Successianus the Praetorian Prefect, Cledonius the *ab Admissionibus*, Aurelian the tribune of the Equites Singulares.

Ballista was shoved forward, his legs kicked out from

under him. Although his hands were bound in front, he landed heavily, the wind knocked out of him. A fist in his long hair jerked him savagely up to his knees.

Shapur leaned forward, the bow in his hands. 'This one I know – the butcher of Arete, the ungodly one who defiled sacred fire with the bodies of true believers at Circesium. He will be the one.'

'No!' Turpio yelled.

A moment later, he landed face down next to Ballista. The *clibanarii* yanked him to his knees.

'He fought you nobly at Arete, defeated your men at Circesium in open battle. A warrior deserves respect!' Turpio roared defiance.

Shapur looked with curiosity at the prodigy of a man that would openly defy the King of Kings to his face. Then his expression changed. He rose. He sprang down from the throne, strode over, grabbed Turpio's right arm. The ornate golden bracelet glittered.

'Where did you get this?' The Sassanid king's voice was soft with menace.

Turpio said nothing.

'You are the one who would have murdered me in my bed, cut my throat as I slept or took my pleasure.'

Shapur stepped back. He called over his shoulder: 'Valash, my son.'

The tall, slim young man in the surcoat emblazoned with big cats came and stood by his father. He rested his hand on his long, straight sword. Shapur pointed at Turpio. 'This one. Do it at the foot of the hill, where all the Romans can bear witness.'

Ballista lurched to his feet. 'No, you bastard, not him!'

466

Something very hard and heavy hit Ballista on the side of the head. A surge of pain. The earth rushing up. A dull collision. The grains of sand unnaturally clear and large close to his eyes. Darkness.

Epilogue (Spring AD260)

The five thousand or so Romans left on the hill held out for over twenty-four hours. During the night, some tried to break out. Many were killed. Most were herded back to the barren hillside. A small band escaped from the valley. They were pursued north by hordes of Sassanid cavalry. The rest lay down their arms.

The day after the surrender, the prisoners were ordered south. Those incapable of walking were summarily executed. The Persians arranged their prisoners in a parody of a Roman triumph. The imperial attendants were rounded up. The *lictors* were mounted on camels; their *fasces* were hung with money bags and some of the more inventive pornography found in the officers' possession. The emperor rode behind them. Publius Licinius Valerian, Pius, Felix, Invictus was mounted on a donkey. He was dressed as a slave, a crown of thorns on his head. His *ab Admissionibus* Cledonius walked beside him, saying in his ear, 'Remember: you are but mortal.' The remaining soldiers followed their emperor. Loaded with chains, their officers stumbled at their head.

Ballista's ankles were raw and bleeding from his shackles before they left the camp. He trudged across the sand. His boots had been taken. The thorns tore his feet. His mind wandered. He hoped his *familia* – Calgacus, Maximus and Demetrius – had escaped. The Allfather willing, they might be safe in Samosata by now. And what of Quietus? Would that repulsive youth also be there? Ballista repeated to himself the vow he had made in Ephesus, the vow he had made again on the barren hillside the other day: *One day, maybe not soon, but one day, I will kill you.*

Ballista's brief moment of optimism, founded on unlikely plans for revenge, was snuffed out by a much darker thought: Julia and the boys far away in Antioch. The idea of never seeing them again. Not to watch Isangrim and Dernhelm grow. Not to discover what sort of men they would become. No! It could not be. *Allfather, Death-Blinder, Deep Hood, Fulfiller of Desire, Woden-born as I am, hear my prayer: I will give whatever is necessary, do whatever it takes, but let me return to them – return to them whatever the cost.*

A stumble and a shock of pain in his ankles brought Ballista back to the present. He and the other prisoners trudged on across the burnt, bare floor of the valley.

As they neared the southern hills, Ballista saw the solitary pike planted stark against the skyline. Halfway up was nailed a man's right arm. It wore an ornate golden bracelet. Impaled on its point was a man's head. Ballista was glad it had been a quick death. No boiling oil. Decapitation. He stopped to take a last look at his friend's face. The quizzical expression had gone. Turpio's face had a look of mild recognition, the look often seen on the dead which can so disturb those left behind to grieve.

A spear point jabbed into Ballista's back. He stumbled on. One of Turpio's favourite poems came into his mind.

> Don't cry
> Over the happy dead
> But weep for those who dread
> To die.

Appendix

Historical Afterword

Third-century History

In addition to the works named in the first novel in this series, *Fire in the East*, B. Dignas and E. Winter, *Rome and Persia in Late Antiquity: Neighbours and Rivals* (Cambridge, 2007) contains a useful selection of sources in translation with informative analysis.

People

Ballista

What little we half know of Ballista (or Callistus, as he is sometimes named) will feature in the third novel in this series, *Lion of the Sun*.

Macrianus and his sons

Sources for and discussion of these men will appear in *Lion of the Sun*.

Places

Antioch

G. Downey, *A History of Antioch in Syria from Seleucus to the Arab Conquest* (Princeton, 1961), is an almost inexhaustible mine of information and inspiration. Although focused on a later period than that of this novel, J. H. W. G. Liebeschuetz, *Antioch: City and Imperial Administration in the Later Roman Empire* (Oxford, 1972) is also extremely useful. The essays and wonderful pictures in the exhibition catalogue *Antioch: The Lost Ancient City*, edited by C. Kondoleon (Princeton, 2000), are powerfully evocative. The one ancient text that tells us most about this city is *Oration XI, In Praise of Antioch*, by the fourth-century AD orator Libanius (translated by G. Downey in *Proceedings of the American Philosophical Society* 103.5 [1959], 652–686).

Hierapolis

The holy city of Hierapolis in Syria and the cult of Artargatis practised there are best known from the strange work *On the Syrian Goddess* by the second-century AD Greek writer Lucian. This should be read with the superb scholarly study by J. L. Lightfoot, *Lucian, On the Syrian Goddess, Edited with Introduction, Translation, and Commentary* (Oxford, 2003).

Ephesus

If you can find a copy, the best place to begin to find out about the history and archaeology of Ephesus is P. Scherrer (ed.), *Ephesus: the New Guide* (Turkey, Eng. tr. 2000 revised from German edition, Wien, 1995). A collection of articles summarizing recent scholarly findings and interpretations can be found in H. Koester (ed.), *Ephesos: Metropolis of Asia* (Cambridge, Mass., 1995).

Ballista's thoughts in Chapter 17 on the Library of Celsus and its surroundings take as their starting point R. R. R. Smith, 'Cultural Choice and Political Identity in Honorific Portrait Statues in the Greek East in the Second Century AD', *Journal of Roman Studies* 88 (1998), 56–93 (esp. pp.73–5).

The stories of Apollonius in Ephesus are drawn from the third-century AD historical novel *The Life of Apollonius of Tyana* by Philostratus (edition and facing English translation in two volumes in the Loeb series by F. C. Conybeare [Cambridge, Mass., 1969]; there is a more recent Loeb version [again in two volumes] by C. P. Jones [Cambridge, Mass., 2005], but see the critical review by G. Boter, and J. J. Flintermann, *Bryn Mawr Classical Review* 2005.09.62).

Edessa

The first port of call when finding out about this city is J. B. Segal, *Edessa: 'The Blessed City'* (Oxford, 1970). Now it is supplemented, and its findings occasionally questioned by S. K. Ross, *Roman Edessa: Politics and Culture on the Eastern Fringes of the Roman Empire, 114–242CE* (London and New York, 2001).

The bizarre Edessan views of ethnography discussed by Turpio, Maximus and Ballista in Chapter 28 are taken from the near-contemporary work *The Book of the Laws of the Countries* (or *Dialogue on Fate*) by Bardaisan of Edessa, translated by H. J. W. Drijvers (Assen, 1964).

Things

Chariot Racing

The standard modern work is J. H. Humphrey, *Roman Circuses: Arenas for Chariot Racing* (London, 1986). Many scholarly and popular misconceptions were dispelled by A. Cameron, *Circus Factions* (Oxford, 1976). A short popular introduction can be found in H. A. Harris, *Sport in Greece and Rome* (London, 1972), chapters 10–12 (pp.184–226).

The day at the races in Chapter 3 draws heavily on Ovid, *Amores* 3.2 and Sidonius Apollinaris 23. 307–427.

Ancient Warfare

Possibly unsurprisingly, I think the best way into this subject is H. Sidebottom, *Ancient Warfare: A Very Short Introduction* (Oxford, 2004).

The Battle of Circesium and the Army of Ballista

As *The Cambridge Ancient History* puts it, 'there may have been some sort of Roman victory near Circesium' (J. Drinkwater in vol. XII, edited by A. K. Bowman, P. Garnsey and A. Cameron, Cambridge, 2005, p. 42).

The army commanded by Ballista is based on one given to Aurelian in a piece of ancient fiction: *Historia Augusta, Aurelian*, 11.3–4.

Ballista's order of march and battle plan is inspired by that of the crusaders at the battle of Arsouf as related by Sir Charles Oman, *A History of the Art of War in the Middle Ages, Volume One: 378–1278AD* (London, 1924), 305–318.

In addition to the works named in *Fire in the East*, G. Clark, *Christianity and Roman Society* (Cambridge, 2004) is an excellent thematic introduction. Specifically on persecution, G. E. M. de Ste Croix, 'Why were the early Christians persecuted?', *Past and Present* 26 (1963), 6–38 (reprinted in M. I. Finley (ed.), *Studies in Ancient Society* (London, and Boston, 1974), 210–249), and T. D. Barnes, *Tertullian: A Historical and Literary Study* (Oxford, 1971), Chapters 11 and 12 ('Persecution' and 'Martyrdom', pp.143–186) are classics of modern scholarship.

The history of persecution is as Valerian explains it in Chapter 13 of this novel – with the exception of Nero, it is a response of the authorities to pressure from the pagan majority until the mid-third century AD when first Decius then Valerian institute empire-wide persecutions (i.e. a 'bottom-up' model is joined by a 'top-down' one). Eusebius, writing his *History of the Church* (a work I have tried for years to convince undergraduates is both readable and fascinating) in the fourth century AD and blinded by the Christian belief that Christians had only been persecuted under bad emperors, was straightforwardly wrong in crediting attacks on Christians before Decius to imperial initiative.

For the details of martyrdoms I have drawn widely, and taken dialogue, from the accounts collected by H. Musurillo, *The Acts of the Christian Martyrs: Introduction, Texts, and Translations* (Oxford, 1972). Roman attitudes to this, including their conceit that any people who initiated dealings with them were in effect submitting to Rome, are explored by H. Sidebottom, 'International Relations' in *The Cambridge History of Greek and Roman Warfare, Volume II: Rome from the Late Republic to the Late Empire*, edited by P. Sabin, H. van Wees and M. Whitby (Cambridge, 2007), 3–29.

So as not to spoil the plot, discussion of this is deferred to the Afterword in the next novel in this series, *Lion of the Sun*.

Previous Historical Novels

As in all the novels in this series, it is a joy to include homages to a couple of those novelists whose work has inspired me and given me great pleasure.

The opening sentence of Chapter 1 contains a deliberate echo of the opening line of Bernard Cornwell's *Sharpe's Fortress* (London, 1999). When thinking about the modern historical novel, the ubiquity of Cornwell's work almost makes it paradoxically easy to overlook. He has written so many, set in so many different periods, and they are all so good. What makes Cornwell stand so far above a horde of inferior imitators is the jewel-like level of historical detail that can only come from a genuine knowledge and love of history.

Two characters that appear towards the end of this novel, Accius of the third cohort of Celts and Camillus of Legio VI Gallicana, draw their names and the Gallic references from the heroes of Alfred Duggan's *Winter Quarters* (London, 1956). One of the great pleasures of Duggan's writing was the subtlety and depth of his characterization.

Various Quotes

When Homer's *Iliad* comes into Ballista's mind, it is in the translation in the Penguin Classics by Robert Fagles (New York, 1990).

The Greek epigrams quoted by Turpio are all to be found in *The Greek Anthology* edited by Peter Jay (Harmondsworth, 1981):

the anonymous one recited in the Prologue and recalled by Ballista in the Epilogue is translated by Peter Porter (No. 775), the Lucian one by Edwin Morgan (No. 627), and the Ammianus one by Peter Jay (No. 593).

Turpio's 'Greek translation' of Virgil *Eclogue* IV is by Harry Sidebottom.

Thanks

It is a great pleasure to thank a lot of people.

First, my family, for their love and support. My wife, Lisa, without whom none of this would be possible. My sons Tom and Jack for all the fun. My mother, Frances, aunt Terry and uncle Tony for the unflagging enthusiasm.

Next, friends. Jeremy Tinton, the man who gave Maximus his nose. Steve Billington for the website. Michael Farley for the office and other stuff. Peter Cosgrove for Ephesus and elsewhere. Özgür Cavus for sorting out the Turkish trip. Ibo and Ramazan for the Turkish driving. My vet, Adi Nell, for teaching me how to kill horses.

Then academe. Various friends. At Oxford, Maria Stamat-opoulou and Andrew 'Beau' Beaumont of Lincoln College, Ewen Bowie of Corpus Christi College, and John Eidinow of St Benet's Hall and Merton College. At the University of Warwick, Simon Swain. Some Oxford students whose tutorials ended up as fiction: Andrew Freedman, Sam Kennedy, and Robert Stroud.

Finally, the professionals, Alex Clarke, Anthea Townsend, Tom Chicken, Katya Shipster, Ana Maria Rivera and Jen Doyle at Penguin; Sarah Day, for copy-editing; and James Gill at United Agents.

Harry Sidebottom
Woodstock

Glossary

The definitions given here are geared to *King of Kings*. If a word or phrase has several meanings, only that or those relevant to this novel tend to be given.

Ab Admissionibus: Official who controlled admission into the presence of the Roman emperor.

Ab urbe condita: Latin phrase meaning 'since the founding of the city (of Rome; traditionally 753BC)'. A method of dating.

Accensus: The secretary of a Roman governor or official.

Agora: Greek term for a marketplace and civic centre.

Alamanni: A confederation of German tribes.

Amicus: Latin for 'friend'.

Angles: A north-German tribe, living in the area of modern Denmark.

Arete: Greek for 'virtue'.

Artargatis: The 'Syrian Goddess'. One important cult centre was Hierapolis.

Asgard: In Norse religion, the home of the gods.

Atrium: The open court in a Roman house.

Auxiliary: A Roman regular soldier serving in a unit other than a legion.

Bactria: Region between the Oxus river and the Hindu Kush mountains, including Afghanistan.

Bahram fires: The sacred fires of Zoroastrian religion.

Ballista, plural *ballistae*: A torsion-powered artillery piece; some shot bolts, others stones.

Ballistarius, plural *Ballistarii*: A Roman artilleryman.

Barbalissos: A town on the Euphrates, scene of a defeat of the Roman army in Syria by Shapur I, probably in AD252.

Barbaricum: Latin term for where the barbarians live, i.e. outside the Roman empire, in some ways seen as the opposite of the world of *humanitas*, civilization.

Bestiarii: A type of gladiator who fought beasts in the *venationes* in the Roman *munera*.

Blemmyes: Barbarian people to the south of Egypt.

Borani: A German tribe, one of the tribes that made up the confederation of the Goths, notorious for their piratical raids into the Aegean.

Boule: The council of a Greek city, in the Roman period made up of the local men of wealth and influence.

Bouleuterion: The town hall in a Greek city.

Bucinator: A Roman military musician.

Bulla: An amulet hung round the neck of a boy at his naming ceremony, taken off when he reached adulthood, the mark of a child.

Caledonia: Modern Scotland.

Campania: Region of west-central Italy, a byword for gentle climate and easy terrain.

Campus martius: Literally 'Field of Mars', a Roman parade ground.

Cardusii: Barbarian people who lived near the Caspian Sea.

Carpi: Barbarian people who lived beyond the Danube.

Carrhae: City in Mesopotamia, in 53BC the scene of the defeat of the Roman general Crassus by the Parthians.

Celeritas: Latin, 'quickness', a quality said to have been embodied in a military context by Julius Caesar.

Circesium: Roman town at the confluence of the Euphrates and Chaboras rivers.

Circus: Latin, course for chariot racing. The oldest and most famous in Rome was known as the *Circus Maximus*.

Clementia: Latin, the virtue of mercy.

Clibanarius, plural *clibanarii*: heavily armed cavalryman, possibly derived from 'baking oven'.

Club Bearers: Men of the Watch at Antioch.

Coele Syria: Literally 'Hollow Syria', a Roman province.

Cohors: A unit of Roman soldiers, usually about five hundred men strong.

Comes Augusti, plural *comites*: A companion of Augustus, name given to members of the imperial *consilium* when the emperor was on campaign or a journey.

Comes Sacrarum Largitionum: Count of the Sacred Largess, very important official in the late empire, controlled mints, mines, monetary taxation, pay and clothing of soldiers and officials.

Commagene: Roman province on the west bank of the upper Euphrates.

Commilitiones: Latin term for 'fellow soldiers', often used by commanders wishing to emphasize their closeness to their troops.

Comus: Drunken procession through the streets at the end of a Greek drinking party.

Conditum: Spiced wine, sometimes served warm before dinner.

Consilium: A council, body of advisors, of a Roman emperor, official, or elite private person.

Contubernium: A group of ten soldiers who share a tent; by extension, comradeship.

Curule chair: A chair adorned with ivory, the 'throne' that was one of the symbols of high Roman office.

Cursus publicus: The imperial Roman posting service, whereby those with official passes, *diplomata*, could get remounts.

Daphne: Suburb of Antioch, famous for sacred sites and notorious for luxury.

Decurion: Officer who commanded a troop in a cavalry unit.

Dignitas: Important Roman concept which covers our idea of dignity but goes much further; famously, Julius Caesar claimed that his *dignitas* meant more to him than life itself.

Diplomata: Official passes which allowed the bearer access to the *cursus publicus*.

Disciplina: Latin for 'discipline'; Romans considered that they had this quality and others lacked it.

Dominus: Latin for 'Lord', 'Master', 'Sir'; a title of respect.

Draco: Literally, Latin for a snake or dragon; name given to a windsock-style military standard shaped like a dragon.

Dracontarius: A Roman standard bearer who carried a *draco*.

Drafsh-i-Kavyan: 'The Standard of Kaveh', thought to have been made by the mythical dwarf Kaveh, who liberated the Aryans from the evil oppressor Zahak; the battle standard of the Sassanid royal house.

Dux Ripae: The Commander, or Duke, of the River Banks; a Roman military officer in charge of the defences along the Euphrates river in the third century AD; historically based at Dura-Europos.

Ecclesia: Greek, political assembly of the people, used as an expression for Christian meetings and the Church in general.

Eirenarch: Title of chief of police in many Greek cities, including Ephesus.

Elagabalus: Patron god of the town of Emesa in Syria, a sun god, also name often given to one of his priests who became the Roman emperor formally known as Marcus Aurelius Antoninus (AD 218–222).

Eleutheria: Greek, 'freedom'.

Embolos: The Sacred Way, main street of Ephesus.

Ephebes: Greek, 'teenage boys'; at Ephesus, a formal society of upper-class young men.

Epimeletai ton Phylon: the Superintendants of the Tribes at Antioch, elected officials of the watch, police chiefs.

Epiphania: A district of Antioch.

Equestrian: The second rank down in the Roman social pyramid, the elite order just below the senators.

Equites Primi Catafractarii Parthi: A unit of heavy cavalry in Ballista's army at Circesium.

Equites Singulares: Cavalry bodyguards; in Rome, one of the permanent units protecting the emperors; in the provinces, ad hoc units set up by military commanders.

Equites Tertii Catafractarii Palmirenorum: A unit of heavy cavalry in Ballista's army at Circesium.

Eupatrid: From the Greek, meaning 'well-born', an aristocrat.

Factiones: Latin, 'factions'. In this novel, applied to theatre factions, organized and often riotous supporters of pantomime dancers, in Ephesus.

Familia: Latin term for 'family', and by extension the entire household, including slaves.

Fasces: Bundles of wooden rods tied around a single-bladed axe, symbols of power of Roman magistrates carried by lictors.

Fides: Latin for 'faith', as in 'Good Faith', keeping one's word to men and the gods.

Franks: A confederation of German tribes.

Frumentarii, singular *frumentarius*: They were a military unit based on the Caelian Hill in Rome; while the name suggests something to do with grain or rations, in fact they were the emperor's secret police, messengers, spies and assassins.

Gallia Narbonensis: Roman *provincia* in southern Gaul, sometimes referred to as just 'the province', roughly, modern Provence.

Galli: Eastern eunuch priests.

Genius: Divine part of man, some ambiguity whether it is external (like guardian angel) or internal (divine spark); that of head of household worshipped as part of household gods, that of the emperor publicly worshipped.

Germania: The lands where the German tribes lived.

Gladius: A Roman military short sword; generally superseded by the *spatha* by the mid-third century AD, also slang for penis.

Gloria: Latin, 'glory'.

Glykismos: Greek, a sweet aperitif.

Goths: A confederation of Germanic tribes.

Harii: A German tribe, renowned night fighters.

Haruspex, plural *haruspices*: A priest who divines the will of the gods; one would be part of the official staff of a Roman governor.

Helkesaites: A sect of Christian 'heretics' who held one could say one thing with one's mouth and another in one's heart, a useful doctrine to have during persecution.

Heruli: Germanic people from the Black Sea.

Hibernia: modern Ireland.

Hippodrome: Greek, course for chariot racing.

Honestiores: Latin for the upper classes, a social distinction turning into a legal one in this period.

Hoplites: A general Ancient Greek term for 'heavily armoured men'; in modern usage more narrowly refers to type of heavy infantry in Archaic and Classical Greece.

Hubris: Greek concept of pride, which expresses itself in the demeaning of others.

Humanitas: Latin, 'humanity' or 'civilization', the opposite of 'barbaritas'. Romans thought themselves and Greeks (at least upper-class ones), and occasionally other peoples (usually very remote) had it, while the majority of mankind did not.

Humiliores: Latin for the lower classes, opposite to the *honestiores*.

Hyrcania: Region to east of the Caspian Sea.

Ides: The thirteenth day of the month in short months, the fifteenth in long months.

Imperium: The power to issue orders and exact obedience; official military command.

Imperium Romanum: The power of the Romans, i.e. the Roman empire, often referred to simply as the *imperium*.

Interamna: Town in northern Italy, in 253AD scene of battle which saw the death of the emperor Trebonianus Gallus at the hands of the pretender Aemilianus. Marching down from the north, Valerian was not in time to save Gallus.

Invictus: Latin, Invincible; by the third century AD a title of the Roman emperor.

Isauria: Ill-defined region of southern Asia Minor, notorious for wildness of countryside and inhabitants.

Iuthungi: Barbarian people who live beyond the headwaters of the Rhine and Danube.

Kalends: The first day of the month.

Kerateion: Jewish quarter of Antioch, near the Daphne Gate.

King of the Saturnalia: Elected King of the Revels, whose whims must be obeyed.

Kontos: Greek, long cavalry spear.

Kyrios: Greek for 'Lord', 'Master', 'Sir'; a title of respect.

Latrunculi: A Roman board game called 'Robbers'.

Lectisternium: A feast offered to the gods, where couches are placed for them to recline.

Legio III Felix: A legion only mentioned in the *Historia Augusta*

(*Aur. 11.4*), and thus most likely fictional. In this novel it is a unit formed of detachments from the historical Legio III Gallica and Legio IV Flavia Felix.

Legio IIII Scythica: A Roman legion from the second half of the first century AD based at Zeugma in Syria; in *King of Kings* a detachment, *vexillatio*, of this legion forms part of the army which Ballista leads to Circesium.

Legion: A unit of heavy infantry, usually about five thousand men strong; from mythical times the backbone of the Roman army; the numbers in a legion and the legion's dominance in the army declined during the third century AD as more and more detachments, *vexillationes*, served away from the parent unit and became more or less independent units.

Lemuria: Days (9th, 11th and 13th of May) when dangerous ghosts walked and needed propitiating.

Libertas: Latin for 'liberty' or 'freedom', its meaning was contingent on when said and who by.

Libitinarii: The Funerary Men, the carriers out of the dead; they had to reside beyond the town limits, and had to ring a bell when they came into town to perform their duties.

Lictors: Ceremonial attendants of a Roman magistrate.

Lupercalia: Roman festival (15th February) where the upper-class priests, naked except for a girdle cut from the skin of a freshly sacrificed goat, ran through the streets striking women with thongs also cut from the goat skin.

Magi: Name given by Greeks and Romans to Persian priests, often thought of as sorcerers.

Maiestas: Latin, 'majesty'; offences against the majesty of the Roman people, under the principate as embodied in the person of the emperor, were treason; a charge of *maiestas* was a grave fear among the elite of the *imperium*.

Maiuma: The May festival held in many cities of the eastern empire, including Antioch and Edessa, nocturnal and orgiastic.

Mandata: Instructions issued by the emperors to their governors and officials.

Mazda: (Also Ahuramazda) 'The Wise Lord', the supreme god of Zoroastrianism.

Meridiatio: Siesta time.

Middle Earth: In Norse religion, the world below Asgard and above Hel, the world of men.

Miles, plural *milites*: Latin for soldier.

Ministrae: Slave women holding some sort of position in the early Christian church.

Moors: In Latin, *Mauri*; indigenous people of western North Africa; much employed as light cavalry by Roman armies in the third century AD.

Mos Maiorum: Important Roman concept, traditional customs, the way of the ancestors.

Mundus: Gate to the underworld, portal between the living and the dead.

Munera: Roman gladiatorial games: a full day would comprise beast fights in the morning, spectacular executions at lunchtime, and gladiators in the afternoon.

Negotium: Latin, 'business time', time devoted to the service of the *Res Publica*; the opposite of *otium*.

Nemausus:City in *Gallia Narbonensis*, modern Nimes.

Nobilis: Latin, a nobleman, plural *nobiles*: a man from a patrician family or a plebeian family one of whose ancestors had been consul.

Nones: The ninth day of a month before the *ides*, i.e. the fifth day of a short month, the seventh of a long month.

Numerus, plural *numeri*: Latin name given to a Roman army unit, especially to ad hoc units outside the regular army structure, often units raised from semi- or non-Romanized peoples which retained their indigenous fighting techniques; thus in *King of Kings* the titles of the units of Armenian, Saracen, Mesopotamian and Iturean archers, and the slingers in the army of the *Dux Ripae*.

Ochlocracy: Greek, mob rule, or rule by the poor; depending on viewpoint, either democracy gone wrong or the opposite of democracy.

Ordinarius: A pawn in a game of *Latrunculi*.

Osrhoene: Roman province in northern Mesopotamia.

Otium: Latin, 'leisure time', the opposite of *negotium*; it was thought important to get the balance right between the two for a civilized life.

Paludamentum: Roman officer's military cloak usually worn over one shoulder.

Parthians: Rulers of the eastern empire centred on modern Iraq and Iran overthrown by the Sassanid Persians in the 220S AD.

Pater Patriae: Latin, Father of the Fatherland; a title of the Roman emperors.

Patrician: The highest social status in Rome; originally descendants of those men who sat in the very first meeting of the free senate after the expulsion of the last of the mythical Kings of Rome in 509BC; under the principate, emperors awarded other families patrician status.

Pax Deorum: Very important Roman concept of the peace between the Roman *Res Publica* and the gods.

Peroz: Persian for 'victory'.

Pharos: Greek, 'lighthouse'; the most famous was at Alexandria.

Philanthropia: Greek, 'love of mankind'; a crucial virtue in Greek, and Roman, thinking.

Pietas: Latin, 'piety'; the human side of the *Pax Deorum*.

Polis: Greek, a city state; living in one was a key marker in being considered Greek and/or civilized.

Porta Sanavivaria: Latin, 'the Gate of Life', out of which spared gladiators were led from the arena.

Portunalia: Roman festival (17th August), holiday for stevedores.

Praeco, plural *praecones*: Latin, a herald.

Praefectus: 'Prefect', a flexible Latin title for many officials and officers, typically the commander of an Auxiliary unit.

Praefectus Annonae: title of official in charge of the grain supply of Rome and of imperial expeditions.

Praefectus Castrorum: Roman officer in charge of the baggage train and camp; normally an ex-centurion.

Praetorian Prefect: The commander of the Praetorian Guard, an equestrian.

Prandium: Midday meal, lunch.

Princeps: Latin, 'leading man'; thus a polite way to refer to the emperor (see *Principatus*), in the plural, *principes*, often meant the senators or the great men of the *imperium*.

Princeps Peregrinorum: Latin, literally, 'The Leader of the Strangers'; the commander of the *frumentarii*, a senior centurion.

Principatus: (In English, the 'principate') Rule of the *Princeps*, the rule of the Roman *imperium* by the emperors.

Proskynesis: Greek, 'adoration'; given to the gods and in some periods to some rulers, including emperors in the third century AD. There were two types: full prostration on the ground, or bowing and blowing a kiss with the fingertips.

Prytaneion: Building which was the symbolic centre of a Greek city (see *polis*); contained the sacred hearth and a state dining room.

Pulvinar: Latin, a cushioned seat, especially for the gods.

Quirites: Formal Latin word for citizens of Rome in civilian context.

Ragnarok: In Norse paganism, the death of gods and men, the end of time.

Res Publica: Latin, 'the Roman Republic'; under the emperors, continued to mean the Roman empire.

Restitutor Orbis: Latin, 'Restorer of the World'; by the third century AD, a title of the Roman emperors.

Rhodion: Greek, literally, 'the rose garden', a district of Antioch.

Sacramentum: Roman military oath, taken extremely seriously.

Salvum Lotum: Latin, traditional greeting at the baths: 'well washed'; used ironically by pagan crowds at the spectacles to tortured Christians covered in blood.

Salutatio: Roman social ritual where clients and inferiors pay their respects in the morning at the house of an important man.

Sarmatians: Nomadic barbarian peoples living north of the Danube.

Sassanids: The Persian dynasty that overthrew the Parthians in the 220s AD and were Rome's great eastern rivals until the seventh century AD.

Saturnalia: Roman festival which started on 17th December and at this period lasted for seven days. It was a time of licence and the inversion of the norms of society.

Saxons: Barbarian tribe living in northern Germania.

Scribae: Latin, 'scribes'.

Scythians: Greek and Latin name for various northern and often nomadic barbarian peoples.

Senate: The council of Rome, under the emperors composed of about six hundred men, the vast majority ex-magistrates, with some imperial favourites, the senatorial order was the richest and most prestigious group in the empire, but suspicious emperors were beginning to exclude them from military commands in the mid-third century AD.

Seres: The Chinese.

Severitas: Latin, 'severity', usually considered a virtue.

Signum: Roman military standard.

Silentarius: Roman official who, as his title indicates, was to keep silence and decorum at the imperial court.

Skoll: In Norse paganism, the wolf who chases, and at the end of time catches, the sun.

Sol Invictus: Latin, 'the Unconquered Sun'; widely worshipped at this period as a god.

Spatha: A long Roman sword, the normal type of sword carried by all troops by the mid-third century AD.

Speculator: A scout in the Roman army.

Spina: The central barrier of a *circus* or *hippodrome*.

Spoletium: Town in Italy which saw the battle which in 253AD brought Valerian and Gallienus to the throne.

Stipendium: Latin, 'stipend' or 'pay'.

Superbia: Latin, 'pride'; a vice often thought inherent in barbarians and tyrants.

Synodiarch: Greek term for a 'caravan protector', the unusual group of rich and powerful men historically known in Palmyra and in these novels in the city of Arete.

Tadmor: The name for the city of Palmyra used by the locals.

Telones: Greek name for a customs official.

Tepidarium: Warm room of a Roman bath.

Testudo: Literally, Latin for 'tortoise'; by analogy, both a Roman infantry formation with overlapping shields, similar to a northern 'shieldburg', and a mobile shed protecting a siege engine.

Tetrapylon: An ornamental arrangement of four columns. Imperial pronouncements were posted on the one at Antioch.

Tribunus Laticlavius: Literally, a tribune with a broad stripe (of purple on his toga); a young Roman of senatorial rank doing military service as an officer in a legion; there was one per legion.

Trireme: An ancient warship, a galley rowed by about two hundred men on three levels.

Tyche: Greek, the goddess Fortune; each *polis* was thought to have its own *Tyche*; e.g. the *Tyche* of Antioch.

Ultio: Latin, 'revenge'; usually considered an honourable motive, hot or cold.

Valhalla: In Norse paganism, the hall in which selected heroes who had fallen in battle would feast until *Ragnarok*.

Vandals: A German tribe.

Venationes: Beast hunts in the Roman arena.

Vexillatio: A sub-unit of Roman troops detached from its parent unit.

Vexillium: A Roman military standard.

Viatores: Roman messengers.

Vicarius: Latin, 'deputy'; as in deputy governor; origin of English 'vicar'.

Vir Egregius: Knight of Rome, a man of the Equestrian order.

Virtus: Latin, 'courage', 'manliness', and/or 'virtue'; far stronger and more active than English 'virtue'.

List of Roman Emperors in the First Half of the Third Century AD

AD193–211	Septimius Severus
AD198–217	Caracalla
AD210–211	Geta
AD217–218	Macrinus
AD218–222	Elagabalus
AD222–235	Alexander Severus
AD235–238	Maximinus Thrax
AD238	Gordian I
AD238	Gordian II
AD238	Pupienus
AD238	Balbinus
AD238–244	Gordian III
AD244–249	Philip the Arab
AD249–251	Decius
AD251–253	Trebonianus Gallus
AD253	Aemilianus
AD253–	Valerian
AD253–	Gallienus

List of Characters

To avoid giving away any of the plot, characters usually are only described as first encountered in *King of Kings*.

Accius: Tribune commanding third cohort of Celts.

Acilius Glabrio (1): Gaius Acilius Glabrio, a young patrician, a member of the emperor's *consilium* in Antioch in AD256, appointed commander of cavalry in the army of the *Dux Ripae* for the Circesium campaign.

Acilius Glabrio (2): Marcus Acilius Glabrio, brother of Gaius, was killed while *Tribunus Laticlavius* of Legio IIII Scythica, commander of the detachment of the Legion in Arete.

Adventus: Marcus Oclatinius Adventus, sometime head of the *frumentarii*, offered the throne on the death of Caracalla in AD217.

Aelius Spartianus: Tribune commanding Roman troops in Circesium.

Aemilianus: A senator, governor of Hispania Citerior, a persecutor of Christians.

Albinus: Prefect of Equites Tertii Catafractarii Palmirenorum.

Anamu: A *synodiarch* (caravan protector) and councillor of Arete.

Antistius: A slave of Aurelian.

Apollonius of Tyana: A philosopher/wonder worker of the first century AD.

Apollos: A Christian 'heretic'.

Appian: Son of Aristides, a Christian.

Aratos: A fisherman from Pigeon Island near Ephesus.

Aulus Valerius Festus: A member of the *Boule* of Ephesus, a Roman equestrian and a Christian.

Aurelian (1): Lucius Domitius Aurelian, a Roman officer from the Danube, known as *manu-ad-ferrum* ('hand-to-steel').

Aurelian (2): Tribune of the Equites Singulares, known as 'The Italian' or 'The Other Aurelian'.

Aurelius Dasius: Roman governor of province of Osrhoene.

Bagoas: The 'Persian Boy', at one time a slave owned by Ballista; he has claimed his name before enslavement was Hormizd.

Ballista: Marcus Clodius Ballista, originally named Dernhelm, son of Isangrim the *Dux*, warleader, of the Angles; a diplomatic hostage in the Roman empire, he has been granted Roman citizenship (AD238) and Equestrian status (AD245), having served in the Roman army in Africa, the far west, and on the Danube and Euphrates. When the novel starts he is returning from the city of Arete.

Bargas: Ballista's standard bearer.

Basilides: A Christian 'heretic'.

Bathshiba: Daughter of the late Iarhai, a *synodiarch* (caravan protector) of Arete.

Calgacus: A Caledonian slave originally owned by Isangrim; helped raise Ballista in *Germania*, and was sent with him into the Roman empire as a body servant.

Camillus: Tribune commanding Legio VI Gallicana.

Caracalla: Marcus Aurelius Antoninus, known as Caracalla, Roman emperor AD198–217.

Castricius: A centurion in Legio IIII Scythica.

Cato: Marcus Porcius Cato, known as 'Cato the Elder' or 'Cato the Censor' (234–149BC), stern moralist of the Republican age.

Censorinus: Lucius Calpurnius Piso Censorinus, *Princeps Peregrinorum*, commander of the *frumentarii*.

Cledonius: *Ab Admissionibus* to Valerian.

Commius: A charioteer with the Blue faction.

Corvus: The *eirenarch* (police chief) of Ephesus.

Crassus: Marcus Licinius Crassus, Republican general who led his army to disaster at Carrhae in 53BC.

Croesus: King of Lydia (*c.* 560–546BC), of proverbial wealth: 'as rich as Croesus'.

Cupido: An ex-gladiator hired by Julia as a bodyguard.

Decius: Gaius Messius Quintus Decius, Roman emperor AD249–251, ordered first empire-wide persecution of Christians, died in battle against the Goths.

Demetrius: The 'Greek Boy', a slave purchased by Julia to serve as her husband Ballista's secretary.

Dernhelm (1): Original name of Ballista.

Dernhelm (2): Lucius Clodius Dernhelm, second son of Ballista and Julia.

Diocles: A charioteer with the Green faction.

Domitian: Titus Flavius Domitian, Roman emperor AD81–96.

Eros: Greek slave, secretary to Aurelian.

Faraxen: Charismatic leader of a native revolt against Rome in North Africa.

Flavius Damianus: Scribe to the Demos of Ephesus, descendant of a famous Sophist of the same name.

Florianus: Marcus Annius Florianus, half-brother to Tacitus (2).

Fritigern: King of the Borani.

Gaius Valerius Festus: A member of the *Boule* of Ephesus, a Roman equestrian, brother of Aulus Valerius Festus, but not a Christian.

Gallerius Maximus: A senator, appointed governor of Africa Proconsularis, a persecutor of Christians.

Gallienus: Publius Licinius Egnatius Gallienus, declared joint Roman emperor by his father, the emperor Valerian, in AD253.

Gillo: A slave of Aurelian.

Haddudad: A mercenary captain who had served Iarhai, Bathshiba's father.

Hannibal: A nickname given to a *frumentarius* from North Africa serving as a scribe on the staff of Ballista.

Heracleon: A Christian 'heretic'.

Isangrim (1): Dux, warleader, of the Angles, father of Dernhelm/Ballista.

Isangrim (2): Marcus Clodius Isangrim, first son of Ballista and Julia.

Julia: Daughter of the Senator Gaius Julius Volcatius Gallicanus of Nemausus, wife of Ballista; also known as Paulla ('little one') to her family and Paullula to her husband.

Lappius: Decurion of Equites Primi Catafractarii Parthi.

Lucian: Writer and satirist of the second century AD.

Macrianus (1): Marcus Fulvius Macrianus 'the Elder' or 'the Lame'; *Comes Sacrarum Largitionum et Praefectus Annonae* of Valerian.

Macrianus (2): Titus Fulvius Junius Macrianus 'the Younger'; son of *Macrianus (1)*.

Maeonius Astyanax: A senator, supporter of Macrianus.

Marcus Aurelius: Roman emperor AD161–180; author of philosophical reflections in Greek *To Himself* (often known as *The Meditations*).

Mariades: A member of the elite of Antioch who turned bandit before going over to the Sassanids.

Maximinus Thrax: Gaius Iulius Verus Maximinus, Roman emperor AD235–238, known as 'Thrax' ('The Thracian') because of his lowly origins.

Maximus: Bodyguard to Ballista; originally a Hibernian warrior known as Muirtagh of the Long Road, sold to slave traders and trained as a boxer then gladiator before being purchased by Ballista.

Mucapor: A young Roman officer from the Danube, friend of Aurelian.

Musclosus: A charioteer with the Blue faction.

Nicomachus Julianus: Gaius Julius Nicomachus Julianus, a senator, Proconsular Governor of Asia.

Niger: Prefect of Equites Primi Catafractarii Parthii.

Odenathus: Septimius Odenathus, Lord of Palmyra/Tadmor, a client ruler of the Roman empire.

Piso Frugi: Gaius Calpurnius Piso Frugi, a senator and *nobilis*, supporter of Macrianus (1).

Plato: Famous Athenian philosopher (*c.* 429–347BC).

Pliny the Younger: Gaius Plinius Caecilius Secundus (*c.* AD61–*c.*112), Roman senator and author; ten books of *Letters* and a *Panegyric* on the emperor Trajan survive.

Pomponius Bassus: Marcus Pomponius Bassus, elderly patrician.

Pupienus: Marcus Clodius Pupienus, Roman emperor AD238.

Quietus: Titus Fulvius Iunius Quietus, son of Macrianus the Elder.

Romulus: Standard bearer to Ballista, died outside Arete.

Rutillius Rufus: Prefect of Legio III Felix.

Saloninus: Publius Cornelius Licinius Saloninus Valerianus, second son of Gallienus, made Caesar in AD258 on the death of his elder brother Valerian II.

Sandario: A young Roman officer from the Danube, friend of Aurelian.

Sasan: Founder of the Sassanid house.

Scorpus: A charioteer with the Red faction.

Sejanus: Lucius Aelius Sejanus, praetorian prefect under the emperor Tiberius.

Shapur I: (or Sapor) Second Sassanid King of Kings, son of Ardashir I.

Successianus: Praetorian prefect under Valerian.

Suren: The Suren or the Lord Suren, a Parthian nobleman, the head of the house of Suren, vassal of Shapur.

Tacitus (1): Cornelius Tacitus (c.AD56–c.118), the greatest Latin historian.

Tacitus (2): Marcus Claudius Tacitus, Roman senator of third century AD (most likely) of Danubian origins; may have claimed kinship with or even descent from the famous historian, but this is unlikely to be true.

Teres: A charioteer with the White faction.

Thallus: A charioteer with the White faction.

Tiberius: Tiberius Julius, Roman emperor (AD14–37).

Titus (1): Titus Flavius Vespasianus, Roman emperor (AD79–81).

Titus (2): A trooper in Ballista's Equites Singulares.

Turpio: Titus Flavius Turpio, *Pilus Prior*, First Centurion, of Cohors XX.

Valash: Prince, 'the joy of Shapur', a son of Shapur.

Valerian (1): Publius Licinius Valerianus, an elderly Italian Senator elevated to Roman emperor in AD253.

Valerian (2): Publius Cornelius Licinius Valerianus, eldest son of Gallienus, grandson of Valerian, made Caesar in AD256, dies in AD258.

Vardan: A captain serving under the Lord Suren.

Velenus: King of the Cardusii, a vassal of Shapur.

Verodes: Chief minister to Odenathus.

Videric: Son of Fritigern, King of the Borani.

Viridius: Prefect of *numerus* of Saracen archers in the army of the *Dux Ripae*.

Xenophon: Athenian soldier and writer (*c*.430–*c*.350BC); author of the *Anabasis* (*March Up Country*).

Zenobia: Wife of Odenathus of Palmyra.

Warrior of Rome

PART III

Lion of the Sun

Read on for a taster of the final instalment in the
Warrior of Rome series

Gone is the trust to be placed in oaths; I cannot understand if the gods you swore by then no longer rule or if men live by new standards of what is right.

Euripides, Medea 490ff.

Prologue (Mesopotamia, north of the city of Carrhae, Spring AD260)

The Roman emperor blinked as he stepped out into the bright sunshine. He seemed to wince as the court official called out his full title in Latin: 'Imperator Caesar Publius Licinius Valerianus Augustus, Pius Felix, Pater Patriae, Germanicus Maximus, Invictus, Restitutor Orbis'. At a sign a horse was led forward. Its bridle shone with silver and gold, and its trappings were imperial purple. Needing no prompting, the elderly emperor walked to where the horse waited. As so many times before in the last few days he got down on one knee, then the other. With a momentary pause, which might be excused in someone his age, he got down on all fours, his elbows in the dust. What seemed an age passed. The horse shifted and exhaled through its lips, the noise loud in the quiet camp. The sun was hot on the emperor's back.

The sound of another man walking towards the horse broke the near silence. From the corner of his eye the emperor could see two purple boots. Deliberately the left one was raised and placed on the emperor's neck. As many times before its owner let some of his weight come down through the boot before he spoke.

'This is true, not what the Romans depict in their sculptures and paintings.' Then he swung himself into the saddle, his weight hard upon his imperial mounting block. 'I am the Mazda-worshipping divine Shapur, King of Kings of Aryans and non-Aryans, of the race of the gods, son of the Mazda-worshipping divine Ardashir, King of Kings of the Aryans, of the race of the gods, grandson of the King Papak, of the house of Sasan, I am the lord of the Aryan nation. You mighty look on my works and tremble.'

Full length in the dust, the posture of adoration enforced by guards and the threat of a beating or worse, Ballista, the Roman general from beyond the borders in the far north, watched. Around him, likewise reluctantly performing *proskynesis*, were the rest of the Roman high command. Successianus the Praetorian prefect, Cledonius the *ab Admissionibus*, Camillus the commander of *Legio VI Gallicana*, they were all there – everyone of importance who had been with the field army. The world had turned upside down, the whole cosmos was shaken. For the first time a Roman emperor had been captured by the barbarians. Ballista could feel the outrage and horror of his *commilitiones* as they were forced to witness the humiliation of Valerian – the pious, lucky, invincible emperor of the Romans, the restorer of the world on his knees and dressed as a slave.

Four days earlier Valerian had been captured. He had been betrayed by the companion he most trusted, the *Comes Sacrarum Largitionum* Macrianus the Lame. The Count of the Sacred Largess had arranged everything. His younger son Quietus had led the aged emperor and his army into a trap and then abandoned them.

Ballista, belly to the ground, furious in his abasement, thought of the repulsive youth Quietus, by now safe back in the Roman city of Samosata, and he repeated to himself a vow he had made twice before. *One day, maybe not soon, but one day, I will kill you.*

Shapur caracoled his mount, its hooves plunging and stamping dangerously close to the elderly man on the ground. Then the Sassanid King of Kings paced his horse along the line of his own courtiers, noblemen and priests, and rode away, laughing.

Slowly, heavily, Valerian began to get to his feet. The butts of spears, freely wielded, encouraged the *Comites Augusti* to do the same.

As he hauled himself up, Ballista looked at the Sassanid courtiers. There, prominent among the priests, was the Persian youth who Ballista had known as Bagoas when the boy had been his slave. How the wheel of fortune turns. Was the youth smiling at him behind that black beard?

The sight of Bagoas turned Ballista's thoughts to his *familia*. Had his ex-slaves Calgacus, Maximus and Demetrius made it to safety? Were they now also safe in Samosata? Or were they already on the road to Antioch? To Antioch where Ballista's two young sons and wife waited, all unaware. The pain of thinking of them was almost unbearable. Ballista spoke in his heart to the high god of his northern youth. *Allfather, Death-Blinder, Deep Hood, Fulfiller of Desire, Woden-born as I am, hear my prayer: I will give whatever is necessary, do whatever it takes, but let me return to them – return to them whatever the cost.*

Part I:

Captivus

(The East, Spring-Summer AD260)

What is it like to lose one's native land? Is it a grievous loss?

Euripides, Phoenissae 388

I

Maximus lay motionless watching the Persians. They were in front of and below him, towards the middle of the small upland meadow where three paths came together. They were not above forty paces away. He could see them clearly, in the pale moonlight men and horses were solid dark grey silhouettes. There were twenty-one Sassanid cavalrymen. Maximus had counted them several times.

The Sassanids were confident. They had dismounted and were talking quietly. They were unavoidably in the way. Maximus raised his eyes to check the position of the sickle-shaped, three-night-old moon. There was not much of the night left. With northern Mesopotamia overrun with Persian patrols, Maximus and the others had to be safe behind the walls of Zeugma by dawn. There was no time to retrace their steps and cast about for another path which ran east-west through the high country. If the Persians did not move on within half an hour, the Romans would have to try and fight their way through. It did not promise well. They were outnumbered three to one. Demetrius had never been much of a one in a fight, and old Calgacus was wounded. Sure, but it did not promise well at all.

Moving slowly, hardly moving his head a fraction,

Maximus looked over at Calgacus. The old Caledonian was lying on his left side, favouring his bandaged right arm. His great domed, balding skull blended well with the white rocks. Maximus was fond of Calgacus. They had been together a long time; nineteen years since Maximus had been bought in as a slave bodyguard to the *familia* of Ballista. Of course Calgacus had been with Ballista since the latter's childhood among the Angles of *Germania*. Calgacus was a sound man. Maximus was fond of him, although not as fond as of a good hunting dog.

Maximus studied his companion; the dark lines of the wrinkled forehead and the black pools of the sunken cheeks. Truth be told, Maximus was worried. Sure, Calgacus was tough. But he had seemed old nearly twenty years before. Now he was wounded, and the last four days must have taken it out of the old bastard.

Four days earlier they had watched Ballista ride out from the trapped army, one of the five *comites* accompanying the emperor Valerian to his ill-fated meeting with the Sassanid King of Kings Shapur. They had done what their *patronus* Ballista had commanded. As the imperial party rode west, they had crossed the perimeter to the south and doubled back behind the east side of the hill. The small group of horsemen – Maximus, Calgacus, Demetrius and eight Dalmatian troopers – had made no great distance north when they were challenged by a Sassanid picket. Maximus, the only one who could speak Persian, had shouted out the password that Ballista had discovered from Quietus, the traitor who had led the Roman army into the trap: *Peroz-Shapur*.

The Sassanids were suspicious. They had been told to let through only one party of Roman horsemen heading north shouting *the victory of Shapur*, and that had already passed. Yet they drew back, their dark eyes scowling, their hands on their weapons.

Maximus and the others had ridden on. Not too fast, to look as if they were fleeing; not too slow, to appear to be flaunting themselves. Against every instinct for self-preservation, they kept to a gentle canter.

Behind them a lone rider, baggy clothes flapping, horse kicking up puffs of dust, had raced across the plain. He spurred up to the Persian picket. There was gesticulating, shouting. The easterners kicked their boots into the flanks of their horses. They gave tongue to a high, ululating cry. The chase was on.

Pushing hard Maximus and the others had galloped out of the valley of tears. They did not see Valerian, Ballista and the other *comites* hauled from their mounts, and, dusty and blood-ied, hustled away into captivity. They had no time to spare a glance for the remainder of the Roman field army of the east, surrounded and hopeless on the hill. They had a large party of Sassanid light cavalry only just over two bowshots behind them. They rode hard to the hills of the north-west.

Darkness had saved them. It seemed an eon coming, then, all at once it was there. A dark, dark night; the night before the new moon. Calgacus, who had been appointed in charge by Ballista, had ordered them to double back to the south-east. After a time he had found a place for them to lie up. The land here was rolling hills. Sometimes they bunched up into mountains. On the flank of one of these was a hollow that was deep and wide enough to hide eleven men and horses. There was a small stream nearby. As he rubbed down Pale Horse, the mount that Ballista had entrusted to him, Maximus approved of the Caledonian's choice. His hands working hard, he tried not to think about the grey gelding's owner; once his own owner, now his *patronus*, the friend he had left behind.

Maximus had been woken mid-morning by the sound of goat bells. Despite all the years since he had been taken as a slave out of his native Hibernia and brought to the southlands, goat bells somehow still sounded exotic. Although alien, they were usually reassuring, speaking of a gentle, timeless Mediterranean order. That morning they had not been. They were getting closer.

Looking round Maximus had seen that everyone was still asleep. Only old Calgacus was awake. The Caledonian was lying peering over the lip of their hiding place. Maximus had scrambled up next to him. He risked a quick look over the top. It was a small flock, no more than twenty head. They were strung out behind a lead animal. They were coming to the stream to drink. The purposeful tread of the leader would take them right by the hollow, would give the goatherd a perfect view of the fugitives.

Maximus had been surprised when Calgacus gestured for him to go to the far end of the hollow. The goats were close; the tinkling of their bells loud. As Maximus moved past two or three of the Dalmatians stirred. He motioned them to silence. In position, he looked back at Calgacus.

Unhurriedly, Calgacus had risen to his feet, and stepped up over the lip of the hollow. He stood still, hands empty by his sides.

Pulling himself up, Maximus had peeked over the top. Through the legs of the animals he saw the goatherd. He was an elderly man with a huge beard and the air of a patriarch. He leant on a staff, calmly regarding Calgacus. The goatherd's untroubled manner suggested ugly, old Caledonians or even *daemons* popped up out of every other gully he passed.

'Good day, grandfather,' said Calgacus.

For a time the goatherd did not respond. Maximus had begun to wonder if he did not speak Greek. He was wearing baggy eastern trousers. But everyone in Mesopotamia did.

'Good day, my child,' the local replied at last. Maximus felt an urge to laugh building inside.

'Is it safe to be out with the goats with the Sassanids all around?'

The goatherd considered Calgacus' question, weighing it up. 'I keep to the higher hills. The goats must drink. If the Persians see me, they may not kill me. What can you do?'

The local had his back almost completely to Maximus. Now the latter saw the point of Calgacus' silent instruction. Quietly he got up. As Calgacus glanced over, he touched the hilt of his sword. There was a pause before the Caledonian gave a tiny shake of his head.

'May the gods hold their hands over you, grandfather,' said Calgacus.

With due deliberation the goatherd turned his patriarchal gaze first on Maximus then back to Calgacus. 'I think they may do already.'

The staff tapped the lead goat on the rump. The herder turned to go. Above the swelling tinkle of bells he called back, 'May the gods hold their hands over you, my children.'

Maximus stepped over to Calgacus. 'If they catch him the reptiles will torture him. Not many men could keep a secret under that.'

The old Caledonian shrugged. 'What can you do?'

Maximus laughed. 'How true, *my child*, how true.'

'Shut the fuck up, and take the next watch,' replied Calgacus quite affably.

In the dusk they had saddled-up. With the true night came thousands of stars and the thinnest of thin new moons. According to the ways of his people Maximus made a wish on the new moon. A wish he could never divulge; for certain to do so would spoil its purpose.

Calgacus had led them to the north-west. Two riders out in front, they took it easy. There could not be many miles to the Euphrates. Unless the Sassanids intervened, they would be in Samosata well before dawn.

They had been travelling for some hours, their hopes were rising, when, as the malignant gods willed it, the intervention came. A Persian challenge, loud in the night. A cry of alarm. More eastern shouts. Calgacus circling his arm, wheeling the tiny column. Everyone booting their horses. All around the rattle of hooves, the ringing of equipment. From behind the roar of pursuit.

Maximus sensed as much as saw the solid black line of an arrow as it had shot past him and seemed to accelerate ahead into the night. A second later he had heard the wisp of an arrow's passing. Momentarily he wondered if it was another unseen arrow or the sound of the first. Shrugging this germ of a huge idea out of his mind, he slung his shield over his back. As he rode it banged painfully into his neck and back. At this short range an arrow probably would punch clean through its linden boards. But somehow even its weight and discomfort made him feel a little better.

They galloped on, over the pale rolling hills, round dark

up thrust mountains, past gloomy vineyards and orchards, through burnt hamlets and by abandoned farms. They crashed through small, upland streams, their beds stony, the water no more than hoof-high.

It is hard to outride men in fear for their lives. The clamour of pursuit had dropped back, faded to inaudibility beneath the sounds of their own movement. One more rise and Calgacus signalled a halt. All the men dropped to the ground, taking the weight from their horses' backs.

Maximus had looked round, counting. There were too few men in the pale light, just seven of them. Four of the Dalmatian troopers were gone. Had they been killed? Were they taken? Or had they chosen a different path, either heroically, to lead the Sassanids away, or out of ignorance and terror? Neither Maximus or anyone else in the party would ever know. They had vanished in the night.

Calgacus had handed his reins to Demetrius and was walking back to the brow of the hill. Hurriedly Maximus did the same. Keeping low, they gazed back the way they had come.

The Sassanids had not given up. Not much above half a mile to the north, strung out at no great intervals torches flared across the hills.

'Persistent fuckers,' said Maximus.

'Aye,' agreed Calgacus. 'Having lost sight of us, they have thrown out a cordon to sweep the country.'

In silence the two men watched the easterners ride over the hills towards them. The undulating line of torches resembled a great snake coiling sideways, a huge mythical *draco*.

'If they want to stay in touch with each other they will

have to go slowly,' said Maximus. 'It will be fine for us.'

'Maybe,' said Calgacus, 'but if they get close we will try the trick Ballista used the time we were chased before the siege of Arete.'

Memories jumbled into Maximus' thoughts: waiting in a stand of trees down by the river, the smell of mud, a scatter of stones, a desperate fight in a gully.

'When Romulus died,' said Calgacus patiently.

Maximus was grateful for the hint. Even the Hibernian's self-regard, well-developed though it was, did not run to priding himself on his powers of recall. Ballista had tied a lantern to a packhorse. His standard bearer Romulus was to lead the Persians away while the rest rode to safety. After a time Romulus had been meant to turn the packhorse loose and make his escape. Something had gone wrong. He must have left it too late. Antigonus had come across Romulus a few days later; what was left of him, staked out and mutilated. Come to that, it had not ended well for Antigonus; not long after a stone from a siege engine had taken his head off. Maximus felt a rush of pity for the companions lost along the way. He steadied himself. As he had heard Ballista sometimes say, *Men die in war. It happens.*

The seven remaining horsemen had pushed south. They rode hard, but not flat out. The stars wheeled and the moon tracked across the sky. Maximus was proved right. There was no need for dangerous tricks with lanterns. Gradually the lights of the Sassanids had fallen behind. After a time they were seen no more.

Calgacus had kept them moving, when they could avoiding the skyline, always aiming south-west. When dawn's rosy fingers showed in the sky the elderly Caledonian began to hunt for a place to lie up. Eventually, when the sun was almost up, he turned aside into an olive grove which ran up the flank of a hill. Dismounted they pushed through some straggly vines and up under the trees.

The dappled sunlight was warm on Maximus' face when Calgacus shook him awake. Unnecessarily the Caledonian had put his finger to his lips. Silently Maximus got up and followed him to a space where the gnarled silver-grey trunks were more widely spaced. They looked down to the valley floor.

One thin column of dust followed by a wide, dense one. A solitary rider was being hunted down by at least thirty horsemen. No one in the olive grove spoke. In the randomness of his fear the hunted man was riding directly towards them.

'The eye of Cronus is on us,' muttered Demetrius. No one else spoke. As the fugitive got closer they saw he wore a light blue tunic.

'Gods below,' said Maximus, 'it's one of us.'

The lost Dalmatian trooper was almost in arrow shot when his horse stumbled. The man lost his seat, slid forward down the animal's neck. Trying to regain its balance, the horse plunged. The trooper fell. His momentum made him bounce once, high in the air, then, limbs flailing, he crashed to the ground. He scrabbled to his feet. His pursuers surged all around him.

There was a moment of stillness. The Dalmatian standing; the Sassanids ringing him. The loose horse ran away to the right. One of the Sassanids went to catch it.

Slowly, almost apologetically, the trooper drew his sword. He threw it down. The mounted men laughed. One spurred forwards. The trooper turned, started to run. A long blade flashed in the sun. There was a scream, a spray of bright blood, and the Dalmatian fell. The Sassanid cantered back into the circle. The wounded man got to his feet again. Another horseman rushed in. Again the flash of a blade. More blood, and again the man went down.

Maximus looked across at Calgacus. The Caledonian shook his head.

After the third pass the Dalmatian remained on the ground, curled up, his arms covering his head. Their sport spoiled the Sassanids called out insults, imprecations. Their prey remained down in the reddened dust.

The Sassanid who had gone to the right returned leading the trooper's horse.

One of the ring of horsemen called an order. They unslung their bows. Another word of command and they drew and released. Almost as one the arrowheads thumped into the man's body.

The watchers on the hill had not moved.

A Persian had slid from the saddle. Tossing his reins to a companion, he walked over to the corpse. A boot on the body, he pulled out the arrows. The shaft of one was snapped, the others he handed back to their owners. The riders laughed and joked, teasing each other about their shooting. One carefully tied back his long hair with a bright strip of material.

Maximus had found his sword in his hand. He had no memory of unsheathing it. So it did not catch the sun, he held it behind his back. He forced himself to look away at the others. Their whole attention was on the foot of the hill. They were all willing the enemy to leave.

Finally, when the watchers had thought they could bear no more, when even discovery and doomed violence had seemed better than the agony of waiting, a Persian shouted a word of command. The easterner on foot remounted and the troop trotted off the way they had come.

Around him Maximus had heard several men exhale noisily. He realized that he was one of them. 'Bastards,' he said.

Calgacus had not taken his eyes off the Sassanids. 'And would our boys have behaved better?'

Maximus just shrugged.

It had not proved easy to sleep having just seen one of their *commilitiones* killed in cold blood, while his butchered remains lay in view. Calgacus had moved them further up the hill. It had done no good. A careless glance through the green leaves still revealed a glimpse of soiled blue tunic. The Greek youth Demetrius had said they should retrieve his body, offer him proper burial, at least a coin for the ferryman. Calgacus had overruled him. The Persians might return, they would be suspicious. But, Demetrius had argued, others might be drawn to the sight. Calgacus shrugged, it was the lesser of two evils.

Twilight had found them more than ready to move. Calgacus had outlined the new plan. Since the gods clearly did not care for the idea of them reaching Samosata in the north, they would go west to Zeugma. They would soon come to a broad high plain, about twenty miles across, then a range of hills from which the Euphrates would be visible. They could do it in one night. Once in Zeugma they would be safe. They had passed through the town on the march out. The walls were sound. They were manned by the 4,000 men of *Legio IIII Scythica* and another 6,000 regulars. Best of all, they were commanded by the ex-Consul Valens, and he was no friend of either the Sassanids or treacherous bastards like Quietus, his brother Macrianus, and their scheming father Macrianus the Lame.

Calgacus had been about to give the word to set off when, boots slipping in the powdery soil, Demetrius ran up through the trees. When he reached them he doubled up, panting like a dog after a run in the hot sun. One of the troopers, the good looking one, helped him up into the saddle.

'Just a coin, a handful of dust,' Demetrius spoke to Calgacus, his tone defensive. 'I know if the reptiles come it will show that we have been here. But I had to. I could not let his soul wander for ever.'

Calgacus just nodded, and gave the word to move out.

It had taken much longer to reach the plain than the Caledonian had implied. When they did it stretched for ever. On and on they had ridden. The stars high above as distant and heartless as the eyes of a triumphant mob. On either side flat, grey nothingness. They were bone tired. They had lived with constant fear for too long. In the face of that immensity, even Maximus had felt his composure slipping, his mind summoning up ghastly imaginings. After a time it had seemed to him that it was the plain that moved, while they stood still. It was like the stories Demetrius told. They were already dead. Their sins on earth had been judged. They had been sent to Tartarus. It was their fate to ride this dark plain for ever, never reaching safety, never again seeing the light.

The grey light of pre-dawn had come all too soon. It

revealed the hills in the west. But they were still a way off. All around them was the emptiness of the plain. There were a few shrubs, the odd wind-bent tree; nothing to hide them. About a mile ahead, stark and incongruous, was a lone building. Anyone with any pretensions to field-craft has always known not to hide in a solitary building. It is the first place searchers will look. Nevertheless Calgacus led them straight towards it. There was nowhere else.

The building was a large, rectangular mud-brick barn. It had contained animals and people. Now it was empty. They led their horses in by the one, wide door. Inside, they hoisted a lookout up on to the beams. Some of the tiles were missing; he pushed out a few more to see all round. The elevation increased the limits of his view. The others rubbed down their horses and searched for food. There was none. There was a well outside. But it might be poisoned. They still had water in their bottles, but they had eaten the last scraps of food the night before. They could cut grass for the horses, but the men would go hungry.

Maximus had taken the second watch. He had to shift around the roof to keep an eye on all the approaches. It was just as well. Falling asleep risked a nasty fall. Another of Demetrius' stories floated into the Hibernian's mind. On Circe's island one of Odysseus' crew fell asleep on the roof of the palace. He tumbled off and broke his neck. Possibly he had been bewitched into a pig. There was a thought – roast pork: hot, blistered crackling, the fat running down your chin. Infernal gods, Maximus was hungry.

Somewhat distracted by the demands of his stomach, it had taken Maximus a few moments to take on board what his eyes saw. The peasant couple with the donkey, the man riding, the woman walking behind, were quite close. Maximus dropped down from the beams. He woke Demetrius and gave him a leg up into the roof. Turning, he found Calgacus on his feet. A word or two of explanation and they walked outside.

At the sight of the strangers the peasant had stopped his donkey with a word and his wife, her eyes all downcast and inattentive, with a stick. His tattooed face registered no surprise. Like the goatherd the other day, thought Maximus, they bred them incurious out here.

'Good day, Grandfather,' Calgacus said in Greek.

The peasant replied with a muted flow of words in a language neither of the other men understood. Now they were closer they could see it was not tattoos on the man's face but dirt ingrained in every line.

Maximus tried a greeting in Persian. An emotion seemed to run across the peasant's face. It was gone before Maximus was even sure it had been there. Quietly the woman began to sob. The peasant hit her with his stick. She joined the men in silence.

With gestures and broken sentences in a range of languages, Maximus asked if they had any food. The man's response, with much eloquent waving of hands and minimal grunting of incomprehensible words, was an extended denial. As far as Maximus could make out, riders had come from the east, they had taken all the food, beaten the peasant and his wife. They had done something else, taken something, a child. Boy or girl it would have not gone well for them.

The woman started to weep again. She quietened at the sight of the stick.

Calgacus then invited them into the barn, but the peasant made it clear he and his wife would remain outside.

There they sat, hands on their knees, outside, up against the wall of what could well have been their own home. As the sun arced across the sky they moved round to keep in the shade. At intervals the woman wept. As his emotions took him, the peasant would either soothe or threaten her. Unable to sleep, Maximus spent much of the day watching them, grieving for their naked misery. Even a man of violence such as himself could sometimes see the bad, naked face of the god of war. Mars, Ares, Woden, call him what you will; war is hell.

As the day faded the men had tacked-up, led their horses outside and swung into the saddle. Calgacus led them off to the west. Neither the peasant or his wife showed any emotion at their departure.

Finally they had come to the hills. Finding an upward path, despite the darkness, they had taken it. As the rocky slopes had further cut down their vision, they had proceeded cautiously, two men out on point duty, fifty or more paces in front. And then they had come across the Persians.

Maximus looked away from Calgacus and back down at the enemy. The Sassanids were relaxed, perfectly unaware they were observed. They stood around where the three paths met, passing a wineskin back and forth. One of them raised his voice in song.

> *'Dreaming when Dawn's left hand was in the sky*
> *I heard a Voice within the tavern cry,*
> *"Awake my Little ones, and fill the Cup*
> *Before Life's Liquor in its Cup be dry."'*

The Persians laughed.

That's it, you goat-eyed bastards, thought Maximus, *drink up every drop. Before Dawn's left hand is anywhere in the sky, in the next quarter of an hour, if you don't move, we are going to try and kill you – and we want you as drunk as possible when the sharp steel gets close.*

Even if they did move it was quite likely there would be a fight. If the Sassanids took the path to the north, all well and good. If they went east, the Romans might hope to follow and, once out of the hills, somewhere down on the narrow plain before the Euphrates, slip past into Zeugma. But if the Sassanids rode west, then there was no choice; there must be bloodshed.

One of the dark grey shadows changed shape, a Persian leapt up into the saddle. He too sang, a voice less mellifluous, but with a ring of authority.

> 'And, as the cock crew, those who stood before
> The Tavern shouted – "Open then the Door!
> You know how little while we have to stay,
> And, once departed, may return no more.'"

The Sassanids all mounted. They milled, sorting themselves out.

Maximus, palms slick, held his breath.

The eastern troop clattered off to the north.